Without a
Conscience
Cat Gardiner

Book 2 of the Conscience Series

YouTube Playlist: https://goo.gl/DAPOgo
Pinterest Inspiration Board: https://goo.gl/pGGXBH

Other Books
by Cat Gardiner

Austen-Inspired Contemporary Romance

Lucky 13 – Matchmaking & Misunderstandings
Denial of Conscience (Book 1 of the Conscience Series)
Guilty Conscience (Conscience Series bonus vignettes)
Villa Fortuna – Pride, Prejudice, & a Haircut
Undercover – An Austen Noir

WWII-era Historical Romance

A Moment Forever

To Kathy
from your book boyfriend,
Fitzwilliam "Iceman" Darcy

Macarena

Pemberley Estate, Leesburg, Virginia

Horse and rider—seemingly sharing a single pounding heartbeat—vigorously galloped. Both reveled in the thrill of four fluid hooves rising in flight across a glorious sea of Virginia bluebells.

Forty miles per hour barely affected the thoroughbred. Elektra's stamina and spirit thrived on the challenge of her owner's command to push her limits—faster, harder.

Fitzwilliam Darcy, fueled by a memory of the Outlaws' song "Ghost Riders in the Sky," coaxed the mare, "Come on. Faster!" A moment later, he laughed, urged to compliment his horse. "You're just like Liz. Fly, girl! Feel the abandon."

Liz wouldn't appreciate the comparison, but this magnificent animal's spirited response was so much like the courageous temperament of his wife of six months. And not too dissimilar from polo pony and rider, he and Liz had formed a true partnership.

His reckless need for Harley-induced adrenaline and speed had been sated by Liz's ready companionship. She had helped him purge the demons of his past—betrayal, fear, and revenge had been heavy armor to wear until she had unexpectedly come along. The love of his life (his beloved, whom he referred to as Lakmé) had helped him to forgive and begin again—at the very place where all the demons were born: Pemberley.

The new direction his life had taken was his salvation—all because of the adoration of one amazing woman. He never imagined, not in a thousand years, that he would be this utterly and completely happy and regenerated, but he was. A year ago, he could not have believed he'd be back on a horse, at Pemberley no less. Back then, he was preparing for a dangerous, government-sanctioned assassination in the bowels of a Bolivian rainforest.

Still, he resisted the troubling urge to acknowledge the cost his past career could have on their partnership, coupled with Liz's own new found need for exhilaration and the inevitable adrenaline rush. He didn't want to explore the possibility of *her* needing more than this tranquil life.

Agile yet controlled, Elektra raced toward the southern paling at the Pemberley estate, ears twitching to his steady instruction. Gloved hands loosely held the reins, allowing the horse freedom in her stride, as he remained centered upon her back, both of them focused toward their goal.

In the nearing distance, the rail fence came into view. Fifty yards beyond it, illuminated in the morning sunlight, three large water bottles filled with bright-red food coloring hung suspended from a thick oak branch.

The horse reacted and obeyed instantly at Darcy's sudden direction to turn. He was on a mission. Still galloping, his former assassin identity re-emerged and deftly withdrew the Baretta pistol from his shoulder holster, firing into the motionless bottles with hoped-for accuracy. It had been a long time since he fired a weapon. The percussion of *bang, bang, bang* repeated as each of the three bottles exploded in instant succession. Red-tinted water poured down like torrents of blood.

Neither Elektra nor he flinched from the forceful blast of the gunshots as they continued along the one-hundred-acre perimeter, again picking up speed.

His mare was no longer a green horse, proving each day to be a potentially superior polo pony than his award-winning Pegasus nineteen years earlier. She was powerful and reveled in playing the game, unafraid of either the high mallet or its combative striking force during the fray—and, now, not even a pistol disturbed her driven focus. Of course, target practice wasn't common training for polo ponies, but on this day it was the beginning of a new exercise drill.

Shifting his weight to give her proper leg cues, Elektra stopped dead on a dime, quickly pivoting. Together, they leisurely trotted back toward the stable.

Gazing up to the cloudless sky, Darcy sighed deeply. The ride was exactly what he needed to clear his mind of his recent worries—worries that had caused him to take up pistol training again. He loathed that his past would impinge on this new life he and Liz were building. He abhorred that anyone or anything might attempt to take away the peace they had found at Pemberley and with each other.

He leaned down and patted the horse's neck. "Don't tell Liz about that little pistol practice, okay, girl? We'll go out again tomorrow, maybe try it at sixty yards. Or maybe, I'll take out my rifle instead and hone some other skills. Sound like a good plan?"

* * *

Three-thousand miles south …

By design, Rick Fitzwilliam looked conspicuously out of place in the City of Palms, located in the jungle plateau of the Amazon, technically, Tarapoto, Peru. His normal fastidious appearance thoroughly sub-jugated, he posed, unshaven and unkempt, as a photojournalist with his atypically long, red hair peeking out from below a Baltimore Orioles baseball cap.

The tropical heat was oppressive. For a man as meticulous in both appearance and hygiene as he prided himself, the perspiration trickling down the crack of his ass from the ninety-degree humidity drove him insane. He shook off the disturbing sensation, deeming it a tolerable, minor consequence in Obsidian's elite world of professional, government-sanctioned hitmen. He'd withstood far worse annoyances.

Deeply entrenched in reconnaissance for Obsidian's Operation Macarena, he was almost unable to suppress a chuckle every time he thought about the name of this assignment. It repeatedly conjured images of the silly dance promoted worldwide by a pair of fortuitous aging South Americans. Where Caroline ever came up with this whimsical stuff was beyond him, but she was seriously talented and at the top of her game—this very real game of espionage and assassination.

As his right-hand at Obsidian, the viper was perpetually ready to strike. She knew every detail of every op and he trusted her perspective implicitly, fully confident that her days of duplicity as a CIA mole were finished. Her loyalty to Obsidian and her discretion were assured.

Operation Macarena's target was the eldest son of the former "Lord of the Jungle" Ricardo Morales, who had met his demise from a solitary shot of the Iceman's sniper rifle ten months ago, taken out during Operation Samba, deep in the Bolivian rainforest. Darcy's hit had been clean, a subject discussed at length a week ago between the cousins.

During these last three days of scouting, rain had fallen relentlessly, making his travel a challenge into the upper Huallaga Valley where the cultivated coca fields lay hidden.

On this op, he had chosen to recon and scout, feeling some pity for whomever would be sniping—probably Bingley. The new recruit, Knightley, was currently on the worst of ops in Sierra Leone in West Africa—a nightmarish, baptism-by-fire field ritual, tagged by Caroline as Operation Viennese Waltz that began at the heart of the diamond mining industry.

Rick nursed a cup of coffee at an outdoor cafe three blocks from the main plaza of this relatively large town, which was considered the commercial hub of northern Peru. Across from him, a group of British bohemians browsed in makeshift open-air artisan shops while local police watched them from a discreet distance.

Nothing evaded Rick's keen observation as he stirred in another teaspoon of sugar, his primary attention remaining riveted on the conversation between two local men seated behind him. They were "falcons" for his target's international drug cartel, La Muerta Mundial. These men acted as ever-present eyes and ears on the street, monitoring the disguised coca-laden trucks driving through Tarapoto and moving onto Colombia twice each day.

Thankful for his past South American tour of duty with the Marine Corps, he translated their conversation with ease, his hearing as keen as a predatory animal.

Laughing, they conversed in Spanish, "America's CIA complied easily enough with our Mexican brothers, four thousand weapons handed over to them."

"Peru will receive more than that. Our fight is larger, covering all the Amazon, three South American countries and rebel forces who are still in allegiance with our rivals."

"Stupid Americans, they give us weapons, and we make addicts of their people." They laughed again; Rick struggled against the instinct to clench his fists.

The men spoke of the new head of the cartel's long absence from Peru and his recent rendezvous in Europe with a spider she-devil. Apparently, a "special package" was on its way to the she-devil for safekeeping. All that remained was the trade off—kilos of arms from the CIA in exchange for the special package.

Rick's measured assessment reasoned that "the package" alluded to a possible kidnapping.

They also referred to a second package. This one was definitely a person, someone who would soon be handed over to La Muerta Mundial *"en bandeja de plata"*—on a silver platter.

Without warning, in primitive English, one of the falcons loudly addressed him, frightening a stray dog hovering at the edge of the café. "You there. Americano. Who are you?"

Rick lowered his cup and turned with a brilliant smile, holding forward his camera and pointed to the press credentials for *National Geographic* magazine clipped to his multi-pocketed fishing vest pocket. In English, he replied with deliberate enunciation, "Journalist. Writing an article on Machu Picchu and the Inca Trail."

Attempting to intimidate him, both falcons stood and moved to station themselves directly before him. One man fingered the press identification dismissively. The other withdrew an eight-inch jungle knife and began to clean under his dirt-encrusted fingernails, a sinister smile revealing the large gap between rotting front teeth.

Ever the consummate front man, Rick motioned to the two seats on either side of him. "Would you like to be interviewed? Please … join me for coffee."

Both men laughed, turned away, and left him to finish his now tepid Peruvian coffee.

The intelligence, as previously laid out by Thomas Bertram, Director of the CIA, initially seemed accurate, but after overhearing this illuminating conversation, clearly the director had omitted some vital information about this sanctioned hit.

With this newly gleaned, staggering information, his reconnaissance had unexpectedly taken a disconcerting detour—one that pointed the way to two possible kidnappings, most likely blackmail, and definitely CIA corruption, not to mention arms dealing and a worldwide network of conspiracy.

As soon as the Falcons left the café, he settled his tab. With any luck, he would be on a flight out of Lima in four hours. First stop: Langley for a little "talk" with Bertram. Last stop: Obsidian's headquarters in D.C., aka The Bingley Dance Studio.

He strolled toward the edge of town, shooting photographs in the process to disguise his observation of anyone tracking or tailing him. Confident that he wasn't being followed, and sufficiently distant from pedestrian traffic or late afternoon commerce, he removed the specially designed, signal-blocking smart phone from his vest pocket and called Caroline over Obsidian's shielded Skype account. Only an hour difference in time, she was most likely at the dance school, teaching. He entered a designated code that scrambled the call, made the IP address un-retrievable, and spiked the signal through three countries and eight different servers.

A flash of shiny red hair came onto his small screen a bare moment before his lover's perfect smile appeared. His heart thumped slightly, as his groin stirred automatically. Yes, he was still stupidly hanging on to her and giving her a pass on all her relationship shortcomings, but the sex was awesome. That had to account for something, right?

"Hey, sugar. I'm headed stateside as soon as I can get on a flight out of Lima."

"You're cutting the trip short? Were you able to accomplish what you needed?"

"Yes and no. I'll discuss it with you when I'm back. First, I have to see Bertram. Listen, gather the team; this is bigger than we thought."

Caroline furrowed her brow. "Bigger as in a job worth more than two million?"

"Bigger as in CIA corruption, and we've been suckered into the thick of it. I'm not comfortable with this. It feels like a set up."

"I'm not surprised. What about Knightley? He's still out in the field on Operation Viennese Waltz."

"Bring him in. Diamond mining despots are going to have to wait until we wrap this one up. I'm sure he'll be happy. Mr. Clean didn't expect this op to take him eight degrees north of the Equator. I can empathize with him," Rick said.

"Hmm, it's protocol. Consider it his hazing ritual. For an ex-SEAL, he'd grown too comfortable and indulged. At least it let him sweat all that champagne and caviar out of his body."

"I've got to go. I'll see you at four in 48 hours."

"Be safe. Watch your back and don't forget you have my favorite new ninja toy with you if you need it."

"I won't need it. I'm outta here." He disconnected and shoved the phone into his deep cargo pant pocket.

He never even felt the needle puncture his neck from behind. He was on the ground in seconds, immobilized and hovering between life and death.

2

Sublime

A distinct low growl rumbled through the quiet morning air from the gleaming black and chrome SuperLow Harley Davidson as foggy mist hung low in the valley ahead, surrounding the rider's destination.

Black rubber tires melded upon the hard pitch pavement where each quick, yellow dash grabbed the rider's attention and led the way like breadcrumbs toward home. Northern Virginia in late spring was the most glorious place, particularly during an early morning ride when the rising sun cast pink and violet shades upon the new green grass. The picturesque roadway was dotted beautifully with trees bursting with the newness of spring, and it tugged at her heartstrings.

As though connected in a symbiotic relationship, the rider carefully and expertly made smooth turns around blind spots that most novices would have a difficult time navigating, but practice had made perfect over these last eight months. The roads toward Leesburg were now familiar and cherished, leading the way to the heart—love, security, and peace—Pemberley.

Eight days had been entirely too long to be away, as though nourishment long denied.

Even in the early morning, music filled the black state-of-the-art motorcycle helmet Liz Darcy wore, shuffling an eclectic playlist ranging from opera's *Lakmé*, *Turandot*, and Rachmaninoff to Bad Company, Boston, and now Steppenwolf's "Born to Be Wild." This particular song loudly demanded she take her new bike up a notch. The powerful lyrics penetrated her core setting her spirit free. Seventy miles per hour hardly seemed extreme, but on these roads, it was enough to defy the grim reaper especially when traversing low, thick fog.

She laughed brazenly at death, unvanquished by the voice repeating within her conscience—that of her overprotective, suddenly cautious husband, *"Slow down. You're taking the road too fast. Trust me, you can't cheat death forever."*

Liz loved the thrill of the bike and its power of velocity. She was born for this, born for speed and adventure. Behind the face shield, she again laughed at how she overcame the suffocating road of life she had foolishly traveled on during the past eight years. *That* was death. *This* is life.

Almost in defiance of her husband Fitzwilliam's resounding words, her black-gloved hand gassed the throttle, pushing the hog's engine revs a little higher still.

Again, his admonition repeated in her mind. Their first real fight happened when she almost wiped out while recklessly taking a hairpin turn too fast around Catoctin Curve. The minute she stopped the hog to calm her heart rate, kicked the rest into place, and lifted her helmet visor, her husband was off his Harley and in her space with his handsome face furiously distorted in anger.

"What the hell did you think you were doing back there? You don't take these turns doing 40 as though you're invincible! How many times have I told you that when cornering you need to look ahead, enter your turn on the outside? At the very least you should have counter-steered!" Throwing up his hands in frustration he walked from her, his heavy, black boots crunching over the freshly displaced gravel. He turned back in fury. *"You never listen to me! You plowed right through that gravel. You should have gone around it, braked before it!"*

"I knew what I was doing … so what if I braked a little late? I had complete control! I didn't lose traction. Stop telling me what to do or I'll crash for sure," Liz defiantly protested.

Darcy stormed back to her and snatched the key from the motorcycle's ignition. "This is not fucking Grand Theft Auto, and you're riding like an asshole!"

She put her gloved hand on her leather-clad hip. "Did you just call me an asshole?"

"I said you're riding like an asshole."

"Look, Al taught me to ride just fine back in Alexandria!"

"Well, Al is not your husband! I've been riding for fifteen years and you're going to fight me because you're feeling headstrong and obstinate? This isn't Monte Carlo Roulette. Riding a motorcycle is Russian Roulette and you're sure as hell not going to be playing either if you keep this up!"

"You can't stop me from riding, Fitzwilliam," she stated petulantly, jutting her chin.

"This is not up for negotiation."

He got back on his bike and forcefully lowered his helmet onto his head. He sat there waiting for her next defiant reply, sure it would come.

"Now what am I going to do? I can't walk home," she asked.

"Get on and I'll take you home. Gus and I'll come back for the bike later."

After that fight, Liz had come to see that it was just Darcy's manner—that Iceman way—that made him so protective. But she had to admit, at times it felt really good and other times, it felt a little like he thought her incapable of existing without his guidance. Apart from the bickering, they'd had six months of marital bliss and harmony; the quiet existence of horse training and occasional travel had brought her back to life. Even things considered mundane became exciting when done together. Laughter filled their home and their passion never tempered.

He'd changed her life and she had changed his. They loved each other deeply. She thanked the day he saved her from making the biggest mistake of her life in almost marrying Bill Collins. Time and again, she berated her then-willful blindness, never recognizing the obvious—her fiancé was gay and she, as his beard, would have forfeited her family estate into his greedy hands. She was a different woman then—afraid to live, afraid to leave, afraid to love, just plain afraid …

The Harley slowed at the final turn when the large, black wrought iron gates bearing the *P* insignia came into view. Home. Within seconds, massive hinges slowly rotated and with just enough width of aperture, the brazen rider who, since meeting Darcy repeatedly tempted fate, squeezed through. Only another split-second passed before she smiled broadly at the scene she encountered: the sublime tranquility of the last kiss of cherry blossoms in spring formed a white welcoming tunnel of heavenly beauty set between two lush, green fields. She felt as though she'd arrived in Paradise.

She gassed the throttle for the two-mile drive toward the mansion, and the Harley bulleted under the tall blossoming tree-lined drive. Tiny white, rose, and green buds surrounded her like a descending halo of heaven-scented clouds. The speed of the bike wheels created a whirl to the fallen petals on the pavement, spinning them into a cyclone in the kicked up wake. It wasn't the surrounding landscape she was anxious for; seven lonely nights was far too long a stretch to be away from this place and the one person whose presence filled it.

As the Harley sped, she noted that Darcy had turned the horses out for early morning grazing in the surrounding green fields. A blurred vision of the stallion Salaam, named for the hotel where they had fused together their healing hearts, appeared to be kissing Elektra in the western field.

Finally, the hog came to a stop beside Darcy's polished red Ferrari on the circular drive before the mansion. After kicking the stand into place, she climbed off, one leg rising gracefully over the seat. With a quick lift of the sleek helmet, she released long, chestnut locks falling loose into the breeze, the brilliant sun illuminating each shiny strand.

Casting unencumbered eyes out across the vast surrounding landscape of Pemberley, a reflective sigh stopped her as she immediately absorbed the tranquility the estate held. If ever she thought Longbourn was the most perfect place in the world, she had been mistaken. Nowhere on the face of the earth embodied such peacefulness as Pemberley. It was breathtaking.

As anticipated, her husband would not be there to greet her arrival. She was sure that the sound of the SuperLow's arrival went unheard because her man was most likely engaged within one particular barn stall and that commanded his full attention—Mallika, her newest mare, was foaling. Hence, the reason Darcy hadn't joined her in visiting her father at Longbourn. Well, and apart from the fact that he abhorred her father.

Resting the helmet on the seat, she removed her gloves then righted her leather jacket and pants before striding toward the barn where she assumed he would be.

Happy butterflies fluttered in her stomach—Darcy's embrace was only a matter of minutes away.

Incredibly reminiscent of their reunion eight months earlier, Liz silently leaned against the post of the stall observing her handsome, jean and T-shirt-wearing husband kneeling within, encouraging her chestnut horse as it groaned, endeavoring to deliver the foal. As much as Liz desired to embrace and kiss him—among other things—she wouldn't disturb him. She believed he'd been nervous about Mallika's delivery, perhaps because the mare was *her* horse. Maybe in some small measure Darcy was projecting. Of course, they weren't even near making those plans, but still.

From the taut tension apparent in his body, she imagined his Iceman expression firmly set in place. Lately, she had seen a lot of that face, but he consistently denied that anything troubled him. Logically, she assumed his concerns were over Mallika's difficult gestation.

From her covert station in the barn, she watched as the horse's body rocked, her rib cage expanding and contracting, birthing her foal. Liz stood fascinated by the process and strength of her mare, as were Darcy and Gus Reynolds squatting beside the horse, awaiting the natural progression of the little one's body to expel within the thin white sac.

She held her breath observing how Darcy resisted the urge to assist in the delivery. The tribal snake tattoo on his forearm moved and slithered as his hand tapped his knee in restless anxiety. She knew that release well. Before the safety and security of his presence in her life, it had been a nervous habit practiced almost every day.

All three watched and waited for the full emergence of the foal. The birth was one more example of how life had come back to Pemberley, particularly this long dreaded barn where death once held its ransom.

"Should we help her, Gus?" he asked anxiously.

"No, she's doing fine. Progression hasn't stopped. It's only been about eight minutes."

Liz remained still and silent, yet unobserved. She almost wanted to pinch herself. Could life get any better than this? She imagined that with the addition of children, it would.

A chill crept up her back and she sobered. For some reason, she couldn't help the niggling fears that plagued her on occasion—now being one of those times. Would this quiet life truly be enough for a man who lived by his own code for so long? Could the tranquil existence of a horse trainer and breeder replace the 007-esque life he had led as a professional assassin? Would he someday feel the need to go back to Obsidian? It had been a few weeks since she last allowed those fears to surface, but the days spent at Longbourn reminded her of the dangerous life Darcy once led.

Seeing him in the barn, enthusiastic as new life emerged, made her push those darker thoughts deep down, assuring herself that he was happy and precisely where he wanted to be: at Pemberley, with her.

Minutes more passed in silence waiting as Mallika patiently continued to birth her little one all on her own.

Darcy laughed, "God, I wish Liz was here to see this!"

Behind him, she giggled loud enough for him to hear.

His head turned with the brightest of smiles and dark eyes filled with joy all for her. As happy as he was about the foaling, it was clear he was overjoyed by her safe arrival home.

"Hey, baby," Liz seductively greeted.

"You made record time ... again," Darcy playfully chastised.

"Hi, Gus."

"Welcome home, Liz. Safe trip?"

"Of course. You know I'm *very* careful."

Darcy laughed, then mockingly used her own signature swear word, "Bulldinky."

"I do believe it was you who once told me and I quote ..." Lowering her voice she imitated his. "Don't be afraid. Danger is real, but if you allow the fear of it, then you'll never enjoy the thrill of the experience."

He gazed up to her twisting lips. "Once again, I'm bitten by those sharp fangs of yours, my serpentine. When I said that, I was *trying* to get into your pants."

Gus laughed. It was good to have them together, bantering back and forth.

Minutes later, Mallika's foal entered the world in a wet, half-covered heap onto the thick straw, his white blaze shining against the black of his hide. The mare raised her head from the straw and looked at her offspring, both curious about the other.

"Hot damn, he's beautiful." Darcy effused low enough not to startle. "Good girl, Mallika."

His gleeful laugh lit his face. "Did you see that, Liz? My God! I'm glad you arrived in time."

She laughed back, "I see it! Good thing I rode like a wild woman to get here."

Gus snorted when she winked at him, clearly sharing his love and penchant to push Darcy's buttons.

Darcy rose from the straw and indicated to Gus to finish the delivery of the afterbirth. He peeled off his latex gloves and in two long strides scooped his wife up into his arms. His kisses were fueled with intensity as she wrapped her legs around his waist, allowing him to carry her into the empty stall beside them.

"I missed you," he growled, pressing her back against the stable wall and attacking the soft skin of her neck.

"I missed you more," she panted.

"I need you."

"I need you more."

"We'll come … back to see the colt later. Okay?" he said, making his intention understood.

"Hmm … colt … what colt?" she purred against his neck.

With strong hands cupping her motor-sore backside, he carried her out into the fresh morning air straight toward the mansion, their lips barely separating even as they took the steps to the master suite.

* * *

From the gourmet kitchen on the floor below Darcy and Liz's bedroom, Ellen Reynolds could discern the passionate vocalizations of the man she practically raised from infancy. Recently, it wasn't anything new to her ears. In fact, she chuckled because it had become rather familiar. She secretly hoped a baby would someday soon fill this home with happiness, because it had been unhappy for far too long. Ellen shook off her dark thought, and turned them to the happiness in "her boy's" life, thanks to his new wife.

After covering the fresh-baked blueberry muffins under tin foil, Ellen grabbed her coat, hung up Liz's discarded jacket from the floor, and left the house to see the new foal. Now that the lady of the house was back, it was time to go home. Those two lovers needed alone time.

* * *

Upstairs, Darcy and Liz were oblivious to the outside world after he kicked the bedroom door shut. With her legs still wrapped around his waist, he pressed her back against the solid oak and continued assailing her neck with suckling kisses.

"You're going to give me a hickey," she objected, lowering her legs to the floor.

"Good."

Immediately, he lifted her sweater over her head, tossing it across the room. His hungry lips attacked her nearest breast through her sheer, delicate, black bra. His teeth tenderly pulled at her nipple in craving, tearing the silky nylon.

She pushed his body away slightly. "Wait ... wait."

"What's the matter?" his voice conveyed disappointment, doubtful that he could survive another minute of not intimately touching her. Slowing his pace, he laid gentle kisses upon her collarbone.

"Don't you want me, baby?" Dejection infused his plea.

"Of course I do." She clasped his hand and led him toward the master bathroom. "I just feel gritty from the road. Shower with me. Let's get dirty while we get clean."

As expected, she didn't need to ask him twice.

The spacious room they entered was both a sitting room overlooking the scenic prospect at the rear of the house and a spa-like bathroom. Streaming sunlight reflected off pristine Carrera marble, which showcased fine bleached wainscoting and teak hardwood flooring. At the far end, beyond a huge, glass-enclosed shower and beneath a wall of windows, sat a claw-footed bathtub charmingly grouped with a white, chaise lounge and matched club chair.

Sashaying away from him toward the center of the space, Liz's tight black apparel presented a deeply erogenous contrast to the bright morning light and fresh purity of the large airy bathroom. He leaned against the doorframe lustfully watching his wife readying to strip for him. Spellbound, he resisted the urge to undress her hurriedly, even tear at her clothes just to touch her, but he could read her determined intention in those vivacious eyes and that lovely pucker of her seductive lips. She wanted to tease him, and she was damn good at it.

Gracefully, she reached to tap the iPad resting in the docking station. It came alive with the riffs of a familiar song that filled the room; he chuckled because she only had one song on the playlist, Joe Cocker's "Leave Your Hat On."

With an aroused blush heating her face, she demurely unzipped her biking pants and rolled the waistband down just below the snake and orchid tattoo on her hipbone; she knew how the slow striptease—and the inked testimony of their entwined hearts—would drive him crazy.

To the music, a circular rotation of her pelvis caused him to groan, especially when she turned her back to him then glanced over her shoulder to see his, no-doubt, hungry expression.

The view she offered of her curvy backside and dimples of Venus enticed him even more. "You're killin' me, Liz."

"I know," she giggled naughtily, turning her head from him.

As soon as she faced away to turn the shower on, he quickly removed his boots, tossing them into the bedroom behind him.

When Liz turned again to face him from the center of the bathroom, she took full measure of his firm body and obvious bulging desire: dilated pupils and slightly parted lips clearly expressed his immediate intention to ravish her. Her eyes seductively traveled his body head to toe, undressing him, stopping briefly at his arousal then proceeding to his bare feet. With a teasing bite to her lower lip, she slowly shimmied down and finally off, the leather encasing her long legs.

She posed before him in matching panties and bra, with silken hair cascading beyond her shoulders, one aroused nipple poked through the mesh fabric where his teeth had torn a hasty breach.

He nearly begged, "Can I kiss you now?"

"Patience, patience."

"C'mon, Lizzy. Please?"

His vixen walked to the linen closet beside him. "Lizzy, is it? Oh, you *are* horny, aren't you? I should go away more often," she snickered. "You know how I love to hear you beg. Do it some more."

"Pleeease?"

She smiled wickedly and with an obvious pretense of removing bath towels, bent to the lower shelf, deliberately displaying her backside up to his appraising eyes and the heat of his cauterizing stare. He was dying now as she dillydallied in the closet just long enough to drive him mad at the sight of her bottom and the beauty mark-like small tattoo of a red heart on the top of her left cheek—her Valentine's Day gift to him.

She rose and turned toward him. Her lips drawing into a self-satisfied grin upon seeing that he now stood completely nude at the threshold of the room; his manhood poised at the ready.

Again, Liz meticulously appraised his perfect physique: passion-filled eyes, chiseled jaw, broad shoulders, sexy tribal tattoos, tight abs, powerful thighs, and finally, his magnificent arousal. Her mouth watered at the image her husband presented.

This time, Darcy did beg when he pointed to his erection with prideful prowess, "*Now* can I touch you?"

She stepped into his embrace and pressed her mouth to his in a teasing, agonizing kiss as she wrapped her hand around his rigid shaft, leisurely stroking him with playful, tortuous intent. Breathlessly, she tormented him with a sinister, "Not yet."

Stepping back from him, she took her time with deliberate seduction, unhooking her bra followed by a downward slide of her panties. Deftly, she kicked the flimsy items directly into his bereft outstretched hand.

She raised an index finger bringing his hot, bothered, and now frustrated rapt attention to her taut nipple where it tantalizingly circled. She batted her eyelashes. "Is this what you want to do?"

"Yeeesss…" he spoke eagerly then involuntarily licked his lips.

Liz's finger traveled provocatively down her abdomen to her bare apex. "Is this what you want to do?"

"Oh, Lizzy," he growled. "*This* is what I want to do." In two long strides, he was in front of her, their lips crashing together, kissing impatiently. Her legs automatically wrapped around his waist when he lifted her into the shower stall.

The warm water from above fell like summer rain, slicking their bodies as heated flesh collided with frantic caresses. The mist within the shower grew quickly into thick heated steam, enveloping them.

The quickness wasn't what Liz had planned, even though she had thought about her shower seduction the whole ride home. The slow, soapy, intimate lathering of each other, the water toys, and the detachable showerhead would all have to wait for round two.

"I missed you, babe," Darcy groaned, sliding her down his body onto his hardness. The moment he entered her, his moan of pleasure and deep pants sounded like music to her ears.

Moving to the shower seat, she straddled his frame, rising and falling as water flowed down upon them. Her wet nipples brushed against his lips with each controlled, teasing glide of her body. Taking one ripe tip into his mouth, he flicked his tongue. "Harder," she panted until he fully surrounded her sensitive peak.

"Harder," she exclaimed again, his mouth working its magic on her. The power of her, much anticipated, orgasm shot through her like liquid energy, and her legs squeezed tightly around him. He couldn't hold back his own rapture and together they crashed, shaking breathlessly, clinging to each other.

Darcy's lips clung to hers as he lifted her from him, then stood, his arms encircling her body, holding her to him. Under the warm, steady spray of water, they faced one another, expressions filled with adoration. She was radiant, her cheeks flushed with the afterglow of lovemaking, not from the steam. Cupping her face, he kissed her sweetly. Their mouths savored one another with measured tempo before separating in profound emotion.

"I love you, Mr. Darcy," she stated, gazing into his eyes.

"And I love you, Mrs. Darcy," he replied, smoothing a wet curl from her forehead. "How would you like for me to wash your hair, beautiful?"

Her smile bowled him over. Liz had obviously missed the languid, gentle intimacy of lathering and caressing.

When his fingers massaged her scalp with loving attention, it fully confirmed to him just how genuinely happy he was.

3
South American Way

Friday nights at Bingley Dance School always attracted an eclectic cast of characters for the weekly Latin dance group class. Three instructors and twenty or so students gyrated and shimmied to the syncopated rhythm. April's dance theme at the school was a new program instituted by Caroline, her cheekily scheduled tribute to Obsidian's Operation Macarena. Tonight was Cali-Salsa—clandestinely, in honor of South America.

Charlie Bingley looked over the two facing lines of students: Men stood with their backs to the mirror, women opposite with their backs to the reception desk where Fanny sat. His eyes traveled to the far end of the women's line, seeking their newest part-time instructor, Jane Bennet. Of course, she barely had teaching experience or any ballroom dance knowledge for that matter, but their private lessons over the last month had paid off wildly. The rhythm she demonstrated between the sheets, in the Cessna, on the beach, and even in a hot air balloon, impressed the co-owner of the school—her lover of the past eight months. He knew, when applied in a different manner on the dance floor, his girl was exactly what the school needed. Her smile and *joie de vive* was perfectly suited to the profession of a dance instructor.

Moving to center of the group he clapped focusing the students' attention. "Okay class. Great turnout tonight. Thanks for joining us. I'm glad you're all excited to learn the Cali-Salsa, which originated in the country of Colombia. This form of Salsa is fast and fun. We're going to learn the basics to dancing socially in clubs. The focus is on the rapid, precise footwork. Let me demonstrate the first part."

He held out his hand. "Jane, would you assist me?"

Her smile told him exactly what she wanted to assist him with. Oh, he could tell his vixen felt very naughty tonight. Now that her sister returned to Pemberley and her father, Thomas, had begun working on a new project, the newly repressed Janie seemed to let loose—finally uncaged like the tigress she truly was.

Tonight, she looked hot wearing a fuchsia, pleather mini skirt and a plunging scoop necked T-shirt. It made him happy to see her dressing like the Janie he knew and loved. Her fashion trendiness began to temper once they came back from Marrakech some eight months ago. It had been a gradual transformation, but he certainly noticed. Most days, in an attempt to be taken more seriously at the International Spy Museum where she worked, she wore staid suits with below-the-knee skirts, and demure French manicures on her fingers and toes. Except for the dance group lessons, gone were the shocking avant-garde styles and colors that screamed, "Take notice of me. I'm Janie and I love to have fun, fun, fun." This was one of the reasons he was glad she came to the school every Wednesday and Friday night. His girl and her pink, press-on nails always showed up in full form.

He adored her trendy looks, and tonight she looked especially delectable—like a pink lollipop he could lick all night. Actually, he mused to himself, she looked quite do-able at this very moment, right here in the middle of the dance floor below the disco ball, surrounded by walls of mirrors. The fact that this scene presented a perfect location for screwing to Teddy Pendergrass's "Love T.K.O," flitted fast through his head. It wouldn't be the first time they did that. Maybe she'd consider a private striptease on that thick rope Caroline uses to practice her upper body strengthening and dexterity. As he thought of Jane's seductive strip, he resisted the temptation to look up at the rope wrapped around one of the beams above the dance floor, in front of all these students. With memories like that, he wasn't sure if he could get through this dance class without a perpetual hard on.

During their next teacher/student private lesson, he'd have to remember to disconnect the new security cameras Caroline installed last year following Operation Two-Step when that crazy one-eyed Texan followed her back to D.C.

Their eyes locked when he firmly held both of Jane's hands between their bodies, but he refocused, and addressed the class, "These are the basic face-to-face steps, if you can, ignore the swivel of my assistant's hips and concentrate initially on the precise footwork. The hip movement comes later."

He winked at the woman he loved, and she smiled back in that flirty-cute way of hers before slowly running the tip of her pink tongue over her lip with that innocent, vixen look he'd grown so accustomed to. She always did that to make him hard at the most inopportune times and it was working.

The studio filled with Latin energy when Caroline cued up the salsa music, and he and Jane demonstrated the various basic footwork.

Just as Jane moved back in line, the happy jingle above the door alerted Caroline that her own participation in dance instruction for the evening had concluded. There was now other business to attend to—real business, life-taking business now that Knightley arrived.

Obsidian's newest member John Knightley sauntered through the front door with his black knapsack slung over one of his very broad shoulders. As usual, the man's steel blue eyes drew her in. His tall, muscular frame mesmerized her—enticing her into imaginings of his virility, his assured prowess. He was all man; that was for sure. Although her current tastes were for a lover of style and class, who paid attention to the details and appreciated expensive wine and clothing, she just couldn't help her lustful attraction to Knightley's rawness. The agent was careless and reckless, living by the seat of his pants, enjoying life with a "dare me" smile plastered on his face. Even his crooked bottom teeth were a source of fascination. She wanted to live dangerously in his arms even though she had, *sort of*, promised never to deceive or hurt Rick again. But real promises required a conscience, and she freely admitted to herself that she didn't have one of those.

From the beginning of her acquaintance with Knightley—the night they rescued Operation Virginia Reel's target, Thomas Bennet, in Marrakech—his energy had captivated her. He was a fine replacement for Darcy; Iceman, unfortunately, had melted, and was now playing house in Northern Virginia with his little woman.

The man before her straddled two different worlds just as Darcy had: life and death. She could tell he goaded death for himself behind that cool, daring persona he conveyed. This, of course, made him excellent agent material for Obsidian. She knew his backstory. Hell, everyone knew his backstory and it wasn't pretty: his son's kidnapping, the fight, the misfire, the guilt, the abandonment by his ex-wife Katie. Three months later, Knightley had replaced his old life with a new country, a new employer, a string of women, expensive habits, and carefree living as the personal bodyguard to one of the richest men in the world. Or so he said; Knightley had never actually named his former employer.

His black sneakers squeaked on the highly polished, wood dance floor as he made his way to the office at the rear of the studio, eyes briefly meeting hers. He raised his hand to his forehead in flippant, sarcastic salute.

"Excuse me, Mr. Knightley," Fanny the studio receptionist interrupted. His rubber soles made a sudden halting noise when he turned to deliver a genuine warm grin.

"Hi, Fanny. What can I do for you?"

"I just … um … wanted to say it's nice to have you back. Will you be staying in town for a while?"

"Probably not. The other dance schools keep me busy around the country." He paused, noting how she wore a little makeup and had highlighted her hair. "You look lovely tonight. New blouse?"

Flustered, she fixed her collar, blushing and stammering. "Yes ... I umm. Yes. Thank you."

He could feel Caroline behind him and imagined her standing with arms folded, tapping one black sandaled dance shoe in time to the Latin music reverberating in the studio. From the corner of his eye, he saw he was right. As usual, the viper looked fantastic, wearing a flirty, black dance skirt and leopard print, clingy top. *That's right, it's Latin night and she enjoys dressing the part.*

"Well, well, well, look who finally decided to show up. We had a meeting scheduled at four o'clock today," she stated, leading the way to the office.

He winked at Fanny before following, deliberately goading Caroline by bemoaning loud enough for her to hear, "Yeah, well you try washing twelve layers of insect repellent off your dick. Some things take time, Viper."

"That's funny, Knightley. You could have called me. I would have gladly helped. I'm sure an extra hand would have been appreciated."

"I don't think Rick would have liked that very much."

She sat down at her desk, examining her perfectly lacquered fingernails with indifference. "He doesn't need to know."

"*I'd* know. Believe it or not, I actually live by a code of honor. I have too much respect for my boss *and* Darcy than to dip my wick into a well-used pot. As I told you when we first met, sloppy seconds aren't my gig. I don't roll that way."

She feigned a smooth smile. "I'll ignore your insult. As for Darcy, he's old news. Whatever he sees in that woman is beyond me. She doesn't have what it takes to keep a man like Iceman tied down to one place long enough. Mark my words—before long, he'll be itching to leave, finding excuses to be away, living on the edge again. People like us need that fuel that Obsidian and living with one foot in hell can provide."

Taking a seat before her, he disagreed. "You're wrong. Darcy loves his life and he loves Liz. Nothing, absolutely nothing, could entice him back into this life of death—not even the devil himself—or his daughter. As for you and me, I suspect we both have reasons for choosing this dangerous career. You, because you *are* actually the spawn of the devil, and me, because I lost my soul years ago and don't give a crap whether I live or die." He grinned widely, enjoying the burn of anger to her face.

He'd never admit (to her anyway) the real reason he chose to join Obsidian. This wasn't a do-over or a reset button. It was, plain and simple, an escape from the death of his heart. The job served to cover the never-ending remorse and sadness he fought every day.

"What happened in Sierra Leone?" Caroline inquired, noting the cuts to his cheek and those upon his smoothly shaven head.

"I lost the target and, after your instructions, started my escape. Somehow, my hide site was compromised. I ran balls out through the rainforest with machete-wielding members of the rebel Kamajors hot on my ass. My only escape was to jump off a cliff and crash into a waterfall and the river below."

"Were you made?"

"Not with rifle in hand. I wasn't spotted until I started my descent down the mountain. That waterproof jungle camo paint that Rick overnighted to me in Austria did the trick at keeping me concealed. And here I thought I'd be wearing a tux in Vienna, not chasing some conflict diamond despot into West Africa." He shrugged, making light of the nightmare he went through. "So, what's so urgent that you called me off Viennese Waltz?"

The concern in her voice surprised him when she said gravely, "Rick called our meeting and while I expected him at four o'clock, our usual meeting time, he has yet to show or even contact the studio. I know he had to stop at Langley, but I can't imagine what waylaid him."

"Did you try contacting him?"

"I did, multiple ways, actually. Nothing. I normally wouldn't worry, but during our last communiqué he had some disturbing news."

"So, Rick's never done anything like this before, disappear off the grid unexpectedly?"

"He has. Once. I think he even overrode the GPS in his mobile just so I couldn't keep track of his whereabouts. He takes his personal life privacy to the umpteenth measure sometimes."

"Maybe he has another woman on the side?"

"Pfft. Rick? Not likely."

He looked through the office window toward the dance floor where Charlie danced with a petite Asian woman. He chuckled, watching his friend smile in that charming way he employed whenever a beautiful woman was within twelve inches of him.

"What does Charlie think about Rick's delay?"

"We're both concerned. Rick is extremely fastidious when it comes to communication and detail during an operation. This op he was sent to recon isn't any ordinary terrorist hit. These people are South American drug traffickers and he's out in the northern Amazon jungle. Sure, he has contingency and escape plans if necessary, but the reality is, he could be dead. I don't say that lightly, contrary to what you may think. Both Charlie and I agree that if we don't hear from Rick before dawn, my first Obsidian order of business is to pay a visit to CIA headquarters and demand answers from Bertram."

"Why would you think the CIA has information on his disappearance?"

"Why? Because Bertram is as corrupt as they come and he was the one who insisted that Fitzwilliam do the scouting on this. Have no fear though—he'll break with the help of some of my little ninja toys," Again, Caroline looked at her fingernails, subtly but immodestly, referencing her skill set.

"Are you just assuming he's corrupt because he gives Obsidian such a difficult time due to his extraordinary disdain of the U.S military?"

"No, I used to work with him—actually *for* him—as a Company mole placed within Obsidian. His background isn't as innocent as the current Administration led the Senate or the American people to believe. No matter the political party, I doubt American voters would stand for a former KGB remnant of the Cold War as the Director of the CIA. However effective he may be when America needs to better understand how the current Russian administration thinks, the fallout from such information would be catastrophic."

"So, he wasn't with the Department of Education before his appointment?"

"Oh he was, but while you were playing with toy guns on the playground, the CIA *supposedly* turned Mr. Thimofai Borislav in the late eighties. That bit of intelligence is so top secret that the State Department conveniently forgot—or ignores it."

Knightley thoughtfully tented his fingers before his chin. "Are you implying that the Director of the CIA could actually be a double-agent for the Russian government? A dangle sitting in one of the highest positions of foreign intelligence for the U.S government?"

"No. I'm just saying that I have known Bertram to deliver *disinformation* on occasion. His loyalties are *suspect*."

"If he's still working for the Ruskies, then that could definitely connect a drug cartel with the CIA. For some time, it was speculated that Russian officials, military, and mobsters were involved with money laundering for the now defunct Cali Cartel, particularly involving them in arms trading. How do you know this about the director?"

Caroline raised both eyebrows. "Let's just say, I didn't get to be a mole, placed within our little organization here without paying my dues, if you understand me correctly. Not every one of my skills belong to a ninja master."

* * *

With only partial faculties operating and only two of his senses functioning, Rick gradually came-to after the kidnapping. He supposed he was located deep in the Huallaga Valley, probably at the jungle base camp of La Muerta's expansive coca plantation.

Both wrists and ankles were securely bound and, with eyes covered, he relied on his hearing and sense of smell. The calming constant rushing of a nearby waterfall was punctuated by crowded conversations amongst the abundant parrot population that thrived within the surrounding jungle recesses. Along with the reminiscent scent of the Amazon's rich soil, the pungent, thick odor of wet and rotting leaves mixed with the sweetness of the flora called to mind his tour of duty in Colombia. Yes, it all confirmed to him exactly where he was: deep within the rainforest.

Even through the lingering fog of the drug's effect, Rick noted that being held hostage deep in the Amazon jungle afforded him the opportunity to accomplish what he hadn't been able in three days of scouting. If he wanted an inside look at the operations, well, he surely couldn't get any more up close and personal than this.

Smelling himself, he crinkled his nose at the distasteful onslaught of wet mule. Its putrid stink attacked his now overly-sensitive olfactory, made stronger by the missing other three senses.

A woman's British accented voice surprised him. "Oi, wake up." She kicked his shoulder lying in straw and leaves, as she demanded again. "Hurry, wake up!"

"Hmm ... What?..." The drug, whatever narcotic they gave him, was starting to wear off. Thankfully so, because the intense hallucinogenic dreams he'd had freaked him out, as well as the fact the he was now temporarily paralyzed. Rick attempted to free his bound hands, but couldn't feel them.

"Who are you?" he asked.

"Sarah Caulfield, *London Times*. They kidnapped me about ten days ago."

"Why would they kidnap a reporter?"

"I was investigating the Amazon's new coca production and its increased trafficking into the UK through Moscow. Who are you?"

"That's right. I remember now ... I read ... about you. I'm Rick Fitzwilliam, *National Geographic* magazine. Are you hurt?"

"Just a broken wrist, but better than you appear to be. Does that gash to your head hurt?"

"My head? I can't feel a ... damn thing yet. I don't have any feeling from this drug."

"It'll wear off. You've been out of it for at least twenty or so hours. They'll be coming for you soon. I heard them talking outside the hut. They said something about you giving them *hielo* for Diablo. Like you're going to bloody-well produce ice in this swamp."

"Ice? I don't know ... I can't think straight. We're in a hut? That's good. Probably their base camp ... cocaine processing lab should be relatively close. Do you smell the ammonia?"

"That's a new smell," Sarah stated, raising her nose in the air.

"It's a good sign. Where there is coca extraction, there are weapons the sicarios leave to protect the goods."

"Forget about escape. We're screwed, dead to the rest of the world here. Unless you have ice, which I'd be stoked if you did, then we're stuck here until both our governments decide *not* to do something."

"I'm not worried," Rick calmly reassured.

"Not, worried? We're journalists, not your bloody MacGyver," Sarah snapped, her fear and worry reaching a final boiling point with the introduction of this delusional man.

"How often do you hear helicopters?"

"Maybe once or twice, but I'm sure they're not looking for me."

"You're right; they're DEA or military looking for the extraction labs below the jungle canopy."

With sensation gradually returning to Rick's head, he winced as he slowly and methodically moved it back, forth, and around, skillfully loosening the binding over his eyes until finally it lay beneath him. His gaze met Sarah's dark blue eyes, blonde hair held in disarray by a ponytail and a pretty smile upon a dirty face.

"Pleased to meet you, Sarah." He smiled that convincing smile of his and positively encouraged her, "Stick with me and I'll get us out of here in no time. First, I have to find out what the hell they want from me and second, I need to get the feeling back into my limbs. Then we're home free."

"Great ... just great. They stick me with a twit who thinks he can easily leg it out of here. Trust me, Mr. Fitzwilliam, we aren't going anywhere and even if we were, I've been told by my informants that the cartel has booby trapped the jungle." She deliberately tugged on her good arm's wrist shackles secured to somewhere beyond the hut's tree-branch perimeter.

"I got news for ya', Sarah. The jungle *is* the booby trap. Have you received your malaria shots?"

She nodded then rolled her eyes.

Rick glanced down to his waist. He still wore Caroline's new ninja belt where three black, steel shuriken throwing stars nested behind a wood inlay buckle. The belt itself comprised of two woven paracords that once untied extended to fifty-six feet, capable of supporting up to five hundred pounds.

"Trust me—I've been in tighter situations than this. Based on the smell in the air, and the strength of the waterfall, the Huallaga River isn't far. After the rain we just had, they'll be some rapids, but it's do-able."

Sarah chuckled again, shaking her head at the overly cocky American.

The makeshift door to the hut flew open and two menacing men stood glaring at them. They were most likely falcons or rebels, one of them wearing a camo fatigue jacket and Rick's Baltimore Orioles cap.

Damn! I loved that hat, Rick momentarily lamented.

The other man, big, burly and bald, grabbed Rick's bound feet, sliding his entire one hundred and eighty-pound frame through the narrow opening into the oppressive green hell of the jungle. A rickety aluminum chair stood conspicuously out of place in the center of the camp into which they carelessly sat him. He didn't fight. His body, formerly dead weight, was only just coming back to life.

Cold eyes inconspicuously examined his surroundings, noting his cell phone tossed on the other side of the fire pit from where he sat. Smashed to pieces on the ground, it could be of no use to him now beyond the fact that Caroline had most likely been alerted to its lost signal once he entered the jungle.

The two captors conversed openly with each other, unaware that the red-headed Anglo understood Spanish even if littered with the local Amazoan dialect. The bald one, most likely a lieutenant for Diablo, addressed Rick in passably proficient English with a thick Russian accent, but not before slamming the butt of a AK-47 into his prisoner's stomach.

"Do you know why we have taken you?"

"For my devastatingly handsome looks, hoping to make me your bitch?" Rick coughed out before grinning like a Cheshire cat.

Again, the butt slammed into his gut.

"La Muerta has been awaiting your arrival. You should know and be very afraid because Diablo has his attention focused on revenge, and your CIA fed you to him like dog you are," the Russian pronounced.

"Yeah, well the CIA and your Diablo can kiss my ass. I'm not afraid of hell or the devil."

A third, more forceful time, the AK-47 made contact. Rick grit his teeth, wincing in pain from the sudden crack within his ribcage.

"We are prepared to release you but first Diablo would like information about this Iceman responsible for killing The Lord of the Jungle," the short Peruvian captor informed him.

Rick looked up, trying not to convey his pain when he spoke. "I know no *Iceman*, but since my balls are sweating, I would like to make his acquaintance." Hiding the terror in his heart for his cousin, he barely managed that front man smile of his—calm, cool, and collected.

"Laugh, make joke, we will draw him to us and then you will both die," the Russian declared.

"What makes you so sure this Iceman even exists or would come to this God-forsaken rainforest?"

The lieutenant laughed. "Because you are here, and he will come for you and when he does I will slice his balls off and feed them to him. Better yet … I will feed them to you and then pull them out of your throat after I slit it. These South Americans have practice called Columbian necktie. Personally, I prefer 'the swallow' of torture we Russian's practice, but when in Rome …"

Rick gazed upward to the canopy of dense jungle where barely a beam of sunlight broke through the tropical palms, but he could tell that the sun was high, indicating mid-afternoon. In a couple of hours, the temperature drop accompanying the darkness would begin to envelope the rainforest. If only he could reach the sole of his hiking boot, but he wasn't physically ready for that. He'd had no recourse but to slip into that mental place of fortitude and bravado to survive this. His life was negligible, but his cousin's wasn't and sadly, he knew that, without a doubt, it would be Darcy coming for him. Protective Iceman would emerge and insist upon it.

"What makes you think this Iceman will come for me? I'm no one important, just a journalist."

"That is not what your CIA has told us. You are the bait, my ignorant friend." The Russian laughed as he slowly withdrew a Spetnatz military blade from its sheath upon his belt. The spider tattoo on the inside of his forearm now visible.

Rick spit. "You've got the wrong guy, asshole."

The knife sliced down his forearm … slowly … the skin separating, exposing muscle as blood began to flow. He was thankful that full feeling to his arms hadn't yet been restored.

The big man spoke again, "We shall see when fever and infection set in. The jungle delirium as the mosquitoes and flies attack will set your lips talking about Iceman. And if not, you will when the jaguar smells your blood at night. Your need to protect the woman will heighten your sensitivities as big cat mews ready to tear both your flesh, ready to eat your squirming body."

"Not likely. I don't give a shit about the woman and … I assure you that before sun up both you and shorty there will be lying dead and, yes, said jaguar will be enjoying morning breakfast as the sun rises over the eastern ridge." He smiled brilliantly, exposing his gritty feeling, pearly whites.

"You Americans have active imaginations—such positive, delusional thinkers. You should know, the world laughs at you." He glanced over to the smaller Peruvian captor. "Put him back in the hut and tie his hands and feet together behind his back—the position of the swallow. He won't be going anywhere when jaguars come."

Rick was kicked onto the ground then dragged back toward the open hut door as the Russian yelled out. "You should pray for the mythical giant anaconda, Mr. Fitzwilliam. Your death will not be as painful once he arrives to crush and destroy."

And you, my friend, *should fear my cousin, the deadly King Cobra whose provoked attack will leave you writhing and dead within minutes.*

4

Distracted

Liz stretched cat-like in Darcy's arms, and he reveled in the feel of her soft body against his after their renewing afternoon of erotically-charged, emotion-fueled intimacy. He'd missed her fiercely and silently vowed that they would not be apart ever again.

The open windows of their bedroom invited the spring breeze to blow the pale colored curtains into the room. It was late afternoon and the sun already began to sink in the sky over the top of the pine trees in the distant field. She pressed further into his embrace with her backside against him. Such peaceful serenity was in that moment, a quiet calm. Whereas earlier, the perfection they found in each other's arms was accompanied by passionate cries that matched the pounding of their flesh and the headboard against the bedroom wall. The sounds of ecstasy from their coupling carried into the wind out onto the estate where only the pines and birds heard them and their professions of undying love and need for comfort. His frenzied lovemaking had given his wife everything, stripping, and emptying himself completely before collapsing upon her.

Laying there in the stillness of the moment, with her limbs entwined with his, his thoughts grew intensely emotional as he reflected upon the perfection of his life with Liz in it. But he couldn't stop his many fears from growing. Could this perfection last? What if she was restless at Pemberley now that she found her freedom to soar? Her daring and adventurous spirit was growing. Would she flee just as her mother had? Worse yet, what if he had to go back to Obsidian, not by choice, but by need?

In fear of alerting her to his thought process, he resisted the urge to shudder at the prospect. Instead, he wrapped his arms more tightly around her waist, pulling her closer to him.

The echoing sounds of a murder of crows outside felt ominous to him and he sought refuge by burying his face into her neck. He moaned, breathing in her soothing, familiar strawberry scent of her shampoo bringing him back to the moment. There was tranquility in that exact moment, not in the foreboding of things to come.

"A week is entirely too long to be without you," he murmured. "Did you miss me?"

"Silly man. I told you I did, and I told you every day at least three times during each text, voicemail, and conversation."

She gazed at him over her shoulder to read the expression upon his face. "Don't you know that I miss you every moment when our bodies aren't touching in some fashion?"

"It's the same for me," he replied, kissing her bare shoulder, his hand smoothing down the flat plane of her stomach, committing to memory that which had already been branded with fire upon his ice.

Darcy knew every tiny curve and space of her body, and he hoped that 50 years from now he would know her soul just as well—all those little things that make up who Liz is. His kisses to that place behind her ear started the fire within her again as he whispered, "Don't leave me again." He suckled her earlobe. "Ever." He nibbled her earlobe. "Til death," he murmured.

"You've consumed me—heart and soul, Liz."

Turning in his arms, she faced him, their lips a hair's breadth from each other, their warm bodies pressed together, sharing one pillow, one heartbeat. His breath hitched before her delicious lips met his.

She purred, "Today was perfect, arriving home to your arms." She kissed him again. "Your lips. I could just stay like this for the next week."

"And what about food?"

"It's overrated, not worth leaving your embrace for."

"But you'll need energy."

"Hmm … yes.

He laughed lightly, thoroughly lost in this intimacy with her, so sure that he could never love her more than at this moment.

"Sometimes, Fitzwilliam, I can't believe this is real and that we have forever to love one another. I never want this feeling to end."

"It never will end, sweetheart, but we will have to eat."

His free hand tickled in gentle wisps down her arm, enjoying the rising gooseflesh, until his hand clasped hers. Overcome by the intensity of his feelings, he opened his heart further. "Do you know how much I adore you?"

"Yes. Every day, every time we make love you speak your heart … so effectively."

She kissed his chin, then his cheek, finally depositing a gentle peck to his lips. "Will you tell me what's troubling you? The last time you made love to me with as much intensity as you did today was when I came back from my first solo ride on the Hog. I can see your trouble etched on your forehead. Talk to me."

Damn. She pulled him out of this tender moment, and he abruptly rose from bed, following one last kiss to her pert nipple.

He knew she'd see that he didn't want to answer. Yes. He was ostensibly running from her to avoid her question, summarily replacing snuggling in the afterglow of lovemaking with his avoidance, but now was not the time to discuss the worries on his mind.

He donned a terry cloth bathrobe and sat beside her prone figure resting on her side. A gentle caress to her brow brushed away the still damp, unkempt hair from her face and shoulder. "Nothing important or worth discussing. Don't worry." Her cheek was baby soft under his finger when it traced the curve down to her chin.

Shifting, Liz laid on her back, gazing up into his eyes, searching for answers, but he silently continued his exploration, his hand traveling down the slope of her waist and hip, allowing the sensation to sooth his thoughts. With gentle caresses, he outlined the orchid and snake tattoo below the bend of her bone.

"You're lying to me," she stated. "I see Iceman in that intense gaze of yours. No matter what you say, no matter what feeling you express during our lovemaking, *that* expression is undeniable when you're weighed down by issues. Please let me share your burden. I might be able to help."

He couldn't and insomuch as told her so when he leaned over her, depositing a sweet kiss to her forehead. "You worry too much, Mrs. Darcy. Everything is fine. My beautiful soul mate is safely home after recklessly speeding on her new Harley. Mallika has delivered a beautiful colt, and Georgiana's wedding is in five weeks. See … tons of good stuff, the beautiful things in life. *La dolce vita, bella.* What more can a man want?"

"I know you, Fitzwilliam Darcy, and I know you always want more. What are you not saying?"

Before rising from the bed, he teasingly grinned. "Oh! I got confirmation from that villa in Santorini for our wedding anniversary trip. Nothing to worry about there."

"That's not what I mean and you know it."

"Hmm … what else am I not saying? What did I forget to tell you? Oh, I know … I didn't kill your freaky black *Maxillaria schunkeana* orchid in your absence."

"If you did, I would kill *you*. I waited months for that orchid's bare root to come from the Amazon." Liz arched a brow. "Is there something else you care to tell me?"

"Hmm … I purchased season tickets to the symphony, and some of UVA's ponies are going to be turning out in the west field next month."

To his retreating back, she called out, "Stop it Fitzwilliam. Are you going to answer me *truthfully*? What *should* you be telling me that you're not?"

Peeking his head out the master bath doorway, he smiled that devastating grin of his and said, "As usual, you're right, Lakmé. I should tell you that I'm hungry. Shall we order in Pizza or Chinese? Then you can tell me all about your dad and the renovations to Longbourn."

The nearest thing to throw was his pillow, which landed only midway between the bed and his laughing face.

Inside the bathroom, his smile turned to a frown. How could he tell her about his insecurities or Rick's phone call ten days ago, which spurred a myriad of fears about being forced out of their idyllic life to address past black ops? No, now was not the time to speak of such things. There were too many details to work out before he spoke to her about Obsidian. For a split second, he wondered if he should make her stay at the house in North Carolina as a precaution until it was time to come back with Georgiana and Justin for the wedding. He shook his head willing himself to think about these things tomorrow. Tonight was a night of lovemaking and sweet conversation after their long separation.

* * *

Darcy came up behind Liz, wrapping his arms around her waist as she dried the last dinner plate in her hands. "You could have left all the mess for Mrs. Reynolds in the morning."

"Nine months residing back in Leesburg and you're already becoming a snob? If you think I'm going to leave Ellen two plates and five empty Chinese food containers, then you're sorely mistaken. Certainly, I can clean our own mess."

He removed the plate from her hands and placed it within the proper cabinet. "Liz, it's what we pay her for. It's what the Darcys have paid the Reynoldses for the last—I don't know—thirty years, maybe more."

"That's a lame argument and if you ask me, I think you take advantage of her goodness. Ellen and Gus are part of the family, not servants."

"No, they're not servants—you're right, but neither are you. Pemberley is not Longbourn and you have spent entirely too many days there, reverting back to that life and your father's …"

"Don't say it. Please. It made *me* happy to take care of him. With eight months of house arrest left, he needs a little t.l.c. The plantation house is still a mess, the contractors haven't been around in days, and he's sequestered himself in my greenhouse listening to Beethoven twenty-four seven. So what if I did a few dishes? It made him feel as though someone cared."

"Yeah, well he should have thought about that before he decided to become a conspirator against America and ..."

Liz's hand flew to her hip, clutching it peevishly. She pursed her plump lips and raised both eyebrows indicating that topic was not open for discussion or censure. Yes, his comment was below the belt and he should have known better than to bring it up. She agreed with him that her father's actions of last year were reprehensible, and further she forgave him that and other things months ago.

The trip to Longbourn had been important, and although Darcy stood before her now with condemnation in his voice, a different scene unfolded a week prior when, in panic, he had insisted she go. Insistent that his reason for staying behind was to help Mallika bring Kalendar Prince into the world. At the time, he tried to convince her that he understood Thomas's depressive needs and how his youngest daughter was a balm to his soul. It was true, that the harsh winter alone in Alexandria had been difficult on him. House arrest in two feet of snow for someone who was already depressed was no trip to Paris, but that wasn't the real reason for his assertion.

He unscrewed a bottle of Jack Daniels in the knowledge that no thanks to him, he put his wife in an agitated state, but he couldn't loosen up, couldn't stop worrying, and he needed to show her what he had worked on while she was gone. No. He'd wait to show her the panic room. She wasn't ready for that yet; she wouldn't understand.

She surreptitiously watched him, he knew, as the rim of his glass touched the bottle, but his mind was already preoccupied, his hand slightly trembling as the whiskey poured.

* * *

To the point of obsession, Rick's conversation replayed over and again in Darcy's mind,

> *"This next op, Darce, Bertram's out for blood. Next week I'll be back in South America continuing the job you completed last June."*
>
> *"I don't remember leaving unfinished business in Bolivia. The job was finished cleanly. I got out undetected, making sure I sanitized my existence at the motel. I know how these cartel assassins operate. There was no way to track me after the hit."*
>
> *"I know you finished the job cleanly. This is new business. It's the son of your target. This cartel is global, named La Muerta Mundial Cartel. Mexico, Russia, Nigeria, Colombia, Bolivia and Peru—they are all one in the same and one man sits at the helm of it all: Juan Sanchez-Morales. He's the son of "The Lord of the Jungle." They call him Diablo and he's undeniably Satan, leaving a not-so pretty calling card to England's Serious Organized Crime Agency (SOCA) when they got too close to his trafficking network into London. SOCA found four of their agents dead, hanging upside down in an abandoned warehouse in Liverpool."*
>
> *The hair on the back of Darcy's neck stood up when he heard that. "Bertram's intel never revealed that Morales's drug business was a family-run operation, nor international for that matter. Did we even know there was a son?"*
>
> *"First I heard of him was when Bertram met me at Tryst for coffee and slid the file in my direction. There's very little intel—the man is a ghost, a phantom. Never in one place long enough to track him, no footprint whatsoever. His lieutenants run the show."*

"Hmm ... well ... then be extra careful when you go down there to scout." Darcy knew kingpins never rested until they enacted revenge. There was no doubt in his mind that this "Satan" would make it a top priority to find the man who killed his father. Hell, Darcy knew acutely what revenge did to a man—the madness, the hate, the cold-hearted actions, the need to assassinate.

With his backside resting against the edge of the marble counter, he swirled the contents of his glass with his left hand. His pensive expression focused intently on the smooth liquor's circling motion. Liz slowly removed the glass from his grasp then leaned onto him, caressing her palm over his bicep tattoo, purring, "Baby... where are you? Come back to me."

Her dulcet voice carried him from his ominous thoughts and he rested his hand upon hers, clasping it under her gentle touch. With a bittersweet smile he replied, "Just thinking. I'm sorry, sweetheart."

In a sudden, rapid movement, he turned her wrist, pinning her arm behind her back, and swiftly rotated her body so that she faced the counter with him directly behind her. Immobilized, she could not step from his overpowering hold.

"Break free," he insisted.

"What? Fitzwilliam, you know I can't break free from your grasp."

"Try. I promise to make it worth your while if you do."

"Why are you playing like this?"

"Because you need to protect yourself in the event I'm not here to do so. What weapons are at your disposal? Be aware of what can assist you," he forcefully instructed, his voice deadly cold.

Liz surveyed the countertop before her. "Um, let see—I can beat you with my yellow dishtowel, chop sticks, or use the macchinetta coffee pot, although I'd hate to ruin that on your thick skull since we bought it in Lake Garda during our honeymoon. It makes such an excellent cup."

"Focus Liz! I'm not playing here. I'm about to kill you or worse. Attack me!"

"No this is stupid. I'm not a ninja Caroline or a viper. I only *watched* the movie *Kill Bill*. I didn't actually live it, remember? Well maybe a little I did, but not enough to know anything."

Damn this was hard for him, but he was determined to teach her, ready her for what may come.

"That's exactly why you need to learn." He slid his free hand up her ribcage to her breast. It killed him to mislead her, but he had a point to make. Her fullness filled the palm of his hand as he fondled her, followed by a pinch to her hardening nipple. She purred when he pressed his hips into her backside. Before she released the moan of pleasure that he knew was forthcoming, he whispered into her ear, "I am not your husband who wants to make love to you. I am an intruder who wishes to hurt you, your husband, or your children. What are you going to do?"

Immediately, Liz's posture became rigid. Her protective instinct kicked in. The newly formed daredevil woman who laughed in the face of death on the back of her Harley suddenly appeared when the reality of what he was saying to her reached down into her core. With her free hand, she instinctively grabbed the chopsticks, thrusting them back toward where she assumed her violator's eye would be.

"Excellent reflex," he encouraged but grabbed that wrist causing her to release the wood sticks, which fell to the floor.

He growled, "Now what are you going to do? I have both your hands."

Liz struggled to get free to no avail, grunting in the process when he tightened his grip, restricting her movement.

"Use your head," he commanded.

"I am! I don't know what to do."

"Liz … *Use* your head. *That's* your weapon. Head butt me, backward—hard!"

"No, I'll hurt you."

"Then, using the side of your shoe, scrape my shin on your way to stomping my foot with all you have."

"I can't do that!"

Darcy released his hold, turned Liz, and wrapped his arms around her. After gently soothing and kissing her forehead, he bent examining her dilated pupils. Calmly he explained, "Lesson number one. There's never room for your conscience when you're fighting for your life and the lives of your loved ones. Your conscience, your moral sensibilities will get you *and* them killed. It'll cause you to pause, to flinch, to second guess. There are no second guesses or second chances. Only one choice before you: life or death. You must remain without a conscience in the fight for life. I was taught to get tough, get down in the gutter, and to win at all costs. There's no fair play, no rules except one: kill or be killed. The villain will prey on your sensibilities. *He* is without a conscience."

He brushed his fingers over the worry lines on her forehead. "Will you let me teach you everything I know?"

Liz nodded, knowing that it wasn't a question but rather a statement. She knew that whatever was troubling him, this would help alleviate his worry.

5
Corruption

Most women have a power color—a color that provides an extra boost to their confidence. A sort of "I am woman. Hear me roar" statement. Red has long been a favorite power color for many women, but it had never worked for Caroline. Instead, yellow was her go-to color. When her cascading copper waves were set against the vibrancy there was no mistaking that her attitude was all business, out for blood. *She* was the power—not the color. Instead, she reserved red for her lips, perfectly outlined and smoothly applied using Chanel's Russian Red— the perfect lipstick for meeting Thomas Bertram. The powerful color will hold his attention when she delivers her verbal assault.

Thirteen hours had passed since her last communiqué from Rick. At two minutes after nine in the morning, she purposely strode past Bertram's incompetent secretary, ignoring the young woman's objections. All it took was Caroline's well-honed, menacing glare and the narrowing of her ice blue eyes to tell the woman to back off.

The door to the director's office burst open, slamming against the wall. She stood within the frame, her presence filling the room even before stepping beyond the threshold. Red polished fingernails menacingly clutched her hip with constricting implication to the man who paid heavily for the expertise that Obsidian offered to the CIA when contracted. Reptilian-cold eyes bore into him.

Bertram sat at his desk; open sugar packets lay scattered beside his coffee mug that read "Boss." The former KGB underling, now Director of the CIA, felt his heart seize with a fear at the sudden arrival of one of the Company's former officers—code name: Kiyohime. He knew that expression upon her face well and knew what usually followed it. Never in all his young years with the KGB or with the CIA, had he met a woman more lethal and black-hearted as Caroline Bingley.

Why he failed to expect that she would seek information about Rick Fitzwilliam's disappearance was beyond him. He knew of her personal relationship with the Director of Obsidian. After all, he was the one who had encouraged her to become involved with the man. Only he didn't think it would last this long, particularly since she most likely still harbored deep-seeded unrequited lust for Iceman.

With as much indifference as he could muster, he greeted the unexpected and unwelcome visitor. "Caroline, what brings you to Langley?"

Taking a seat opposite him, she withdrew the CIA insignia pen from its holder at the edge of his desk followed by its baton-like twirl between her nimble fingers, a habit *he* had always employed in his intimidation tactics. An appropriate action for Caroline since her threat was based on her specific skills set. The ninjutsu warrior in her couldn't resist the unspoken threat.

"You know why I'm here, Thimofai."

Again his heart slightly seized. "You know well, that's not my name, *Kiyohime*."

"Do I? Surely after our history, you can't possibly still think all my skills are restricted to Sai fighting sticks and manriki chains?"

He narrowed his eyes, glaring into hers. "What is it you want? I have to be in a meeting with my team in thirty minutes. Do you have questions about Operation Viennese Waltz or Operation Macarena?"

"As a matter of fact I do. Where is Rick Fitzwilliam?"

And there it was: the question that could very well get him killed by her if he didn't answer truthfully. He remembered all too well how she ruthlessly killed one of their former officer-turned-radical-terrorist in Pakistan. Having traveled with her to bring him in, Bertram had been rendered speechless watching her stand over the traitor as the fierce *kunoichi* fanning herself in feigned heat from the excruciating South Asian temperature. The moment he made a brash move, Caroline's red, steel Tessen war fan sliced his jugular in one swift sideway move.

Visions of the spurting blood out of the rogue agent flashed before Bertram's mind's eye. He replied nervously, "How should I know where Fitzwilliam is? You're the one with Obsidian, not me. Once we placed Operation Macarena into your organization's hands, Company involvement washed its hands clean of knowledge or intelligence. This op is black, highly classified. Only a handful in the administration know of it."

Foolish to challenge her like this, but what else could he do? Too much was at stake. He was the only one that knew anything about the bogus Operation Macarena, and silently prayed she wouldn't see through his lie.

Caroline sighed deeply, rotating the pen in her fingers one last time before she snapped her wrist, flinging it in one swift move past his ear. Upon contact with the wall behind him, it bobbed in the air after sharp impact.

"That could have been between your eyes. I want answers and not this game. Either you're working for La Muerta and have sold Obsidian out because of Operation Samba last year or you're working for the Russians. I won't ask again. Where is Fitzwilliam?"

"I ... I don't know!" he exclaimed accidently knocking over his coffee in the process, the liquid rushing across his desk in her direction.

No doubt she saw the unmasked panic in his eyes and the slight tremble to his hand when he attempted to clean the mess.

She stood, walked around the desk, and sat at the corner. Her long legs crossed one over the other beside him, slightly hiking her yellow skirt. He couldn't help but notice the alluring sexiness, a tease of garter peeking from the edge. Deadly as she was, she was still one hell of a sexy woman.

With perfect balance, the *kunoichi* leaned toward him. Her fingernail grazed deeply into his cheek, leaving an indentation mark. "Tell me or I'll blow the whistle on you to every right-wing, fanatical group and news organization in America telling them that the Director of the CIA is ex-KGB who is still loyal to mother Russia. When I'm through with you, they'll eat you alive for being the lying Communist scum that you are and always have been."

"You wouldn't dare because if I go down so do you. I'll expose Obsidian to the world as traitors to the American people, drug smugglers for La Muerta Mundial cartel."

The sudden grip or Caroline's left hand around his throat caused him to gasp out in panic, "They've … they've kidnapped my daughter! I made a deal—for her release."

"Who or what did you bargain with—traitor?"

Bertram tried to look away from her steely gaze, but her grasp tightened along with the sudden grip to his crotch with her right talons. The hidden smile behind her venomous demeanor disappeared the moment he blabbed, "Weapons to Peru … and … Iceman. Diablo wants Iceman for killing his father. Fitzwilliam is the bait to draw out Darcy, get him to Peru. I couldn't very well tell you that!"

"Iceman? What made you so sure I'd call him in on this? He's retired from black ops. What made you so sure that I wouldn't send my brother or go myself to get Fitzwilliam?"

The second she released her neck hold, his hand flew to his throat in a coughing fit between gasps.

"You'd never … send in your brother at the risk of losing him, and as for you, if Fitzwilliam were killed that could only mean your rise to Director of Obsidian. Don't forget, I know how mercenary you really are."

"Maybe I'd send our new guy. Why didn't you just give up Iceman? You know his name. Hell, you handed me his dossier when I went undercover in Obsidian. You know everything about the man and his little woman. Why the ruse? Why use Fitzwilliam as bait?"

She took a seat again, watching the signs of defeat cover the director: slumping of shoulders, cloud of uncertainty, hesitation, even self-recrimination having never expected his corruption to spill into his family.

"Because with Darcy back in Obsidian, there was a chance that both he and Fitzwilliam could survive in the Amazon and find my daughter. Maybe she's held there, too. They're the best at what they do."

"Oh, I have no doubt they'll survive, and I have no doubt that no matter what you've promised La Muerta, they'll still kill your daughter, wherever she is."

Bertram rested his head in both his hands and bemoaned, "It's over now that you know. They'll kill her for sure when you blow the lid on what I have done. Selling arms to the Peruvian branch of the cartel following the last administration's ATF scandal of "Quick and Dead" arms to Mexico would ruin the president's re-election for sure."

"Have you supplied the arms to Peru yet?"

"No. The DEA has their eye on cartel trafficking into Chicago, and I've held back so as not to draw any unwelcome inquiries, but time is of the essence ... they took Julia a week ago, and I can't bring any of my people in on this. Diablo wanted Darcy outright, but I hedged, feigning lack of intel on Obsidian's team members. If the drug lord found out where Darcy resided, he'd send one of his men for him, his family, everyone he knew. You think I want that on my conscience?"

"Oh, now you have one?" she sarcastically said. "I'm sure it's more like you didn't want to take the chance of La Muerta sicarios' passport and fingerprints getting flagged by ICE at customs. Then this Diablo's cartel would deliberately lead the trail directly back to the Company—to you."

"And kill Julia."

Caroline shook her head in distaste. "Always protecting your own ass, Bertram. You disgust me. You put your daughter in danger to further your greed." She hated to see a grown man tremble in fear—especially one with a formidable career made from intimidation and violence along with espionage and covert underhandedness. Try as she might, she could find no compassion for the traitor who had put his family, the nation, and Obsidian's team members in jeopardy.

The now Acting Director of Obsidian stood ominously before him and pointed her index finger at him accusingly. Speaking low and deliberate, her crimson lips turned downward in cold threat. "They will survive, and they will execute an exfiltration op to find your daughter, and you will go down as a traitor to this nation. I expect every exacting detail that you were holding back to cover your involvement with La Muerta and Juan Sanchez-Morales. I want his associates and his trafficking routes and I want this intelligence in the next two hours. If I'm going to send my men in to save your ass and your daughter's life, I expect the truth."

"I'll give you what I have, but there is very little."

"Surely the CIA at least knows where we can find him?"

"You can't find him. He's a ghost. I don't even meet with him."

"Find something!"

Bertram solemnly nodded in agreement. "And what do you want as payment?"

"Your resignation and, if I don't get it, mark my words, Bertram— you will get yours. I can almost promise you that when Darcy learns of your activity, he'll be coming for *you* when this is over, and if he has suddenly acquired some moralistic scruples, I have a new collection of war fans."

She glanced down at her Patek Phillipe diamond wristwatch. "Time's up. I guess you have to run to your little meeting of corrupt government underlings." Nimble fingers grabbed the black, retractable pencil sitting next to the already vacated penholder and she flung it into the wall, whizzing by his other ear. "You'll be sorry you ever messed with Obsidian, but, rest assured, Operation Macarena is a hit that will be seen through to the end."

She laughed and turned to face him as she neared the closed door to exit. "I didn't think you'd cave that easily, Bertram. Perhaps you should consider going back to the Department of Education. It's safer there for a man like you."

* * *

Liz had been home for two days, and during that time Darcy rarely left her side. Supermarket? He pushed the cart. Hairdresser? He sat in the chair next to her and read a two-year-old fashion magazine. Good Lord, he even went with her to get a manicure, sat next to her and conversed with the manicurist in Vietnamese! Who knew he even spoke the language? She had traveled across the globe with him, to some of the most dangerous of situations, and he had vowed to keep her safe. She knew he would do so until her last breath, but his sticking to her like glue seemed a bit much. Granted, he wasn't one to overreact about anything, particularly danger or adventure. Asking him again why his protective nature was out in full-force was of the question. Rather than feeling oppressed or peevish or bitchy about his behavior, she decided to rely on that trust she had placed in him very early on in their relationship. Confident that, in due time he would tell her his troubles, she simply enjoyed his company.

She wrapped her arms around his waist, reveling in the renewed feeling of riding with him instead of beside him on the back of his Harley. It didn't bother her that the vintage bike wasn't well suited for two while touring; the feeling of her body pressed against his back was all she cared about. Earlier this morning at her proclamation of, "I think I'll ride to the park with you on the Classic," he wordlessly answered her with two long strides to her, embraced her, then kissed her deeply. As usual, she could tell his mood by his kiss. He was that transparent—always had been, since that first kiss in her hotel room in Seville. Domesticity hadn't changed him in that regard.

Now at the park, under a majestic oak, they reclined on a picnic blanket at the bank of the Shenandoah River, listening to the gentle lap of water at the rocky shoreline. All around them green buds and blossoms burst forth and the new leaves of spring displayed a vibrant green from the recent rain.

Her head rested above Darcy's heart, its beat attempting to lull her into slumber in time with the birds chirping in the surrounding park. With eyes closed she reflected upon the picturesque ride on the two-lane Route 9 from Leesburg, Virginia to Shannondale Springs in West Virginia. Under a clear blue sky on a spring fever type day, country roads and sleepy towns had inspired Darcy's choice of Classical music. Piped into their helmets through the specially designed wireless walkie-talkie and sound system, the "Allegretto" from Beethoven's Seventh Symphony seemed to have relaxed him.

With his leather jacket rolled under his neck, Darcy's upper body leaned against the tree as he read from his iPad held aloft by his right hand. His left arm held her close to him. He lay long and lean with blue jeans and heavy motorcycle boots spread out before him, crossing at the ankles on the blanket. Making small circles on her shoulder, even etching letters onto her bicep it was as if he hoped to make a tattoo imprint. "My love," "beautiful," "4ever" was his subconscious way of speaking to her even if he wasn't in the mood for conversation.

Only once, when he opened his tablet and began to read, did she break their companionable silence. "What are you reading?"

Darcy sniggered. "You'll yell at me if I tell you."

"Oh, well now you have to tell. You've piqued my curiosity. What is it?"

"*The House of the Dead*," he replied before grimacing, sure of what her comment would be.

"Dostoevsky? Now I know something is wrong with you."

Darcy laughed and she comfortably settled back down into his arm ready to drift to sleep. "Goryanchikov killed his wife," she stated with a yawn.

"I venture to guess life with her would have been a more pleasant sentence than Siberia."

"He ended up having great empathy and sympathy for his fellow captives," Liz sleepily reflected.

"Yeah, and it took a gulag to bring that about. When faced with the lack of conscience of his captors, he was able to have a spiritual awakening of sorts."

For the next thirty minutes, Liz relaxed and Darcy read until his deep voice startled her awake. "How is your sister? Has Jane adapted to your father's situation?"

Liz surmised his reading turned his thought process to her father and his last year's fascination with *Crime and Punishment*. "Yes, Jane's adapted so much I hardly recognize her. When I saw her last month, I didn't realize that it was a permanent alteration. It seems she and I have exchanged personas."

"How so?"

"For starters she threw away the 1970s sofa in the den and then burned dad's crochet blanket. Even her clothing has morphed into a more serious, professional look. She purchased a couple of Donna Karan suits to wear to the museum and goes for manicures in neutral colors. Maybe Charlie has had an influence on her—I'm not sure."

"More like guilt, baby. You carried the burden of Longbourn all by yourself for a very long time while Jane enjoyed herself and her freedom. She may have been a support for your emotional needs, but she certainly steered clear of the responsibility of both taking care of your father and the upkeep of the estate."

With her left index finger, Liz traced the midline of Darcy's taut stomach muscles. "I suppose. She doesn't seem to be bothered by the change in her lifestyle though."

"Again, probably the result of her guilt. Jane's stepping up to the plate now. It's all good. Also, I'm sure Charlie's career is sobering to her. While most of the time, he may live life on the carefree edge, he is very serious about what he does for Obsidian. Your sister *needs* to be grounded and understanding. She needs to remain focused in the knowledge that what he does out in the world can and most likely will at some point come back to roost."

Liz raised her head, resting her chin upon his pec. She searched his face, which still seemed intent on reading. If, in fact, he was actually reading. She wasn't sure. "Will yours? Come back to roost, that is?"

"There's always that chance." Darcy turned his head and smiled warmly at her, his way of attempting to disarm her fears, particularly when he pulled her closer to him. She settled down beside him once again, tucking under his arm.

His fingers toyed with her hair. "I never counted on you coming along. After exacting my revenge on Wickham, death was always a preferable option than giving away my heart to a woman. I was sure that no woman could possibly protect it and love me in earnest, but then you and that perfectly arched eyebrow, seductive smile, and sharp wit changed all that."

"And what happens if evil does come calling?"

"Well thankfully, all of my ops met their demise at the end of my rifle, but in the event that something does happen, you'll know everything I know about defending yourself. Remember, I always told you that you have skills, Liz. Given the right amount of training, you would have definitely been an asset in and out of the field."

A group of laughing rafters floated down the chilly river, disturbing their peaceful sanctuary. The joyful cacophony seemed in direct contrast to the disturbing subject matter of the conversation.

"Is this the reason you're going to teach me? Because something has happened? Is that why you've been acting so erratic these last two days?"

"Erratic? Me? I'm about as consistent in my behavior as any man."

Liz laughed. "Any man? Yeah … right, that's why you went to the hairdresser with me. *Any* man wouldn't do that."

"Don't be so sure about that. Charlie and Rick are both extremely attentive to the women they love."

"Charlie loves Jane?"

Darcy looked surprised. "Sure, doesn't she know that?"

"I don't think so. I know she's in love with him, but I'm not sure he's ever expressed the same sentiment—not that *she's* ever told *him*. But

I know as her sister, she's hoping for the happy ever after with him: marriage and children. She wants what we have."

"Maybe that further explains her subtle transformation. Perhaps she's hoping that if she and Charlie settle down, marry and then children enter into the picture, he will look at his career in a different light. I did, particularly when I realized that you and I could very well have conceived that wild night in the gazebo. I never told you but the thought of you pregnant in my dangerous life, scared the crap out of me. That wasn't and isn't what I want for our family. I'd give my life protecting you and our children."

He put his iPad down then slid beside Liz, holding her to him as he gently kissed her soft, yielding lips. His hand smoothed against her backside, pulling her into him so he could wrap his leg over hers. "Everything in my life can be replaced but you. Without you, I'm nothing."

Her hand slid over his snake tattoo, then bicep, upward to the dark curls at his nape where she thread her fingers into his locks. "I feel the same way. Did you say children?"

He wiggled his eyebrows, his lips forming that mischievous smile that always stopped her heart. "A passel of them."

"Starting when?"

A glance over her shoulder to see how far the rafters had gone preceded his seductive words. "Soon, so let's have fun practicing." That wicked smile she loved so much lowered toward her earlobe, nibbling it in spite of the small silver earring. "How much of an exhibitionist do you feel like today, my love?" he whispered.

Before Liz could answer, a special ringtone on his phone indicated to him, not her, who was on the other end of the call. Darcy sighed, and as soon as his arm reached out for his phone, she sighed, too.

"Bad timing as usual," he said into the phone, shedding no light as to who the interloper was.

Still entangled within his embrace, surrounded by the peaceful cadence of the park, Liz watched how every word the caller spoke, brought forth the Iceman. Darcy's lips grew taut; his body went rigid in her arms. When he finally clicked off without even having voiced a word into the phone, the affectionate man, who moments before was about to seduce her beside the riverbank, was gone. That moment and the man were lost when he abruptly stood, held out his hand to assist her up, and with clipped tone said, "We have to go."

"What is it? Is everything okay? Is it Gigi?"

"No. We'll talk about it when we get back to Pemberley."

Liz sat behind him on the back of the motorcycle riding with a song she had never heard before pounding her ears within the helmet. Since knowing Darcy, she had yet to hear him play this music. She spent twenty-five miles traveling across the state line, listening to hard-edged heavy metal music screaming something about bodies hitting the floor as her husband rode in impenetrable, focused silence. Finally, she turned the volume in her helmet off and held on for dear life as Darcy rode like a bat out of hell toward home.

Liz had thirty minutes to think about all the possible things discussed in that mysterious phone conversation. What had caused not only such intense speed, but also an enormous amount of anxiety rolling off Darcy's body? A hundred different conversations crossed her mind, all speculation, but her gut told her it had something to do with Obsidian.

Vast and splendid newly plowed farms and lush green valleys became blurs when the Harley flew past with invasive dual exhaust noise. Sleepy little country towns with unexpected slowing traffic from tractors or pedestrians became sources of frustration whereby the occasional swear word escaped Darcy's lips in haste and aggravation, and she wondered what images supplanted this idyllic landscaped scenery.

Twenty minutes into the ride home, his gloved hand finally found hers clutching tightly to his abdomen. He held onto her as though trying to protect her even at that moment.

6

Confession

The Harley came to rest in the circular drive at Pemberley beside Ellen Reynolds's white Audi and once Darcy cut the engine and lowered the kickstand, Liz quickly jumped off, removed her helmet and firmly stood her ground. He seemed to lollygag almost in fear of what awaited him—the expected wrath of his wife. He sat straddling the bike, removed his helmet, yet still did not turn to face her.

"Who was that?" she demanded.

He turned, playing ignorant. "Who was what?"

"On the phone, by the river. Who else would I mean? I want to know who made us leave such a beautiful day spent in each other's arms, not to mention the re-emergence of a man I haven't seen in at least six months, a man I thought long gone—your cold alter ego. What's going on?"

Darcy rose from the bike, unzipping his leather jacket. He held his breath as his jaw clenched, distorting his features in stern reply, torn between smothering his wife within his embrace and ignoring her demands for an explanation. Frustrated, the Iceman was ill equipped for this, unable to deal with the straddling of two polar-opposite worlds at the same time. Tenderness and death dealing had a difficult time cohabitating in one mind. Operation Virginia Reel taught him that months ago.

He was used to remaining stoic and cold once his mind began to focus like a laser on his enemy. At this moment, surrounded by the vast beauty of Pemberley and the vision of his loving wife with a burning fire in her eyes, he didn't want to admit that his mind already left on the first plane to Lima in search for his cousin, even knowing it was a trap.

His heart demanded he leave, taking the threat with him, away from Liz. He didn't know what to do; his options were limited. Taking her on this search and rescue was not an option, leaving her home without him wasn't one either. The Iceman did the only thing he knew how to do well: withdraw into himself and focus on the target at the end of the rifle.

He was petrified that Diablo would come for him—here, at home—and would hurt Liz. Shutting off his emotions, trying not to give into the fear bubbling deeply within him, he coldly replied. "Not here, not now. I have to think this out."

Liz glanced at the clenched fists at his side, then up to his dark gaze. Her lips, pouty. "Think what out? Talk to me, *please*! Have a little faith in me—trust me—I might be able to help you. I want to share this with you!"

A flash of Ellen's blonde head peeked out the dining room window in curiosity at the raised voices, and although embarrassed Darcy couldn't help shouting. "Please, Liz! Stop!" He scowled, promptly sliding into his familiar, safe behavior by storming away in vexation.

Thunderstruck by his inability to express himself or share with her his burden, he left Liz standing in the middle of the drive, arms dejectedly at her sides.

Equally exasperated, she called after him. "Fine. Go hide in your stable. I may or may not be around when you do finally decide to share with *your wife* what in the heck is going on!"

She stormed to the front door and entered the mansion in a huff now faced with having to explain herself to Ellen. The poor woman waited dumbfounded in the archway between the foyer and the dining room.

A too-forceful tug to her jacket's zipper felt like she'd break it as her heart hammered in frustration, until she finally stopped, took a deep, much-needed breath and said, "I'm sorry, Ellen. Please forgive our rudeness. Fitzwilliam isn't quite himself today."

"Today? Honey, that boy hasn't been himself since he was twenty-one years old. Don't you worry, whatever is bothering him will come to a head and he'll be running to you for a solution. Trust me on this. He values your opinion above all things. It just takes him a bit longer to get there then most men."

"I hope you're right. This is only our second fight."

"Is that all? I'm sure it was over a very trivial thing then. Did he leave the toilet seat up?"

"No, nothing like that," she reassured, placing her hand on Ellen's arm. "Thank you. I'm sure everything will be fine. In the meantime, I'll be in my greenhouse if you or Mr. I Can Handle It On My Own needs me."

* * *

For nineteen years, Anne Darcy's greenhouse had remained barren and neglected with overgrown strangling weeds and vines. Upon Liz's first inspection, when she took up residence at Pemberley, only the memory of death and betrayal, representative of the dead foliage, lurked everywhere near the structure that once held fond fragrance and recollection for her new husband.

Slowly the hothouse transformed, lovingly restored like the rest of the house and grounds. Together new husband and wife brought it back to life through attention and care along with the cultivation of several varieties of orchids. Slipper, Moth, and Dendrobiums filled the large glass structure. Newly installed shades and overhead lighting, along with ambient lights in her personal space where she sketched and read, completed the last of the renovations.

Before long, love replaced death and the first time Darcy made love to her on a snow-covered winter day, sitting on the club chair in her reading corner, this place became forever reborn.

Furious and worried, Liz sat at her workbench and pressed play on the Bose. Tapping through several pieces of music, she prophetically chose Puccini's "Un Bel di Vedremo" from the opera, *Madam Butterfly*. The aria filled the glass structure. For a second, she felt transported back to Longbourn, both in frame of mind and escape to her peaceful domain. It was the first time since her arrival at Pemberley that she felt the need to run and hide to a place of sanctuary and tranquility. She had yet to feel this way at any time in the last eight months since committing her heart to Darcy.

Almost in defiance of his obstinacy and stoicism, Madam Butterfly's heartfelt promise of "One Beautiful Day," conveying hope and constancy, competed with loud Led Zeppelin rock music coming from the tack room. She knew that it must have been deafening within the stable if she could hear it in the greenhouse. Lifting her eyes to heaven as though in silent prayer to her mother-in-law for whatever was bothering Darcy to ease, she prayed he had put both Mallika and her colt out in the field before his head-banging escape into the world of Iceman. "Whole Lotta Love" rocked the stable, and she was sure he held a tumbler of Jack Daniels.

Furiously she began to sketch the fountain of the Roman Goddess Flora beside the koi pool then insolently raised the volume of the aria, so sure Darcy could hear it. It was a battle of wills and expressive voices lasting until both passionate songs ended in rising crescendo five minutes later.

Following Robert Plant's scream, the aria's orchestra slowly faded into tranquil rest.

Silence ensued.

Minutes later, her husband stood at the top of the steps leading into the open door of the greenhouse. She gazed up into his dark, pain-filled eyes; his hair was in disarray and he looked to be on the verge of tears. With one hand resting on the side of the doorframe, his other hand raked through his long locks. Her heart clenched when she noted his pronounced swallow then the purse to his lips. It was clear to her that he struggled to give voice to his troubles.

She wanted to yell at him, take him to task, but she couldn't do it. As mad as she was, her husband had come to her. He needed her. She wouldn't give him reason to turn away.

A slight quirk to her lips at the agonizing image he posed was her way of saying, "You're forgiven—I love you." That small smile was all it took before he rushed forward and knelt at her feet, his head rested upon her lap, his strong hands clutching her hips.

"I'm so sorry, baby. Please forgive me for shutting you out since you've come home from Longbourn. I'm so sorry," he implored.

Her fingers ran through his hair soothingly. "It's okay... I'm here whenever you want to talk. I know whatever is troubling you, we can work out together. We've done it before—we've faced incredible odds together, right?"

Darcy gazed up into her hazel eyes, now shiny with checked tears. "We have and we will again."

Rising, he held her to his chest. "I ... I ... there's so much I need to tell you, but ... but I need for you to follow me, sweetheart. There's something I need to *show* you."

Hand-in-hand, he led the way with determined strides, entering the back of the house into the atrium sunroom in the south wing, passing Mrs. Reynolds who hunched over a coffee table, dusting. She smiled at the couple and Liz meekly smiled back.

Following Darcy down a deep flight of stairs, they then turned to another small hall, followed by three steps and a narrow passage, which led under the house. At the end, they stood before a steel door.

"Umm ... when did you put this hallway here?"

"Most of it was here. The previous house that stood on this parcel of land was once a stop of the Underground Railroad before the Civil War. I made modifications while you were gone."

Before unlocking the door, he kissed her and then intently held her gaze when he asked, "Do you trust me?"

"Of course. I always have." She tugged his arm when he turned toward the numeric keypad beside the door. "Why? Don't *you* trust *me*?"

He faced her, eyes warm with assured sincerity. "I do. Implicitly."

In astonishment, she watched how he went through a series of security measures, first numerical passcode and then voice recognition. A light flashed green and he said, "Fitzwilliam Darcy."

"The code is Lakmé, backwards. We'll program it for your voice later."

The sudden unlocking of what she assumed were metal bolts within the door itself slid back. This measure of security made her both curious and uneasy. What the heck was this room? What could be so secretive to have such authentication? What was next? Retinal scanner?

The door popped open and Darcy flipped on the overhead fluorescent lights. One by one, they flickered on, revealing a long security bunker of sorts. It smelled of fresh paint and gun cleaning solution. On one side of the expansive open area were different sized punching bags and a thick, black tatami sports mat. On the other side, several targets and different sized padded bull's-eyes hung securely to the wall. Against the third wall rested various multi-drawer cabinets that crafters employ for organization.

"What ... I don't understand. What is this room?"

"This is your panic room—*our* panic room. Reinforced in steel around the entire stone and concrete perimeter." Stepping toward one of the punching bags, he pointed to the far right corner. "You can't see it because it is camouflaged, but over there is another room, which is also accessible from a specially-designed floor in a new secured closet safe in my office one and half floors up. That ante-room has everything you need for survival up to ten days. It is also fireproof."

Shocked, she slowly traversed the perimeter, touching everything, attempting to absorb the world she had just entered. Part of her wanted to pick up the spear-tipped Bo stick and throw it toward the bull's-eye and attempt to make contact. Secretly, she had always admired Caroline's skills. But that other part of her (the Lizzy part), the one she was sure had been banished for close to nine months, began to surface. Even after everything they had been through last year and all she had seen and done, even given the adventurous married woman she had become, she was still uneasy about self-defense. "Why do we need this training bunker and panic room, Fitzwilliam?"

"Because I'm determined to keep you safe in the event of anything. No matter what it is—an intruder, a fire, a tornado."

She snorted. "We hardly get tornadoes in Virginia."

"Whatever, Liz; you know what I mean." He cleared his throat. "I did this also in the event my past seeks retribution. I will not put you in danger because of Obsidian. I need to know that you have a safe place to come to, even skills to fall back on if necessary to defend yourself. This room is impenetrable."

Liz mumbled to herself, running a hand over the workout dummy, "This is more than simple self-defense." After a moment of thought, she turned to her husband. "What kind of skills? Your kind of skills or Caroline's kinds of skills?"

"Both."

Darcy observed her and could almost see the wheels turning in that pretty head as she walked to one of the cabinets then pulled out the top shelf. Within lay various pistols of all sizes, perfectly spaced and lined one next to the other, all locked and fully loaded. From afar, he watched as her eyes widened when she slid out the second drawer where different sized combat blades lay carefully placed on blue fabric: small pics, boot knives, hunting knives, a Marine Kabar knife, a Fairbairn. Of course, she didn't know the names of them, but her index finger touched the handle of each one in consecutive order. He smiled knowingly; Liz's words may have conveyed one thing, but her body language told him something else. She was intrigued.

Wrapping her hand around his favorite boot knife, the one that killed Omar on the train to Seville, she removed it from the drawer. "I remember this."

"That's the one." He came to stand beside her, observing the changing expressions on her face when pretending to thrust the knife away from him into the air. Intrigue had turned to fascination.

"Do you like knives?" he asked, encouraging her.

She placed it back on the blue fabric and simply said with a small voice, "Maybe."

He slid open the drawer with the pistols, removed the magazine from the 9mm Glock 17, and then pulled the slide back. The previously chambered bullet popped out onto the floor before he handed the gun to her. "How does this feel? Too heavy for you?"

"I'm not so sure about a gun. I was uncomfortable with the one you gave me in Marrakech." She promptly handed it back to him. "You want me to learn to shoot?"

"Absolutely. Gun safety first then the basics: target practice, mechanics, firing in combat, but I don't have the time to teach you. Everything you see in this bunker will be taught to you over the next week or so while I'm gone and then our lessons will commence when I return."

"Gone? Your return? We never discussed any trip."

"I'm leaving for an op. I'm temporarily going back to Obsidian. This is the last time. I promise."

Unable to find words, Liz's mouth went slack, her eyes widening as her posture stiffened.

"I know … I didn't discuss it with you, Liz. That phone call was the catalyst to my decision." His voice was grave. "Rick is missing in Peru, and it has to do with a hit I made prior to accepting the op at Longbourn."

Her hand went to her mouth in horror. "Oh no! Rick!"

"You understand what I'm saying, right? I'm going to get him."

"Why you? Why not someone else? I mean, I know he's your cousin, but you're not part of that world any longer. The Iceman melted long ago." Her hand reached out to his folded arms as she begged. "Don't do this. Don't go."

Sighing, he turned from her, causing her arm to drop lifelessly before her. Taking a seat on a tall leather stool, he clasped his hands before him, locking his eyes with hers. "As long as Rick is with Obsidian and as long as my mark has been made on the criminal world through Obsidian, it will always be some part of me. I can't leave the responsibility or the obligation to clean up to another just because *I* decided to retire. True, I'm not that angry, half-dead man any longer, but I can't just turn my back completely away from the consequences or fallout from the actions of my past. It would be unfair to send Charlie or now Knightley into a fight that I received a shit load of money to see through from beginning to end."

"This was why you felt yours and Charlie's past may catch up with you? Because it has already?"

"Yes. The man I killed in Bolivia during Operation Samba was an international drug cartel kingpin. His son is trying to draw me out and has kidnapped Rick in that endeavor. The intelligence is sketchy, but Knightley will bring me up to speed when I meet him at the safe house on U Street. I won't be going into this alone if that eases your worry."

"So what you're telling me is that you're giving this kingpin exactly what he wants … you!"

"Not exactly, he'll have to catch me first."

He reached out to touch her forearm to draw her into his embrace, but she rebuffed him, moving from his reach. He could see how she struggled, unsure how to handle this wrench in their idyllic life. Biting her lip, she mindlessly stared up at the paper target, an image of a gunman ready for battle.

"When are you leaving?" she coldly asked, folding her arms across her chest.

"As soon as possible. As soon … as … I have your blessing to get our cousin."

Eyes flashing, she turned to him and snapped, "You obviously don't need my approval. Clearly you've made up your mind already."

"Liz … I need to go with your understanding why I have to do this. I can't leave with things not right between us."

With an exaggerated sweep to her arm, she challenged, "And this room is supposed to make me feel safer in your absence, a few steel doors, and a couple of knives and guns that I don't know how to use?"

"No, I thought you'd be safest back in North Carolina where this type of room is already set up. Because of possible CIA corruption and involvement in this, sending you to Longbourn is out of the question because Operation Virginia Reel compromised it. I did consider sending you to your sister's, but in the end I knew you would fight me tooth and nail, insisting to stay here, particularly since Georgiana's wedding is only a few weeks away. I know you—you'll want the details solidified before my aunt arrives to screw everything up."

She turned quickly. "I'm not going to stay here without you. Gigi can finish everything when she arrives. She doesn't need me. I'm going with you. That's how you can best protect me. We did this before and I was fine."

"This is different."

"But didn't you just tell me earlier today that I'd be good in the field? That I have skills?"

"Yes. You will. After training." He shook his head. "There won't be any casinos, or high-speed luxury trains, no tango in the moonlight or lovemaking in exotic ports. That was James Bond stuff with a beautiful brunette on my arm. This is a trip into the bowels of the green hell of the Amazon jungle where the villain's codename is Diablo, a man who wouldn't think twice about viciously killing you after raping you—a man who has no sense of right or wrong."

Petulantly, her fingers clutched her hips. "I'm going whether you like it or not."

"No … I forbid it."

"You forget, Mr. Darcy, I don't respond well to *'I forbid it'*."

This tactic of defiant obstinacy wasn't working for her. He seemed impenetrable, as unmovable as the Iceman of old. She considered how she got him to bend the first time around in Longbourn's greenhouse.

Bearing a flirtatious smile, she stepped into the gap between his seated, spread legs and wrapped her left arm around his waist. Her right hand ran up his rock-hard thigh as she kissed his neck, alternating between nibbles and pecks.

"It won't work this time, seductress."

Her hand smoothed over the outline of his flaccid member, which was not about to become aroused as he willed his mind to remain detached from his wife's allure. This wasn't the greenhouse back at Longbourn, and he wasn't so easily swayed given the evil that faced them.

"Please," she purred.

"No."

"I promise to be good and won't take things into my own hands like last time. I promise, I'll do everything you tell me."

He snorted, taking her hand in his. "That'll be a first. No, baby. I have to go this one alone." Setting her back from him, his eyes and his smile conveyed the contriteness in his heart. "You'll be safer here with Charlie protecting you."

Like a peevish child, she pulled her hand from his then, again, crossed her arms before her chest, retorting, "I don't want Charlie."

"Liz, I understand your reservations, but … but you're acting like a child."

"Child? Did you just call me a child?"

Oh Shit. "What I meant was, you need to think this out logically— rationally. Look, Jane is coming here with Charlie, and together the two of you will learn self-defense."

"I don't want Jane. I want to be with you, wherever you are. That's the only place I'll feel safe."

He hated to say it, but he had to make her understand the enormity of what he was about to do. Brushing his thumb against her soft cheek, he said, "But *I* won't be safe. My focus has to be one hundred and fifty percent on finding and saving Rick and taking out this Diablo. Bringing you will weaken my heart *and* my conscience to do the things I will need to do. Messy things, things that you never need to know about or witness."

His fingers wrapped around her folded arm and he gently tugged her to him until she wrapped her arms around him. "Please understand."

She finally nodded in acquiescence, and they kissed claiming one another with the uncertainty of never seeing each other again.

Breathlessly he said, "Upstairs … now … before I make love to you here."

* * *

Liz lay naked, sound asleep on their bed. The sun was descending behind Pemberley, setting the sky aflame with burnt orange and grey wispy clouds. Darcy leaned against the doorframe of the master bath admiring his angel-of-a-wife slumbering, her hair spread over his pillow and her hand tucked under her cheek. The image before him represented everything he loved about his life: serenity and filled with love. The pinkness of her taut nipple brushed against the smooth cotton sheet. He was fully tempted to crawl back into bed beside her and love her again and his heart clenched thinking this could possibly be the last time he gazed upon her. The violence of his love almost caused him to turn his back on what lay ahead of him, but that same violence caused him to go forward. He had to stop this evil before it harmed the one thing in life worth living for: his Lakmé.

Even if Charlie was driving out tomorrow with his promise of beginning both hers and Jane's self-defense classes, he was overwhelmed with a sense of foreboding. He hated to leave her.

He vividly recalled watching her sleep in Seville, bidding her adieu shortly after. In love with her then, he had tried to protect her, but in the end, separating his heart and mind from her had proven impossible.

Dressed in stealth black, he glanced at his Sunto watch. The grave reality reminded him that Rick had now been off the net for two days, and a flight to Lima beckoned him but not before meeting up with Knightley to go over the intelligence and op details.

He walked toward Liz's sleeping form, sat at the edge of the bed, and faced her, watching her eyes flicker in R.E.M sleep and the rise and fall of her chest in gentle breaths. He smiled slightly thinking she was dreaming, maybe of him. Hating to wake her, he couldn't leave without hearing her voice one more time, hearing the words that would carry him back home to her.

The palm of his hand smoothed over the curve of her waist and hip to the cool sheet draping her thigh. Pulling it up to cover her, he committed the image of her shapely body to his mind's eye. The back of his fingers caressed, molding over the delicate slope of her neck to her shoulder until she unconsciously shifted in her slumber, laying on her back and slightly opening her right leg. He smiled sweetly, knowing that his wife had been so accustomed to his midnight lovemaking that her body naturally responded in welcome whenever he touched her while she slept.

Slowly, she opened her eyes to see him smiling down at her.

"Hi, sleepy head," he softly said.

"Hmm … you're going?"

"I am, sweetheart."

Liz tried to get up but he held her shoulder. "Stay just as you are. I just … want to see you like this before I go. You look so ravishing."

A tear trickled out the side of her eye, rolling sideways and landing in her strewn hair on the pillow. Promptly, he brushed its wet remnant away with his thumb.

She sat up, unwilling to stay reclining in the face of his departure to an unknown, uncertain fate. Smoothing the wayward curl of hair at his forehead, she said nothing.

Conflicting emotions played in her eyes. She didn't need to speak; he felt the same way as her. Finally, with her hand cupping his cheek, she whispered, "Come back to me."

His arm scooped her bare body close to him, only the waffled texture of his black Henley separated them. "I promise," he said before his mouth captured hers in an earth-shattering kiss that both didn't want to end; they were lost in the emotion behind the expression. His devouring lips lingered as they tried to separate from hers, savoring the last of the sweetness that her tongue deposited.

Her tears continued to escape as he reluctantly ended their kiss.

"I love you and I'll be back in a week or so. I'll call *you*. It might be dangerous if you try to telephone me. Okay?"

"Okay, I'll be waiting."

He pressed his forehead to hers. "After I return and after the wedding, what do you say about escaping down to the Florida Keys, maybe Little Palm Island? We'll spend the rest of the summer there and

I'll teach you to scuba. Just you and me, far from everything and everyone."

She nodded, tears streaming down her cheeks. He kissed their tracks then stood with a final smoothing of his index finger down her moist cheek in his usual endearing fashion.

He whispered, "Don't worry, baby," then headed toward the door.

When he neared the threshold, she called out to his retreating back, "Fitzwilliam!"

He turned toward her and reminiscent of last year's parting in Tangier, she blew him a kiss. "Be safe."

Wordlessly his eyes told her what she needed to hear. She never thought she would see the retreating back of the stone-cold assassin ever again, but life had a funny way of throwing her curve balls. Before crying herself to sleep, the last thing she heard was the Harley kicking to life, its distinct muffler fading with each quarter mile down the drive away from her.

The last thing she felt was the Glock he left for her under his pillow—just in case.

7

Arrivals

Had anyone been watching, they would have seen Liz appearing like an ethereal vision when she exited the back door of the mansion. The descending moonlight illuminated her knee-length nightgown, and despite the chill, she seemed unaffected. On her way toward Anne's greenhouse, she stopped at the edge of the koi pool, gazing down into its shallow depths, her hands wrapped around a lukewarm coffee cup. Darcy had once told her that her beauty was a life-like comparison to the cold contrast of the marble effigy of the Roman goddess beside her. She glanced at the statue; the water at stone feet rippled as though moonlit shards of electric beams danced upon the surface. At that moment, she only felt akin to the inert, emptiness of the lifeless effigy.

After long minutes, she mindlessly—as if sleepwalking—made her way to the stone and glass hothouse.

Waiting for sunrise and Charlie and Jane's arrival seemed interminable and she sat distractedly in her quiet space at the back of the building with her now tepid coffee, the goose pimpled flesh rising on her chilled arms. She stared out the small panes of glass, barely observant of the deer family on the other side of the pool, a sight that would have normally filled her with glee, but not that early morning. There wasn't even a place for the classical music that usually filled the greenhouse. Her sketchbook, now cast aside without thought, lay open to a drawing of the dead vines that once clung to the side of the structure. The sadness of both the sketch and her heart matched one another. She felt hollow now that Darcy had left toward danger. A chill suddenly permeated her bones.

At four in the morning, her single-serving mini Keurig was being called upon to help pass the hours of loneliness and worry. Not that she needed the coffee to keep her awake, but she just needed something to do with her hands; uninspired to do anything but tap her thigh with her fingers, she began to think about ways to break that particular habit.

She picked up the letter he had left for her where he knew she would find it—her special place in the hothouse—and ran her index finger over his name for what seemed the one-hundredth time. Suppressing the rising fear that this mission would be the end of their future together, she read between the literal lines and wondered if he felt the same way.

Dear Liz,

Thank you for supporting my decision to go to Rick. I couldn't have gone with confidence in what lies before me if I knew you were unhappy with me. Believe me, this was the hardest decision I have ever had to make.

That's how much you've changed me. Have I ever told you how much? I meant to, but as you know, deep emotional words are sometimes difficult for me to express. I'm a different man than the one you met last year. I know you're thinking that my return to Obsidian means that I haven't changed at all, but you are wrong. The <u>reasons</u> for my going have changed. It's like I told you in the kitchen the other night—I will do whatever it takes to keep my loved ones safe. Leaving you is the hardest thing to do, but knowing that I'm taking the fight to <u>them</u> means the risk is less to you here. I know you wanted to join me, and selfishly I wish you could have, but too much is at stake. Your and Georgiana's safety is paramount—as is Rick's. I would give my life to save and protect you all.

Sweetheart, please don't cry. Channel those emotions when Charlie is teaching you. I have faith in you and your latent skills. Know that wherever your heart is, mine is right beside it. Our love is so deep, so destined that not even separation can part us. I will be home before you even know it and then we'll pick up where we left off – building our future and living life as planned – happily ever after.

I love you, Liz. Please stay off the bike until I get home. It's a small thing, but please do this for me. It'll make me feel better since you're such a hell on wheels and are hell bent at ignoring every lesson I have attempted to give you.

All my love,

Fitzwilliam

Liz's thoughtful smile conveyed the small amount of humor she found in his last paragraph. Even in his absence, he was still telling her what to do. His concern tugged at her heart. She folded the letter and placed it in between the pages of her sketchbook wherein she also placed her emotions and tears. With resolute swipes to her cheeks, she dried the wetness and with renewed strength placed the CD of Rimsky-Korsakov's "Scheherazade, 1st movement" into the Bose. Of all the pieces of music they shared—their tango, their operatic arias, their rock—this was their symphonic suite. They made love to this piece in Marrakech and it would forever be symbolic of their oneness and abiding love. She picked up the charcoal pencil and began to sketch, not the statue by the koi pool, but her husband's face beside a *Coelogyne ochracea* orchid. Their fragrant orchid, the one he cut and saved before they met—the one tattooed to her hip, erotically entwined with his tribal snake and the imprint of his name.

* * *

Charlie's favorite residence, even more than the villa in Capri or the apartment in Prague, was a secluded houseboat docked on the Anacostia River in Maryland where he and Jane were happiest playing house. He knew she loved her converted warehouse loft in Georgetown, but she spent very little time there and, on more than one occasion, he had considered working up the nerve to ask her to move in with him, only to discount it. His high-adventure and dangerous life called him to live like a vagabond; the only two things grounding him to earth and DC were Jane and Caroline's dance school, which was, in fact, the best damn cover for Obsidian. It wouldn't be fair to Jane to ask her to accept that if they took their relationship to the "next step."

The sun wasn't up yet, and she was still sleeping as he stood on the deck of the boat, immune to the river's rocking below. Already dressed for the day ahead, he looked out onto the eastern horizon watching for the first signs of life to come upon the earth. Their bags were already packed, his mind prepared to leave DC for as long as necessary—but he couldn't dispel the unsettled feeling he had about this operation and Darcy coming out of retirement. During the four years of Darcy's tenure with Obsidian (and he suspected much longer), Iceman had behaved as though his blood was frozen in his veins, but a few months of marital bliss and quiet living in Leesburg had thawed him substantially. Charlie couldn't help but wonder if his friend's game might be off. Returning to an assassin's life—for a high-stakes rescue mission no less—might spell disaster. Death-like disaster.

Unexpectedly from behind, a T-shirt clad Jane wrapped her slender arm around his waist and snuggled her face into his neck. He loved when she did that, followed by her sensual purr in his ear. "Good morning, lover."

"Good morning, kitten."

"You like when I purr in your ear?" she cooed.

He put his arm around her shoulders and gave a small, smiling peck to her lips. "I *love* when you purr. You're my favorite pussycat."

She chuckled, "I better be your *only* pussycat."

He gave a chortle, neither confirming nor denying her suspicions. Jane noted his silence but didn't remark on it even though her heart sunk a little. Of late, she noticed how his attention seemed to wander at the dance school. The Asian woman in their Cali-Salsa class was an ideal example. A territorial woman in love never forgot how her man once remarked that Chinese woman were the best lovers, even though he later added how she changed that opinion. Of course, they were skinny dipping in the Grotto Verde in Capri at the time. What else would he say? That trip, on their way to rescue her father, was some of the best sex she ever had, but things were new, fresh, and exciting between them. Life and all its responsibilities following that trip had tempered their passion and she feared the worst.

"Are we leaving for Lizzy's soon?" she groggily asked after yawning, not expecting to wake at this ungodly hour.

"Yeah, we should leave at first light. You should get dressed and grab a cup of coffee so we can make tracks."

"So early."

"I don't think we should leave your sister alone for too long, and I've a lot to accomplish with you two once we get there. My buddy Wentworth is scheduled to arrive late sometime today to take up security on the perimeter of the estate."

"Wentworth? I don't know him."

"No, you wouldn't, he lives down south. When he left the Army, he found some secluded cabin in Tennessee. I only call him in to help me when we're a man down. Great guy, but lives and breathes the outdoors, even sleeps under the stars if he can. He's like frickin' survivorman."

"Hmm … and Caroline? Is she coming to Pemberley, too?"

"She'll be arriving tomorrow to teach you girls some of her *particular* skills."

Immediately, Jane felt excited by the prospect. She secretly wanted to *be* Caroline, but not only did she lack the physical acumen but she also lacked the cutthroat demeanor to be as effective as the spitting cobra. That didn't mean she wasn't trying. Other than her moonlighting as a dance instructor at the school, the admittedly flighty girl in her attempted to adopt a more focused persona, trying to portray a serious demeanor. Spending every day of the workweek playing with espionage artifacts and spy gadgets as one of the curators of the International Spy Museum in DC while actually dating an international assassin for the CIA, she couldn't help to be attracted to the intrigue of it all. And now, with the unveiling of the museum's newest exhibit "007 Bond Villains," her fantasies took over, making her more determined than ever to learn the tricks of the trade. After listening to interviews with notable Cold War women spies such as Shirley Perry and organizing and sitting in on the different lectures and classes, she fell in love with some of the 1950s and 60s famous counter-intelligence equipment: various concealment devices, tiny cameras in buttons, eyeglass frames that held a poison tablet, and best of all—the lipstick gun. Several of these items she'd already "borrowed" from the museum's storeroom with the intention of learning how to use them.

Charlie looked at his girl's beaming smile, noting how it complemented the vivacious look in her eyes, even at that early hour.

"You're excited about this?" he asked, peering curiously at her.

"Hell yeah! I want to *be* Caroline!" She bounced on the balls of her bare feet and he saw the excitement lit in her eyes. "Can I? Please?"

"Really? You're totally serious?"

Suddenly, she started to wield her arms in front of her, karate chopping the air, attempting to quell her effusive grinning. "Yes, Charlie. I'm serious. Picture it: you and me on an international espionage assignment, kicking ass and taking names ..."

He couldn't help himself from playing into her fantasy, enthusiastically adding, "... You wearing red leather, skintight pants, and a plunging halter-top while dismembering the bad guys like one of my favorite *DC Comics'* heroines Tarantula. You know, she's ex-FBI and willing to do anything to get what she wants. She wears leather hot pants. Or ... or I'll call you 'Pussy Catnip,' named after a 1940's comic heroine."

Jane squealed in the moonlight. "Yes! Oh my God! This is so great ... maybe I can be like a Bond chic. You can call me 'Pussy Galore'! I miss red leather and hip hugger hot pants. I'll wear wigs and learn how to use a whip and you can teach me to shoot a small pistol, like the ones in the museum, tucked into my garter belt. I can be all serious and deadly, exuding a bad ass persona as Obsidian's newest femme fatale!"

He laughed. *So this is where my Janie went and this is what will bring her back to me.* "Baby girl, you have skills and talent to dismember any man without Caroline's cold reptilian manner."

She furrowed her brow. "What do you mean? It's Caroline's severity that makes her so effective both in and out of the field, isn't it? Her bitchy hard-edge is extremely intimidating and successful. Hell, I'm scared of her most of the time and she's not even trying to kill me."

"True, but that's not you and trying to embody her doesn't become you. It'll be your frivolity and fun-loving spirit that'll blindside any man. They won't expect my deadly kitten purring up at them—braless with hot pink nail polish, hoop earrings, and wearing those furry Ugg boots of yours while you're sucking on a lollipop. That's your style, not my evil sister's."

"Gee, I didn't think about that. You really want to teach me, Charlie? You really want me to be part of your dangerous world? A Bond girl?"

Charlie slid his hands down her slender waist to rest upon her hips. "Yeah, I do. Jane ... I love you. We're a great team."

"You. Love. Me?"

"Sure. Don't you know that? I might flirt a good game at the school, but *you're* the only girl I want. You think I'd let just any woman into my heart let alone Obsidian's intimate circle?"

Jane wrapped her arms around his neck and asked with a frisky smirk. "And what about China-doll the other night?"

"Oh her. That was just to make you jealous. You know, I could ask the same thing of you—what about that guy at the museum? What's his name ... I think you called him Hercules?"

"Are *you* jealous, Charlie?" she teased before swiping her tongue across his lips.

Swiftly, he lifted her to sit on the deck railing before him, spreading her legs to accommodate him. "I was insanely jealous, Janie."

With a teasing smile, her hands smoothed up his chest, settling into the hair at his neck. "Good, I meant to make you jealous."

His own hands slid up the outside of her bare thighs as he growled into her neck, "Naughty girl. I know what you want."

At the sublime feeling of her lover's touch, she closed her eyes and moaned. "Yes I am, baby. I'm *your* very naughty girl."

* * *

Hours later, Liz and Jane dressed in shorts and tank tops stood at attention in the center of the training bunker below Pemberley. It was clear to Liz that Charlie's stern countenance was employed for his role as "combat instructor." For obvious reasons, she was distracted no matter what he said and Janie had gone off half-cocked with effusions at becoming a Bond girl. Only her sister failed to grasp the part about her training balls-out to become one. He stood authoritatively with his hands on hips, staring them down until Jane's eyes wandered to the hanging paper target of a man with a drawn pistol directed at her. She giggled then promptly covered her mouth.

"This isn't playtime, Jane," he admonished.

Liz couldn't help concurring with the sentiment behind her sister's silly reaction. Her life certainly had changed and now would yet again. "It's okay, Janie. *I* give you permission to laugh at Pemberley. If it weren't so deadly serious and if Fitzwilliam weren't in such danger, I'd laugh too. You and I are a far cry from Longbourn and this is definitely a different life than what we both led a year ago. I don't know about you, but I feel like Snowflake the cat. How many lives and reinventions does one get?"

She walked from the "at attention" line then removed Darcy's boot knife from the open drawer beside her, noting how some of the knives previously within were now gone. She resisted the sudden urge to shudder.

Charlie turned to her, his expression conveying the gravity of the situation, his voice delivering a menacing tone. "You're right, Liz. This is deadly serious and I'm going to need one hundred and fifty percent of both your attention and cooperation. Combat training isn't for wimps so I'm going to be demanding and Army tough on you. Like a drill sergeant, I'm going to strip you bare."

"Oh, Charlie, you're going to strip me?"

"Not now, Jane." He narrowed his eyes making his point, causing her immediate reaction. Her body posture and smile sobered until he winked at her, softening his admonition.

Liz knew he hated making her sister sad or mad at him, but this was training for her to enter the world of espionage, and if Jane was going to be successful—a weapon herself—she needed to take it more seriously. She also knew that Charlie was trying his best to distract *her*, keeping her mind off what was going on in Peru. No doubt Darcy had left him with those instructions.

A glance down into the open knife drawer must have been his tip off to her fascination over its contents. She couldn't resist her curiosity and picked up the eight-inch military throwing knife, examining it and attempting to hold it properly.

"Knives serve their purpose," he stated, startling her, taking the knife from her hands. "But they are not the best for self-defense. Unless you're extremely accurate from a distance, you cannot guarantee death when throwing them. We are not in the game of wounding; we're in the game of death-dealing. End of story."

She then opened a slender, black pouch lying beside one of Darcy's belt buckles, which concealed a pick knife behind it. "What are these?" she asked, withdrawing a slim steel stick.

"Ah … those are shuriken throwing spikes. Caroline will teach you to use those when she arrives tomorrow." He removed one of the spikes from the pouch then cradled it in the palm of his hand. With a forceful wave and push of his arm and wrist forward, he flung the spike through the air directly into the wood target at the far end of the room.

"Caroline uses pens and pencils because not every situation accommodates her steel spikes. I think she sometimes uses the sticks as hair thingies, too."

"Great idea," Liz gathered her hair back, coiling her tresses upward. With her free hand, she then stuck the spike through the mass of tendrils, securing it in place. "I like this!"

From behind them they heard Jane snapping the bullwhip that had been hanging upon the wall. She giggled, snapped again, then whimpered. "Ouch!"

A bang on the security door sounded, startling them all. They silenced, knowing that both Mr. and Mrs. Reynolds were previously instructed to use the intercom. Liz ran to the monitor on the wall. "It's not the Reynoldses," she whispered. "It's a guy. I don't know him." The stranger knocked again using the side of his fist, and Charlie removed a Glock from the second drawer of the cabinet before looking at the screen himself.

Liz's heart thundered. Had Darcy's enemy already come for them, here? But then Charlie laughed opening the door to reveal a cowboy-esque type of guy on the threshold.

"Well ain't that a fine howdy." The guy chuckled, eyes falling on the pistol that Charlie still held.

"Wentworth!" Charlie exclaimed, placing the pistol on the counter as both women sighed in relief then looked to each other as they rose. Liz could tell right away by the gleam in her sister's eyes that Jane appreciated the amazing-looking "Wentworth" and that rugged appeal of his.

Sporting a groomed stubble goatee and mustache, he was dressed in denim jacket and jeans. His magnificent smile revealed adorable laugh lines and straight, pearly whites. A bit windblown, his dark hair stuck up in an alluring mess.

He stepped into the bunker then shook Charlie's hand, "Good to see you, Crash!"

Again, the sisters looked to each other both knitting their brow and mouthing in surprised humor the unfamiliar nickname "Crash" at the same time.

"Liz, Jane, this is my good friend, Dave Wentworth. He's going to be helping us out until Darcy's return."

Cowboy shook their hands and with a sexy, southern drawl greeted, "Good to meet y'all. I hope it's okay that I came down here. Your housekeeper told me where to find y'all."

Liz warmly welcomed him but made a mental note to speak with Ellen about having directed him toward the secret panic room. She'd have to explain the importance of security again; this time without beating around the bush. "That's no problem. Welcome to Pemberley, Dave. Thanks for coming to assist us from ..."

"Tennessee. I left at about three this morning."

"You drove the Apache six hundred miles? Is it out front? I gotta see it!" Charlie exclaimed.

Wentworth laughed. "It's in the drive." He looked to Liz when he added, "I restored a '59 Chevy pickup and Crash has been lusting over it for the last two years."

"Ah, I see. That's impressive. I had an old '78 Jeep Wrangler that could have used a bit of restoration before I drove it to the junkyard last month. It near killed me to part with it, but it was time."

"I think you did the right thing trading it in for that racing red Ferrari out front."

"Actually the Spider belongs to my husband. I traded the Jeep for a Harley SuperLow."

Jane stood silently intrigued by the exchange between Liz and this new hottie on the scene. Although, not apparent by her sister's words or demeanor, she wondered if Wentworth's gentlemanly, southern voice washed over Liz in the same manner that it did to her. Did his vibrant, blue eyes mesmerize Liz in the same way as they did her? Not that either would act on an attraction or knee jerk impulse to lick, taste, and swallow his southern pralines, but Wentworth was candy of the finest caliber. Yummy, scrumptious, down and dirty, hard candy whose laid back vibe said, "Let's do it in a lake," or better yet, "Let's do it on the flatbed of my pickup." *Yee Haw! Ride 'em cowboy!* Jane wanted to shout aloud. She'd never gone bull riding before.

But Charlie's observation of her reaction and most likely expression of famished temptation for the fine hunk of meat in front of her, pulled her back.

Serves him right; he had a similar look the other night at the dance studio dancing with Miss Chinese, Chu Mei food.

He then territorially draped his arm around her and she chuckled. "We're going to train Liz and Janie in combat arts. My girlfriend has a hankering to be a Bond chick!"

Liz wanted to laugh when Jane licked her shiny, pink lips, followed by her sudden blurt. "Pussy Galore! I want to be Pussy Galore!"

Charlie snorted.

Wentworth nodded with a slight embarrassed smile. "And what about you, Liz? Which Bond girl are you?"

Her husband's dark Iceman eyes suddenly flashed into her mind. "Frost. Miranda Frost from *Die Another Day.*" She quickly changed the subject, feeling uneasy in the way Wentworth's eyes examined her face. "Well, shall we go upstairs? I'll have Ellen prepare a guest room for you, Dave. I'm sure you want to wash up after a long ride and get comfortable before eating."

"Oh don't worry about me. If it's alright with you, I'd prefer just to drive the truck to the far perimeter of the estate and sleep in the flatbed during my stay. The outdoors does me just fine, and the weather is supposed to be magnificent this week."

"Sure. That's no problem. Just pull around to the south field, because the horses are currently let out on the west and east fields and Gus is training some new ponies. The truck might spook them."

Charlie led the way out the bunker and looked over his shoulder to Wentworth. "Did you bring your pistol over state lines? Do you need anything? Gear? Ammo?"

"Hopefully, we'll have no need for the latter, but I'm good. Knives are my thing lately, so I came prepared. Although it looks like you have quite a set up and quite a variety to effectively train with." Wentworth's scanned the contents of the bunker, eyes settling on the open drawer.

"Yeah, Darcy spared no expense in getting everything we need. Hmm, knives you say? That's great because Liz has expressed an interest in learning how to use them. Maybe you can teach her."

Wentworth's eyes met Liz's and he smiled warmly. "I'd be mighty happy to teach you."

She tried to ignore the heat of the blush to her face. "Sure. That would be great."

8
Calculated Objectives

Caroline's silver, convertible Jaguar kicked up a dusty fog as she drove down the dirt road leading to Longbourn Plantation—the estate that had been home to seven generations of Bennets. With the top down, the wind pulled at her cream-colored scarf covering and securing her copper locks. Designer sunglasses and ruby red lips added to the attractive picture she painted as the warm afternoon sun shined down upon her.

To her right, she noted the large oak tree and the newly installed wood swing attached to a thick branch above. That hadn't been there when she visited four weeks ago. Subtle changes had taken place around the estate, and it annoyed her to know that most likely Darcy and his forty-six million dollars, made by his work with Obsidian, were footing the bill for the restoration. It further grated her nerves that she had to make this trip to Alexandria in Rick's unexpected absence. Dealing with an American traitor who had once attempted to sell a diabolic weapon to terrorists was loathsome business.

"All to save this piece of shit land," she said aloud with a shake to her head, uncaring and unappreciative of the two-hundred-year history of said "shit land."

"They should have locked Bennet up and thrown away the key."

Then again, if the Feds had actually sentenced Thomas Bennet with a harsher punishment than an eighteen-month house arrest, she wouldn't be making this little visit and Obsidian wouldn't have any new toys to employ out in the field. Some of their recent operations were taking the team's objective in a different direction. Therefore, they needed cutting-edge gadgets, especially given the obvious path of Operation Macarena. For that op, they required every type of high-tech espionage equipment they could get if they were going to successfully locate and rescue Bertram's daughter.

After parking the luxury car at the rear of the house, Caroline stood at the back door with one hand perched on her hip, knocking and waiting. She heard the overture from Mozart's *Magic Flute* playing behind the screen door. She knocked louder pursing her lips tighter in each passing second of impatient frustration.

Bennet, wearing his usual brown wool cardigan, sweat pants, and torn flannel slippers, shuffled down the hallway toward her stylish form. His black-rimmed eyeglasses rested upon the tip of his nose and his silver-gray hair stood up in an unkempt mess. They were a study in contrasts: well-worn and barely holding on, up against put-together and commanding wrapped in a gray Tahari suit.

"Miss Bingley, I'm sorry to keep you waiting. Please come in, come in. I expected Mr. Fitzwilliam last week," he greeted in a welcoming manner, obviously happy for any visitor in his house imprisonment.

Immediately assaulted by the musty smell of old books and antiques mixed with new construction, she entered Longbourn, scrutinizing the obvious layer of dust on the antique pier table.

"Yes well, Rick has been detained in Peru, so I'm assuming the temporary role as Director of Obsidian. Is everything completed?"

Bennet rubbed the palms of his hands together. "Follow me to my study. I think you're going to be very pleased with our prototypes."

She stepped over a tile-cutting saw in the middle of the hallway, and resisted the urge to look at the two photographs hanging on the wall, bracing her hand below them. No, she didn't want to see her former lover married to the daughter of this man. The visual hurt her brain and eyes. The new Mrs. Darcy was an insignificant kindergarten teacher who knew nothing about the kind of life the Iceman led during his employment with Obsidian.

"I hope we *are* pleased, Mr. Bennet. Obsidian has put ourselves on the line in recruiting your services. Of course, you and I both know that deceit is the name of the game in this violent world. Your technical knowledge and impressive skills, coupled with our expertise, afford us the opportunity to act without a conscience …" She raised an eyebrow. "… for the good of our nation, of course."

"Yes, of course, that is why I consented to Mr. Fitzwilliam's offer. I think I have learned a valuable lesson from the events of last year."

To Caroline, Bennet was still a traitor no matter what he did in recompense or his sudden regrets. She had no compunction in using the tools of his trade and drawing him into Obsidian's dangerous game of assassination because, simply put, the man—and his daughter—were expendable.

Entering his book-laden room, she resisted the urge to crinkle her nose at the stale aroma lingering in the stuffy confines. Although the open heavy curtains exposed the room to resplendent daylight, she could see the dust particles floating in the stream of sunlight. Situated to her left, a bulky mahogany table was covered with two desktop computers, three monitors, and various componentry amidst papers. She assumed that within the open, black suitcase were the completed prototypes—the booty she had traveled twenty miles outside the Beltway for.

Before speaking, she removed from her purse a small counter-surveillance device and beginning at the perimeter of the room, slowly scanned the bookcases with the high-frequency bug detector. Bennet stood watching her "dry clean" his office in the standard security sweep protocol, which she assumed Rick explained to him some six months ago. It was at the beginning of their business relationship, following Operation Shag down in South Carolina when they realized they needed an industry edge.

Satisfied that the room was clean of any listening devices, Caroline pointed to the table. "Are these the completed handheld EMP devices?"

Beaming with pride, he puffed his chest. "Yes, they are. Focused Electromagnetic Pulse with variable settings from 150 joules to 400 joules depending on the size of the facility. These prototypes, however, will only allow for one use, but I'm working on that."

She picked up the stainless-steel pistol-like pulse gun. "Impressive. It resembles a Desert Eagle .44 magnum. No one could tell. Oh, and this one! — a pistol small enough to be tucked into my clutch handbag. It's a Lady Derringer."

"Exactly. Mr. Fitzwilliam gave me the handgun hardware components." He held the lightweight, derringer, admiring it before handing it to her. "Eventually, they will be programmed to activate by only biometric fingerprint recognition. Once I obtain your agents' impressions, I'll then program and initiate but for right now, the prototypes are usable and ready to engage."

She held up the Desert Eagle, using the attached red dot laser to hone in on a book upon the shelves across the room. "So, all I have to do is point and shoot and then the building's electronics, lighting, and security system become fried?"

"Yes. Although heavy, it's very easy to deploy. Of course, you don't need the laser for the EMP detonation, but I liked the way it looked. It's an excellent subterfuge, but so as not to render the red dot laser totally useless, I did give it the capability of heat-guided laser as well."

"Heat-guided laser? What does it do?" Caroline asked, her curiosity piqued and her interest definitely engaged.

"Just aim the laser and press the small button on the grip of the pistol. The red beam generates enough concentrated heat to blow up any person or thing up to fifty yards away."

"Vehicles, too?"

"Yes, there is enough concentrated energy in that one burst to take out even an armored car. It's cutting edge, I assure you. Not even the military has something like this in so small a delivery."

"This is no small pistol, Mr. Bennet."

"For the power it generates, it is."

"Well, well, quite the diversion that just may be necessary at any given moment. You're to be commended."

"Oh, but there's more. I took it upon myself to create a few incognito doo dads to take with you into the field." He handed her a pair of trendy, hot pink, bubble glasses.

She couldn't help rolling her eyes. "Doo dads? Concealment devices for intel-gathering are referred to as camo communications, Mr. Bennet, and you've got to be kidding about *these*. There is no way I am wearing pink lens glasses." She gazed down her nose at the repugnant accessory.

"I know, I know, they're more suited toward my Janie's style, but you may change your mind, Miss Bingley, when you hear what it can do. I have designed an elaborate camera, programmed with facial recognition software within the hollow frame. Triggered by a touch to the temple tip, it feeds the photo back to Obsidian's server."

"Ingenious. And this gold saucer-shaped item? Is it a woman's compact?"

"Yes, but don't be fooled. It's not to be used lightly." He flipped the lid up then pointed to the mirror. "Concealed below is a miniature computer screen that, with fingerprint impression to the glass, will transmit through to Obsidian's mainframe, gathering intelligence from Interpol, NSA, Homeland Security, and a myriad of other databases. Within seconds, you should receive the entire worldwide dossier on your suspect."

"Amazing."

"I know. Isn't it? There's more. The cosmetic is actually tinted powdered chloroform that doesn't need to be inhaled. A little dab on your villain's face and he or she will be drunk as a skunk and lights out."

"Clever, very clever," Caroline stated, finding herself unwillingly impressed by the aged man beside her. "No wonder they employed you at the Pentagon. I must say—I should have given you more credit. Is that all you have for Obsidian?"

"No, just a few small things remain." He opened an innocuous-looking, engraved pillbox, then with a push of his index finger, resettled his eyeglasses at the top of his nose.

"Adhered to the inside cover of the pillbox are a listening device and its ear canal receiver, both in the guise of black beauty marks. You will notice that the back of each is a different color. It's very simple—red for listening, black for microphone. They will both transmit over Obsidian's secure communications network once activated. Further, they also are outfitted with military grade GPS satellite tracking.

He coughed and looked away from her questioning raised eyebrows.

"I … um … sort of hacked into a few governments' satellites … but anyway, this little microdot will firmly stick on anything, even fabric, but I rather like the way it looks on a woman's soft cheek. It's very authentic looking, I assure you." He held out his hand, palm up revealing two different colored pills. "Now, what do you see?"

"Simple pharmacological pain suppressors."

"Very good. Under the deliberately mislabeled guise of two popular over-the-counter acetaminophen and ibuprofen brands, you now have morphine in the orange one. In the event you can't get to the doctor. And this blue one is the strongest form of epinephrine; when consumed, it will immediately enter your bloodstream. Not as effective as a shot in the heart, but it'll work fast. In your line of work, one never knows what anaphylaxis you may encounter." Bennet handed her the pillbox.

"True. You have done your homework and I see you concur with my opinion that in our business we must act outside the parameters in order to achieve results."

He didn't answer as he began to take apart the components to the EMP guns, demonstrating their easy assembly in the event of air travel. He then placed each piece back into its grey foam cutout, which fit perfectly into her titanium case.

"So, what is your fee for this service you have provided to Obsidian? We are prepared to pay handsomely. You've done well, very well, indeed, and I'm sure Rick will want to compensate you in thanks."

"No thanks necessary, Miss Bingley. I only ask for Obsidian's continued confidentiality. I would greatly appreciate it if you kept our relationship private … more specifically, concealed from my son-in-law and two daughters, if that's okay with you. They wouldn't understand that this is my way of redeeming my traitorous actions of last year."

Ordinarily, Caroline's smirk would have given her away, but she knew he would fail to recognize (as he did with Henry Crawford and Al-Hanash the year before) that on that issue, she couldn't be trusted. "Oh, you have my word. I wouldn't dream of it."

* * *

By Rick's calculation, he had been missing off the grid for close to forty-eight hours, twenty of which were unaccounted for because of his drugging. He was sure by now that Caroline already executed the standard protocol for when an agent didn't check in, and, knowing Caroline, she went straight to Bertram. He counted on that. What he hadn't counted on was the presence of Sarah, nor two broken ribs and two festering wounds, one to his skull and one to his arm. With any luck in the light of day, the flies would get at them and lay their eggs. He welcomed maggots, but not fever; time was of the essence. Especially since he knew Obsidian's protocol would dispatch rescue—confident that it would be Darcy coming for him directly into the lair.

But all things considered, the odds were in both their favor. Two sentries were a laughable opponent.

Lying on the floor of the makeshift hut, his eyes focused through a wide slit in its perimeter. He watched the sun when it occasionally broke through the forest canopy. Focusing on a bamboo sapling, he observed the surrounding shade on the ground like a compass, calculating the Southern Hemisphere and his last known whereabouts latitude and longitude. He listened to the conversation of his captors who, becoming lazy and bored, talked of returning to town before dusk was upon the jungle. By his estimation, there were only a few more hours of sunlight remaining on a forest that grew ever darkening, inhibiting his and Sarah's effective escape in the light of day. There was nothing on earth like the blackness of the Amazon, particularly without a single beam of light, either from the moon, stars, or man-made. The jungle, already inhospitable to interlopers, meant certain death at night.

Hog-tied with his hands and feet bound together behind him and his painful rib cage stretched to accommodate his bindings, Rick rotated his body to look at Sarah. He noted how she examined him in curiosity.

"Do they feed you?" He asked grimacing in pain and breathing heavily from the exertion.

"Yes, once a day, usually at sunrise."

"Good. They'll have no reason to enter the hut again until tomorrow. That should buy us some time."

"What if I have to go to the bathroom? They'll come in then," she logically asked.

"Piss in your pants. I won't care and they sure as hell won't either."

Voices grew outside the makeshift hut. Again, Rick shifted his body through the dirt and straw to peer awkwardly outside the slits of wood. Men and women flooded the camp. Some with machetes, some with military-grade machine guns, and others held baskets filled with food. All wore knapsacks and pistol side arms on top their jungle apparel. These cartel members were rebel forces. Each individual looked menacing, several of whom, to Rick's trained eye, looked downright evil.

He allowed his head to fall back to the ground, and he closed his eyes from both the shooting pain and the need to think through the tenuously changed circumstances they now found themselves in. The odds had suddenly shifted and not in their favor. At least thirty cartel members kicked up the fire and began to settle in for the afternoon and most likely the night.

"What is it?" Sarah whispered.

"A lot more cartel guerillas than even I can handle. Our odds have significantly changed," Rick replied shimmying closer to her.

"Mr. Fitzwilliam, I don't mean to be rude, but did you really think you could get us out of here, all by yourself and in the condition you're in?"

He sighed. "It's Rick and yes I do, Sarah. It's important though that you follow my directions. I'm not really a journalist. I'm ex-military and know this jungle very well. I possess a very special set of skills and so do my people, who will be coming for us."

As he said this, his fingers worked furiously to remove the bottom of his heel.

"What kind of skills, if you don't mind me asking?"

With labored breath he spoke, "You don't want to know. Listen to me carefully … I'm going to turn my body and I'll need you to slide back the heel of my left boot. Your shackles are looser … than my bindings and you can effectively see what I need you to do."

Hesitantly she agreed, complying with him to reveal a digital device within the rubber heel. "What is this?"

"A homing device. What do you see in the shoe?"

"Some sort of digital scanner and three buttons," she stated tilting her head to the side to examine it more closely.

"Great, okay. You'll need to press the center button, which will engage the fingerprint scanner. It'll turn blue … and once it begins to flash, twist my right hand and place my index finger on it, holding it steady until the flashing stops. At that point, the screen should turn green if it reads accurately. You'll have four seconds to press the far left button, which will send the signal."

Sarah did exactly as Rick instructed. Her nervous fingers attempted to make quick work as she held his finger to the small blue screen then released it. "Done. Who gets the signal? NSA? America's DEA or CIA?"

"The CIA?" He sniggered. "No, not the CIA. *My* people will get the signal and with any luck they've already mobilized for my extraction, but we can't stay here. Once the gunfire begins, both of us will be killed without question."

"So, we're back to square one then." Sarah groaned, "For God's sake."

Calm and reassuring, Rick refocused her attention. "Look at me, Sarah. We're not as far up shit's creek as you think. We have to get evacuated and quick, but I *cannot* let my team walk into this ambush.

Between your wrist and this cut to my arm, not to mention my broken ribs, we need medical attention. In the jungle, I can make a poultice for my wounds, but I have to get there to do so. The first thing we need to do is to get me out of these ropes, then your shackles, and then you've got to stop the bleeding in my arm so we can dig out of this snake pit. We can do this. *You* can do this."

Sarah nodded, realizing that this guy was the best thing to happen to her and the only option she'd had since her captivity began. As much as she hated the idea of entering the dense rainforest on foot, she knew escape was her only hope. "First tell me what the other button in your boot is for."

"You really want to know?"

"I wouldn't have asked otherwise. Have you forgotten that I'm a reporter?"

"When pressed, it arms the boot and the plastic explosive within it. The whole shoe is an explosive device, but unfortunately in the jungle I need both my boots."

"What's in the heel of your other boot?"

"American dollars, just in case."

"Forget MacGyver. You're like bloody James Bond. Well then … what do you need me to do?"

Rick shimmied his torso again, thankful for his rock-solid thighs to move him in a circle until his waist and groin rested against Sarah's legs. "If you dare," he said with a smirk. "I need you to unbuckle my belt … and no funny business."

"Ha. Ha. What's below your waistband that you need me to attend to?"

"Sarah, are you flirting with me and under such dangerous circumstances?" Rick flirted back, loving her British accent and pleased to see she had a sense of humor in such a tenuous situation.

"Hardly, Rick, but these types of dangerous situations always bring out the cheeky in me."

"Well, I'm glad to hear that because once you unbuckle the belt, there's no turning back."

"And why is that? I'll be so dazzled by what I find inside?"

Rick laughed. "That's two for two. I'm impressed, but unfortunately you won't get that far—not today at least. Tucked within the buckle are two steel stars, gingerly pull one out. They're sharp so take care. If you can, slice my rope bindings. It may take a few passes, given their thickness. See if you can slide the cuff of your shirt sleeve down into your hand to protect your fingers."

"Shuriken stars? What are you a ninja assassin, too? Are you going to go all Bruce Lee once we get out of these bindings?" she joked and even though he knew she was a journalist who could expose Obsidian, he met her query with a raised eyebrow.

Thirty minutes later with the sun hovering at three o'clock in the afternoon and La Muerta's cartel sufficiently relaxed in their siesta, Rick's restraints lay concealed under the heavy straw flooring. He now set to the task of picking the lock of her shackles, using a rusty nail he pulled from a board in the hut.

Furtive glances between the wood slats revealed the quieted security force, at least three quarters of whom were asleep in the heat and humidity. With the nimble fingers of her good hand, Sarah used her small hair clip to pull at the soft dirt under the boards of the hut. He couldn't help but notice her messy, cascading blonde locks and her determined expression. Even with a dirty face, she beguiled him. Her new, positive attitude buoyed him through his own sweat and pain. With his hand wrapped in his torn shirt, he quietly used the edge of one of the stars to saw the bottoms of the thin wood board perimeter to create a means of escape.

It seemed to take hours as they worked side-by-side, making whispering small talk about family back home, marital status, and to Rick's benefit, slowly extracting what information Sarah knew about La Muerta and its connection to Russian trafficking. This intrigued him the most because Caroline had once shared her knowledge that Bertram, in his early twenties, was a former KGB underling. Rick hoped that, now acting as head of Obsidian, her subsequent visit to Bertram revealed enough intelligence to track this Diablo and bring down the cartel and

Bertram in one fell swoop. He further hoped that if the trail led to the east that Knightley and Bingley would be willing to go to Russia to finish Operation Macarena, if need be.

With a muffled snap, the last of the four boards on the western wall of the hut gave way. Rick and Sarah quickly repositioned their bodies to cover the gaping hole. They sat still, waiting, just in case the rebels heard the noise. He clutched a shuriken star in each hand at the ready to fling them if and when the door opened.

Time seemed to freeze as they waited, their breaths caught in anticipation until the moment passed and the second hand resumed for them to continue digging.

The escape hole was ready.

"Sarah, you go first." Searching beyond the hole, he whispered. "Head to the south, straight into the forest until you get to that Walking Palm about fifty meters in. Can you see the top of the tree in the canopy? It's the tallest palm."

"Yes."

"Hide in its stilt roots and I'll catch up to you there."

"But you need help."

"Don't worry about me. I can manage and I'll be right behind you." He opened his boot heel, and then withdrew a stack of one hundred dollar bills, shoving them into her palm. "Take this. If we get separated, keep heading south. Follow the increasing scent of the chemicals. At the lab, there will most likely be peasant workers who, for a price, will help you and lead you out of the jungle."

He stuck his head out the hole, checking to see if the coast was clear, then handed her one of the two ninja stars. "Go and don't look back!"

Sarah lay on her back, and using her feet, pushed herself head first through the narrow aperture, then made a mad dash for the trees.

The hole was small, but thankfully, he was slender. Rick ignored the pain in his chest and his shortness of breath. He disregarded the dirt encrusting and penetrating his open wounds. All he focused on was getting out of that hut and guiding Darcy, via the homing beacon, as far from this camp as possible.

With one final push, he broke through to freedom and ran balls out to where Sarah waited for him in the dense jungle. Together they would traverse the rainforest toward the cocaine-processing lab.

9
Dangerous Liasions

Obsessive worries laid heavy upon Liz's heart and mind as she went about her day trying to distract herself. Try as she might she couldn't escape playing out all the worst-case scenarios in her mind of what may go down tonight in the Amazon. Darcy was good, there was no doubt, but he was also out of practice in the field, no thanks to her and the soft life she had forced him into. Was going back to "that life" like getting back on a horse? Would he just slip back into Iceman's deadly skill set? God, she prayed so.

Sitting astride his black stallion, Salaam, she wondered if her husband might be off his game for this dangerous mission to search for Rick. That had deadly results for all involved. As beautiful as the scenery and as leisurely as their walk, her stomach knotted, oblivious to the tranquility of the landscape before her.

Thoughts turned to her exciting training. As usual Darcy knew what he was doing when he instructed Charlie to educate her in self-defense and weapon management; it was the only way to keep her mind refocused away from niggling fears and what ifs. She understood his strategy. When it came to her protection and safety, he was acutely transparent and fiercely focused.

The vast empty field ahead beckoned Salaam—and her—to kick up their pace a notch, but just like when riding the SuperLow, Darcy's voice echoed in her mind. *Straighten your back. You're not ready to gallop—only canter!* This was not the day to fall off and break something. Today's ride was only a means to get to her destination at the southern perimeter of Pemberley.

Wentworth's vintage pickup sat parked horizontally along the tree line, but he was nowhere in sight. Most likely, he was acting sentry within the lush forest. Nearing the rear of the truck, she noted his bedroll and a large cooler sitting in the wood-floored bed. Like Darcy's lifestyle had been with Obsidian, his was foreign and it intrigued her.

"What do you think, Sal? Should we go back?" she asked, bending down to pat the horse's neck. "No, I guess not. I have to learn knife throwing."

Tugging at the reins, they stopped. A slide down the horse preceded a casual, unhurried walk toward the front of the truck, examining it with curiosity, her hand dragging along the warmed metal edge of the pick up's bed from back to front. She couldn't resist the temptation to peek her head into the driver side's open window and reach in to finger the black-trimmed military dog tags hanging from the rearview mirror.

The clearing of a man's throat from behind her startled her and she jumped, banging her forehead on the window frame. Embarrassed, she abruptly turned to see Wentworth, with his hands resting on his hips, watching her trespass. He wore a humored smile and she thought she saw something else flicker in his eyes—admiration? Enjoyment? Attraction? How long had he been observing her?

"Are you alright?" he asked, walking toward her with an outstretched arm.

"I … I'm fine. Oh, I'm so embarrassed. I didn't mean to be so nosey. I'm sorry." She felt the flush to her cheeks rising.

Wentworth chuckled. "It's okay, Liz. Don't worry about it. You were just curious. They're a buddy's dog tags."

Subconsciously, she continued to rub her head, more from embarrassment than pain.

"Let me see that," he offered, reaching up to her hand to remove it from her brow. Her eyes locked with his crisp baby blues and Wentworth promptly stepped back. "You're okay. I'm sure you won't even have a knot."

He smiled warmly, however the slight flare of his nostrils and subtle parting of his lips made her uneasy, if not somewhat self-satisfied that a man other than her husband would be affected by her nearness. Not that it was solicited, or even wanted, but it was certainly nice for her ego.

Flustered, she quickly brushed past him and headed for Salaam's saddle pannier. *Focus, Liz!* she reprimanded.

"Um, I brought you a couple of sodas and water. I wasn't sure if you had anything out here in this unusual heat."

Wentworth didn't indicate whether he had refreshment or not, but took what she offered. "Thank you. That's real thoughtful of you."

"Your truck is impressive. I can see why Charlie covets it. You did all the work yourself?"

"Yes, ma'am. She was a junker when I got my hands on her." His rugged hand smoothed over the oak laid within the flat bed. "She's my darlin'; suits my lifestyle perfectly."

He stepped away from the truck with a wistful smile, as though the truck came with memories. Perhaps his friend's dog tags had something to do with it.

"So… are you ready for our lessons, Liz?"

"Ready as I'll ever be. Apparently, my husband gave strict orders to turn me into a Navy SEAL."

"From what I understand, Darcy was one of the best."

"He still is," she quickly defended.

"Of course. I'm sorry. I only meant …" he stammered.

"It's okay. I know what you meant."

Obviously uncomfortable by his inadvertent implication and eager to move the conversation to something more pleasant, the man opened the truck's passenger door and removed a leather case from under the seat.

"We'll practice with these knives, using that thick oak as our target. Have you ever worked with knives before?"

"Only in the kitchen."

He chuckled. "That won't do. Dicin' and mincin' aren't part of our syllabus."

"Darn. I'm pretty skilled with a Ginsu," she joked for levity but was surprised by his switch of gears, his serious tone, and she sobered, just like they had done with Charlie.

"I don't know what Crash explained about knives, so I'll work on throwing technique with you. It's important that you understand that knife *fighting* is different from knife *throwing*. When one introduces a knife into confrontation, it's for the sole purpose of assassination. Your attacker doesn't want to *fight* with you, he wants to *kill* you."

Holding out a small knife he said, "Feel how light it is."

"Yes," she replied in barely a whisper.

"Pinch the handle between your forefinger and thumb, then face the tree," he instructed.

"Now this is just the basics, getting comfortable with your weapon. Lesson number one: never throw your knife unless it's an absolute emergency. It is part of you, an extension of your hand."

"I understand."

Wentworth moved beside her, then leaned forward, placing his hands upon her right knee, bending it and dragging her foot back about twelve inches from her left. His hand slid a few inches down her left thigh, lingering where he pressed slightly. "Bend your knees while placing most of your weight on your back foot. When you toss the knife, your weight will shift from back to front, right to left."

Despite his relaxed tone, his closeness, his hands upon her, made her nervous—flustered actually.

She focused on the knife, attentively listening to his instruction and attempting to absorb everything he said. He moved behind her, mimicking her body posture as his arm and hand molded to her straight throwing arm.

He was so close; she felt his warm breath tickling her ear. It smelled sweet and she couldn't help wondering if he chewed tobacco.

"Like this," his southern drawl guided, pulling her backward before guiding her arm and body in a forward shift and release.

The knife soared through the air, falling short of the target.

"That was good. Let's try it again," Wentworth said.

Feeling on edge, her fingers tapped upon her thigh. "I'd like to try without your help if that's okay?"

It was more for her protection than for her tutelage. This gorgeous stranger, in this carefree setting, at this vulnerable, worrisome time was more than she could handle. Wentworth, without his even knowing it—or maybe he did—affected women with just that winsome smile and delicious accent.

"Absolutely. Remember to keep both arms out toward the target and follow through with the movement."

Liz did as he instructed, then tossed the blade with surprising skill. It soared toward the tree and made contact at the bottom of the trunk. Clearly impressed, he grinned and handed her a third knife, making small talk.

"How long have you been riding motorcycles?"

"Not long. I just learned, really. My husband is an excellent teacher even though I have a proclivity to ignore his advice and suggestions. He says it's my one and only defect." She snorted a laugh. "I doubt that. Stubborn and reckless are *two* character flaws in my opinion."

She turned her thoughts to her husband, and then tossed the knife with steely determination.

"A lot of men actually find those characteristics in a woman extremely sexy. I know I do. Darcy is a lucky man—a very lucky man."

"I think he feels that way, at least I hope so. I know I'm a very lucky girl."

He came to stand beside her again. "Here, let me show you another trick on how to hold the knife at close contact. If the situation warrants and you're forced to engage in hand-to-hand, you'll need to maneuver with greater ease."

He cradled her hand in his calloused one and placed a fighting knife diagonally across her outstretched palm. "Grasp the small part of the handle and place your forefinger on the largest part, like so."

As his fingers molded around hers, she could feel the heat expending from his hard body. *Good God!* His allure and her innate desire to reach out and touch the stubble of his beard battled with the happily-married-to-a-super-hot-man, rational woman she was. Awash with guilt, she took a deliberate step away from him. Their eyes met for a brief moment.

Wentworth smiled regretfully. "I'm sorry … I, um … Let's continue," he stammered, obviously upset with the small temptation and liberty he had taken.

* * *

The scar running from just below the left temple to the corner of Juan Sanchez-Morales's lips only made his appearance more sinister when coupled with menacing beady eyes that closed to mere slits whenever he was displeased. If not for his dynamic smile of pearly white teeth, there was nothing particularly appealing about his looks. However, none of that bothered the woman who had been sharing his bed for the last three years as they worked together to build his father's drug empire in Europe.

Morales was powerful, feared, and educated, and he had made her millions after enticing her with a substantial offer to leave her miserable cold life of little pay as a Bio Engineer for the Russian Federation. The man she loved to call by his alias "Diablo" had separated her from her then-lover (Alexei Petrov, also with the Federation) and their tiny apartment near the Tom River in Siberia. After settling her into a luxurious palace in the "secret city" outside of Moscow, she re-invented herself, assuming an alias: Nadya Karakurt, carefully selected for her skills. She prided herself on being as deadly and poisonous as the Russian lethal widow spiders she collected as pets.

Unlike Diablo, blood and guts weren't her method, instead preferring toxins to usher in her brand of evil: paralysis, flesh-eating bacteria, delirium, lunacy, and when necessary, truth-seeking. All of those formulas she concocted in her personal laboratory using the neuro-toxins of her beloved black wolf Karakurt spiders.

Educated by the Russian Ministry of Defense for the diabolical purpose of the design of binary chemical warfare agents, she earned three PhDs in microbiology, toxicology, and virology. The government put her to work in her home village where secret testing began in the Tomsk Oblast. However, once the title of doctor was employed for her *own* interests, her scientific acumen was put to another type of death dealing. Her expertise employed for Morales was in the formulating and design of Peru's newest crop of specially hybrid coca for growth in the swamps and unique environment of the Amazon rainforest.

There was nothing ordinary about Nadya. Beyond possessing the intellect of a prodigy, she possessed a beauty that left men spellbound. A tall woman in her late thirties, she wore her jet-black hair in a surprisingly utilitarian long braid down her back. Rare violet eyes, the color of highly sought-after Siberian amethysts, hinted bluish reflection. Both her hair and her eyes were unusual for someone from Tomsk.

She possessed beauty, brains, and a strange taste in men.

Morales was also only one of a handful of men vicious enough to arouse her. He created the rules and punishment and bent the world to his will—all within the shadows he hid. They both spoke three languages and loved to watch their victims die by the gruesome methods they deemed appropriate. Death was foreplay to their sexual exploits of BDSM. Only who played the Dom and who played the sub was often inter-changed following their latest kill. As kindred as they were, though, he was not her only partner in the bondage world—nor in the criminal world—and she made sure to keep many of her "business" dealings a secret from him. That was one thing that Nadya prided herself on: she had no loyalty to anyone other than herself and was not ashamed to use sex as her form of manipulation. In fact, that was her desired means to getting what she wanted and needed.

With temperatures hovering around freezing, the winter thaw had yet to come to Moscow, particularly within the dense forest of the secret city on the outskirts. So secret that only Russia's wealthiest billionaires sought seclusion and concealment within. Her home, a twenty-million dollar art deco structure of ten thousand square feet was impenetrable, particularly the sub-basement, two stories down.

After pressing the elevator button, she turned a key and placed her right index finger within a hidden panel to scan the print, allowing access to below. Following her normal protocol, she tapped a button on her wristwatch initializing the various security cameras' relay of the ante-chamber. Before the lift's door slid open, her lips curled, noting the armed guard seated at the end of the cavernous steel-lined hallway she was about to enter. He had defied her for the last time.

Upon exit into a small space before the hallway, she bent toward a device upon the wall, placing her thumb to the biometric screen disarming the seven motion-triggered acid showerheads suspended above the passage leading to two prisoner cells, her lab, and her personal BDSM dungeon. The cells were hardly used, but past occupants had included obstinate government officials and uncooperative *militsiya* as well as the occasional rival cartel leaders who failed to relinquish their drug business to La Muerta Mundial. Today it was guarded for the package within: one Miss Julia Bertram, the CIA's director's twenty-three year old daughter.

Expensive, high-heeled shoes below the wolf spider tattoo upon her foot clicked against the marble flooring as she made her way down the metal hallway. She smiled disarmingly at the guard, but he had obviously grown accustomed to her manner. He promptly straightened his posture and fidgeted to conceal the Cuban cigar he smoked.

She internally sneered at the filthy habit emitting a thick, putrid cloud of lingering smoke. Her fingers wrapped around the offensive, lit stogie crushing it within her fingers. Sensation had been long gone in her right hand since beginning a love affair with the spiders whose nerve and incapacitating venom had exacted their toll over these many years.

With a tone brooking no opposition, she disciplined the guard in Russian. "I have told you—no smoking. It vill kill you!"

He abruptly stood at attention. "Yes, *Diablesa*. Forgive me."

She turned her back from him, laughing at her joke, because surely he understood that it would be *she* who would kill him if he did so again. Several steps brought her down another hallway and she stopped before a windowless metal door, pointing her finger. "Open."

The guard ran to her, nearly stumbling over his feet. He pressed a series of numbers on the wall keypad outside the sliding pocket prison door.

Once inside, she stood at the entrance of Julia's cell, looked at the untouched food tray on the wood table then stared down at La Muerta's captive. Miss Bertram was the ransom for a cache of arms large enough to keep Peru's drug enforcement military at bay. From her perspective, the young woman's usefulness was for that purpose alone. Her focus was on cocaine trafficking, not Diablo's personal revenge for this Iceman. She could care less that this woman was meant as a form of extortion to catch the CIA assassin.

Julia sat huddled in the corner of her cot with knees pulled to her chest. She was afraid of the black widow woman, and with good cause. It had taken four days to come out of paralysis and stupor. Upon her arrival, she had not felt the electrodes pressed to chest and neck, but heard the Russian, "New drug for experimentation purposes will keep her silent and immobilized. I vant her vitals monitored at all times. She is valuable commodity."

"Are you well?" she asked Julia in clipped perfect English, which was answered with short successive head nods.

"You have not touched food. You must keep up strength since your stay may be many more days."

"I'm ... I'm not hungry."

Nadya stepped further into the room and the door slid closed behind her. "Are you obstinate or just not hungry? It is important you convey your physical condition to me. Do you have blisters? Swelling in armpits? Double vision? These things you must tell me."

"I'm fine."

"Good. That means anti-toxin has worked well."

"Why have you taken me?" Julia begged.

"You should not ask such things. If you continue to cooperate without conflict, your eventual death will be painless. I promise you, *Lapushka*."

"Why would you kill me? I don't know you. I've done nothing to you. Please let me go."

"Yulia. Such beautiful Russian name." She ran her index finger along the edge of her captive's chin. "How appropriate. It means youthful." Nadya laughed at the irony. "Death is only a matter of consciousness. Do not fear it—it comes to us all—no matter what age. Some quicker than others. Your abduction was business decision. So do not concern yourself with the details. Soon it will be over, I promise you."

She patted the petite woman's delicate hand as if trying to comfort her. "Do not worry so."

"I'll do anything, whatever you say. Please don't kill me."

Nadya turned from Julia, walking back to the threshold of the door. Glancing over her shoulder, her eyes met her captive's and she raised an eyebrow. "You would do *anything*? Well, Yulia, there just may be further use for you after business is completed with your father. Many men would pay handsomely for your virginity."

"I-I-I am not a virgin."

"There is no need to lie. I have confirmed you are still intact." She laughed maniacally, a lightbulb decision having been triggered. "Yes. I have other fate for you and an old friend who can take care of the arrangements. You are rarity and your chastity will prove very lucrative. Thank you for your prudence." She cackled again, her heart and mind filled with glee. Although it had been some time, renewing her relationship with her former lover, Petrov could be advantageous to everyone. He had connections in such matters as human trafficking.

Glancing at her Rolex, her laughter turned into her best smile. It was time to leave for Paris; she had another playmate to meet at her favorite fetish club. Morales's lieutenant could wield a bullwhip like none other.

10

Exfiltration

The distinct overwhelming thump, thump, thump of the helicopter's choppers drowned out Darcy and Knightley's voices following take off from an abandoned airfield outside of Tarapoto: the last known location of Rick. Since the DEA, regionally headquartered in Peru, wanted nothing to do with the extraction, Obsidian organized the mission with the help of Peru's national police. The covert Operation Macarena, now in search and rescue mode, commenced bribing officials to look the other way with one-hundred thousand hard US currency. Darcy thought nothing of it when he slid the small duffle bag across the broken desk.

Through military headset walkie-talkies, the two-member elite team conversed sitting at the open door of the armored helicopter. Dressed in jungle fatigues, Kevlar vests, and tactical backpacks, they were both armed with a side arm and a semi-automatic rifle. Dusk was settling favorably upon them when Darcy noted the intermittent blip growing in strength on the wristwatch-sized device he held.

Holding it out to Knightley he said, "There it is again. He's alive." His heart rate surged, but his demeanor remained cool and focused. Iceman wouldn't assume what the conditions below the canopy were and he was damn happy they had their night vision goggles for what lay ahead.

"It's stationary, six klicks east of the river," Knightley confirmed.

"Let's hope it's him and not a diversion."

"Either that or he's been moved or escaped. He's at least two klicks from where his cell phone signal went dead."

After sharing the coordinates of Rick's homing device, the pilot turned the helicopter south in compliance. Once they repelled into the jungle, they were on their own until extraction in three hours by this same pilot.

Flying over the green forest, Darcy's attention remained riveted on the swaths of land cleared for coca production, a patchwork of green to brown acres upon the hillside. "You're a far cry from Monte Carlo."

"I wouldn't have it any other way—seems like I'm always destined to follow in the footsteps of the Iceman."

"Apart from my mistake with Caroline, I wish that for you." He smiled thoughtfully. Try as he might, he could not put Liz out of his mind.

"If I wanted an evil woman, I would have stayed married to Katie. She was a God-damn ball breaker."

The helicopter crossed over the Huallaga River and Darcy observed a lone boater slowly making his way across the rapids to the other side.

"Mark my words—one day you're going to find an angel like Liz. You're a good man plagued by memories, but the right woman'll help you deal with your past just like Liz helped me to deal with mine."

"Yeah, if only I could find a woman like your wife … someone who'd melt my frozen heart, too."

"I didn't melt entirely, just slightly *thawed*, thanks to her. I haven't lost my edge if that's what you're getting at."

"I'm not implying anything. Don't get defensive. You're as much a bad ass as you were before Liz—only a slightly better conversationalist now." Knightley smirked.

Darcy's lips twitched into a half smile. "Are you seeing anyone?"

"No. No time, but I do have my eye on that receptionist at the dance school."

"Really? You're serious?"

"Yeah. What's wrong with Fanny?"

"Nothing. I just thought you went for a little more flash."

"Flash is overrated."

"Yes it is." He thought of the wholesome, captivating, surprising woman who had been locked inside Longbourn. There had been nothing flashy about Liz, and she had him by the balls the moment she raised her defiant chin in the dance school. "So they've slugged you with a code name, I hear."

"I hardly call 'Mr. Clean' original, but it does seem apropos to this new profession and my baldness."

He nodded, changing the subject to the mission. "Let's hope this mission ends here with Morales dead and Rick and Julia Bertram safe."

"The man's a ghost. There is no guarantee he'll be here."

"Maybe he will be. A man like him wants to enact revenge on his own. That aside, we have to keep focused on this mission's objective: Rick and Julia Bertram. If I were Diablo, I wouldn't be foolish enough to keep the girl captive here in the jungle. The rainforest could very well taint the goods. Most likely, he's thinking that after he kills me, he'll promise to return the girl to her father, get his arms from the CIA, then traffic her in Eastern Europe. The first place to start would be to locate his mistress. She'll lead us to finding Bertram's daughter."

Slathering his neck with more insect repellent, Knightley agreed. Damn, he hated the jungle. Twice in as many weeks Darcy had made him eat his words. He did wish he was on his boat racing on the Liguria Sea, but Rick needed him and that kept him focused. His hand made another swipe of repellant upon his cheeks, before applying the black and green swaths of camo paint. He spoke against the flapping wind into the fuselage, "Viper Caroline is having difficulty dredging up any solid intelligence on this Nadya Karakurt broad referenced in Bertram's report. Neither Interpol nor Russia's FSB have knowledge of her name, her past, her involvement—if any—in the drug trade. She's a mystery.

We don't even have photographic intel. If you ask me, we need a little more to go on before this wild goose chase for Bertram's daughter."

"A ghost, just like Diablo. Thankfully, Caroline has her share of seedy contacts in Russia, maybe a Company sleeper asset or two from her days with the CIA. She'll come up with something, I'm sure," Darcy replied, painting his face black.

"Are you going to go after Bertram when Macarena is finished?" Knightley asked.

"Probably."

"Probably?"

"Yeah, that's the best I can say. Unfortunately, at my *slight* thawing, I seemed to have grown some scruples. I'm not too keen on the idea of taking out an American government official for personal revenge. Kick his ass, yes, but not execute him. Damn Dostoyevsky. Liz would laugh if she heard me say that."

"He's ex-KGB."

"Dostoyevsky?" Darcy asked, humored by his joke.

"No Bertram."

"Why am I not surprised?"

"Will you at least continue the op to take out Morales?"

"I haven't decided yet. If I don't, then he won't stop trying to find me and I can't risk Bertram spilling his guts even if we bring his daughter home safely. That jackass knows where Pemberley is and knows about Liz."

One hundred feet below the helicopter, the setting sun cast an eerie shadow upon the emergent layer of trees. They were almost at the coordinates and the homing signal was now steady. The men silently prepared: removing their headsets and donning black tactical helmets, Bluetooth communication, night vision goggles, and then finally the rappel harnesses.

Knightley withdrew his side arm followed by a lift to the black grip.

Darcy watched with keen fascination as his friend tapped a couple of buttons within the handle. "What the hell is that?" he asked with raised voice over the deafening chopper.

"It *was* my custom .45, but now it's jacked-up with some computer gadget. It's a thermal guiding system installed by some computer geek Rick has working on specialized weaponry for us." He shrugged. "Guess it'll be of use tonight."

Warning bells went off in Darcy's head. "What other kind of computerized weaponry?"

"Alls I know is that Caroline was going to retrieve the prototype of a hand-held electromagnetic weapon for compound infiltration."

Darcy rested his head back against the doorframe. "Did you happen to catch the name or background of this *computer geek*?"

Knightley shrugged. "Used to work for the Defense Department. Why? You know I'm too new to the team for Rick or Caroline to part with that kind of intel."

"Yeah, I guess you're right. I just know someone who specializes in weaponry like that." *And when I get back to Virginia, Liz is going to freak out when I tell her about her father's duplicity. And when I find Rick, he's going to get a piece of my mind.*

The pilot signaled to the men and pointed below to a large coca field in a valley. In Spanish he said, "I will pick you up here at twenty-one hundred hours sharp. If you're late, I'm gone."

Darcy nodded then promptly registered the coordinates within the GPS.

An ominous silence settled within the chopper as both men shifted deep within their tactical mindset. Both began the process of freezing their hearts, effectively putting aside all emotion so they could focus solely on the mission: escape and survival for all three of them.

The helicopter hovered a mile south of Rick's signal with the chop, chop, chop of the blades slicing through the air. The loud drone within the fuselage grew and the pilot signaled their drop over a small separation in the trees. They neither heard nor saw anything below the canopy. It was so dense that not even Darcy's thermal riflescope penetrated through to the ground one hundred and thirty feet below the tops of the inter-locking trees.

He inspected Knightley's rappelling seat and equipment before shouting, "I'll see you on the ground," then gave him two thumbs up before throwing the nylon ropes down into the jungle below.

Both men clipped onto their respective ropes, took hold, then hung precariously outside the door, jungle boots poised on the chopper lands. Side-by-side, Obsidian's elite faced the interior of the helicopter until Darcy gave the "go" command. Pushing off, they propelled eight feet a second into the silent, deadly jungle below.

Operation Macarena had officially begun.

* * *

They cleared through the rainforest's entwining canopy of trees, landing unscathed in the dense jungle. The Amazon was ever blackening as the sun descended, and the two immediately employed the night vision goggles attached to their helmets, switching the forest from the growing gloom to vivid green. Neither felt the chill already enveloping the forest, but they immediately became assaulted by the deafening sounds of nighttime. Frogs, crickets, and birds created a coordinated symphony around their stealthy figures. Against the otherwise eerie stillness, the deadly ex-Frogmen hunched low, getting a fix on location and direction.

Vibrant orchids, that Liz would appreciate, and ferns, hung beside vines—all of which became a source of obstacle. The moving jungle's inhabitants: large scorpion spiders and bats, tarantulas the size of rodents were visible in the night vision. The dead, rotting ground below their military jungle boots squished soft and muddy with each deliberate step forward.

Darcy tracked, attuned for signs of previous human trespass. Apart from the GPS strapped to his wrist, he relied on his training and experience for such an operation.

He whispered into his communications Bluetooth, "One klick left," then signaled with his fingers for Knightley to move to the flank.

Their rifles remained poised and ready, their muted footsteps lost within the cacophony of the jungle. Stealth was of the upmost importance. To become the forest, one with the surroundings whether in recon or combat mode was essential to any mission.

One thousand meters to traverse hardly seemed any distance at all for SEALs conditioned to withstand intense rigors, but progress was deliberately slow within the density. Their sight was hindered by the limiting fifty-feet the goggles provided.

The pungent smell of coca leaves soaking in bleach grew stronger, overpowering the freshness of the rainforest. Darcy raised his goggles and with the flip of a switch on the side of his riflescope, changed his view to thermal heat seeking, giving him a broader picture of a jungle alive with small mammals, now aglow in red and orange.

Muffled sounds breached the surrounding trees and enormous leaves. The distinct pop, pop, pop of pistol fire and repetitive rat-a-tat-tat of AK47s alerted him that Rick was still alive. He and Knightley spread out, moving faster from tree to tree until finally he picked up the guerrilla stronghold some twenty meters ahead. Ten cartel rebels, that he could see, surrounded what was most likely a cocaine processing lab. Pistol fire intermittently repeated from a small outbuilding at the forest edge of an expansive clearing. Its muzzle flashes illuminating the darkness. Rick's homing signal confirmed his location within.

It was only a matter of seconds before all hell broke loose in the Amazon.

Darcy's first bullet hit a sicario in the center of his forehead—his signature kill shot. The Iceman was officially back in death-doling business.

Flanked on both sides of the hut, Darcy and Knightley moved their positions, alternating cover after each shot. Executed with sharpshooter skill, they picked off cartel members one by one. In the pitch black of the jungle, a melee of gunfire surrounded the flammable contents of the cocaine paste-making building. The acetone and kerosene could blow this place to kingdom come and them with it if they weren't careful.

Diablo's Russian lieutenant was correct, the mythical giant anaconda had arrived to crush and destroy, and Rick seized the opportunity to grab Sarah's hand. Together they laid flat on the muddy floor. His team, more than likely his cousin, had arrived and was drawing the sicarios gunfire away from the shelter and its explosive contents.

Knightley rushed around the rear of the lab, his night vision showing him his enemy along the forest perimeter and one after the other they fell in his wake through the trees. The closer he drew to the hut, the less opposing firepower he encountered, which alerted him to the fact that Darcy was now in the thick of it and that extraction of Rick was viable.

"Going for the objective," he spoke with exertion into the Bluetooth, ready to breach the building after positioning himself strategically at the doorway.

"Copy that. Three more bastards and I'll meet you on the eastern perimeter."

Knightley spoke low and forcefully into the door-less hut, "Fitz."

The ground below his feet came alive with two coca leaf and mud-covered figures, one obviously a woman. Her British voice pled, "He's hurt; help him."

Although Rick couldn't see him, he fell into Knightley. "You're late, baldie," he joked with short wheezing breath.

Draping an arm over his friend's shoulders, he buoyed, "Hang on there, Fitz. I got ya'. Darcy's not far behind."

"That sounded like only half of them. There's at least 28 that I counted back at the camp. We gotta get out of here."

"That's the plan boss."

Gunfire continued around the escaping threesome, becoming more sporadic. Knightley looked to Sarah's green and white form enhanced by his night vision lens. He withdrew his .45 and placed it directly into her hand. "You may need this. Are you Julia Bertram?"

"No, Sarah Caulfield."

She held the pistol, unable to even see it.

Rick breathed heavily. "Her left wrist is broken. Chamber the round for her."

"Are there any others?"

"No. Just us."

After pulling back the slide of the pistol, Knightley then switched sides with Sarah, making sure her injury was on the outside of them. "Get Rick's other arm over your shoulders, Sarah. We'll do this together. We're going to move left into the forest and find cover until my team member's rendezvous with us."

He spoke to Darcy. "Objective and a woman secured. Making for rendezvous point."

"Copy that. Bertram's daughter?"

"Negative."

With one cartel shooter remaining, Darcy seized the opportunity to obtain intelligence before Operation Macarena went half-cocked around the world for Bertram's daughter.

He aimed and fired at the burly rebel's shoulder, blowing back his body and knocking him off kilter. The man's defense was now weakened and Darcy quickly closed the gap between them. He circled behind the wounded rebel with deadly silence, simultaneously, withdrawing the Kabar knife sheathed at the side of his thigh.

Two quick steps brought him directly behind his enemy. He knocked off the scum's night vision goggles with one hand and wrapped his other around his neck, the sharp blade held to the rebel's throat.

Darcy's captive couldn't move, restrained from fighting within a locked arm hold.

"You move, I slice. *Comprende?*" he breathed with venomous intonation into the large man's ear.

In Russian, the bald rebel called Darcy an American piece of shit. To which, Darcy replied also in Russian with a faultless Georgian accent. "I believe you have been expecting me."

"Iceman," the heavily accented voice said, assured in his guess.

"You're quick. Where's the Bertram girl?"

"I tell you nothing."

Darcy tightened his hold. "Really? You're sure about that?"

"Diablo will kill you."

"I thought that was supposed to be your job. I'd say that's an epic fail on your part." He tugged on the wounded arm. "I'll ask again, where is Diablo holding the Bertram girl?"

The Russian spat in reply and Darcy's blade broke skin in answer as his securing arm contorted to reach for the pistol holstered upon his hip. "Where is the girl?"

"¡*Yob tvayoo mat.*"

"Wrong thing to say," he stated, pulling his Baretta. He fired into the back of his enemy's knee, dropping him to the muddy ground. "No one but me, says shit about my mother. Now where is the girl?"

"You will not find her here," he laughed.

The scorching barrel of the pistol pressed firmly against the rebel's temple, singeing his flesh into a burned circle. "I'll spare you if you tell me where to find Diablo or his mistress."

"You will never find him, he is *prizrak* but he will find you and slice your balls off."

Darcy turned him then punched him in the face, breaking his nose. The barrel of the gun, swiftly repositioned to the Russian's forehead. "This is my last offer—give up Nadya Karakurt."

The rebel knew he was defeated. He couldn't see his enemy in the pitch dark, but the cold, steel edge in his voice matched his knife. This Iceman would, in fact, kill him like he had killed the Lord of the Jungle. But still, he laughed aloud. Nadya would torture this American scum, and that knowledge alone was worth divulging the information.

"L'Enclave, Rue Thérèse … Paris."

Darcy sighed. Damn, he hated the avant-garde, salacious underground of Paris.

"She will kill you even more viciously than Diablo, and I will dance on your grave."

"Dance? Not with that knee."

Now faced with the dilemma of killing the Russian or keeping his word, he did the only thing an assassin who had grown a conscience could do: with a powerful sweep of his arm, he pistol-whipped his enemy, leaving him unconscious and at the mercy of the jungle and its inhabitants.

He holstered his pistol and looked sixty feet away at the cocaine processing vats where the coca leaves soaked. He spoke to Knightley. "Is the objective secure?"

"Affirmative."

For a split second, he thought to blow the lab to smithereens, but this wasn't a Bang and Burn mission and the explosion would only serve to alert any remaining cartel rebels still within the jungle. In the end, it would compromise their objective and they still had two miles to traverse toward their coordinated extraction in the coca field.

Covered by the large, thick roots of the kapok tree, Knightley rested his rifle at the top of the wrapping buttress root, waiting for Darcy and ready to provide fire cover if necessary.

"Where's ... extraction?" Rick whispered.

"North, three klicks at twenty-one hundred hours. Can you make the hike?"

Rick smiled and looked toward Sarah's barely discernible silhouette in the dark. "Are you up for it, Sarah?"

"I'm going home, so yes, I'm up for it. It's only a broken wrist. You sure show a girl a bobby dazzler time, Rick."

"So would you consider this our first date? It might be a tough act to follow, but number two would certainly be less dangerous."

Rick didn't see her beaming smile, but he felt her delicate hand rest upon his bicep. "We'll talk about date number two *after* we get out of this jungle, you heal up, and then give me an exclusive on who you and your team are."

Keeping his eye fixed through the riflescope, Knightley chuckled at the banter, thinking this just might be the catalyst for Rick to kick Caroline's tight ass to the curb.

Rick coughed with labored, straining breath. "Why did you ask Sarah if she is Julia Bertram?"

Knightley glanced at Sarah. "I'll let Darcy fill you in, when we get outta here."

"Iceman? Is that Bertram as in the Director of the Central Intelligence Agency?" Sarah asked, but both men silenced.

The large ferns and tropical plants parted before them and Darcy emerged with night goggles in place. He rushed to kneel beside his cousin, doubled over and favoring his left side.

"Damn good to see you alive, Rick. What a fucked-up op this is."

"No kidding. You coming out of retirement and me with a couple busted ribs and a laceration down to muscle on my forearm. Right now, the only thing holding it closed are the heads of several army ants."

"We gotta get out of here." Still in combat mode, Darcy looked his cousin over with a tight smile.

Rick grasped Darcy's forearm. "Thanks, for coming … to get me, Darce. *You* were the target; I was the bait. It's revenge for Operation Samba."

"So I learned. One of your friends back there says the girl's not here. Did you see or hear anything about her before we leave this godforsaken place?"

"She's not here. It was just us."

Darcy opened his backpack, withdrawing a jacket and a spare night vision headset, handing them both to Sarah.

"Put these on and stay close. Do you know how to use that pistol in your waistband?"

"Not really; we don't use the things in England but I watch a lot of American television."

Rick smiled at her honesty but quickly winced when Darcy and Knightley helped him up.

After removing his camo jacket, Darcy helped his cousin into it, but in spite of his Iceman persona, he couldn't resist showing some humor. "What the hell? Is that mud on your head? You smell like shit."

"Don't bust my balls … please. I've been drugged, slung over a donkey, beaten, cut, shot at, and just took a bath in stinkin' coca leaves. You'd smell like hell, too, if you had to make a poultice out of a castor plant. In fact, you *do* smell like hell. What's your excuse?"

"Rescuing your sorry ass. Obviously, your stench didn't stand in your way from wooing the pretty girl."

"Yeah, she is a pretty girl and a damn good nurse, too."

In the green illumination of the night vision lens, no one saw the blush to Sarah's cheeks.

Darcy nearly carried Rick the entire distance to the rendezvous location, and Knightley took scout point with Sarah walking between them. Finally, they stood winded and impatient in the vast coca field surrounded by small green bushes laden with kilos upon kilos of contraband ready to harvest for Peru's illegal drug trade.

The sky above them hovered as black as the jungle from which they emerged, but the cloudless view expressed welcome especially when the Peruvian National Police helicopter noise filled the stilled Amazonia air. As the chopper lowered and the four survivors climbed aboard, gunshots rang out from the rainforest's thick perimeter.

Along with sixteen sicarios of La Muerta, the big Russian, with splinted leg and bound shoulder, exited the jungle's tree line, firing at the helicopter.

The helicopter lifted off in the nick in time.

Just as Knightley handed Rick the satellite phone to notify Caroline back at the dance school, Darcy noticed Diablo's Russian lieutenant with mobile phone in hand.

Standing in the center of the coca crop, watching the helicopter and Iceman make their escape, he shouted above the roar of the chopper blades into the phone, "Iceman is …" but failed to finish the sentence.

He fell dead by a single bullet between his eyes.

Darcy squatted in the helicopter one hundred yards above him with rifle poised into the field at its target. He knew the Russian—possessing no conscience of his own—would have ultimately compromised Operation Macarena and most likely would have found Liz back in Virginia. Russians, like drug lords, were known for revenge.

With one free hand, Rick removed his boot, flipped the switch in his heel and threw it out the open side of the helicopter.

The coca field below them exploded into smithereens.

It was only then that Darcy pressed his Bluetooth and the hard rock riffs of his new signature song filled his ears: Led Zeppelin's "Bring it on Home." He was one-step closer to returning to his serene life at Pemberley with his wife.

11

Sleepless

L iz couldn't sleep; the worries and speculation overwhelmed and plagued her troubled mind. Over dinner, Charlie mentioned that Operation Macarena was scheduled to go down tonight and now, she lay fitfully in wait, in hope for Darcy's phone call. Was he safe? Was it successful? Was Rick alive?

She tossed and turned alternating between smoothing her hand over the cool, vacant linen beside her and sitting up only to plop back down in an anxious huff. Her heart rate felt as though she had consumed two double espressos before going to bed.

Worried beyond measure, she impatiently kicked the bed covers from her legs, again, then rose from the bed, clutching her cell phone in anticipation, as though willing it to ring. She padded barefoot in the dark into the bathroom to curl up in the sitting room overlooking the back of the house. Apart from the greenhouse, the sitting area held many joyful memories of her and Darcy, and she felt a modicum of relaxation there but not enough. A snifter of brandy would help.

Both Charlie and Wentworth had reassured her that the search and rescue would go off without a hitch. Wentworth explained that he had a similar operation when he was in the Army at the start of the Iraq War.

Although an entirely different enemy, the jungle's environment was equally as inhospitable as the arid desert, but Darcy's intense training and career as a SEAL would guarantee their success. She knew in her heart that he was right, but couldn't control the anxiety.

Settling into her chaise lounge in the darkened room, Liz looked out at the Olympic-sized swimming pool below the window, noting how the moon reflected off its surface like glittering diamonds. It was one in the morning, so she was surprised to see Wentworth, wearing only black briefs, dive into the dark water and begin laps. She figured he most likely assumed everyone was asleep in the house and since he had been on perimeter watch for seven straight hours, he probably needed refreshment once Charlie took the next shift as sentry.

A welcome distracting focal point at that moment, she couldn't help to admire Wentworth's swimming form and the sinewy muscles of his arms with each reach of the crawl across the length of the pool. His presence at Pemberley, while unexpected, provided an interesting diversion—for Jane who hadn't stopped staring at him since his arrival. Wentworth was a beautiful man, that was for sure. Of course, he wasn't as handsome as Darcy and she was violently in love with her husband, but she couldn't help admiring the man now gliding through the water with such ease, the moonlight catching his dark hair as it skimmed the surface. She thought of the man's honeyed voice, that lazy drawl oozing with laid-back sex appeal. It was most likely the undoing of many women, and she wondered if he was single.

Their lesson this afternoon had made her uneasy, and she rightfully resisted the knowledge that she might be ever so slightly physically discombobulated by him. Freely admitting that she was inexperienced with men, at first she couldn't ascertain if he flirted with her or was it just southern, gentlemanly charm. Lord knows, she had missed all the signs of Darcy's early interest when they trekked across Europe in close quarters. However, when Wentworth revealed that he thought "stubborn and reckless" were "sexy attributes," her suspicions of his interest and intent grew more decided with each encounter. Yes, she was flattered. Apart from Darcy, no man had expressed a true interest in her. In almost all ways, she was thankful her first was her last—and best. But … the unexpected attention strangely made her feel attractive this afternoon when her spirits were so low. She wondered if that was normal behavior given she was happily married and felt completely guilty even in just her speculation.

As though in admonishment of her musing, her cell phone vibrated. It was Darcy.

"Hey, baby," she greeted on the verge of tears from relief. "Are you safe? Tell me you're safe."

"We're all safe. We found Rick." He sighed heavily into the phone, controlling his voice from cracking. "Damn, Liz, your voice is music to my ears."

"Same here. I miss you so much. I was so worried."

"I know. Me, too. Is everything quiet there, no strangers showing up? Is security tight?"

"Everything is fine. Charlie and Wentworth have been very diligent. Even Gus is in protection mode. He seems to think he's in an episode of *The Walking Dead* the way he has that rifle draped over his shoulder."

"Good."

Straight to the point, she nearly begged, "When are you coming home?"

"I don't know. Rick was in a pretty bad way when we found him: broken ribs, cracked sternum, and a couple of deep lacerations. His body is fighting infection and fever, so they have him on IV antibiotic."

"Oh God! Please give him my love. Where is he now? Is he still in Peru, in a hospital?"

"He's being taken care of, but Knightley and I would feel better staying here with him until he's comfortable enough to make the flight home. The area is volatile yet."

"So then you'll come straight back to Pemberley once he's ready to travel?"

"Yeah, I'll be home soon."

"Bring Rick here. We'll care for him in the sanctuary of Pemberley. I'm sure Ellen would just love the chance to see him and care for him. I know I would."

Darcy chuckled. "Well, he might have company. Turns out that even kidnapping and beating didn't stop him from charming another prisoner. It seems they're quite taken with one another."

"Unfathomable how these dangerous situations bring people together. I'll never regret you *almost* assassinating my father."

"Me either, sweetheart. In more ways than one. How are you feeling?"

"Restless and anxious, but now that you've called, I'll get some sleep."

Liz heard the rocks settle within the glass he held close to the phone, and she knew it had been a rough night.

"What are you wearing?" Darcy suddenly asked.

"Fitzwilliam, are you flirting with me over the phone?"

"Yes. What are you wearing?"

"One of your T-shirts. Your scent is all over it. It's comforting." She could almost hear his smile in his silence, imagining that alluring quirk to his lips.

"It's strange. Previously … after an op … all I wanted to do was decompress with a whiskey and hope that sleep would take me quickly. Tonight, the whiskey has no effect. My only desire is to hold you in my arms and caress you. All I need is to fall asleep with your body wrapped around me."

"Then finish your whiskey and try to get some sleep. I'll be waiting for you in your dreams. We can hold each other all night long there."

There was a long silence and she bit her lip before blubbering, "Baby, hurry home. I miss you and love you so much." A tear trickled down her cheek.

"I love you, my Lakmé. Sleep tight and don't worry. I'll be home as soon as I can, okay?"

"Okay. I'll be waiting. Call me as soon as you can."

"I will; I promise."

She waited for Darcy to disconnect the call first then she tugged the afghan from the quilt rack beside her before curling deep into it. Her vision gravitated out the window, noticing Wentworth climb the ladder from the pool. The moonbeams reflected off his glistening hard body. He brought the towel over his chest with one hand, and ran the other through his wet, messy hair.

Sipping the brandy, she stared out at his retreating back, the vacated black pool, and the man in the moon until sleep finally overtook her.

12
Poisonous Snake

G reat, Liz!" Charlie encouraged over the blasting music meant to fuel her and Jane as they went head-to-head on the mats. Linkin Park's head-banging "One Step Closer" accompanied each executed self-defense move. Combat arts was his favorite to teach: basic kicks and defense posturing, strikes and unexpected blows while holding a weapon. Sure, he enjoyed the seductive movements of the cha-cha-cha and the rumba, but the takedown on the mats he truly loved to teach Jane. Of course, he would consider some additional instruction when everyone was asleep tonight—naked wrestling type instruction.

Drenched in unladylike perspiration, the sisters seemed to tap into their hidden frustrations, attacking with unusual ferocity for two who loved each other so much.

"Is that all you have, Jane?" Liz baited.

"Hardly, Lizzy-dear."

Jane gave her one of their mocking, teasing smiles then snapped her leg up into her sister's shoulder, pummeling her backward with a loud oomph onto the mat below them.

"Ho, Ho!" Charlie exclaimed, clapping his hands. "Get up, Liz! Now! Strike back!"

Liz jumped up, coming at her sister with bare-fisted punches and low kicks, some actually making contact. She felt alive and strangely even more liberated than usual, as though clearing out any lingering cobwebs of animosity toward Jane that she may have buried. In turn, Jane's deep-seeded, private envy toward her sister's beautiful marriage and eventual escape from Longbourn seemed to be coming to the surface.

Finally, she grabbed Jane in a neck hold, contorting her long and lean body. "Submit. Do you yield to my greatness?" she taunted like a teenager.

"Never!"

Jane stomped her heel on Liz's foot, causing an unexpected literal knee-jerk reaction into her backside.

"Ow! Dirty pool, sis-sy!"

Charlie laughed, lowered the music, then clapped, again. "Okay, let's take a break."

With chests heaving from exertion, hair in disarray, and flushed cheeks, they separated, standing an arm's length apart, both feeling satisfied by their rumble.

"If Darcy could see what only three hours of work produced, he'd be proud, Liz. Hell, I'm proud and you're kicking *my* girl's ass."

"Charlie!" Jane exclaimed.

"Oh, you gave it back good, Jane. Who the heck knew you had this lethal streak running through that sweet blood of yours. You both did great."

Liz snorted. "Sweet? You didn't grow up with her. She put a firecracker up our childhood cat Snowflake's ass. Thank God my mother found it before Janie lit the fuse."

Charlie threw his head back in laughter. "Gives a whole new meaning to Pussy Galore."

"Ha. Ha, I'll have you know, Lizzy told me to do it. She even held the cat's tail up while I slid it in like an enema."

"You girls are sick." Charlie tossed them each a small towel. "Catch your breath, kitty killers, we're going to cover the basics of pistol safety next. Then Liz, later you'll work with Wentworth on pistol basics while Jane and I go over the proper usage of a mini-bullwhip."

It was clear to Liz that his intention to slam them busy today, keep their minds focused on what they were accomplishing in Virginia and not what Operation Macarena was up against in Peru. Apart from what she shared of her and Darcy's conversation the night before, Charlie didn't know all the details yet. However, she knew Caroline would be filling him in once she arrived with any newly acquired intelligence.

From the intercom on the wall beside the bunker door, Ellen's voice came through loud and clear, "Liz, there's a woman at the door." By the terse tone, she could tell there was dislike laced within the drawn-out syllables of 'woman.' "She says her name is Caroline."

"I'll be right up. If you can seat her in the living room, I'd really appreciate it. Thanks, Ellen."

Charlie made to leave the training room with her to greet his sister, but Liz insisted he stay with Jane. "I'll bring Caroline downstairs after I show her to her room, Charlie. Why don't you work with Jane some more? Her right hook sucks." She laughed wickedly, turning her back to her sister then exited.

Upstairs, Caroline stood in the formal living room, hating to admit that its Colonial-styled elegance made for a welcoming, light-filled home. She scornfully wished this was *hers* and Darcy's domicile, not the Bennet woman's.

Just being in this home angered her, but she kept it concealed below the surface of her cool demeanor. She wasn't a fool and rarely fooled *herself*, freely admitting that she still harbored feelings for Darcy. The lingering memories of his sexual prowess never left her and, sadly, she'd wasted her time on many men attempting to find a suitable replacement. Even Rick failed to "penetrate" to the core of her soul as Darcy had. As much as she vocally claimed indifference to him, he had inadvertently claimed her and it infuriated her to know that the daughter of an American traitor had succeeded where she had failed.

Maintaining a disaffected air, she sauntered to the fireplace and ran her finger along the mantle expecting the little woman to be remiss in her housekeeping. There was a tinge of disappointment when her clean index finger stared back at her.

Having only been in Liz's company at the dance school during the infamous wedding lessons to that Bill Collins, as well as the night Obsidian rescued her father in Marrakech, she hardly knew anything about the new Mrs. Darcy. Well, apart from the fact that she had melted and captured the elusive, cold Iceman. However, those limited amiable meetings with the woman didn't stop her from forming preconceived opinions—not to mention acute jealousy. Yes, she admitted that she was that, too. She despised having to teach Liz some of the tricks of her trade—tricks that set her apart from other women in their chosen field. And now Darcy had asked the nearly untenable, but such was the deal they'd come to: her protection and tutelage in exchange for any active field duty on this operation—alongside him, if and when the time came.

Liz stopped abruptly just before entering the living room. She furrowed her brows, curious by what she witnessed: Caroline's almost territorial command over the room. Charlie's sister examined picture frames displayed upon the mantle, picking them up and rearranging them, placing some to the forefront and others behind. Feeling every bit violated in her own home, Liz raised her eyebrows when the presumptuous woman reached for the Millefiori glass vase, scrutinizing it as though to fault-find. She thought she even heard a "pfft" exit the woman's downturned lips. The coup de grace was how she sat in the center of the cream-colored loveseat, smoothing both palms over the cushioned fabric as if imagining it was her home, her furnishings.

Straightening her posture followed by a nervous fix to her messy ponytail, Liz glanced down at her sweaty workout clothes then walked into the room, suddenly feeling inferior and insignificant compared to the gorgeous redhead wearing camel-colored trousers and a stylish blouse. The fashionable assassin appeared to have emerged from *Vogue* magazine, right down to that perfect, red manicure. The only thing missing was a pearl-handled mini revolver clutched within her grasp.

Liz extended her arm for a confident handshake, chin held high. "Caroline. Welcome to Pemberley."

"Thank you. I was just admiring Darcy's home. It is lovely. I wouldn't imagine his tastes to be so … so traditional." Caroline walked toward her until palms met. Her ice blue eyes bore unblinking into Liz's even though her smile conveyed genuineness in spite of the obvious insult in her voice.

"That's sweet of you to say. My husband has a keen eye for style and detail."

"You're a far cry from Longbourn Plantation."

"I am, and I'm very happy—*we're* happy here. Much like the tranquil beauty of my childhood home, this time of year is particularly breathtaking at Pemberley. Did you notice the last of the cherry blossoms along the drive?"

Caroline stepped toward the bow window, glancing out. "Charming. I've never been one for horticulture but I suppose they lend a certain appeal—very Japanese and *that*, of course, I do appreciate."

She turned her attention to the fireplace mantle. "I see your wedding portrait was taken on the front lawn of the estate beside the pond and footbridge. Did you re-enact it?"

"Re-enact? I'm not sure what you mean. Fitzwilliam and I married in a private ceremony this past October on the footbridge. The photo was taken by my sister-in-law that day."

Caroline snorted. "Fitzwilliam? I thought you married in Seville."

"No. I don't know what gave you that idea. Marrying in Seville would certainly have complicated our three-week separation following Marrakech. I don't think either of us would have agreed to it otherwise. We're hardly separated at all." Her hand flexed at her side, but she continued to employ a welcoming smile and convivial tone to her adversarial house guest, who was Jane's employer, and an Obsidian team member.

Caroline circled around the wing chair, coming to stand before her.

Venom oozed through an obviously contrived sweet smile, and the assassin delivered her bullet. "Then I suppose your father would have had a different sentence if you refused the CIA's deal."

"Yes, you're right, but it all worked out in the end, didn't it? They got their justice and media victory. My father received unexpected clemency and Fitzwilliam and I said 'I do' shortly thereafter." Liz smiled brightly but her stomach churned inside, attempting to redirect her need to tap upon her thigh. She rubbed her earlobe, toying with the small silver hoop earring.

Caroline noticed the body language immediately. In that simple gesture, Darcy's wife conveyed an aversion to the topic of her father's traitorous action. Oh, this was going to be good. She had discovered a weak spot that could be exploited another time and boy did she have explosive ammunition. Bennet's subsequent involvement in the same crimes that put him under house arrest in the first place was information she would take joy in imparting when the time was right.

Turning from Liz's sickening sweet smile as hostess with the mostest, Caroline glanced around at the picture of domestic bliss and normalcy conveyed by the well-appointed furnishings and expensive décor. She bent and picked up a magazine from the coffee table, casually fanning the pages with a sneer. "I'm amazed the Iceman committed to marriage. He must be going stir crazy in this existence of calm domesticity. You have to admit, Darcy's not the model of the suburban life featured in *Better Homes & Garden.*"

"Oh, I wouldn't say that at all. *My husband* loves Pemberley and enjoys working once again with horses, even riding. He plans to enter the polo circuit next year. In fact, he has a subscription to *Horse and Hound.*"

"Hmm, things he enjoyed before Liz Bennet showed onto the scene."

"These things he enjoyed before joining the Navy and subsequently Obsidian. We share his love of Pemberley and horses *together.* We ride motorcycles together, and I'm teaching him how to cultivate orchids."

An uncomfortable silence settled between the two women until Liz blurted, "Would you like something to eat or to see your room?"

"What I would like is to see Charlie. He and I need to go over Obsidian business and the status of Operation Macarena." She wrapped her slender talons around the handle of her titanium briefcase.

"Sure, follow me. He's down in the training bunker my husband installed before leaving for Peru. Don't worry about your suitcases; I'll have Gus bring them upstairs for you."

"If possible, Liz, would you mind securing this particular case in a safe? Its contents are classified."

"That's not a problem at all. I can put it in Fitzwilliam's office safe." Liz turned her back, walking through the living room to a connecting door. "Just follow me."

Caroline's eyes traveled the length of Liz's backside and long legs, looking for fault in an attempt to resist every urge of envy. She failed in that endeavor. Although, her own breasts and body she considered attractive and pleasing, she unfortunately lacked the tight curviness of the woman before her. Not only was Darcy's wife physically alluring, but she proved able to handle a *kunoichi's* ways very well. She couldn't help being impressed, just as she had been during her meeting with Bennet the traitor.

Darcy's study was furnished in similar traditional décor to the formal living room. Mahogany floor-to-ceiling book cases encased half the room, surrounding an ornate Chippendale partner's desk and two matching damask arm chairs. Although more masculine, there were feminine touches everywhere and it got under her skin.

"Have a seat. I'll be just a minute," Liz said.

Regrettably, she handed over the briefcase carrying the electromagnetic weapons and camo communications to her nemesis.

Liz pressed a few buttons on a keypad followed by a biometric scan of her thumb upon a print reader. A second later, a hidden pocket door slid open. "There's a safe in here, so don't worry. No one will be able to breach the security. Besides, we're all family at Pemberley." She stepped into the room, the door closed and she was back out in minutes.

"I'm impressed by the standard of security here; obviously the Iceman hasn't thawed entirely."

"Don't be so sure. My husband prides himself on that. Thawing doesn't mean he's still not the best at what he does. It just means that he allows his conscience to guide him on substantive issues."

"Hmm. Like those issues of the heart?"

"Exactly."

The viper trailing behind Liz didn't miss a thing as they left the study, walking through the hallway, kitchen, den, and finally the solarium. The woman sneered in jealousy, even speaking aloud in mock fascination, inadvertently or deliberately feeding the insecurities that plagued Liz of late.

"Amazing." "TV? I'm absolutely shocked that he can sit still long enough." "Quaint, in a *Leave it to Beaver* sort of way."

In contrast to the squishing of Liz's workout shoes, Prada pumps tapped along the wood flooring, clicking as they descended the steps, until finally reaching the bunker's steel door. Again, as though the most natural thing, she tapped in Lakmé backwards then spoke her name into the device. The security bars hidden inside the door pulled back with a loud thump.

"Here we are," she declared with feigned cheerfulness.

Now this room Caroline appreciated. Almost immediately, she sensed the Iceman's presence, and as she usually felt—it overpowered her. The cold steel and hard edge of weaponry seemed to emit his raw perspiration of virility and strength. Her eyes raked over the punching bag and she imagined each forceful thrust of his arm, which of course, led her to remember other thrusting.

"Caro!" Charlie greeted, rising from the mats where Jane lay.

"Charlie. Jane. I see you've been busy. Excellent." She traversed the cabinets, inspecting everything through narrowing eyes. "Now this is a room where I'm sure the Iceman feels very much at home and happy. It's probably what keeps him from killing himself with boredom."

Jane noted the placid, amiable look upon Liz's face, not to mention the fake smile plastered upon her lips. Oh, she knew that expression well, particularly Liz's slightly jutting chin. It was a look her sister had expertly employed when she dated her ex-fiancé, Bill. Jane now used that same expression when working at the spy museum beside her demanding administrator—and, of late, used it when in her father's presence.

Charlie laughed, even though nothing, particularly Caroline's insult, was funny, but he was a master at levity and redirection from his sister's barbs. "We've been very busy. Wait'll you see these two. I'm amazed at their quick progress and once they work with you, I'm sure they'll be agents in the making."

"Hmm…" Caroline grunted.

Jane raised her eyebrows in her sister's direction. Their eyes locked and, as usual, spoke with one other through their eyes and body language.

Already fatigued by the goading and ill-prepared to enter into all-out war, whether it physical or verbal, Liz walked to the door, promptly seeking escape. "Excuse me, Caroline. I need to check on your room and then lunch, so I'll leave you and Charlie since you have work to do anyway. Jane, would you mind giving me a hand?"

"Sure, no prob." She kissed Charlie's cheek, pinching his backside. "See you later, Crash."

The moment the door closed behind the sisters, Liz grabbed Jane's arm, nearly dragging her up the staircase, through the solarium, and out the back door, straight to the greenhouse.

She raised her arms and voice the second the glass door shut behind them. "What. On. Earth was that?"

Some unknown opera piece filled the hothouse when Jane's subtle reply was to press the play button on the Bose as cover to their conversation.

"You know that's her way, Lizzy."

"What's her way? I invite her into my home and from almost her first sentence, she belittled me and the life Fitzwilliam and I have? Implying that I'm the little woman who's hogged-tied him to Pemberley against his will. She didn't treat me with such disdain at the dance school."

"Well, you weren't married to or even interested in Darcy then. You weren't a threat to her."

"Me? A threat?"

"You married her former *lover*, Lizzy. What did you expect?—a gracious greeting from the losing, scorned woman? That's the way things work with exes. Well, not yours since he played for the other team but you know what I mean."

Liz stood shocked and silent, her mouth agape at her sister who deftly turned from her avoidance of the conversation.

Jane picked up a Keurig pod and examined the label. "Obsidian? The coffee is named Obsidian? That's hysterical. Where did you get these?"

Fast footsteps stormed across the greenhouse. Liz grabbed the pod and catapulted it across the room, smashing it against the stone wall. "Fuck Obsidian! Fitzwilliam bought that stupid coffee. What the hell are you implying about him and that bitch?"

"Wow. Did you just say the *F* word?"

Liz's glare burned through her sister.

"Liz, it's simple: Caroline's jealous of you. You have what she always wanted, and clearly it's killing her to see how Darcy has changed, let alone how happy he is." She deliberately turned her back from her sister's widened eyes and flaring nostrils, then nonchalantly popped another pod into the coffee maker. The silence that ensued was deafening. No doubt Liz was boiling over, ready to throw an even larger fit.

Surprisingly she remained frozen and silent—breathing hard like she just got punched in the gut. Jane made an exaggerated grimace. "Ahhh … you didn't know about their sexed-up affair? Oopsie."

"Oopsie? You think this is an '*oopsie*' moment, Jane? Seriously? Oopsie, I forgot to tell you and so did your husband but he had been screwing that bitch before you came along? Oh, and by the way—she wants him back!"

Liz plopped down onto one of the workbench stools; devastated, she attempted to breathe in the calming fragrance of her orchids. "He lied to me. My husband lied to me."

"Sissy, not *telling* you is not *lying* to you. They are two totally different things. Like, for example, when Charlie asks if I had an orgasm, I'll never reply with an emphatic 'no'. I'll just tell him how satisfying his touch was. No need to be cruel and hurt the man. The sex is great, but it's not the end of the world if I don't get off—although that rarely happens, but it does. Sometimes, I have other things on my mind and I just can't relax. Surely, you can understand that … dealing with dad is a real mood killer."

Jane's rationale was met with a sardonic chuckle and head shake of wonderment. "Big difference here. This is about my husband and *another* woman's orgasms. He did lie. When we were on our honeymoon, I specifically asked him about his relationship with Caroline. That day in Marrakech, before they left to get dad, I sensed there was tension between them. I wanted to believe it was professional jealousy, but I just had a gut feeling it was more.

"Come to think of it, it was in Marrakech when he used that same ridiculous rationale of *not telling* versus *lying* when he concealed the fact that he was an assassin."

"Well, so now you know. Does that change anything between you and Darcy? If you ask me, I think it only helps to know how to deal with Caroline. I know she's Charlie's sister and my boss at the dance school, but truth is she's a deceitful woman, Lizzy. Obviously, you can't trust her or take any of her insults seriously. Hello, news flash … she's an assassin and a spy. Charlie tells me that she was even a CIA mole in Obsidian! His own sister spied on him! She makes her living surrounded by deception. Caroline is a quintessential femme fatale." Jane held her chin a little higher. "I know these things. I studied women just like her at the museum."

Absentmindedly, Liz fanned the pages of her sketchbook lying on the workbench. "The thing is Jane … Lately, I've been thinking a lot that Fitzwilliam is *not* happy. Caroline succeeded in touching upon a sensitive nerve." She hesitated, afraid to give voice to her greatest fear. "My worry is that life at Pemberley may *not* be enough for him—that *I* may not be enough for him. It was only a matter of time before he went back to Obsidian and the fast-paced, dangerous life he led before me and my orchids came to Leesburg."

Taking a seat on the stool opposite her, Jane reached out, grasping Liz's hand. "Are you afraid of him cheating on you?"

"Not particularly but more to the point of him feeling tempted by women in that life—women like Caroline who might stop at nothing to try to steal him. It's the lure and the eventual realization of his unhappiness that I'm afraid of."

"Hmm ... the lure ... the temptation ... sort of like you and Dave Wentworth."

Liz snapped her head up and was met by Jane's mischievous smile.

"What? I don't know *what* you are referring to, Jane. I am not tempted by that man!"

"Bullshit. I saw you last night and how you could barely keep your eyes off him at dinner. I near expected you to start playing footsie under the table. Either that or lunge for him over the sea bass and lick him as though he was the mornay sauce. Lizzy, he flirted with you through the entire dinner and you seemed to like it."

Blushing profusely, Liz's hands flew to hide her face. "Oh my God, I didn't mean to! What did I say? What did I do that he misinterpreted? That *you* misinterpreted?"

"It wasn't any one thing. It was the way you bit your lip. Oh, and you did bat your eyes once, and let's not forget the way you licked the whipped cream from your finger. Coy seems to work. I should try it more often."

"I'm so embarrassed. I have to talk to him, make it clear to him that I didn't mean ..."

"No you don't. Look, that man is so hot he could explode the sun. So trust me, I totally get you fantasizing about screwing him senseless. If you didn't, then I would be sure that you and I are not actually blood sisters, or it just may convince me that this ho-hum life at Pemberley has affected *you* more than you think it's affected Darcy."

"But, but ... I don't want Dave to think that I'd cheat on Fitzwilliam. I may find him attractive; I mean, who wouldn't, but I never imagined anything like you're implying. I'm head over heels in love with my gorgeous husband."

"It's okay if you admit it. You're human and he's a god."

"No, Fitzwilliam is a god. That man's sex appeal isn't worth tempting me into destroying my marriage or hurting a man I would die for. I would never cheat. There is no need to. Ever. *Especially* knowing the devastating toll it would have on Fitzwilliam. His past, his mother's infidelity is only just healing within him."

Jane nodded knowingly. "And let's not forget your own past, our mother's betrayal when she abandoned us for a life other than what she led at Longbourn as mother and wife. That's why you are afraid of Darcy's discontent. You're afraid he'll abandon you."

Realizing the truth, Liz spoke in a small voice. "Yes. You're right. Where did you pick up such wisdom? This is new for you."

"It's fleeting, so take my advice while it still makes sense. Of course, *I* may not take my advice. That man *Wet*-worth looks downright tasty, and I'm sure worth the wetness."

She slapped her sister's arm. "You're so bad. You know as well as I do that you'd never cheat on Charlie."

"You're right, but I can look and so can you. It's not cheating."

"Jane, I know I have nothing to fear when it comes to Fitzwilliam's constancy and devotion, nor does he have anything to fear about mine. Other women may tempt him, but in the end, he will always come home to me and the life we've made together. I do trust him. I really do, and I know this, *rationally*. But, e*motionally* … I'm insecure."

"It's no wonder you are a mess. You just don't have experience with men, and you are so in love with Darcy that you can't think straight. Emotions are emotions and we can't fight them. You're worried about Darcy and his happiness here. At the same time, this Wentworth—with his dreamy eyes and hot body and amazing accent—arrives on the scene. And he's clearly hot for you. I can't advise you on any of that, but I can caution that whatever you do, don't let Caroline see anything she could misinterpret and use to her advantage."

"Advantage?"

"Yeah, like using it to drive a wedge between you and Darcy by filling his head with bullshit lies about you and Wentworth."

13

Ruses

Following Liz and her sister's ninja lesson, their early dinner was an awkward, uncomfortable disaster—one where she fought her spirited self, wanting to lash out in verbal self-defense at every insult and passive-aggressive comment. The asparagus was too hard, the soup was too bland, or the beef was overcooked—and Caroline voiced each and every complaint with a sneer, while her ice blue eyes watched and waited for a reaction.

It was when Charlie laughed for the eighth unknown reason that Liz became convinced it was a nervous tick. Wentworth attempted damage control with praise to the cook and thanks for the hospitality, coupled by his astute deflection of compliments to Caroline's acumen in the fight ring. Liz continued to smile that interminable smile demanding to Jane "Kill me now."

Further, she had avoided making eye contact with Wentworth, ignoring him like the plague, cautiously assuming that Caroline's skills of observation would pick up on his attraction to her. The last thing Darcy needed to hear were lies about her and Charlie's friend. It would unequivocally destroy him if he thought she was unfaithful, even in her thoughts, which weren't the case at all. After her conversation with Jane in the greenhouse, she postponed her pistol practice with Wentworth and any other training Charlie had scheduled between the two.

Following clean-up in the kitchen with Ellen and then bidding the Reynolds goodnight, she had retreated to her bedroom to await her husband's phone call. She needed a place of refuge from the unwelcome, disruptive circumstances to her normally peaceful life—not to mention needing to avoid any interaction with Wentworth that could be misconstrued, which only served to remind her of Darcy's lie about Caroline and his past hurts where women were concerned.

She waited with baited breath for his call, the phone tucked in the back pocket of her jeans, until it finally vibrated against her butt.

"Hi, sweetheart," she said with worried excitement, her heart thundering.

"You sound happy to hear from me."

"You know I am. I've been worried sick. How are you? How is Rick?"

"He's better than he was last night, but still not ready to travel. We'll be down here a few more days."

"Hmm. How many is a *few* more days?"

"Another five or so. I'd just feel better staying beside him. The Peruvian police have suggested that he and I remain under tight security, and well, you know how I've become so proficient with my Baretta."

"Oh have you now? Since when?"

"Right. I guess I forgot to tell you about my and Elektra's daily practice sessions."

Among other things, she thought before replying, "Yes, you did, Mr. Darcy. Apparently, the Iceman has been hanging around longer than you alluded to."

"We'll talk about it next week. I promise, babe." He deliberately changed the topic. "How is your training going? Have you worked with Wentworth and Caroline yet?"

Liz swallowed hard and slightly hesitated, biting back her need to discuss Caroline or the other consuming question of, *How does it feel to be back in the field?* "I trained with both. Apparently, they think I am skilled in the use of knives. Who knew?"

"I did. Has Caroline behaved? Given you any trouble with that slithering tongue of hers? I know how difficult she could be."

"Nothing I can't handle as the proper, hospitable Mrs. Darcy. Don't worry I didn't slash her jugular with one of my new toys if that's what you mean."

"See, you are skilled. Purposeful self-restraint makes the attacker believe you are weaker than you really are. Thanks for putting up with her and humoring my worries by training with her. And Wentworth?"

"Um ... he's fine, I guess. He taught me how to knife throw."

It became clear to her that Darcy was distracted when he replied, "Good, good. I'm sorry, but I have to cut this call short. There are some things I need to take care of on this end and I need to take Rick's friend, Sarah, to the hotel."

"I understand. Fitzwilliam, when you get home can we maybe discuss our future? Make some plans about starting our family in the fall and how it will work in with your playing polo again?"

Darcy glanced at his watch, then over his shoulder at the strange man exiting the elevator on their secured floor.

Narrowing his eyes, he quickly replied without thought, "Yeah, sure. I gotta go, Liz. Sleep tight."

"I love y—" Her word died when he clicked off his cell phone and her heart clenched slightly at his brush off.

* * *

Darcy's black-clad menacing form towered above the small stranger dressed in a cheap suit. It was too late in the evening for any type of business and since there were no other patients on the second-floor ward, the man's arrival put him on alert.

"Can I help you?"

The British accent was an immediate tip off that he was either with the British Embassy in Lima or MI-6 coming to debrief Sarah.

"I'm looking for Sarah Caulfield. I'm Attaché Branson of the Foreign and Commonwealth Office." He handed Darcy a business card. "I'd like to discuss with Miss Caulfield her return to England. She has yet to appear at the British Embassy."

"What did you expect? She's traumatized and required medical care."

"Yes, but we have protocols."

Darcy rolled his eyes. "Follow me."

Darcy led the way to a small sitting room at the end of the hall. He instructed Branson to wait for Sarah to come to him rather than take him into Rick's hospital room where she sat on one side of the bed, holding his hand with Knightley on the other side holding his .45 pistol upon his lap.

Peeking his head around the door, Darcy signaled for Knightley and Sarah, explaining the presence and purpose of the visitor. "You two go; I have to talk with Rick. And, Knightley, don't let her out of your sight."

"Hey, Sarah …" Rick moaned. "Think about coming back to the States with me." He winked. "I'm an excellent cook."

"Only if I get that exclusive you've promised."

He chuckled. "Oh, you're going to get an exclusive, alright."

Darcy took her recently vacated seat beside his cousin. "Enough, you two." The door shut and he promptly asked, "So, what about Caroline? I don't think she'll appreciate you arriving home with a replacement on your arm."

"Whatever. I don't care what she'd appreciate or not. It's time for me to move on. I might ask you the same thing. What about Caroline?"

"I'm putting off calling her, but I have to. Are you sure you're okay with me activating her as a field agent?"

"I don't see how I have a choice," Rick said, his voice grave.

"It's probably just as well that she joins the op out in the field. I sense from Liz that the woman is giving her a hard time."

"Exactly why I'm dumping her. A man can only stand so much. She's like a fucking boa constrictor, squeezing the life out of everything and everyone around her."

"It was my understanding that you were in love with said boa constrictor."

"Love? Let's just say I was mistaken—caught up in the sex, little head over big, ya' know?"

"You have very low standards, Cousin. I don't kiss and tell but that woman was nothing but a shed snake skin in bed."

"To each his own. Listen to me, it's my duty to caution you about meeting up with her in Paris to capture Diablo's woman. Caroline's not over you by a long shot and may well put you in a compromising position."

"It wouldn't be the first time. I'll handle her. Look, Knightley and I need her skill and Company intel. If there was any other way around it, I'd take it, but I'd rather drag my balls through broken glass than walk into a fetish club with Mr. Clean as my date. Iceman's masculinity can't withstand *that* cover."

"What did you tell Liz?"

"That I'll be here for a few more days. It's best that she doesn't know I'm extending this mission. What she doesn't know won't hurt her about my temporary activities with Obsidian. I don't want to worry her any more than she already is and, really, it's for her protection. Liz understood my coming here to get you, but I can only push her generosity so far." He paused and looked away in thought; the enormous reality of lying to his wife unsettled him. "Yeah, it's best that she doesn't know. If I were to tell her that I'm going to Paris to attempt to locate Bertram's daughter, I have no doubt that she'd be on the next plane to De Gaulle."

"You lied to your wife … man, you're screwed if she finds out."

"It's a chance I have to take to protect her."

"So you're going after Morales then? Following the rescue of Julia?"

"Probably … If I can find him."

"He's a ghost. I'm told that he's never in one place long enough to track him. Hopefully Karakurt will give him up. Are you sure you want to complete Operation Macarena if she doesn't?"

"I have to because if I don't, everyone I love is at risk. You've already been targeted, and I refuse to draw breath if Liz or Georgiana are hurt because of my past. Morales is my sole responsibility."

Rick took hold of his cousin's forearm. "Do you want to come back to Obsidian permanently? I could use you, and well, you seem to enjoy being back in the field. I'd talk to Liz and explain how it is."

"Always the deal maker. No way. Rick, I've never been happier. Being back at Pemberley, bringing it to life once again, and enjoying everything with Liz by my side are more than a man could ask for. We birthed a colt this week and in every way it represented my rebirth. Liz wants to discuss starting a family when I get back."

Rick nodded, smiling thoughtfully. "You're a lucky man. You'll make an excellent father."

"I hope so. Although, sometimes I wonder if family, right now, is what Liz *really* wants. The tighter I hold onto her and try to keep her safe, the more she seems to want to fly recklessly. I'm afraid that life at Pemberley maybe too much like life was for her at Longbourn. She's restless and I hope not restless like her mother was."

"She's also newly married, in a relatively new relationship that made her wealthy beyond measure. Give her time to adjust to all of the change. Life with you is hardly boring, and Liz is only just learning to live life on the wild side."

"We're both adjusting; this is new territory for both of us."

"True. You've never been a relationship sort of guy. Listen, before Sarah comes back … when do you and Knightley leave for Paris?"

"In about five hours, on the ten o'clock flight. I've arranged for the national police to continue with your protection and then escort you to the airport tomorrow for your flight back to Washington. A limo will be waiting for you to take you back to the safe house for recuperation."

"And your arrangements?"

Darcy leaned forward, clasping his hands between his spread knees. "Knightley has contacted one of our assets, Peter Andrews, at the Hotel de Paris in Monte Carlo. He was invaluable during Operation Cancan last year. So, he's making arrangements for our hotel, VIP admission to

L'Enclave, and suitable apparel. Knightley's connections are impressive. He's an excellent addition to Obsidian."

"Yeah, he's working out well. This Enclave club … are you ready for what that'll entail? I hate to call your attention to the obvious, but you are a happily married man and you're going with *Caroline*. Why not have Knightley take point?"

"Because in the months I've been away from Obsidian, you've updated all your intelligence equipment to this high-tech spy crap that I don't know how to use. I'm just a trigger man. I need him in the cam-car for intelligence collection and surveillance on the laptop. I'll do what I do best: action, cloak, and dagger."

Before Rick could reply, Sarah came back into the room, a stack of forms clutched in the hand unencumbered by the new cast.

Darcy rose. "I better go place that call to the boa constrictor."

"Good luck."

As he neared the door, he turned back. "Oh by the way, when we get back to the States, you and I are going to have a long, honest discussion about my father-in-law's new employment."

Rick pursed his lips, slowly nodding his head in understanding.

* * *

Liz might have considered it fortuitous to be walking past Caroline's room at the exact moment she did, but given the overheard conversation, she cursed not only Caroline, Operation Macarena, but her husband as well.

At the first overheard words of "Paris, Rambo?" Liz froze in her tracks, having previously been told of Caroline's sometimes moniker for her husband. The slightly ajar door allowed half of the painful conversation to breach the parameters of confidentiality.

"Did I hear you correctly?—you and me in the most romantic city in the world? Be still my heart, Darcy," Caroline cooed.

Liz's left hand flew to clutch her heart, ostensibly shielding it from each stabbing word spoken by that bitch. Like the thrusting daggers she held only hours before, they eviscerated her, striking at the gold ring of fidelity upon her finger.

"And Knightley will be there, too, and don't get it into your delusional head that a *Ménage à trios* is on the agenda. Business, Caroline. I need for you to meet me at L'Enclave."

"L'Enclave? I'm shocked. You want me to meet you at a fetish club? Had I known the Iceman was interested in a little BDSM … well, then … that certainly could have been a game changer for you and me. You have me excited to enter into the dark underworld with you. You, me, and a manriki chain—the thought of which does things to me. I have just the little black lace and leather number to wear. You always did like me in lace."

Liz's two fists clenched as she pulled her lips together into a taut, painful line, trying to turn their trembling into anger. *Yeah, he does love leather and lace … bastard.* Tears brimmed, ready to spill but she held them back.

"Stop it, Caroline. I only need you and your skills as my cover at the club. Can you fly out tonight?"

"There is a non-stop Air France flight to Charles De Gaulle at nine from Dulles. I'm sure I can get a seat. I have a connection at the airline. And what about, Rick?"

The knot in Liz's stomach rose like bile up her esophagus, feeling the burn in its ascent. *Poor Rick! Of course they don't want him to know!*

"He'll be headed back to Washington tomorrow. He's in pretty bad shape but he's tough."

"Where are we staying? Somewhere romantic, I hope."

Darcy cringed when he said, "I have reservations at the Hotel Scribe, but I booked a room for you on another floor."

Liz peeked through the crack of the door into the guest room catching a glimpse of Caroline standing above her suitcase, assessing her "appropriate" apparel.

"The Scribe? Oh, Darcy you *are* sentimental, aren't you?"

"Don't flatter yourself. And listen, don't go shooting your mouth off to Liz about the direction this op has taken. The last thing I want is for her to worry."

"Of course I'm not going to tell your wife. I'm not an idiot." She sighed. "Do you remember the last time we were in Paris during Operation Mazurka? With the exception of you dragging me to that ridiculous opera across the street, it was unforgettable. Seeing you in a tuxedo was worth all that shrieking."

This last statement broke Liz's heart. Her face burned red, ready to blow—the lies, the deceit, the obvious secret rendezvous, his sharing the passion of opera with his paramours, demeaning it in their relationship to commonplace, obviously a seduction ploy. Darcy's earlier words to her—*Purposeful self-restraint makes the attacker believe you are weaker than you really are*—kept her from charging into the room to grab the phone from the viper's ear. There was now no question or doubt in her mind: Darcy and Caroline's relationship had been confirmed and resurrected.

She turned from the image of the black negligee the woman folded then placed into her suitcase. Bolting down the hall, she quickly ran to the only person she knew who would help in her immediate decision and already forming knee-jerk reaction: Jane.

Darcy replied to Caroline. "Don't be ridiculous, Medusa. The Scribe is only a ten-minute walk from Rue Thérèse and the club. That and the fact that my op asset in France made secure arrangements are the only reasons I chose it. Let me make myself clear—apart from our earlier agreement in your teaching Liz, besides my unfortunate need for your skill set, there is absolutely no other reason you are needed—or wanted—in Paris."

Nearly hyperventilating Liz pounded upon Jane's door, but had no patience to wait for a reply and threw it open. "Jane!"

Sitting with her back against the headboard, a myriad of items were spread out beside her upon the bed. Strangely, her sister wore a black, shoulder-length wig and heavily made up black-rimmed eyes. She sat cross-legged reading one of Charlie's vintage comic books, *Tarantula*.

"What the—?"

"I'm getting into the role," Jane giggled.

"We need to talk. It's important."

Jane recognized the graveness in Liz's voice and that miserable expression, but when she noticed the unshed tears and the way her sister's fingers bounced against her thigh, she knew trouble loomed.

She promptly pulled the wig off her head, readying for another serious talk. She hoped to God, she had another round of sage advice in her, but seriously doubted it after just reading how Tarantula licked a bloody blade. "What happen? Did he kiss you? You look like you've seen a ghost or does he have one of those carinatus snakes like Darcy?"

A tear fell. "Where's ... where's Charlie?" Liz stammered.

"He's out scouting the perimeter. Why, what is it, Lizzy? What happened to make you cry? Is it Darcy or Rick?"

Only stone-cold silence met Jane's query until Liz seemed to vomit the words all at once, her resolve shattered once her assumptions and accusations spilled forth.

"Oh God, Jane. I just heard ..." She hesitated and looked down at her hands.

"Yes?"

The tears fell. "I ... Caroline was just talking to Fitzwilliam on the phone. He lied to me. He's not in Peru, he's in Paris and he wants her to join him. She's taking a flight out tonight and he's made reservations for them to meet and then go to some fetish club. He's rendezvousing with her for an affair! He's having an affair! Now I know why he blew me off the phone earlier. He couldn't wait to telephone that bitch. And she's in my house! I knew it. I knew he wasn't happy and that he was bored with life here at Pemberley—bored with *me*!"

Liz's hands covered her face and she sobbed like she did when their father told them that their mother wasn't coming home. "She said that to me when she arrived at Pemberley! Caroline told me he was unhappy!"

"He's not unhappy." Jane immediately reacted by taking her sister into her arms, holding her tightly and rubbing her back. "It's gonna be okay, Lizzy. We'll get answers; we'll face this together."

"What a bitch. What an evil woman! How could she do this to Rick? How could my husband do this to *his cousin*? To *me*!"

Liz's tears and sobs wracked upon her shoulder for several minutes until Jane felt the need to interrupt the heartbreaking intensity. "A fetish club? Darcy's into BDSM? Wow, I never would have expected that. I guess that whole biker thing. Does he like whips? Maybe Charlie should be teaching *you* the bullwhip instead of me."

"Jane! This is serious!"

"I know. I'm just trying to get you to stop crying." She wiped the tears from Liz's cheeks. "Okay, sissy, so you heard what you heard and based on that look upon your face, I can see you're determined to do something about it. Let me ask you this though: is there *any* possibility that you either heard wrong or are jumping to conclusions? Eight hours ago you were sure of your husband's fidelity. And honestly, I just don't see Darcy as a cheater."

An abrupt turn of Liz's head indicated that she was suffering from immediate tunnel vision, not considering any other explanation for what she heard. She avoided Jane's intent gaze, instead staring mindlessly at the black wig now lying on the floor. "I'm sure of what I heard."

"Well, baby girl, what do you want to do? Call him, confront him on the phone or …?"

Hazel eyes met Jane's soft blues. With tears packing away and a determined set to her mouth, Liz stated, "I'm going to Paris, Jane. There is no possible way I will sit here playing the rejected, shunned wife while he wines and dines that viper in the La Ville-Lumière. I'll be damned if I'm going to remain at Pemberley, playing the clown or the fool while he takes *that* woman to the Palais Garnier for *I Pagliacci* or *Cosi Fan Tutte* and then some sex club for DDSS! No frickin' way!"

"Beyond 'sex club' and 'frickin' I have no idea what you just said. And it's BDSM, not DDSS."

"Stop it, Jane! I need real help, not your stupid levity! I need a plan. I need you and that devious kitty-killer brain of yours to help me get out of here without anyone knowing. That cheating, rat bastard is going to get the surprise of his life when his obstinate, headstrong wife stands before him and his evil leather, lace, and manriki-chain-toting home-wrecker. Maybe I'll be the one wearing leather while whipping his cheating butt into submission!"

"Are you going to leave him, Lizzy? Leave all this for a misguided indiscretion?"

Liz looked aghast. "Leave him? No, I'm going to *fight* for him before he does anything foolish. If it's adventure and daring that he's craving, well then it better be with me." Her eyes welled with tears again. "I love him. I'd die if I lost him. Please help me."

Jane bent down, picking up the black wig then carefully lowered it onto her sister's head. "First thing you need to do is get yourself on that flight to Paris with Caroline and see if you can get a room in their hotel. Second thing we need to do is go through my luggage and find you some suitable clothing."

She rose from the bed and walked to the closet, then removed a black travel case resembling a multi-layered cosmetic box. "You're going to need some tools of the trade if you're going to assume an incognito identity."

"Excuse me?"

"You heard me. Lizzy, you just can't get on the same plane as Caroline without her noticing you, and if you want the element of surprise on your side, you need to change everything about your appearance—an alias. Trust me, I've learned all about this in the Spy Seminar Series at the museum. Haven't you ever watched that TV show *Alias*?"

"What?"

"This is gonna be great!— a few disguises and you can pull off the greatest honey trap."

Liz fingered the ends of the wig, feeling the naturalness of the strands.

"I know what you're thinking," Jane remarked. "It's real hair. Cost me a dang fortune along with this little one." She pulled out a blonde bob-styled wig from the bottom drawer of the case.

"Janie, why exactly do you have these?"

"Because I'm determined to join Obsidian and get the hell away from Longbourn."

"You devil! You're miserable helping dad. You made me believe you were content helping him."

"All part of the act, my dear sister. That man is ruining my sex life. If I spend the rest of his house arrest tending to him, I'll never have an orgasm again." Jane removed the black wig from her and replaced it with the blonde one. "Oh, this is adorable on you."

Liz shifted her weight and bent to look at herself closely in the mirror. "Wow, this totally changes the way I look. If I add a little pink lipstick, I could pass for you before you grew your hair out."

Handing Liz two lipstick tubes, Jane encouraged. "Try one."

After popping off the top of a three-inch silver tube, she turned the base, surprised to find that hot pink gloss didn't emerge from within but rather, a sharp pick knife. "Where did you get this?"

"I ... um ... borrowed it, along with some other things from the museum's storeroom and now I'm glad I did. You're going to need this stuff." Jane slid out another drawer to reveal a mace perfume mister and a stun gun disguised as a hard box of Marlboro cigarettes.

"Borrowed it? Is anyone in this house honest about anything? Jane, you *stole* this stuff."

She shrugged and handed Liz her iPhone. "Make the flight arrangements and then, with these lock picking tools, we'll go break into that case Caroline had you lock up. She's bound to have something in there pertaining to Darcy."

Liz's chin slacked. "I don't know how to pick a lock."

"No? I'll teach you." Jane flashed a brilliant, mischievous smile.

"And what are we going to tell Charlie about my sudden departure? He's bound to call Fitzwilliam right away and warn him. I swear, my husband has lie radar *and* sonar. He doesn't miss a thing. There is no way he won't suspect something is up or at the very least worry that something has happened to me. I need the element of surprise if I'm going to do this."

Jane sat at the edge of the bed, thinking of the possibilities. "Well, then we just won't tell him that you've left. No one will even know you are gone. You'd be surprised just how well I can manipulate my man."

"I'm beginning to see that. Do you really think this will work? This *has* to work!"

"Let me hear you do a deep southern accent."

"Darlin', I might could do that," Liz said batting her eyes as her fingers toyed with a strand of blonde hair.

"Perfect! You can do this. If you rode a Harley and got two tattoos, you can do anything."

"But can I become Caroline?"

"Not only can you become the ninja but you can also kick her ass to the curb."

Two hours later, under the guise of needing to go to the supermarket for tampons, insisting on privacy, Liz left the house thirty minutes before Caroline. Now, standing at the Air France check-in counter, she smacked gum and blew bubbles as only her sister would through shiny pink lips. With fuchsia, silver-sparkled polished nails (sans her wedding ring), she handed over her Elizabeth Bennet passport. The blonde wig was firmly secured atop her brown locks and jumbo, silver hoop earrings hung, larger than life, to her shoulders. Elizabeth wrapped up her new look with freaky aqua blue contact lenses, heavy black eyeliner, and pink-tinted bubble eyeglasses (conveniently lifted from Caroline's titanium case). A newly-purchased international cell phone was tucked in the back pocket of a borrowed pair of Jane's hip-hugging, skinny blue jeans.

She rested one of Darcy's briefcases on the counter then checked the two locks to make sure that the stolen contents from Caroline's case were all secure—not that she really knew what she'd use them for, but what girl couldn't use a compact and a mini pistol. "Can I check this along with my other baggage?"

"*Oui, Madamoiselle.*" The red-haired airline attendant placed both pieces of luggage on the conveyer belt then turned and tapped away on her keyboard.

If Liz weren't so upset, she'd laugh at the shirt she wore: another procurement of Jane's from the spy museum. Pink and oversized it read: "I Have Mad Ninja Skills."

"You have had quite a transformation in appearance, Miss Bennet," the woman remarked glancing up and down between the staid passport photo and Liz's new persona, her eyes settling on the bling skull and cross bone two-inch ring encircling her index finger.

With fingers upon the corner rim of her eyewear, she removed them, and spoke with a mock southern accent. "Good golly that was before I learned there was a big, wide world out there beyond daddy's farm. Blondes *do* have more fun." She winked poorly, feeling the crinkle to her newly installed beauty mark and then put the pink glasses back on.

"*Oui, chevoux roux* is also exciting. So, you are traveling for pleasure then?"

Although scared out of her mind with a furiously pounding heart, Liz cracked her gum followed by a contrived giggle. Her fingers drew up to her collarbone where they nervously fiddled with the diamond, snake microphone necklace Darcy had given her in Monte Carlo. "Of course pleasure, sweetie. I'm fixin' to live it up in gay Pa-ree and get me some shuga. Tall, dark, and dangerous type of shuga. Maybe I can find me one packin' a pistol in his pants."

"I hope you have fun, *Mademoiselle*."

"Oh, I will. A friend recommended L'Enclave. I recon you've heard of it?"

The attendant playfully raised her eyebrows. The sly smirk to her lips indicated that she did. "*Oui*. It is exclusive, but a good concierge will call the establishment to put you on the VIP list. It is very secretive, so make sure he understands it is your one desire, otherwise he will deny its existence."

"Secret? Why in tarnation would it be a secret?"

"Because at L'Enclave they cater to your *every* pleasure, every one of your senses will be awakened as never before." The ticketing agent moved forward, close enough so as not to be overheard. "Sophistication, desire, even music—erotic slow dancing to the sensual French tango by candlelight."

"Darlin', that sounds like my kind of place. I do so love a tango." she fumed behind her sugary sweet smile. *Rat bastard.*

14

Ooh, La, La

B londe and playfully vixen, even if contrived, Liz squeezed into an economy seat on the upper deck of a superjumbo Airbus. After official check-in with the helpful attendant, she did a bang-up job of asking about an *ex*-friend of hers also flying to Paris on the same flight. The kindred spirit of the French redhead was only too happy to comply with seating her near the restrooms and bar—in the middle of the plane—on the deck above. Of course, Caroline was situated in Le Premier Class on the lower deck at the front of the plane in one of their luxurious shell suites. The champagne and caviar, not to mention the Michelin-starred menu, was as refined as the dust bags for the woman's friggin' Prada shoes. *Bitch.*

It seemed a good plan at the time of seat assignment to deliberately sit as far away from Caroline as possible. But in light of her seatmate's stinky feet, Liz was regretting that decision. Sitting next to the shoeless man for the eight-hour journey might kill her before this ruse even began.

With the tip of her index finger, she poked at the baguette lying on the dish beside her cold chicken and remaining potato leek soup. *Well, at least the bread is exemplar. Of course, it would be and so was the cheese, as stinky as the guy's feet.* She fought the urge to grab the white paper bag tucked in the pocket below the TV screen.

As much as she adored travel, she vowed to kill Darcy for this. His shit list was getting longer by the minute. So much for their plan to visit Paris and go to the opera next year. Never in a million years did she expect to go alone and certainly not for the reason of keeping her husband from having an affair. And, she definitely did not plan to travel in Voyageur class for said trip. Having grown accustomed, not to mention spoiled, by flying with him since her very first flight *ever* to Monaco, she never expected to sit in economy class again. Having done that for all of two hours on their first flight, it was enough. *All this suffering—to catch him in the act.*

Further, on the issue of his promised romantic getaway to the Florida Keys following this nightmare: he was sorely mistaken.

She resisted the impulse to scream or cry as she watched Sylvester Stallone pummel a villain's face on the small TV screen before her. Thoughts drifted to Sly as Rambo, which of course, drifted to Darcy and Caroline. Damn, the rose-colored glasses on her face weren't doing a blessed thing to temper her heartbreak now turning into furious anger with each passing minute of uncomfortable inactivity. She wondered if trans-Atlantic economy class did that to people in their restlessness, feeling like caged animals needing to tear at and feed on someone's hide.

"Excuse-a-moi," she said to the flight attendant as he bustled toward the galley. "I might could do with a little brandy, darlin.'"

Southern seemed to have grown on her, so she decided to keep up the act. In truth, she was enjoying the freedom of existing within an alias persona, especially one as carefree as Jane had lived 24/7. Shoot, Liz was used to living within another persona. Before life with Darcy, she had lived eight years at Longbourn as the unassuming, acquiescing, dutiful daughter. She could pull off flighty, southern crassness mixed with a large measure of Jane Bennet. In a small way, she felt like her husband must have in what was *supposed* to have been his *former* career. The whole hiding in plain sight thing was titillating.

"*Oui Mademoiselle*, cognac or Armagnac?"

She falsely giggled. "Ooh, la, la – cognac, of course, *garçon*."

He shook his head at the bubble-headed, bleached-blonde American and continued on, complaining under his breath in French, "*Garçon?* Pfft. I am not a waiter; I am the assistant purser, *darlin'*."

She hoped to God this flight ended soon. In truth, it wasn't the economy class or the stinky feet and armpits—although those in and of themselves were causing her eyes to water. It was the simple fact that her heart was shattering into teeny tiny pieces and her world was crashing around her. Fighting with her subconscious rational mind that demanded to be heard was taking a toll on her. *He* is *happy* and *in love with you. He would* never *cheat.* However, the emotional, irrational, insecure woman buried deep inside fought for dominance. Not to mention, at that present moment, she happened to be trapped thirty thousand feet in the air beside a smelly, fat man while her husband's *affair d'amour* was spread out like the Queen of Sheba one deck below her. Her eyes narrowed to menacing slits. *Bitch.*

The flight attendant placed a clear, plastic cup on her pull-down tray and removed the half-eaten chicken and cold soup. He offered her one of those fast, fake smiles she and Jane always exchanged.

"Thank ye' kindly, shuga britches," she replied with an equally satirical smile of super glossy pink lips. *Plastic? Sixteen hundred dollars for this last-minute flight and I get a plastic cup?* She wondered if her chastisement to her husband three days before was more suited to herself. Was she becoming a snob in their peaceful, affluent existence?

After switching the overhead light and TV off, she attempted to settle down for the night, hoping the cognac and earbuds would take away the slow, miserable churning in her stomach. Unable to discern whether it was the vichyssoise, the feet, or the altitude, she finally resolved that it was the fact that her seemingly perfect life with her beloved man was slowly turning to shit thanks to Operation Macarena. *Frickin' stupid dance. Figures. Caroline always thinks up the op names.*

After pressing the music play list on her Shuffle, she lowered the seat back and began to listen to one of her favorite opera playlists.

"Naturally," she sarcastically said aloud when Placido Domingo's first aria was "Vesti la giubba" from *I Pagliacci*. She knew the translation by heart and it was never more apropos than now as she, obviously the clown, dressed like her sister behind a façade at the ready to break out into tears. *Laugh, clown at your broken love!*

A woman's familiar haughty voice snapped Liz from the agonizing place her mind and the song had taken her. "Excuse me, *monsieur*."

The viperous bitch called out to *garçon* Assistant Purser stood in the aisle beside foot guy who leered at her, his eyes fixed upon her crotch.

Oh Shit! Liz slid down into her seat, attempting to look toward the shaded, small window, her heart rate increasing exponentially at the possibility of being caught on the flight. Unfortunately, her attention continued to draw toward Caroline and her chic, albeit too tight, travel outfit. Again, insecurity and a morbid sense of curiosity toward her competitor caused her to dissect her husband's lover.

"Yes, *mademoiselle*? How may I help you?" the purser replied, happy to assist someone who clearly sat in Le Premiere class.

Caroline flicked her hair over one shoulder. "Can you direct me? I was told the mezzanine has an art gallery for those of us in first class …"

With disdain, the woman glanced down at the crotch staring man then quickly scanned Liz behind the pink bubble glasses. Caroline furrowed her brow, and promptly crinkled her nose when the onslaught of b.o and feet rose to her perfectly shaped nose.

"… and this clearly is *not* first class," she added, her lips downturned and pursing.

Liz, again, turned her head to the shaded window and pulled the white bag from the seat pocket. She held it to her face, pretending to vomit.

"Follow me. I'm happy to escort you to the electronic gallery. It is in the Affaires Cabin," the flight attendant said.

"Of course it is. Clearly, I don't belong in this section of the plane."

Hidden in the bag, Liz chortled a wry snicker, *Affaires—bitch. You don't belong anywhere near my husband either.* She fumed, but try as she might, couldn't stop the steady stream of silent tears down her cheek.

* * *

"She's sleeping?" Darcy asked Charlie, hoping to catch Liz before he got on the flight to Paris. "I've been calling her for the last thirty minutes. She's a light sleeper and would have picked up. Did you check on her?"

"Darcy, I'm not going to barge into your wife's bedroom because she didn't pick up your call. She's safe; she's sleeping. She had a busy day working with Wentworth."

"Check on her. Liz never goes to bed before midnight." Running his hand through his already tousled hair, he paced back and forth before the long plate glass window looking out onto the tarmac below.

Charlie chortled. "Man, you're a worry wart. She's fine. Jane told me Liz wasn't feeling well—you know that monthly thing. She went out for … you know … feminine stuff, earlier."

"She what?"

"It's cool. Calm down. She's home and now asleep."

"Hmm, well, it does wipe her out. Maybe she took something to help her sleep, but don't think you're off the hook for letting her leave Pemberley. Did Jane at least go with her?"

"No, but Liz came back safe and sound. Jane tucked her in and made her some tea about an hour ago. Don't worry so much. The girls are in good hands and doing a great job. Even Caroline can't help but to be impressed at them being such fast learners and you know what a difficult feat it is to impress my sister."

Darcy continued to pace, his hand making hurried tracks against his scalp. "Did Medusa leave yet?"

"Yeah. She split a couple of hours ago, tried to tell me that you want to rekindle your romance. What's up with that?"

"Nothing. Just keep her delusions between you and me, okay? I don't want Liz jumping to wrong conclusions. It's bad enough she's always suspected my past relationship with your sister."

"You told her the truth, right?"

"What are you on drugs? Tell my wife about how that blood-sucking snake and I were an item before I dumped her sorry ass … Sorry, I forget sometimes that she's your sister."

"Join the club. You really should tell Liz."

"That's on a need to know basis, and my wife doesn't need to know that Caroline was getting too close, too clingy, and too obsessed with sex to warrant Iceman's severe reaction."

Charlie laughed. "You know that's not the only reason you ended it with her. It was because she showed up in Paris during Operation Mazurka and blew your cover. Don't you remember?"

"I remember. She better not do it again during this op. This time, her hands will be nowhere near my balls."

"Yeah, that'll be quite an unusual thing in a sex club. I think you're the one on the drugs for not going this op alone."

"Can't be helped, the club doesn't allow men in without a date, but damn I wish it were you on this op and not me."

"Seems to me I got the sweeter deal. Here with your gorgeous wife and my wild Janie versus me making out with my venomous sister in some BDSM club."

Behind Darcy, Knightley signaled to him as the boarding announcement filled the airport. He pointed to the McDonalds and headed in that direction. Darcy waved, signaling his end of the call.

"Take care of Liz, Charlie. She's my life."

"Then I'm honored you entrusted me. Hey one last thing, I spoke with Georgiana like you asked. She's headed out to California, something about surfing in Santa Cruz to burn off wedding stress."

"Good. The farther she is away from her normal routine, the easier I'll rest. Thanks for making the call. Listen, I gotta board the plane. If Liz wakes, tell her I called and that I'll call her in the morning."

"That's it? Gee you're such a romantic."

Embarrassed, Darcy sheepishly smiled. "No … Tell her I love her."

* * *

161

As the airbus prepared for its final approach into Charles de Gaulle, the assistant purser vacated his position in economy for an urgent matter in Le Premier class. He stormed up and down the first class aisles brandishing a weapon, an orange disinfectant spray, with an equal measure of ferocity and repulsion. The set to his lips was understood and expressed by all who sat in the luxury section.

Time was of the essence. In a matter of minutes, the first class cabin would be overrun and crowded with passengers departing the plane, and given the slow nature of debarkation, traveler traffic would be at a standstill.

Monique, one of the flight attendants in the luxury class, nodded when he stopped beside the sleeping red-haired American, who he recognized from the night before in her search of the art gallery. He waved his arm in the air above her, viciously spraying as the orange aromatherapy fell in a fine mist onto white Egyptian cotton sheets.

A quick escape was tantamount and he nearly ran with a huff, firmly placing the bottle in Monique's outstretched hand before bolting up the spiral staircase two at a time.

Monique's other hand pinched her nostrils as demurely as she could, approaching the sleeping passenger. Leaning over she shook her shoulder. "*Mademoiselle*, zee plane is landing. Wake up, *si vous plait*."

Caroline stirred and slid her sleep mask up and off. She stretched her arms above her head and her vision settled upon the flight attendant's pinched face of discomfort.

"Please *madamoiselle*. Prepare for arrival," Monique barely commanded, holding her breath.

She promptly turned her blue-suited back to the passenger, running as fast as she decorously could toward the front galley where two other seat-belted flight attendants sat gossiping about the rancid smell within the first class cabin.

Caroline swiveled in the leather chair just as she heard the Boeing's wheels lower. "Huh?" was all she could manage before her lips started working. They seemed to be stuck together with glue. Her mouth was parched like the Sahara. Overall, she felt like a train wreck, groggy and out of sorts, like she had slept for a thousand years. Her vision was blurred and she could literally feel the bags under her eyes. Every one of her senses was thrown off-kilter. She surmised it must have been that last bit of cognac she consumed when she awoke in the middle of the night. Apparently, it had knocked her on her ass, which was highly unusual given her practiced immunity to all forms of alcohol, narcotics, and toxic drugs. The ninjutsu master could withstand anything off the market.

She leaned forward and lifted her purse from the console storage compartment then removed a compact from within, to take in her appearance. Her hair was askew and her eyes were nearly swollen shut. She signaled Monique for a bottle of water but was promptly met by her turned head in answer before the attendant sat and belted herself onto a jump seat for landing.

An older, sophisticated woman beside Caroline leaned toward her with a crinkled nose, but she spoke kindly. "Dear, do you need some Gas-X. It just works wonders for my constitution and controls the flatulence."

"Um ... no thank you."

"Accidents happen. Don't you worry. I'm sure it was that Vichys-soise. A good bowel movement will set you right."

Still, Caroline failed to understand the nature of the statement. Her surroundings spun, and there was a growing stench in the cabin that her olfactory was just awakening to. *What the hell is going on?*

The Boeing touched down and taxied for what felt like forever to her. Now that *some* sense of clarity was coming back, she grew excited to see Darcy tonight, but she needed beauty sleep and an anti-inflammatory to bring her facial swelling down. She had plans above and beyond their rendezvous at L'Enclave or the capture of Diablo's woman. She glanced at her wrist with the intention of logging into her specially designed Smart Watch. She wanted to check for his text message and instructions. Only the delicate bones of her wrist stared back at her. The watch was gone. In her fog, she imagined that perhaps she had packed it in her suitcase and not worn it at all. *Damn, what the hell was in that cognac?* She couldn't remember anything.

Monique and the others opened the airplane door and took their obligatory stance as well as a much-needed breath of fresh air for their goodbyes at the exit. As each passenger shuffled toward them, they were bid adieu with a pleasant smile and congenial, "Please fly Air France again."

Caroline's disembarkation farewell was different.

Carrying her Louis Vuitton travel case, she noticed how the passengers behind her kept back several feet as though she was an emergency vehicle. She observed Monique spraying that overpowering orangina into the air when she neared the galley. Even the pilot, who looked gorgeous with that silver fox hair of his peeking out from the pilot cap, seemed to cover his nostrils with his thumb and index with each step she took closer to the cockpit.

Fifteen feet behind Caroline, standing in the middle of the staircase leading down from the mezzanine, Liz waited for the crowd of passengers below her to move. She leaned her back against the railing and through the rose-colored glasses watched Caroline and the facial expressions of all those she encountered.

The assistant purser pointed to Caroline as she shuffled nearer to the exit door and Liz overheard him tell another flight attendant that the *Americain* smelled like poo-poo.

Normally, Liz would have been highly agitated by the standstill wait coupled with the acute suffocation, particularly since her dirty bomb deed was starting to waft in her direction, but watching how people reviled Caroline was worth the wait and the odor. She could be patient and observant—Darcy had taught her that. She lifted a Kleenex to her nostrils and peered over the white tissue with a look of mischievous innocence. God, it felt good to be Jane for a change.

Glancing at her newly acquired, chic-looking Smart Watch, she quelled the impulse to check Caroline's texts. That was something she needed to do in private. Lord knows what her cheating husband had sent his paramour, and she vowed not to cry in public. The second the wheels of the plane had touched down, her nerves unraveled further. She was so riddled with fear over what she would see and discover that she felt on the verge of a breakdown. Her hand slightly trembled as it held the tissue to her nose as her eyes fixed on her nemesis. She refocused, thankful for the distraction that Caroline and the kryptonite toxic warfare provided. Finally, her nerves gave way to anxious laughter.

At first, she started slowly chuckling between the cracks of her bubble gum. Then she outright cackled, so damn proud of herself, particularly when smelly feet man behind her complained that his socks had been stolen and no one would help him locate them.

She laughed and, again, thought of Jane and how proud she would be of her antics. In the time that Liz stood waiting, she reflected on the events of the night before like a pleasing balm to her frazzled and very cranky soul.

> *Like previous international flights, she had awakened in the dead of night. Except for the man snoring beside her, the cabin was blissfully quiet. In truth, it wasn't his snoring that had awoken her. Hell, she had long been used to Darcy's freight train when he was exhausted from horse training all day. Still groggy, she looked over to her seatmate and noticed how the smelly white socks lay draped over the outer armrest on the aisle. He was barefoot, and she resisted the urge to grab the white bag before her.*

> *With the exception of the few overhead reading and red emergency aisle lights, it was eerily dark. The seatmate stirred, scratched his balls, and then vacated his seat. Liz assumed he had to use the lavatory and she seized the moment to quickly get up to make her escape. She was still too upset and wound tight to attempt sleep again.*

> *In the center row of seats beside her, a young mother sat changing her infant's diaper. A little boy about three lay curled up in a third seat. Liz smiled at the woman when their eyes met. She was amazed at her skill in occupying the two children, who were thankfully unaffected by the altitude.*

> *"How old is your baby? She's adorable," Liz whispered.*

> *"Seven months," she replied while pulling down the front of the poopy diaper. At which both Liz and the woman leaned away—one with a "Whoa," and the other with a "Yowza" at the stench rising like a toxic*

mushroom cloud.

Through watering eyes and held breath, the woman gave her a sheepish smile. "Sorry … it must be that new Gerber's Smartnourish I'm feeding her. She's been like an atom bomb."

Liz grimaced, "More like kryptonite. It looks like vichyssoise."

"Smells like andouillettes. Well, her daddy is Parisian. He loves those foul-smelling sausages."

The baby laughed.

"That's right, my little stinky pooper, we're going home to daddy," the woman cooed as she pulled the offending diaper completely out from under the baby's tush. She leaned back again, assaulted by her baby's stink bottom.

"My God that's lethal," Liz declared.

The mother rolled up the diaper, placed it in a plastic bag and looked around the seats and down the aisle for the obnoxious purser. "Do you see the flight attendant? I think this should be put someplace, and hermetically sealed for everyone's sake. I don't want Emily to be responsible for an international incident aboard a trans-Atlantic flight."

Like an instantaneous light bulb had illuminated over Liz's head, she quickly offered, "I'll take care of it for you. No worries, I know just the place to put it."

Being a former devious kitty-killer had its benefits, she surmised, thankful for the experiences of childhood spent beside one of the most notorious pranksters she knew: her sister. Only her plans at that moment had nothing to do with enacting a playful prank, but everything to do with immature, impulsive behavior enacted by an insanely jealous wife.

The mother handed the bag to her with apologies and gratefulness.

"Oh, it's no trouble at all." With that, she quickly stole the smelly socks draped over the armrest then stealthily made her way down the aisle toward the staircase leading to first class. Good Lord, she almost skipped in glee to get to her destination.

The *Le Premier* cabin was dark when she peered around the blue curtain separating classes. Snores emanated all around her, and at that late hour, she noted very few passengers awake. Within the luxury accommodation, she surmised that the absent flight attendants were sleeping since all eight passengers slept comfortably.

A quick movement placed her on the opposite side of the curtain, and she silently made her way toward Caroline, nestled as though in a cocoon in her shell-suite bed.

Standing over the woman's sleeping form, she resisted the urge to pull up the ridiculous eye mask wrapped around her redhead then snap it back against her face with force. Keeping her hands from enacting that little eye whiplash, she held onto the diaper as tightly as she could stomach. Beside her nemesis, a crystal glass of half-consumed liquid invited her to enact something even more sinister. She smirked, lifted the pink skull on her big ring and removed a small white pill. Although the woman was already sleeping, on the off chance she awoke needing a drink, she dropped the over-the-counter sleeping pill into the glass before quietly kneeling at Caroline's feet. Confident that generic medicines were not part of her drug resistant regimen, that little baby was going to give her one hell of a morning.

Surreptitiously glancing over a shoulder before raising the lid to the storage cabinet, she made sure no one watched. Her heart hammered but she remained focused on the target of Operation Dirty Bomb: Caroline's travel bag, a new and very expensive *Louis Vuitton*. She wanted to laugh in a devious, malevolent tone but bit her lip as she slowly slid open the zipper inch by slow, creeping inch until she was able to reach in. Her hand felt around the contents until finally her fingers grasped Caroline's Smart Watch—a most excellent find that quickly got shoved into her pocket. Her hand's second descent into the bag discovered a hard sunglass case. *Dolce Gabbana* black sunglasses were the first covered victim of the baby's excrement. Two dark lens' now covered in "vichyssoise" would meet Caroline's revulsion and horror in daylight.

Liz held her nose when she quietly placed the diaper at the bottom of the travel bag, rearranging the contents to conceal its covert delivery. She zipped closed the bag, so sure that each of its contents would be permanently violated in the airtight compartment. Next, she removed the stinky socks from the plastic then stealthily tucked them in the outside compartment.

Quietly, the intrepid mischief maker rose and lowered the cabinet lid with its putrid contents secure, ready to percolate until the plane landed, growing stronger and more lethal with each passing hour.

Standing over Caroline, she smiled wickedly, thinking, "Ninja masters have nothing over the diabolical superpowers of baby poop."

15

Masquerade

C harlie leaned against one of the bunker cabinets, watching Jane practice cold-firing the .38 Special at one of the targets. Even though he held the iPhone to his ear, he couldn't stop admiring her long legs displayed by black biker shorts. "I'm sorry, Darce but Liz has been out working with Wentworth all morning. According to Jane, she awoke refreshed and ready to tackle pic-knife fighting with a vengeance."

Darcy paced the small balcony of his hotel suite. His brow furrowed, his cheeks flushed. "Did you see her? Is she feeling better? I don't want her overtaxing herself after feeling so poorly last night."

"No, I didn't see her, but Jane tells me she's feelin' groovy."

"Charlie, this isn't some disco song, this is Liz we're talking about. She's a master at bullshit when she's hiding something. I want you to go out there and check on her. Find her cell phone and bring it out to her or find out why she's not picking up. She hasn't even responded to my texts. What the fuck is going on over there?"

"There's no need to freak out. She's in good hands with Wentworth. She's most likely practicing her hand to hand with him and can't get to the phone. He probably has her in some submission take down move, pinning her legs and—"

"He better not!" Darcy stopped dead in his pacing, running a hand through his hair.

He stalled in his tirade at the edge of the wrought iron balcony, observing couples gather before the Palais Garnier Opera house during the intermission. Damn, he wished more than anything to take Liz to see the performance tonight instead of leaving in fifteen minutes to meet Caroline in the lobby. Something wasn't right; he felt it in his bones. "She's spending a lot of time with Wentworth. I don't like it. You hired him to guard the estate not to seduce my wife. Damn, fucking southern boy!"

Charlie firmly raised his voice, turning his back to Jane and staring at the target above his head. "Calm down and focus. I have everything under control here. Listen to me. You're losing your edge. I had a feeling this was going to happen—you're getting soft. Focus, Iceman. You need to go into Enclave thinking about Operation Macarena and finding the target and the objective, not thinking about another man shagging your wife. Liz is my concern, and she's in good hands. Wentworth isn't trying to get into her pants, so chill out."

"I'm not getting soft."

"Yes, you are. You're blinded and compromised. Focus on the fact that Liz and Georgiana are the reasons you are there. I'll be waiting on this end for yours and Knightley's incoming intel. Stick that receiver in your ear and patch in some AC/DC to get your head back in the game."

"It's Led Zeppelin now, not AC/DC."

"I don't give a shit if it's the Village People singing 'In the Navy!' Where's that 'The only easy day was yesterday' SEAL attitude?"

It was on the tip of Darcy's tongue, but he held the expletive. It wasn't Charlie's fault, and he was one hundred percent correct in his assessment. The Iceman *had* melted. Fire did that to ice. Liz did that to him. Now that Rick was secure, all he desired was to get home to his life and his wife and pick up where they left off: making love with the sun rising and setting upon Pemberley. His voice suddenly turned cold and lacking inflection. "You're right. As soon as I've made contact with

Nadya Karakurt, Knightley will feed you the intel for analysis. Until then, be on standby."

"That's more like it. Talk to you later." Charlie disconnected the call before Darcy could reply.

A pounding upon his hotel room door caused him instinctively to move to his pillow where he had placed his pistol, since he couldn't take it into the club. He walked through the luxury suite as someone's fist meeting wood continued its assault. He peered through the peephole. It was Caroline and the set to her red lips told him trouble loomed. For her to break protocol before they even arrived at the fetish club was unexpected.

He opened the door widely and with a welcoming flourish to his arm, said nothing to her as she entered like a woman on a mission. There was nothing alluring or seductive about her gait. Wearing that Burberry trench coat, and he didn't want to imagine what was below it, she looked all business. Beautiful but business, and that was fine by him.

Angered by her presence, he closed the door, hoping that her foolishness in coming to his room wasn't any indication of things to come. He was in no mood for her to screw up this op like the last time they were in Paris together. "Already you're gonna blow this cover? We're supposed to meet in the lobby? Didn't you get my text?"

She snapped, "No, I didn't get your text. We have a problem—a security breach, Rambo."

"We're back to that, again ... Medusa?"

"Apparently, your wife is up to something." She laid her titanium case on the desk and began to unlock it.

"What are you talking about?"

The lid popped open to reveal a near empty case. "I'm talking about the mysterious disappearance of some of this case's contents, and the not-so-small issue of my stolen specially programmed Smart Watch, designed for Obsidian's security network. And don't get me started about the horrific diarrhea diaper that mysteriously showed up in my travel bag, its contents covering and ruining my custom Dolce and Gabbana sunglasses. Your wife is a certifiable lunatic!"

Her voice had risen to dangerous levels. In Darcy's experience when dealing with that particular lethal tone, he took a step backward but his voice lowered an octave. "I've killed for less, Caroline. You're walking on thin ice, here."

"Do you have any idea what was in this case? Do you?"

Darcy peered in melodramatically. "Your dildo? What did you do, short circuit it?"

"Very funny. No. Two handheld EMP devices. This one is a Desert Eagle but the other—the missing one—is a .22 derringer, as well as various other camo communications that Obsidian recently commissioned."

"From my father-in-law." He raised an eyebrow, stealing her thunder.

"Yes, from Bennet and it seems that the only person with access to your safe has helped herself to some of its contents. I guess, like father like daughter. It must be in the Bennet gene pool, traitorous actions."

Now beyond livid, he hoped Caroline saw it when his eyes bore directly into hers. Cutting like a sharp-edged razor he said, "I don't appreciate your blaming Liz for *your* failure to secure such volatile equipment. Did you not examine the case before you left Virginia as a security precaution?"

"I, er, didn't think to do so. Your wife assured me of its safety stating *'we're all family here at Pemberley'*. Apparently not."

"Do not *ever* imitate or speak ill of my wife again. Do you understand me?"

"Fine, but you must face facts that she's as traitorous as her father."

"Caroline, Liz would have no knowledge or need to take Obsidian property or open your briefcase. Admit it, this isn't because someone sabotaged your designer eyewear, this is because you're steamed and jealous over my marriage."

He took two full steps closer to her, rising to his full 6'2" height. "I won't have you disrespecting my wife or her family because of it. It is *never* going to be renewed between you and me."

"Get over your high and mighty Iceman intimidation tactics." She removed one of the two remaining pieces of equipment from the case and placed her fingerprint on the biometric scanner. She handed it to Darcy with a smug look upon her face. "If you don't believe me let the evidence speak for itself."

With the swipe of his finger, photo after photo rolled by, revealing the people associated with someone's air travel. A red-haired Air France ticket agent, a fat man aboard an airplane, a male flight attendant, a woman changing a diaper, Caroline sleeping with that stupid eye mask he recognized, and finally a concierge at a luxury hotel.

"All this tells me is that someone took a nice trip. Why do you think this is Liz? She doesn't even know I'm in Paris and, further, has no need to come on her own. I just spoke with Charlie; she's at Pemberley training with Wentworth."

Caroline chuckled, "Oh yes, Wentworth. If I didn't see Eliza wearing a disguise *on the airplane* myself, then *that* I might believe. Those two couldn't keep their eyes off one another. Looks like you've married quite the little woman, Rambo. The minute you take off for Peru, she's hot for teacher, maybe even getting a little extracurricular activity in. I've seen that Wentworth and he's one fine stud. Maybe he's planning to meet her here. Did you consider *that?*"

She could see she touched a nerve. Darcy's fist tightened at his side and his jaw clenched ever so slightly. He withdrew the iPhone from the inside pocket of his suit, turned his back to Caroline then walked to the balcony. He hit redial.

"Yello."

"Charlie, I don't want a single argument from you. I need to speak with Liz, urgently. We're leaving for the club, but I expect to hear from you or my wife before we get there. It's important." Darcy clicked off and turned to see Caroline standing before him with her red talons gripping her hipbones. The smug look and snide curl to her lips pissed him off even more. Liz wouldn't cheat, never. "Fuck you, Caroline."

* * *

On Rue Thérèse Liz paced back and forth on the sidewalk opposite the wood entrance doors of L'Enclave and other long vacated businesses and shops. The narrow street was eerily deserted except for a small delivery van parked half on the sidewalk and half on the street twenty or so feet from her and the occasional club patron seeking admission.

For five minutes she had been having a silent argument with herself. Fact was, she was terrified to confront what she didn't want to see. Her hands shook and her heart raced. She was one step away from chickening out, but having arrived sufficiently early before Darcy and Caroline, Liz knew she had time for a drink or two to calm herself. She also knew she'd need to get adequately drunk in order to remain at this den of iniquity so she could enact her plan to wrest her husband from the viper's fangs.

She purchased her apparel from the lingerie shop in the hotel lobby; her choice of the red satin and black lace bustier was made with him in mind. The two colors, the two fabrics met in feminine, provocative union like the lustful tango that she and Darcy experience in one another's arms. A pencil skirt enticingly hugged her curves, narrowing slightly above her knees. Sheer, jet thigh-highs accented five-inch black Louboutins with ankle straps. She knew this ensemble would unhinge him. Completing the look was another discovery from Caroline's case: an obsidian black beauty mark, which was now situated to the left above her chin. She hoped that she looked alluring and mysterious, particularly since the feathered Venetian mask covering half her face only revealed plum-colored lips, startling blue eyes and her newly adhered disguise.

She still burned with anger recalling how earlier after logging into Caroline's Smart Watch having figured out the password (her husband's name), his text to the bitch read *"Lobby ten o'clock sharp."* It was now nine thirty; her heart slammed so hard she could hear it in her ears.

At the darkened vestibule of the club doors, a statuesque, raven-haired woman approached, sliding a black mask down over her eyes. She seemed at ease in her arrival as though L'Enclave was well known to her. *Perhaps she is a regular.*

The patron glanced over to her where she continued to pace and wring her hands together. Before gaining entrance to the club, she saunterd to her with long, elegant strides, her long braid, draped over one shoulder. Even though partially masked, Liz thought the patron was the most exotic looking woman she had ever seen, and she considered that her stares could be misunderstood. At a place like this kink club it wasn't unusual to gape.

A square-necked, black leather dress and lace up stilettos added height to an already graceful body and with each long stride, Liz's eyes drew down to the detailed tattoo of a spider and web inked at the top of the woman's foot.

A heavy Russian accent comforted her, "Don't be so timid, *dorogaya*. Is this first time?"

Noticing a black crop in the woman's hand, Liz replied as confidently as she could. "Is it that obvious? It *is* my first time, and I have no idea what I'm doing here. I must be crazy." She adjusted her mask more out of nervous release than anything else.

The woman chuckled, her eyes twinkling in the moonlight. "There is nothing to fear within L'Enclave, and if it is the discovery of your identity you fear, vell, we have strict code inside. Do not worry." She touched the long, black tendril cascading from Liz's wispy, updo wig. "Do you desire women or men?"

"Um ..."

"No need to answer. It is just that even behind your stunning mask, I can see you are beautiful, so feminine and delectable that I am sure many will vant to experience those plump lips. Should you decide that women may be your interest tonight, my name is Nadya. Come find me in the Libertine Room. I will be there until daybreak." Nadya leaned toward her ear. "I promise, the only pain you feel will be pleasure. The candles are not just for ambiance. The wax can be highly stimulating."

Oh my God. "I'll ... I'll remember that. Thank you."

The Russian ran her index finger down Liz's cheek. The legged point of a two-inch long gold spider ring, nearly scraped her flesh. "Would you like me to escort you inside? My usual submissive is ..." Her voice trailed and she glanced over her shoulder at the van parked on the street.

"unfortunately missing tonight. I would enjoy introducing you to several who will make your experience everything you desire."

Liz looked behind her to see what it was that drew the woman's attention. She felt as though someone watched the exchange. The street seemed darker, more tenebrous then before. All that was missing was a rolling, growing mist clinging to the cobblestone. Perhaps it was just the licentious offer that put Liz on alert, making her even more uneasy. "You're very kind, Nadya, but I'm just not ready yet."

"I understand, *lapushka*. Just remember, it is not all bondage and discipline. That is within dungeons on first floor only. You can watch, of course, if you are not ready to partake in good pain."

Good pain? Liz nodded, trying not to imagine what a dungeon looked like, let alone what took place in it. Immediately, a medieval rack torture device popped into her head. "What's on the second and third floors?" She looked up at the darkened windows of the building.

Nadya laughed. "Curiosity is good. When you are ready, I will take you. You will come find me, *da?*"

"Yes."

She ran the tip of her crop across Liz's breast then turned, leaving her standing where she found her, in the middle of Rue Thérèse and more anxious than before. The quicker she found her husband, the better. Surreptitiously, she watched how Nadya gained entrance by ringing the old bell. A small window revealed itself when its door slid back. She thought she heard the word "Karakurt."

The moment the mysterious stranger entered through the doorway, she sighed in relief then began to buoy herself. *It's now or never—do it—be Jane—be brave—save your marriage.*

Needing a dose of Jane's inappropriate levity and bolstering confidence, she promptly tapped her sister's cell number into the mobile phone. It rang and rang then finally went to voicemail. *Damn! She said she would be at the ready for my call. WTH?*

It was now or never and she took a deep breath before walking to the door. In the black of night where only a red glow illuminated from the palladium window above the doors, she depressed the old bell, her finger trembling when she did so. An annoyed, heavily accented voice addressed her through the intercom. "Yes?"

It was as though the Lizzy of Longbourn had reappeared and the reborn Liz Darcy had disappeared when she stuttered terribly doing exactly as her hotel concierge instructed her. She gave her alias name, "Flor … Flor… Floria," then waited, shifting her weight from one foot to the other for what seemed like long minutes. *Oh God, what are you doing, Liz?*

Her black-gloved hand ran down the side of her coat in nervous release until her fingers settled upon her thigh. She began to tap them, like she used to do before Darcy calmed the tornadic activity inside her. Her sister's bling skull ring bounced up and down.

The Frenchman slid the small window in the door open. She couldn't see him; it was obviously one-way glass. "Good, you have your mask on."

She had donned the mask the moment she exited the taxicab at the corner of Rue Moliere. On the off chance that Darcy arrived early, she didn't want to risk getting caught. The whole point of this was to confront him during his liaison, and she didn't want him to see her until the moment of truth. Not that he would recognize her. There was nothing remotely familiar about her appearance, right down to the blue contact lens' she wore.

"Yes, I was told that …"

"*Arrête !*" He abruptly cut off her sentence with a quick slide of the door.

She looked up at the three innocuous stories before her. No one would suspect that one of Paris's most risqué clubs hid behind this unassuming appearance. A chill ran up her spine at the thought of what she would encounter when she went in. Was it truly as Nadya had suggested? It wasn't curiosity that posed the question in her mind; it was the fear of entering a salacious world so wholly unknown to her.

Liz paced before the doors waiting for the rude doorman to allow her entrance. Her mind focused on what her hotel concierge had explained to her when he called to add her to the VIP list. It was "*Eyes*

Wide Shut' night. The promise of an evening of highly stimulating, erotic fantasy entwined with the mystery of anonymity was an overwhelming and scary thought for the former peaches and cream woman. Behind the palm of his hand, he explained quietly that disguise would open the door to experiences of pleasure otherwise not attained.

"*Entre, si vous plait*," the voice ominously stated.

One of the two doors opened and Liz stepped in, no longer in view of the bald observer in the van.

* * *

Red. Everything was covered with a palette of shades of red—and darkness—and illuminated by candles. The sweet aroma of roses wafted in the air, immediately assaulting Liz. She supposed the scent, to some, might act like a pheromone, but it did nothing to mask the smell of sex. The flicker of flame cast shadows onto the plush velvet walls and ceilings. Even the music in the entryway sounded sensual and provocative in a slow tantalizing way. From the moment she had entered the fetish club, every one of her senses awakened. Strangely, the gothic ambiance felt welcoming, and unexpectedly arousing, but none of it took away the anxiety threatening to immobilize her.

This world and what went on in it frightened the sensible woman in her and the fact that her husband had scheduled his liaison in it dismayed her. He had never shown a bent toward this type of sexual excitement or activity before.

Nervously, Liz relinquished her handbag, cell phone, and coat. Insistent on keeping her newly acquired compact, she slid it up the edge of her bustier. But there was another accessory, one she had carefully hidden at the small of her back—Caroline's derringer pistol from the case. Not that she knew what she was going to do with it, but instinct propelled her to bring it to L'Enclave.

The brusque Frenchman pointed down a red carpeted and walled hallway where glass votives flickered from their stations upon small shelves hanging on the wall. "You will find the bar area at the end of the hall. Your entry fee includes unlimited champagne."

He snapped his fingers and a masked, shirtless, beautiful specimen of masculinity entered the foyer, promptly handing Liz a slender flute of Cristal.

"Enjoy, *mademoiselle*. The safe word for the evening is 'red'," the doorman said.

"Safe word?"

He rolled his eyes. "*Oui*, so that a dungeon monitor can stop a scene immediately … when you have reached your hard limit."

A scene? "Right." Liz had no idea what the hell he just said. She clutched her champagne like it was a godsend.

As though in a trance, she slowly traversed the dark hallway with trepidation, noting that between each set of double shelves were red padded doors with small windows. She assumed for patron viewing pleasure.

Curious, masked eyes peered in. Liz's jaw slacked. She resisted the urge to cover her mouth in shock.

A man she assumed was a dungeon monitor observed the play of two men and a woman as minimal leather and exposed flesh collided with hard slaps and groans, and an eager mouth received its fill.

Oh my God.

The crystal glass in Liz's hand trembled slightly in unison to the rising bubbles when she brought the drink to her lips then consumed the entire contents in one long gulp.

Her morbid sense of curiosity brought her to stop before the next door where another masked, shirtless waiter seemed to magically—or intuitively—appear in the shadow. Twelve sparkling flutes of champagne on a tray beside her left shoulder invited her to partake.

"Would you care for another, *Mademoiselle?*"

"Oh God, yes." Liz exchanged her empty glass for a full one. "Thank you."

If the previous scene had imprinted upon her mind's eye, the next room's torrid sexual role-play replaced it.

Two blindfolded, nude women kneeled bound together at their backs before their Dominant acting as their kidnapper in an unnerving scene of bondage and submission. He was dressed in all black, including his mask, and looked quite the villain standing before one of the women while holding a clothespin. He bent down toward her erect nipple.

Liz abruptly turned away not waiting to see what he was going to do with the pin. She shuddered, resisting the urge to clutch her breast as an impulse to protect or soothe it from the clamping that was sure to follow in the dungeon had she remained.

Passing by a third dungeon, she heard strange noises from within and halted in her footsteps at the "whack" sound of a paddle against something. Another "whack." A loud moan of pleasure breached the padded door. Liz froze, resisting the inclination to give into the curious creature within her by looking through the window. Then another strange sound emanated from the room, and she continued down the hall as fast as her Louboutins could take her. Already, the bubbles in the champagne were taking a toll on her composure—or was it what she had just seen and heard? She felt lightheaded and tried to focus, making her way to the bar area by walking through the hanging red curtains at the entrance archway.

With the exception of the restaurant, it was the central room in the club. The location where hook ups happened and numbers exchanged. Dancing, music, and stripping all took place in the exotic, plush space of shadow and mystery. Varying shades of pinks and reds covered every part of the room like a Moroccan explosion. All accented by low-hanging, red crystal chandeliers, and the diffused lighting of flickering candles set before framed mirrors.

Liz reached her free hand out to feel the soft tufted wall beside her as she stepped into what she referred to as "the den" in her mind. Again, lingering and mixing with the scent of burning candles, the heady smell of roses in the center of small tables surrounding the dance floor greeted her arrival. Couples and threesomes drank, groped, and flirted on the cushioned sofas lining the wall. She noted how everyone was dressed to the nines, even in their masquerade, but then again, everything about

L'Enclave was a masquerade. It was seduction and carnal wrapped in a roux, gothic veil of elite sophistication.

The glass behind the bar's liquor bottles was backlit against mirrors and the brightest spot in the room surrounded by red and gold votive candles. Liz figured, like her assassin husband, the best place to blend in was out in the open, but she felt out of place—alone—voyeuristic, and she chugged the second glass of her champagne down in anxiety.

Another shirtless god on the other side of the counter came to her assistance, holding a gold bottle of Cristal and promptly refilled her empty flute. She smiled meekly.

This experience was like nothing she had even *read*. Not that she was a prude, but erotica books had no appeal to her. She thought she and Darcy had an extremely active and fulfilling sex life. *She* didn't need to venture into this fetish world as an aphrodisiac. Their deep love was the fix she needed in their lovemaking. At least it *had* been until she learned about Caroline.

Liz felt the burning stares of those around her. Were they mentally undressing her? Whispering about her? Imagining secret machinations to woo her into a submissive role? She didn't want to know; she was on a mission of her own and could not allow herself to worry about others' plans.

Within minutes of settling herself at the end of the bar, an older man with a congenial smile approached her. The warmth of his voice felt like smooth caramel and strangely did wonders in quelling some of her anxiety.

"Would you care to dance?" he asked as she held tightly to the slender flute while leaning forward upon the countertop.

Remembering to employ her southern accent she said, "Not just yet, but thank you very much." Her lips touched the cool glass of protective diversion.

Her admirer ran his finger down the side of her bare bicep, his eyes riveted on the fullness of her breasts made more enticing by the narrowness of her waist within the bustier.

"You are an exotic lovely. Perhaps, you would care to visit the Sensual Room with me and my date? We have reserved the third floor's boudoir for the evening."

In the dimly lit room, Liz's eyes drew to the couple behind him. Even concealed by both the shadow and the woman's dress, she could tell they were having tempered sex against the wall. *My God, I'm a long way from teaching kindergarten, Longbourn, and Pemberley.*

She smiled apologetically so as not to offend the libertine standing beside her. "Maybe later, but thank you for asking."

"This song, 'Temptation' certainly invites us to indulge and that is why you are here, no?"

Her fingers played with the gold chandelier earring swaying against her neck. "It does. I enjoy Diana Krall. Her voice is so seductive, but I am waiting for someone. Our preference is the tango, and I'm sure he will be here shortly."

Mimicking his action and trying so hard not to shake from this role-play she found herself in, she ran her finger down the lapel of his fine suit jacket.

He captured her opera length gloved hand in his and placed her index finger in his mouth, sliding it slowly and seductively out between his encasing lips.

Her heart raced a mile a minute and it took every ounce of composure she could muster to play without causing suspicion. "But, if he doesn't show then I just may take y'all up on your offer. I do so love a man wearing Armani."

He leaned into her and his beard tickled her cheek. "I won't be wearing my Armani, enchantress."

"Pity."

"If you change your mind, come find us," the man said with a wink before moving on. He glanced back over his shoulder, eyes undressing her from top to bottom one last time.

Alone and left once again to her voyeuristic devices, the candlelit ambiance was enough concealment for her observation of the *in flagrante delicto* taking place within the swingers' club. Many patrons were, in fact, also just watching and admiring as well as planning their attack—just as she was. Apart from masking their identities, everything was unabashedly out in the open.

A nude, small-breasted woman clung to the stripper's pole at the far end of the room near the DJ. Her willowy, lean body moved like artistry in motion against the cold sleek steel as Diana Krall's music continued to cast a spell of eroticism.

The dark wood floor separating the stripper and Liz was void of dancers, which gave Liz a clear view of the goings on at each small round table and cushioned sofa of patrons. She curiously speculated what was going on in the boudoirs on the second and third floors, but after witnessing the scenes within only two of the six dungeons, she internally shuddered at the thought.

The black masked, half-naked bartender came up beside her again, noting how she watched a group of patrons in the left corner of the room. He re-filled her empty glass.

"Do you like what you see? You could join them. They prefer x-somes," he said in an obvious fake French accent.

"X-somes?"

"More than three, not your run-of-the-mill ménage. That group there enjoys a full-fledged orgy in the Fantasy Boudoir."

Liz thoughtfully nodded, trying not to let her shock show. She drank deeply from the flute.

"I like your ring. It's cool the way the skull catches the candlelight."

She snorted. "It's my sister's. I thought it would give me courage tonight."

He smiled and nodded. "Awesome."

"You're an American?" she asked tipped off by his slang usage.

"Yup. I fell in love with this place a year ago and I never left. Of course, my girlfriend at the time couldn't understand it. Hence, she is now my *ex-girlfriend* living back in Idaho."

"Frankly, I can understand her trepidation. As a first timer, it's freaky and overwhelming, odd to see people so exposed in their intimacy." The alcohol appeared to be working its magic, her apprehension diminishing slightly.

"I know it seems outlandish at first but you should let yourself enjoy the experience. Mostly, L'Enclave provides a sanctuary for women to explore and indulge in their femininity and hidden desires. They only admit men who meet the requirement. Look around, everyone is attractive, and they're all here for your pleasure. If you're not comfortable with a fetish club, then why are you here?"

Liz leaned closer to him. "To catch my husband in his affair."

"Ah. I'm sorry to hear that. So what's your plan ... what are you prepared to do?"

"Anything and everything. That's why I'm here." Feeling slightly brazen, she was ready to meet her husband and his mistress head on.

The alcohol combined with the pornographic exploits playing before her like a movie had made her skin flushed. Strangely, the entire hedonistic club and its exhibitionism had begun to titillate her every sense within the short span of thirty minutes. Her inhibitions were shedding and her desire was growing.

She once again glanced over at the couple still having sex, only this time the woman sat straddling his lap, slowly rising up and down. It appeared to her that both were prolonging their orgasms. At the display, her womanhood clenched and it only served to heighten her need to see Darcy. She was so aroused that it hurt—need coupled with the real pain of knowing that her husband was about to enter the club at any minute to lick, touch, and thrust another woman.

Her head snapped to the right when Darcy walked through the curtain, holding Caroline's hand. Her heart clenched and she bit her lip to keep it from trembling. Even through his silver mask, she'd recognize him anywhere—the blackness of his hair, the wave at his forehead, the sensual curve of his lips, and that distinctly purposeful walk of his. He looked fabulous, wearing a dark suit and oxfords she hadn't seen before. He had cut his hair, and she resisted the urge to run to him, kiss him wildly and—slap him and beat the crap out of Caroline. Liz tried not to let her emotions show, but damn if her heart wasn't breaking at the sight before her. Then he smiled at Caroline, and the bitch laughed back at something he had said. His radiant smile and the jubilant cadence of his laughter nearly unhinged Liz. God how she loved him, but she chastised herself for foolishly believing he felt the same way. He had done this to her once before, but then they had yet to form a relationship. Sighing, she thought, *Once a deceiver, always a deceiver.*

He looked so happy with that evil redhead on his arm that she thought for sure he didn't have any qualms or conscience about being here with her.

"Is that your husband?" the bartender asked.

She nodded as Darcy walked across the dance floor in her direction.

"She doesn't have anything over you and certainly too uptight for kink. You want my advice?"

"Please. A second ago, I was ready, but seeing him has vanquished my nerve to do anything. In about five seconds, I'm going to be running out of here. A minute ago, I was prepared for battle. Now, I don't think I can stand the pain. Seeing him with her is …" She shook her head, stopping herself from voicing her agony, but her eyes remained locked on Darcy and Caroline, settling into and snuggling beside one another on a red sofa. Liz's gloved hands clenched like her jaw.

"Here's what you have to do. A burlesque striptease. Pick a song. Go to the pole and spellbind him so that his eyes remain on you, not her." He reached over to the top liquor shelf and removed a bottle of Chivas, pouring her a shot. "Here, no charge."

She pulled the warm liquor then gave him a beaming smile, even though it wasn't from her heart.

"Would you like another?

"Yeah. I need it."

He complied, filling the glass, and she shot it back before giving him a newly bolstered, "Thanks, Joe."

"Joe?"

"Yeah, isn't that what you call a bartender who advises lovelorn patrons?"

He laughed as she pressed her beauty mark, making sure it was adhered firmly before her little dance.

"Good luck," Joe said.

She made her way with newly bolstered confidence across the empty dance floor.

You can do this, Liz. Just like you did in the bathroom. Remember how he loved it when you stripped for him?

Sauntering steps—no, strutting strides—approached the DJ sitting in a darkened corner spinning seductive tunes.

In the van parked on Rue Thérèse, following a piercing, static noise, two words came through Knightley's headphones. "Good luck." Someone's microphone was now transmitting to Obsidian's secure network. "What the hell? Where's this coming from?"

He thought to himself that if anyone needed luck, he did. Sitting in this hot van watching the couple having sex across from Darcy on his computer monitor was going to be the death of him. He tapped a few of buttons on the keyboard and, with the mouse, zoomed in on the lounge through the button camera on Darcy's suit. Maybe he could match the transmission's spoken words to the person in the club, using lip reading.

Darcy couldn't help his attention gravitating to the leggy, raven-haired woman approaching the DJ. She reminded him of Liz, and he wondered if it was because he was so upset still awaiting Charlie's or her phone call. Apart from the woman's cinched waist and voluptuous breasts, her curves were similar to his wife's, a tantalizing balance of seductive indentations. His gaze lingered on her spilling bust line and he considered how Liz might look in such a sensual bustier. Once she passed by him, his eyes traveled to her backside encased in form-fitting black satin, and he felt a tinge of guilt at doing so. Her sexy legs sheathed in black, back-seamed stockings were so like Liz's that he was sure he was going crazy from missing her. The woman crossing the dance floor made him ache with need for his wife.

For a passing second, he thought he detected his Lakmé's distinct perfume—the one he had made for her in Germany. The scent of their *Coelogyne ochracea* orchid. No doubt his imagination was conjuring every recollection of her.

Caroline snuggled against him, turning his chin in her direction to garner all his attention. Her gold cat's eye shaped mask made her ice blue eyes look even more sinister. "Maybe that's her. My asset said she is tall with long, black hair, and violet eyes. She is here tonight, but arrived wearing black leather. Perhaps she changed her clothing."

He looked back over at the woman talking with the DJ. She didn't look like she could be as evil as the Russian in Peru had indicated. Then again, she was wearing a mask. And if his past was any indication, he sucked at discerning women.

The woman glanced over her shoulder in his direction and he said, "Her eyes are blue, not violet," grimacing internally at Caroline's closeness to his body.

Within his ear canal Knightley finally made communication.

"Iceman, we're getting a strange audio transmission from the club. Are you sure, we don't have a sleeper or any of Caroline's contacts within wearing a wire?"

Darcy fixed his mask, bringing his diamond, snake cufflink up closer to his mouth. "What kind of transmission?"

"Some southern woman with a cheating husband."

"Probably, a cell tower's cross signal transmission. Don't disregard it entirely. Just monitor it. Listen, I need you to get Crash on the line, patch him through. We had to give up our cell phones when we entered."

"Copy that."

The bartender approached Caroline and Darcy and bent offering a tray of sparkling champagne flutes.

"My, aren't you handsome," Caroline cooed.

He replied with an obvious fake French accent. *"Merci beaucoup."*

"Tell me, is Nadya here tonight? We were supposed to meet for our little ménage, and I haven't seen her."

"I'm not at liberty to identify a patron by name, particularly during tonight's masquerade, but if you are referring to the spider woman, she's here but hardly frequents the bar area."

Darcy raised an eyebrow at the moniker "spider woman" and thought to himself, *Thank God she's not called snake woman. One of those in my life is more than enough.* He noted how the bartender's eyes scanned over Caroline's gold lame sheath dress when he delivered a much-appreciated passive-aggressive insult. Iceman wanted to chuckle aloud.

"*Pardonne-moi*, but you don't seem her type. She enjoys exotic spices, but ginger has little appeal to her." The bartender's attention drew to the red bustier and the spilling tops of the woman taking her place beside the pole. "She prefers the hot, spicy curves of the red cayenne pepper."

He moved the tray over to Darcy. "I would think that is your taste as well, *monsieur*, no?"

Darcy smirked following the man's gaze. "Yes, it is." His vision remained locked on the beauty whose shapely back was turned to him. Her black, gloved hand caressed the pole suggestively as though grasping and sliding up and down his manhood.

He couldn't help the involuntary reaction in his groin when he hardened at the sight, recalling Liz in the bathroom after her return to Pemberley last week. That day when her hand wrapped around him, teasing him until he nearly burst, precipitated hot, wild sex that lasted for hours until exhausted and satiated. Even now, the thought of his wife caressing him firmly and watching that woman do the same to the pole, made him physically uncomfortable in the tight confines of his trousers. He shifted his weight, resting his ankle upon his knee.

The bartender's lips twisted slyly, and he moved on to the next table.

Caroline nuzzled Darcy's ear, sliding her hand below his suit jacket.

His arousal immediately softened.

She pretended to purr lustful words, "We should look for the objective. Damn, I wish I had that compact Bennet made for us. I could locate her, get a fingerprint, run an identity check and track her every footstep back to Julia Bertram and Diablo."

Cringing at the feel of Caroline's talons against his pectoral, he growled, "Don't. Touch. Me. like that," and she removed her hand from his nipple.

The DJ spoke into the mic wrapped around his head. "Ladies and gentleman, I give you the exotic Floria."

With the exception of the flickering candles around perimeter of the room and a dim, recessed beam above the pole, the lights in the room extinguished. Only a single, red glowing bulb shined down upon the stage. The color of deep cayenne lit the striking beauty who shared the heroine's name from the opera *Tosca*. Floria was the jealous lover prepared to do anything for the man of her heart.

The DJ spun the seductive, bluesy sound of violins to Nina Simone's "I Put a Spell on You."

Darcy's attention drew, once again, to the alluring goddess on the small stage who circled the pole with long, slow, deliberate sashays, and foot drags. One hand remained at her grinding hip while the other continued to smooth up and down upon the pole, gloved fingers caressing shiny, red-tinged silver.

She stopped with her back facing him when the keys of the piano tinkled. All he could see of her face was a masked profile in the silhouette of the roux light. The glow to her bare skin seemed to radiate sex from every pore. The champagne no longer appealed to him, and he licked his lips thinking of Liz's sweet nectar and how whenever she climaxed upon his suckling mouth, it was a delectable rush of ambrosia.

When the first sensuous, claiming lyrics rang out about captivation and ownership, "Floria" slowly rotated her hips, charming him. He was unable to tear his eyes away from the curves of her figure enhanced by that provocative movement. He thought of Liz again and the figure eights her hips slowly employed when she sat upon him.

16

Confrontations

The fact that Knightley sat in the van awaiting intelligence while Caroline sat to Darcy's right and both of them were on a mission to find Nadya had absolutely no importance in Darcy's mind at the moment. The burlesque stripper "Floria" dancing and clinging to the metal pole before him had garnered all his attention. The powerful blues lyrics were made even more provocative by the way she moved to them. Clearly, she felt the song.

Every sensual motion she made under the red spotlight left him spellbound and feeling immensely guilty. It frustrated him every time he came close to glimpsing her masked face when it emerged from the shadow, only to abruptly turn before he could view those inviting lips and beguiling beauty mark of hers. Everything about her made him yearn for Liz and it taunted him.

The swing of her sparkling, gold chandelier earrings seemed familiar, but he couldn't put his finger on the recollection. It was a small detail lost when Floria raised one gloved arm high above her head, spread her fingers then lowered her body with a swivel to her hips—knees bent to black and red stilettos to the seductive saxophone. It was as though she was sliding down onto his hardness, especially when both her hands clasped the pole, gliding up and down.

Like the song lyrics, she had put a spell on him. He shifted uncomfortably in his seat.

"Harrumph" from beside him alerted him to the fact that he was being watched, made obvious when Caroline's hand traveled up his thigh. She leaned toward him, dropping kisses to his neck, but he quickly captured her nearly grabbing fingers before they reached the now fully erect, nine-inch booty she sought. He surmised she knew the state of his flaming arousal because his eyes never left the burlesque dancer's each and every hip rotation.

"I'm leaving," Caroline stated in a huff. "If you're not going to do the job we came for then I will. I'm going in search of Nadya. Too much is at stake to sit idle because of your base instincts."

Darcy grunted in reply, pleased for her imminent departure. What he wanted to say, but dismissed when his vision locked on Floria's hand sliding down her now outstretched leg, was *You wouldn't mind that base instinct if it was directed at you, viper.*

Before rising from the booth, Caroline's venomous words spewed. "I'm sure your little woman at home would be curious to learn of your philandering nature."

"I'm sure, she'd be quite pleased to know that my condition is only because I'm imagining *her* beneath me—not anyone else and certainly not you."

He snickered when she rose in a huff and quit the room.

Floria rose as well, twisting her hips until she stood legs apart, her back to him. A coquettish glance over her shoulder at him stopped his heart. She puckered those pouty lips he had admired when she had walked past him toward the stage. Was that kiss directed to him, he wondered. He already felt as though she danced for him because even her seductive body movements were in his direction, each swivel exacting their explosive toll on him.

She bent at the waist, giving him the full expanse of her raised derriere, her gloved hand encircling the champagne flute waiting for her on the platform, bubbles rising in the roux lighting.

Floria stood with delicate fingers wrapped around the glass. She raised it to her welcoming lips that kissed the crystal. Even that did things to him as he admired the muscles move in her slender neck as she drank. This was a provocative, suggestive act of fellatio. She was making love to the glass, grasping it, taking all of its contents into her mouth. *My God!*

He smoothed his hand down his thigh and uncrossed his legs, his arousal near explosive levels.

The stripper sashayed around the pole before placing the flute back on the floor. To the saxophone riff, she reached around her back, slowly unzipping the skirt in time with the music.

The black satin dropped, pooling at her high heels, and he drank in the fullness of her bottom. The familiarity of her curves encased in black lace and red satin panties were uncannily identical to his wife. The alluring lace-topped thigh high stockings were nearly his undoing. The glimpse of flesh below the hiking edge of her panties caused a physical response. That exposed delicate slope of her bottom had him licking his lips and clenching his hand. To his complete mortification, he was fighting the urge to touch himself, so filled with hunger for his wife.

The stripper turned to face him, and Darcy drank in her full hips. He watched as her pointed toes wrapped around the fabric lying on the floor and with a seductive snap of her leg, she sent the skirt flying toward him. Sliding across the floor, it landed at his feet.

The listening device, settled deep within his ear canal, beeped snapping him from his fantasy—more like memories, and his near salacious reaction to do something he hadn't done in years.

Charlie spoke as soon as Darcy tapped the receiver.

"She's gone, Iceman. Liz isn't here."

He sat upright, looking away from the tempting woman who now lifted her knee to straddle the pole.

"Um … I'm sorry, Darce. It didn't take much coercion to extract the truth from Janie. That woman's a sucker for oral sex. One lick and she's spilling the truth like the Exxon Valdez. The two of them played me like a fool."

"What happened? Where is she?"

"Um … where are you?"

"You know where I am. Where. Is. Liz?"

"Well, she's *there*, too."

Darcy's head snapped to the woman doing perfect body rolls. *That* enticing movement, she didn't realize, moved her bustier, exposing the gorgeous snake and orchid tattoo on her hip. His name written in the tribal skin of the viper stared back at him. He snickered then his face darkened when he realized that *his wife* was dancing and stripping in the most notorious fetish BDSM club in Paris! *What is she doing here? And why is she dancing like this for strangers!? Oh God, is she cheating?*

Coldly the Iceman replied, "Right. Thanks. I found her. Gotta go."

"Don't you want to kno—"

There was nothing Charlie could tell him that could make her deception acceptable. He disconnected the call with a tap to his ear, his face burning with anger at all the conclusions he was jumping to.

He knew he had to regain control of the situation, but after a long minute of debate, he found himself torn. Unsure whether he should run to her, cover up her half-naked body and scold at her for doing exactly what he told her not to do—leave Pemberley—or sit back and enjoy her performance and later give her a tongue lashing worth giving because that's what he damn well needed to do. Unable to stop himself from chuckling, he shook his head in wonderment. All this time, he had been lusting over his wife! *Damn she is good. The perfect femme fatale. She must be drunk; she would never do this otherwise.* His girl couldn't hold her alcohol, but to do this?

He settled back in the sofa for a moment thinking this through carefully. Sure, he was madder than blazes, infuriated actually, but he couldn't deny the fact that he was happy Liz was here. This intoxicating masquerade of hers was highly titillating and, in truth, he wanted to watch her dance some more for him. He wondered if she knew it was him. After all, he was wearing a mask and as far as she knew, he was in Peru, caring for Rick. Suddenly his heart sank with the overwhelming reality of why she was there, obsessing him as he sat there watching her move against the pole. *Is she cheating? Had she left her ho-hum life at Pemberley for adventure, just as her mother had?*

Liz watched Darcy's shadow from the corner of her eye. She couldn't believe she was actually stripping before all these strangers, but truly there was no one in the room but her and her husband. She focused solely on him and occasionally noticed in the dim light the way he tugged at his collar. With heady, intoxicated euphoria, she knew she was succeeding in undoing him. Caroline had fled in a huff, and he had uncrossed his legs and shifted his weight repeatedly. Liz knew her husband well enough to surmise that he strained uncomfortably. She thought she even saw him touch himself when she flung her skirt in his direction.

She was so turned on that she was sure this dance would end with them having sex on that sofa just like the couple on the other side of the room. He'd forget Caroline in a heartbeat when she held him in her arms. She'd *make* him forget.

Toward the end of the song, Darcy rose and purposefully walked to the DJ. As he passed her in the dim red glow, she slightly bent her legs, pushed out her backside and extended one leg out with toes on the floor. She reached her arm out, rotating her hand and fingers with a come hither invitation to him, but he ignored her.

Now she was curious, and her heart rate sped up, wondering if he wasn't interested after all. Panic nearly set in, and the lightheadedness she felt from the alcohol and music had taken its toll on her reason and logic.

She rose, turned with a shimmy to her spilling breasts and noticed how the DJ smiled at Darcy, placing a record on the turntable. Gotan Project's "Epoca" tango began to play. Her heart nearly stopped. Was even their tango something he shared with others? She immediately wondered if he knew it was her after all, especially when he stood before her in the middle of the dance floor, one hand clutching his hip, the other outstretched to her. What was visible of his expression told her nothing. She had seen this set to his lips many times. It was his Iceman persona, and the silver of his Venetian mask seemed to enhance the coldness rolling off him.

In time with the music, she seductively stepped from the stage into her husband's firm embrace.

Immediately, the connection was made not only between their upper bodies but also between their souls. She felt it instantly, that intense feeling of coming home, that electrifying synapse that only being next to Darcy charged to life in her. Liz hoped he felt it, too. Hoped and prayed he would come to see that his presence at the club with Caroline was all wrong. She hoped he would be filled with regret and longing for *her* instead.

Nevertheless, the question remained in the back of her mind. *Does he know it's me, or is he perusing yet another? The tango was what wooed me when first we met.*

At first, he led her with long glides in a close tango frame with his pelvis against hers. His erection enflamed her all the more. The music flowed within their souls, wrapping a spell over their cocoon of intimacy. Their masked eyes remained locked through small apertures until he turned her in a promenade under his arm.

Darcy smiled slightly at how far Liz had come in her dance skill and how this masquerade of hers was so well suited to the tango. "Floria, as in *Tosca?*" he asked.

Her southern accented reply surprised him. "You know your opera, darlin'. Yes, Floria—a woman prepared to do whatever is necessary."

Knightley listened within the van at the exchange, assuming that Darcy had found Nadya, now surprised by the familiar accent from the earlier transmission.

Darcy guided Liz across the floor, his forehead pressed against hers. Their legs brushed one another in heated friction to the seductive staccato beat, both of which were in unison with the sound of his heart. He pulled her closer to him. "Prepared to do anything? Such as a striptease?"

She ignored the question. "Is that your wife with you tonight?"

"No, my *obedient* wife is back home in the States."

"Obedient? Or y'all just assume she's a trusting fool?"

Liz left his hold, ran her gloved hand down the side of his masked face, then sensually circled him. At his back, she leaned into his ear, draping an arm over his shoulder. With grazing wine-colored lips upon his lobe she purred, "Hmm, you're quite the libertine."

She continued to circle him with an inviting caress across his shoulders until he finally grabbed her back into their tango frame.

Liz looked away, unable to meet his searing gaze as her legs kicked and hooked between his with rapidity.

"Does my wanting you make me a libertine?"

"This club, three women, and that cocky swagger of yours does."

He smoothed his hand down her suddenly raised knee resting upon his hip, smirking as he enjoyed the feel of the silky thigh under his palm. His dark eyes stared through her blue contacts, searching for the hazel irises of Liz Darcy—not this masked Floria. "There's only one woman for me and that's *you*. You're stunning perfection."

Their lips stilled a hair's breath away from touching, and he felt the warmth of her gentle pant upon his when she said, "And what of that cold-lookin' redhead? Clearly, shu-ga, you're cheatin' on your wife already."

He turned Liz quickly, bringing her back flush against his chest. They stood in the center of the dance floor halted, one of her arms raised; her hand clutched the back of his head with spread fingers. Surrounded by flickering candlelight, their reflection looked back at them from a mirror at the edge of the dance floor.

A tilt of her chin brought upturned lips to his; he resisted the urge to consume them. His wife's orchid fragrance was tantalizing and he struggled against its captivating siren call. No. He needed to play her game, live in her fantasy awhile longer and find out why she was there. He was simultaneously intrigued and heartbroken. Was she there to meet her lover or to find a new one?

His spread fingers slid provocatively down the satin and lace of her slender waist. Brazenly, his tongue glided over her top lip before whispering, "The redhead is no one, and lusting after you is *not* cheating on my wife. What of you? Are you cheating on a husband?"

Eyes locked in the reflection of the mirror, his hips pressed against her bottom as his hand descended to her panties, ready for exploration. Her head dropped back against his shoulder and he was overcome by the vision of her closed eyes and expression of pure rapture when his index finger brushed over her panties.

"Yesss," she answered with a throaty moan, and he was confused if it was in response to his touch or in answer to his question. But when she arched her back against his chest, tilting her pelvis to encourage his tease, he knew.

"I want you," he seduced in a husky moan, moving his hip again. "Now. Come with me to a boudoir." His voice dropped to barely a whisper before nibbling the curve of her ear. "I want you hard, and I want to make you scream in ecstasy."

He saw her lip quiver when she moved from his embrace but even in her dismay, her hand slid down his chest to his arousal. Darcy nearly groaned aloud when she caressed him, clutching around the girth and gently squeezed.

Her eyes searched his, and he knew that he couldn't continue toying with her like this. He took his wife into a firm hold, his splayed hand traveled down over the laces of the bustier to the small of her back, and it was then that he felt the small pistol. With one foot back, he executed rock steps, their bodies moving in shared weight with slow back and forth rhythm. Terror struck his heart in anticipation of her answer. Could he withstand hearing the truth from her lips? He must. He had no choice. His voice almost trembled when he asked, "Why are you here, Lakmé? Because you want to cheat?—maybe with Wentworth?"

Stunned, Liz's body went rigid in his arms. Her chin dropped.

She wanted to cry, promptly biting her lip in an attempt to keep her emotions in check in this masquerade's finale. Relief washed over her— her husband *knew* her. But even that knowledge could not prevent her words from sounding meek and wounded; the need for anger and bravado in this gambit no longer existed. "Went ... worth? I'd never cheat ... never ... I came to catch *you* in the act."

What?

Unsuccessfully, she tried to leave his embrace but Darcy grabbed both her wrists, turning her around with a snap. He pulled her into him as he continued to dance her across the floor with basic tango steps and slow circular footsteps at each pause of their movement. Liz's forehead burned hot under his gently deposited kiss. "I'm hurt, baby. You came all this way because you don't trust me. *I* would *never* do that to you?"

"Then why are you here with *her*?" Her voice cracked, and she turned her face from his searing, dark eyes, her own now pooled with tears. "I heard you on the phone with her. I heard everything."

Their bodies circled one another's although they remained touching with hands, eyes, and hearts locked. His heart broke seeing and hearing her pain but now was not the time for consoling or reassuring. At that moment, their trust in each other was tenuous, at best. The romantic music surrounding them belied their emotions. He sighed deeply. "You only heard one side of the conversation. I needed her cover and contacts for Operation Macarena. Bertram's daughter has been kidnapped by the same people who had kidnapped Rick. The trail led here."

"Then why did you lie to me?"

He gently pushed her away, directing her into a rapid turn before grabbing her back into his embrace to execute a corte. His voice was practiced control and anger. "To protect you, Liz. Why else would I not tell you everything? But again, you refused to listen to me in your usual obstinacy. Further, you didn't trust my professional judgment. And now you're smack in the middle of danger, just where I didn't want you! This is Monte Carlo all over again!"

"You're right, but you didn't trust me enough to tell me! A marriage is two people—remember? You shut me out!" she angrily snapped, the alcohol giving free reign to her pent-up emotions letting them run their course.

Damn. She was right about that. He had shut her out time and again. "Did you steal Caroline's Obsidian watch?"

She ignored him.

"Where's the wire?"

By the set of her mouth, it was clear to him she wasn't going to answer anything, especially when she turned her head away from his glare. He wondered if her furrowed brow at his question meant that she didn't know she was wearing one.

"Did you take the dangerous contents of her camo case from my safe?"

She looked away in the other direction and bit her lip.

Again, he sighed, lunging back into another corte dance step. "We need those things, particularly that pistol you have tucked under your bustier. What else do you have? What is pressed against my hip?"

"Nothing!"

"This isn't the time for your petulance, Liz. Look, we're tracking a target, a woman named Nadya Karakurt."

Darcy released her, and in response to his information, she rotated her body then slid her leg down his, seductively wrapping it around his calf. A knowing quirk appeared on those kissable lips of hers.

"Nadya? Then it's a good thing that I continue to defy you because I *know* Nadya and *know* where to find her tonight. She's not going anywhere until morning. In fact, she's probably tied to some bedpost as we speak. And there is nothing more than a compact under my corset. Well … and maybe a derringer, too." She kissed him full on the lips before he could say anything in reply. Their mouths crashed in consuming heat, exploding in pent up desire in the middle of the dance floor.

They didn't wait for the music to end. Darcy entwined his fingers with hers and led her decisively from the dance floor. Trailing behind him, teetering in her four inches, she had just enough time to scoop up her skirt from the floor as they hurried by. "Where are we going?"

"You started this."

"Where are you taking me?"

"You'll see."

She smiled at how his Iceman persona had delivered short sentences of focused reply. It was like the night in Seville when he made love to her for the first time in the gazebo. Yeah, she knew what was on his mind. Lord knows, she felt it press against her hip when they had danced.

Darcy spoke into his cufflink as they made their way across the crowded room of lovers and would-be lovers. "Mr. Clean, the target is here, but we've got a blowback. I'm going dark for about thirty minutes, but keep your listening surveillance on Viper."

"Well, that's sort of an insane situation right now. Currently, she's being whipped by some Swede whom she keeps referring to has Thor, the god of lightning orgasms."

"What?"

"You heard me."

"Has she been burned?"

"Not literally, but that may be next. That crazy bitch would enjoy it though."

Darcy chuckled. "Well, keep an ear on her to make sure she's safe. I have something urgent to attend to." He looked back at Liz's deep merlot lips and the beauty mark on her chin. "Apparently my wife, the provocateur, had decided to set a honey trap for me."

"Yeah, so I heard—and saw. Damn if I don't hate that camo camera of yours. Did you find out where her wire is?"

"No, but I will."

"All right, copy that. You've got thirty minutes of audio and visual silence, any longer and I'm coming in there hot, guns blazing."

For purely protocol purposes, Knightley resisted the urge to keep the listening device feed from Darcy's cufflinks and Liz's hidden wire transmitting, but he switched them and the camera off knowing what would follow. The last thing he wanted to hear or see was another man screwing a beautiful woman. It was bad enough he had to listen to Caroline's pants and moans, but he knew he'd be screwed if two women were panting inside his ear canal. That was more than any sexually starved man could take. Mr. Clean couldn't help thinking how he consistently got the shit end of every job. Operation Macarena: reduced to a voyeur sitting in a van with a hard on for Iceman's wife.

With masks still in place, they exited the main room into a pitch-black hallway lined with more dungeons. Not even a candle flickered from a wall sconce or candelabra. Thin red lines bled from under each door's threshold but did nothing to offer illumination. That didn't stop Darcy in his determination to find a suitable location to make love to his wife. Every door was unlocked, and he opened each with unabashed shame, revealing provocative, kinky acts within. Perversely, they only served to fuel his appetite for the expressions of love he and his wife shared. Being there with her was not only extremely arousing in its own right, but also the opportunity to experience something new and erotic with her was even more exciting. Moreover, he had to seize the opportunity to show her the depths of his love.

Open elevator doors at the end of the hall beckoned, and he could see the wall sconce within flickering in seductive invitation. He continued to pull her gently behind him toward the light and the moment the doors closed, he was all over her, barely restrained from tearing the remaining lingerie from her body. One of her hands tugged at his necktie, the other grasped the back of his head, pulling it toward the tops of her breasts.

His lips branded her neck with nibbles turning into full-fledged bites seeking to taste and devour. "I am yours, Liz. Only yours," he murmured. His right hand traveled, once again, to her heat where two fingers entered, immediately finding that sensitive spot deep within. She responded. Moans and mews of ecstasy were her aria, and he desired nothing more than to love her fully right there.

Spurred on by the champagne, the salacious environment, and the masquerade play they had continued off the dance floor, Darcy's words of lovemaking weren't his usual endearments—rather they were scandalous and raw words he used only when he was feeling absolutely naughty. They turned her on all the more.

With her back pressed against the elevator wall, she panted, on the verge of releasing him into her hand when suddenly the elevator doors slid open and a wave of whimsical music and French lyrics greeted them.

They froze in a shocking position, but given where they were, it was tame. He could have bent her over and screwed her right there and no one would have batted an eye. Both chuckled at the lighthearted, playful song filling the hallway as though they had arrived in a Quentin Tarantino movie.

He groaned then chuckled. "C'mon, Floria, my possessive wife, let's find a room."

They exited the elevator into a dimly red-lit hallway. Long tables lined velvet-covered walls displaying candelabras, champagne, and bowls of condoms neatly arranged for boudoir patron usage. Liz stopped before a door surrounded by ornate gold molding.

"What's the matter?" he asked, nearly bursting, not able to wait a moment longer.

She hated to say it but after all that champagne it was inevitable. "I have to pee."

A deep chuckle preceded the release of her hand. "I'll wait *right here.*"

"You better, darlin'."

She started for the door when Darcy abruptly blurted, "Liz?"

She turned, smiling at the endearing quirk to his mouth. The hallway swayed slightly in her intoxication.

"Hurry back," was all he said before winking at her.

17

Bondage

Hot pink and gold accents were juxtaposed against hard, black granite but the look of the luxurious restroom was strangely harmonious and feminine. A long vanity, surrounded by a decorative, antique-styled triptych mirror, lined one wall where candles flickered and reflected in the dim ambient light, but Liz didn't take the time to explore or admire. Dizzy from the bubbly, she quickly ducked into a commode stall, anxious to get in and get out. Beside her, a toilet flushed and a woman hummed.

Seconds later, she exited, freezing at the door. An unmasked Nadya sat at the vanity beside a damask pink and black chaise. Gold chains and cuff shackles hung from the wall above, just in case anyone wanted to "play" in the *toilettes des femmes*. Her heart thundered with panic at the sight of the Russian dragging the bristles of a black cosmetic brush down the length of her neck. Suddenly, any bravado Liz had about *anything* ceased to exist. With the effects of the alcohol in full-force, she began to panic; she felt a full-blown anxiety attack coming on when faced with the dangerous woman her husband was in this club to capture, follow—or worse. Rendered immobile with fear and unsure what to do, she continued to wash her hands over the crystal bowl sink. In her mind, she rapid-fired several knee-jerk responses: yell for Darcy, run, or stay and play it off as coolly as she could until she could call for her husband.

The woman's face lit up when she recognized her in the reflection of the mirror. "You look as intoxicating as I imagined. Red and black against voluptuous curves of your body are highly arousing." Nadya rose, walking to her saying something in Russian that she did not understand but the gleam in her made it clear.

Why Liz suddenly felt embarrassed by the outfit she wore was beyond her, but she smiled sheepishly at the appraising gaze of this villainous femme.

A form-fitting black leather bodysuit exposed the woman's full breasts by a sheer *v*, which extended downward to a point, revealing a small patch of pubic hair. A leather, silver-studded collar encircled her slender neck. Nadya's shiny red lips curled into a satisfied smile when she noted her stare upon her body. "You like vhat you see. I can tell."

Liz looked away from the object of her curiosity, considering, for just a moment to remove the small pistol from under the back of her bustier, but instead removed the compact from under the front, so sure that in her drunkenness the woman could easily disarm her of the weapon. She nervously began to tap her nose with the soft pad covered in powder.

"Hi Nadya. That's … that's an incredible outfit."

Fitzwilliam's prey stood beside her in front of the floor length mirror, and she couldn't deny how stunning she was. She smelled of sex and musk coupled with the heady aroma of the roses rising from four crystal vases upon the sink's countertop.

"You came to find me, *da?*"

"I um, came to find an empty boudoir."

Nadya smoothed her hand across Liz's décolletage; Liz's panic reached a near crescendo.

"Beautiful. Are you having a good time, *lapushka?* Are your nerves soothed by flowing champagne and beautiful men and women, or are you in search of *right* partner to initiate you?"

"I am having quite a night. My ... I did meet someone, and he's waiting for me outside the door."

"Perhaps he will join us." She ran her black crop up Liz's leg sliding over her small panties to tickle and rub her sex from front to back as the crop slid over her apex. "Is he dangerous?"

"Yes ... very." She reminded herself that a wrong move could mean death. It was bad enough that the room was starting to spin, but she held her cringe inside, poker face in place. If her husband had been the one enacting this, it would have been highly erotic, but she felt repulsed watching Nadya's nipples harden as her tongue slowly slid over her top lip. Regretful for leaving her skirt on the elevator floor, Liz stammered, tightening her grasp on the compact. "I'm not ready for that yet ... but thank you, Nadya."

"Vhat a shame we are not in my private dungeon back in Russia. My cottage has special toys for your pleasure," she cooed, continuing her seduction, ignoring Liz's polite decline. "Abandon your confining conscience. Both you and your dangerous playmate will enjoy yourselves in the Libertine Room."

Liz panted, her body betraying her in her drunken state. "I can't."

The dominatrix retracted the crop, smiled, then removed the compact from Liz's grip, depositing her thumbprint on the mirrored interior when she clutched it in her hand to admire her lipstick.

In the van on Rue Thérèse, the silent, inactive laptop computers came alive before Knightley. Lines of intelligence and photographs flashed before his eyes on the small monitors. Immediate identification from Interpol, France's DGSE, America's Homeland Security, and NSA. Finally, the world's largest fingerprint database in the world, the IAFIS, confirmed what all the others laid out, *someone's* fingerprint was Valentina Donkova, former high-level bio engineer for the Russian Federation. Specialty: biological toxins and entomological warfare. Wearing a white lab coat, the brilliant woman was knock-out gorgeous and lethal.

Liz took the compact from Nadya, her eyes drawing to the chains upon the wall over the settee. She stammered. "Actually, Nadya ... I've been trying … um to visualize something one of the patrons talked about downstairs. Could I … um… try it on you?"

In the van, Knightley activated audio and visual transmission with Darcy, bracing himself for what he would hear and see on the other end. Apart from the French music, he heard nothing but saw the red hallway and the bowls of condoms through the button camera as the Iceman paced back and forth.

"Of course, *lapushka*. What is your heart's desire?" Nadya replied, a tell-tale twinkle lighting her eyes.

Liz pointed to the golden cuffs dangling from the wall, momentary clarity overcoming her. "Can I try my hand at bondage?"

Nadya laughed. "I am good teacher—and sub. Chains and whips bring me most pleasure and I am sure you will find the power of bondage highly satisfying. Follow me to settee and I will demonstrate."

Knightley spoke in measured breath. "Iceman, sorry to break radio silence but for some strange reason my computers are flooded … we've got identification and a shitload of intel on *someone*, and it's all coming in from fingerprint analysis. I don't know how or where it's originating, but we've hit the mother lode. What's going on?"

"I have no idea," Darcy said. "What's the name?"

"Valentina Donkova specializes in neurotoxic spider peptides and biological warfare for the Russians."

"Black hair? Violet eyes?"

"Yep. Drop-dead gorgeous. Is this Karakurt?"

"Could be. They call her spider woman."

"Where's Liz?"

"She's in the ladies' room." … *and has a compact. Caroline's fingerprinting one from the case?*

Knightley turned on the audio transmission from whatever was feeding her wire. "Let me patch her audio feed to you."

Within his ear canal, Darcy heard a seductive Russian voice loud and clear, up close, and too personal for comfort. The woman said, "That is it. Very good. See, bondage is powerful feeling. I am near climax feeling so helpless to your control. Would you like to use crop?"

A chill ran up Darcy's spine. Iceman fell back in place; a dark shroud covered his masked countenance.

"Get Viper. I'm going in for visual confirmation. Upon facial recognition, forward the intel to Charlie then prepare for immediate extraction of the target."

"Copy that."

Within seconds Darcy entered the restroom, eyes flashing but demeanor calm. Panic wouldn't help Liz, only quiet restraint. One false move and this woman could hurt his beloved if put on the defensive.

The door swung closed and he stopped abruptly in his steps. The image before him caused a wry half-smile. Violet eyes filled with passion: Nadya laid wrists and ankles bound on the settee, her legs spread wide with Liz standing beside her, holding a black crop.

"Pardon me, I didn't mean to interrupt your foreplay but I've been waiting for you, Floria," he said, gaze traveling down to the spider tattoo on the woman's foot. Yes, his girl had skills.

Knightley said, "Yup, that's her."

"Is this what they call you, *lapushka*, Floria?"

"Yeah." She dropped the crop, then slid the pistol from its hiding place. "It's my role play name."

Darcy could tell she was nervous, her hand shook when she pointed the derringer at the Russian. He walked toward Liz and winked slyly but allowed her to continue to hold the weapon, knowing that she'd feel safer with it.

"So this is how it is, *da*? You are not so innocent in the ways of sadomasochism after all."

Liz shrugged a shoulder. "Looks can be deceiving, *dorogaya.*"

She looked up at him and his heart thundered, not because he was facing this evil woman, but because Liz was here to see what he was going to do to her. It pained him that she'd be witness to the vicious side of him.

"Do you know who I am?" he asked, his voice razor sharp.

A slow smile spread on Nadya's lips. "Take off that mask. Let me see."

"I'd rather not."

"You would like to play. I like it rough."

"I like it rough, too, but not like you think. I quite enjoy torture. By the way, your Ruskie friend in Peru sent me to tell you good-bye before I put a bullet between his eyes and blew up his coca field."

Now enlightened, she laughed. "I wondered what happened to Ivan. He never misses play time." She examined him up and down, eyes narrowing when they met his. "I had feeling you would come for me, Iceman, but did not think you would arrive with such alluring plaything."

"She's not with me, just some toy I picked up for the night. For an exchange of favors, she's suddenly in my employ."

Instinctively, Liz pressed the barrel against the woman's temple, her brows furrowing, her lips drawn to a thin line clearly frightened for him. God, he felt proud in that moment. She was so brave.

"Floria likes it rough, too," he added, folding his arms and towering over the prone figure. The woman's sex and breasts stared up at him, but it did nothing for him. "I'd like for you to tell me where Julia Bertram is."

"She is inconsequential to Diablo. It is you he wants. He will hunt you and your family until his revenge is satiated."

"News flash—he won't catch me." He fought the urge to glance at Liz, afraid he would give her up. "And I have *no* family. I'm a lone wolf and his worst nightmare. Look, if you want to play this game, I can make you talk, *Valentina*."

"You have done your homework. And what will you use?—that power between your legs to make my mouth move or vill you beat me into submission with it?" Dilated pupils locked on his loin and both Nadya and Darcy were taken aback when Liz immediately raised her arm and in one fell swoop pistol whipped the side of the spider woman's head, knocking her out cold.

"That's my husband, *bitch*," she hissed to the unconscious woman then lost her balance.

Darcy caught her arm before either the gun went off or she fell onto the hot pink carpet. "What the—?"

Liz pulled off her mask with frustration. "I'm sorry, Fitzwilliam, but your questions were getting tedious. Sheesh. Is this what it takes to get stone-cold silent Iceman talking? Besides, I'm sick of women fawning all over you, commenting on your sexual prowess, staring at your carinatus. It fucking grates on my fucking nerves."

"You just swore … twice. How drunk *are* you?"

She snorted. "Drunk enough. It must have been that last glass of champagne. I think it sent me over the edge."

"Yeah. I know what you mean. Your performance with that glass sent me over the edge, too."

The ladies' room door swung open revealing Caroline. She stopped in her tracks, stunned by the sight before her as a snippet of another whimsical French song breached the room. Both Darcy and Liz gaped at her askew hair and the red welts upon her neck.

"About damned time, Medusa."

"Oh goody! The not-so-perfect little woman is here. And I see she has my derringer … and beauty mark. Thief, just like your father."

He was about to say something—or plunge his fist into her face, but Liz beat him to the punch.

"Shut up, Caroline. And for the record … keep your grubby ninja hands off my husband if you know what's good for you. You can't have him back!"

Darcy's head snapped to his wife. *Shit! She knows.*

"The Iceman and what he's packing is too much for a simple country girl like you to handle," Caroline spat back.

"Don't be so convinced of that. I'm sure he never made love to you while galloping on a stallion."

"No, we did it in *style* in my brother's Cessna numerous times."

The smug look on her face set Liz off. "Big deal! You wanna talk style? You never had sex in his new Spider Ferrari doing 75 around Catoctin Curve. Further, I get free and ready access to what he's *packing* 24/7!"

"A Ferrari? That's impossible!"

"Don't be so sure of that. I'm far more limber than you think and my husband is quite a *driver*."

"Ladies! I'm *right* here!"

Liz looked up at him, her eyes narrowed. Yeah. When they got home, hell was going to be unleashed. Caroline's fake laughter filled the room.

"Don't mock me, Viper. Not only is Iceman mine, but *I* just pistol whipped the villain while *you* were laying down on the job, obviously getting pistol whipped yourself! Looks like I'm the hero here." Liz raised her chin in absolute defiance. "Tell me, did the baby shit come off your sunglasses?"

"You're certifiable!" Caroline shouted.

His wife was ten sheets to the wind, schnockered, shit-faced, wasted. There was no way in hell she'd challenge a ninja master without a lot of Dutch courage coursing through her veins.

"Enough! We'll talk about this later. Liz, put the pistol down," he cautioned, guiding the barrel away from Caroline's direction until it was safely tucked under the corset again. He tapped his ear. "Knightley, the target's down. I need a diversion near the front door. We'll meet you in the back alley for extraction with the target."

"Copy that."

He looked over at the settee where Caroline stood at one side with Liz on the other, both unshackling the Russian, both shooting daggers at the other across her limp body.

"And we have ourselves a situation."

"So I heard. God, I love a cat fight, even if it is over you. If you ask me, Caroline has it coming."

"I fear I do, too." He glanced at his watch. "See you in four minutes and don't forget to fry our mobile phones still at the reception desk."

"Right. Oh, and thanks for that eye candy laying on the sofa. You are one cruel son of a bitch, man, tormenting me with a body like that."

"You'll see her in the flesh in a couple of minutes, but keep your hands to yourself."

He turned to the women, his voice low and stern. "If anyone asks, the three of you are going home with me to continue our little orgy. Your friend here has had a little too much to drink. Caroline, if she comes around, you know what to do."

"Yes I do."

"What will you do?" Liz asked, the venom in her tone suddenly gone, overridden by curiosity.

"A simple little pinch to the carotid artery works just fine. That should keep her lights out for about thirty minutes given her height and weight."

"Hmm, you'll have to teach me when we get back home," Liz replied, draping Nadya's arm over her shoulder.

Darcy was thankful that Caroline's only response was a snigger. Lessons definitely would *not* be continuing between these two.

Outside on Rue Thérèse, an explosion shook the old building. Car alarms filled the deserted street with ear-splitting wails. The overhead lights in L'Enclave suddenly burst on, illuminating the halls, exposing half-nude and all-nude patrons running from dungeons and boudoirs in panic, scattering like cockroaches exposed to light. A loud fire alarm pierced the air and emergency exit signs pulsed in the hall. Knightley had done well.

They dragged Nadya into the elevator.

As soon as the doors slid open on the first floor, the burly bouncer blocked their exit, his fists balled at his side. "*Arrête !,*" he commanded but his menacing order was met with Darcy's right hook. The man fell backward, but not down.

Again, no one expected Liz's fast movement. She brazenly removed the pistol then fired it in the direction of the thug.

Everything went dead from the immediate EMP pulse.

Silence.

Blackness.

The building's lights cut off when 400 joules shorted the electrical system. The alarm deadened and all emergency lights ceased. With the exception of trace candles burning down the hall, it was pitch and patrons ran wild, screaming.

"Did I do that?" Liz innocently asked.

"Yeah, baby. You did. Your father made it an EMP. Remind me to thank him when we get back home."

Another punch to the bouncer's jaw, laid him out like a rug.

"Gimme that," Caroline demanded, one hand trying unsuccessfully to pull the gun from Liz's grip.

"C'mon. We have to get out of here," Darcy said leading them through the club's main lounge—the den—the scene of Liz's erotic performance still backlit with the glow of red candles.

"Joe!" she called out to a bartender, much to Darcy's surprise.

"Hey, I see you got your man back and you found the spider woman. Guess that fabulous strip tease did the trick."

"It did, despite the bitch." She turned, eyes boring into Caroline's again. Darcy snorted.

"Great! You guys are going the wrong way. You have to exit the club out onto Rue Thérèse."

"We are leaving, but we need the back door. Can you tell us where it is? It's … it's important," she begged.

He nodded, giving them all the once-over. "Sure. Go down that hall, make a right into the kitchen. The door to the back alley will be on your left. Be careful."

She dropped Nadya's weight onto Caroline then walked to him, swiveling her hips. Darcy watched in silent submission as his wife kissed another man. "Thanks, Joe. For everything."

"The name's Tony."

"You're a sweetie, Tony." She kissed him again and Darcy cleared his throat, narrowing his eyes at her.

Again confirming that his girl—sober—could be quite the effective decoy. "We have to go, *Floria*," he groused.

"Oh Fitzwilliam, don't be jealous. I'm just thanking him properly." She yawned, and her gloved hand sleepily dragged across her eye.

Two minutes later in the cobblestone alley, he slid back the surveillance van's door and the girls dumped Nadya's sleeping body onto the metal floor.

"Close your mouth, Mr. Clean," Darcy said when Knightley's eyes fell on Liz's spilling bosom as she climbed in. He removed his suit jacket then placed it on his wife's shoulders before opening the front passenger door.

"Hi, John," she drowsily greeted, pushing her arms into the sleeves. She rested her head on the stool, sideways vision scanning the inert computer screens on the makeshift counter. She yawned again then closed her eyes, but held onto that pistol with her life. No one was getting that baby from her grasp. She'd taken a liking to handling a firearm.

"Hey, Liz. You were pretty bad ass in there," Knightley complimented turning in the driver's seat. "I like that EMP trick you pulled. How'd you manage to shackle Karakurt?"

Caroline huffed.

"Oh that was easy. Janie the kitty-killer would be so proud … these last 24 hours have really been exciting." She reached out, bracing herself on the floor. "Fitzwilliam, why is the van driving in circles?"

Darcy valiantly tried to maintain his serious mien, but how could he? They hadn't even started to drive and well … this was Liz, the love of his life, and she repeatedly broke his reserve. He'd never seen her this drunk before. She needed him. She'd done the unthinkable today and was now more vulnerable than ever. He climbed from the passenger seat and moved to the back of the van.

"Caroline, go sit up front."

"Yeah. Right. This is what I've been saying! She's a lightweight! She's even lost the camo communication beauty mark!"

Liz's hand flew to her chin.

"*That's* her wire?"

"Yeah. A little something her father made along with the hot pink photo intel sunglasses."

"Daddy? Oh I loved those. It was like looking through life with rose-colored glasses—until I glanced at you. Can I keep them?"

"No!" Caroline exclaimed.

Iceman's expression brooked no opposition and the viper finally switched seats, following a final pull of the cable zip tie around Nadya's bound wrists.

Sitting on the floor beside Liz, he wrapped her in his arms and kissed her head, supporting her body with his. "Now do you see why I couldn't take you with me?"

"Hmm… yes, but you smell so good. I like your new suit."

He smiled wryly. "Thank you. Now can I have the pistol?"

"No. I like guns after all. Honey, can we go home now?"

"Not yet, Liz. Soon. Right after I torture the spider woman."

"Good. She touched me inappropriately with her crop. Make her pay."

"What do you mean she touched you?" Caroline asked, surprised by this statement.

Liz yawned. "She's hot for me. She wants my bod."

A little sigh left Darcy's lips and he looked down at the Russian's still lifeless body beside them. It was going to be a long night. "Drive outside the city to Vincennes—The Zoo. We'll interrogate her there."

Knightley glanced over his shoulder. "No way. No one in their right mind would go there."

"Exactly."

"And what about the little woman?" Caroline sneered.

He kissed Liz's forehead again. She had passed out. "Don't worry about my wife. She's my sole responsibility, and she's coming with me whether you like it or not."

18

Safe House

The Obsidian safe house on U Street in Washington was the perfect place for Rick to covertly convalesce. No one but the team and Sarah knew of his return home. His Henry Tilney identification had served him well. With Bertram's corruption and treason, Obsidian couldn't be guaranteed of his silence to La Muerta Mundial—even if his daughter had yet to be rescued. He'd always hated that man, but took the jobs as they came, only pushing back on the ones he had a bad feeling about. How many of them had been legit hits? Were they all just assassinations to further Bertram's political or deceitful agenda? Sure, he knew Operation Cancan and Bennet's traitorous actions had been real, but he had disapproved of the political motives behind taking out *any* target—particularly an American citizen. What about some of the other ops? Mazurka, Polka, Tarantella?

Although it felt good to be back in his clothes, he still needed a haircut and his body ached. His broken ribs and cracked sternum made moving difficult, and even though the wounds to his head and arm were bandaged, infection was still present. IV antibiotics every eight hours was starting to piss him off, too. In other words, he was a mess, but thanked the powers above that Sarah had agreed to return to the States with him.

Her nursing skills and attentive care took away the sting of inactivity—*and she's cute, too.* He sat in the office, putting some order to his vacillating emotions. As he sipped a glass of Pinot Grigio, his thoughts were filled with worry for the team in Paris, as well as anger at having been used as the pigeon to draw Darcy out. He simultaneously felt elated that Sarah had the same attraction as he did, obvious by the kiss they shared when they'd landed at La Guardia Airport.

"This is an interesting apartment you have," she called out from the living room, her refined British accent washing over him. "Are you sure you live here?"

"Why do you ask?"

Her voice drew nearer. "It's just that there aren't any photographs or artwork. It's void of anything remotely personal. The place is nice, but cold and you're not a cold sort of bloke."

"I don't like clutter. How do you know that I'm not cold?"

"While your cousin is frozen, that Knightley fellow is chilly, but even in the worst of situations, you had a warm smile and kept your humor. You made me feel safe—in spite of my thinking you a twit. No, Rick, there's nothing cold about you."

He smiled, punched in a few numbers and letters on his laptop, then patched into the intel that Bingley had forwarded to him about this Valentina/Nadya Karakurt woman. The hairs at the back of his neck stood up when he read "binary biological warfare."

"Say, Sarah. Do you have a minute? I'd like to discuss something with you."

She turned the television off and when he glanced up she was standing in the doorway, shoulder rested against the frame. "Interview time?" she asked.

He chuckled. "No. Not yet. Is that the only reason you returned to Washington with me?"

"Of course not. You're my knight in shining armor. Playing nurse is the least I can do."

"You're serious?"

"No, silly. I came with you because … well, if that kiss in the plane didn't tell you why then I'll just have to give you another."

He cocked an eyebrow as she approached him with a saucy smile. Caroline's snug-fitting blue jeans clung to her hips and he resisted the urge to lick his top lip and pull her onto his lap. Her attractiveness was the complete opposite of Caroline's. Sarah was naturally pretty without make-up or hair dye. Unlike the viper's ice blue eyes, Sarah's were deep blueberry, bright and clear. She seemed to be a good person with a caring heart and was committed to exposing lies. This girl was his kind of woman, and the cast on her arm was the battle scar to prove it.

She bent down and deposited a soft, lingering kiss on his ready mouth. The feel of her supple flesh against his felt like coming home. Her left hand traveled through his hair when her lips parted against his, the kiss turning more expressive, her tongue touched his with unhurried strokes. Something in his stomach fluttered. *That* had never, ever happened, and the marine in him refused to acknowledge that he felt like a chick on a first date.

"Now do you know why I came with you?" she breathed.

"Too bad I'm too incapacitated to continue that kiss in another room."

"In due time, Rick. I'm not one to rush to bed."

"Good. I'd like to take it slow, discover each other. See if Great Britain and America can remain allies."

She smiled before giving him a peck on the lips. "What did you want to discuss with me?"

"Have a seat. I find myself in need of some help, and because of that, it means I am forced to tell you something about my team—my organization … off the record, of course. You might have information that could help us save someone's life."

"Your organization is clandestine, isn't it? Black ops for the American government? Maybe something like Blackwater?"

"No comment."

"And this is a safe house, right?"

He laughed. "You watch too much television."

"Then why can't I leave to get us a pizza across the street?"

"Because ... um, DC is dangerous?"

"Deny it all you like, but I'm good at what I do."

"If I didn't know that, I wouldn't need your assistance in this matter. Can I have your word that whatever I discuss with you, will remain in this room and not be sent to the *London Times*?"

She considered what he asked, then ran her hand down the side of her face, an index finger settling on her lips in thought. He knew he was asking a lot, but also knew that she'd be honest in her answer. Call it instinct or the fact that her kiss felt like none other, he knew he could trust her.

"Well, Rick, I'd like an honest answer to a few questions before I give you my word."

"I expected you'd have conditions. Okay, what's on your mind?"

"Back in the jungle, was I correct about Julia Bertram being the Director of the CIA's daughter who is in trouble?"

"Yes. She was kidnapped by the same cartel who took us. There is corruption involved and blowing the lid on that—right now—would be ugly before the girl is rescued."

"And Darcy and Knightley went to Paris to find her?"

"Yes. They have a lead from Peru. They're the extraction team, along with one other."

"Your girlfriend."

Shocked, he stopped typing. She was to the point.

"How ... how did you know?" he asked.

"I overheard your cousin on the telephone when I went to use the loo at the hospital in Peru."

"Yet you still came home with me knowing that I'm in a relationship?"

She sighed, and he took a sip of wine. "I did. Even with the little I know about you I have a feeling that you would not have flirted with me if there were anything meaningful between you and this Caroline. And judging from Darcy's end of the conversation ..." She looked away, stopping herself from completing the sentence.

"Yes?"

"Your girlfriend is interested in *him*—not you. I'd hardly consider that a relationship worth having ... or keeping."

"Like I said, you are good at what you do. She's been infatuated with him for quite some time, and I've been unhappy in that knowledge. Caroline is a good ... *team player*, but not good girlfriend material."

"Does his wife know?"

"That he's in Paris and working with her, given her feelings for him?"

She nodded.

"I'm sure he'll tell Liz after the fact. No sense in needlessly worrying her. They haven't been married very long."

"Right. Well, now that we addressed whose jeans I'm wearing ... I'm happy to give you my promise for secrecy. What can I tell you?"

He tossed a photograph of Diablo onto the desk. "We were handed zero intelligence on the whereabouts of Juan Sanchez-Morales, the head La Muerta Mundial. But perhaps you can shed some light on him. Have you discovered anything that could possibly be considered his home base of operations?"

"I wish I could help, but the man is an enigma even if he leaves a trail of death wherever he goes. Whether he's delivering the destruction himself or it's his henchmen, it's difficult to know." She picked up the slick image, examining it. "This is the first time I've seen him. He's frightening. Where did you get this?"

"An official with Peru's Interior Ministry just before we left the country. He wanted to help ... unofficially, of course."

"Hmm ... What I do know is that some of the cartel's traffic routes begin in Afghanistan to Moscow with shipments passing through the Ukraine, Prague, then finally Scotland, funneling down into London for wide distribution throughout England and Wales. But that's heroine. Coca production begins in Peru and Bolivia."

"That's quite a network. I wish we had this Intel early on, but our source had too much at stake to be honest. He claimed most of his contact was made through Morales's lieutenants."

"Yes. My sources have indicated that. A man such as Diablo, responsible for six percent of the Russian population being drug addicts from a $6 billion drug trade business in that country alone, will operate from the shadows."

"My team and I are operating on hunches and cold trails. The closest lead we have is through Valentina Donkova, a Russian bio chemist and lover to Diablo … in Paris."

"I haven't heard that name before, but women are a sure-fire way to get to the man."

"That's what we're hoping."

Shifting in her seat she considered another option then nodded. "I do have a 'friend,' someone heavily involved on the inside of the drug trade business, but he's only a valuable informant for the right amount of money. It's been a few months since I last heard from him, but I'll reach out, see what I can dig up." She snorted. "He seems to believe that sharing information with a journalist is completely different from being an informant for drug enforcement agencies."

"That would be great."

"Are you willing to put up monetary incentive? I warn you, he's not cheap. We're talking six figures."

"I am prepared—as much as it would take."

"So, you're going to kill him … Morales that is."

"Not me, but Darcy most likely will. My cousin's future happiness and safety for his family is dependent on it."

* * *

Strict instructions guided Jane toward the one and only entrance at the back of the Obsidian safe house. She'd been there only once before, and that was following all hell breaking loose on Liz's first wedding day to that Bill Collins. Of course, she didn't know then that the enigmatic biker god who took her and Liz here was a hitman employed by a black ops organization outsourced by the CIA for assassination. The minute Darcy's body had crashed against Liz on her wedding day, she knew that man was going to change both their lives. And he had. And so had Charlie.

She considered this her first "mission." As unimportant as it seemed, bringing groceries and medication to the director of Obsidian as he healed in secrecy was a huge step forward, especially since she now had some skills under her not-yet black belt. But she still fretted slightly, knowing that she had to discuss something important with Rick—something that could end her career with Obsidian before it really even began. From within her vintage Mustang, she depressed a button on a remote control ("Guard it with your life, Jane," Bingley had warned her), which, she was told, would trigger the disengagement of the door's six-inch thick, internal security bolts. Another button activated the door's opening. The garage was empty except for one of Iceman's motorcycles (concealed beneath a black cover) and the fireproof steel door that led up to the apartment.

Once the car was parked, she quickly hit the button to close the door and re-engage the bolts, careful—just as Charlie had explained—to check all angles and make sure that she hadn't been watched. So far, so good. In her mind, this was her first op: Operation D.C. Swing. Sure, it wasn't officially on the books and she was only a messenger, but she loved that she had been trusted to go to the safe house. A pop of the trunk, the gathering of the two grocery bags, and a turn of the key following the pressing of a series of numbers on the door and she was in, the door quickly slamming behind her when she took her first step up the staircase.

"Rick?" she called out, so as not to get shot. Maybe Charlie hadn't informed him of her arrival. "Ms. Caulfield? Hello? It's me Jane Bennet. Lizzy's sister."

A rather plain girl wearing too-tight-for-her-hips jeans showed her smile at the top of the staircase. "Hello!" she greeted with a very cool British accent. Jane made note to practice it for future reference. Most Bond chicks had accents.

"Oh, hi! You must be Rick's friend, Ms. Caulfield."

"It's Sarah, and it's lovely to meet you. You're a God-send! We're famished."

"Sure! No prob."

Sarah removed one of the bags from her arms and together they walked to the kitchen. Jane's eyes scanned the large den, recalling that fateful day and Liz's indignant shock as well as absolute distrust and dislike of Darcy. She audibly snorted also remembering the sexual sparks flying between them from the first time they met.

"Did you say something?"

"No. I was just thinking about the last time I was here. My father had just been kidnapped by terrorists and the boys came to the rescue. Obsidian is bad ass."

"Obsidian?"

Jane playfully grimaced. "Ooops. I guess I shouldn't have said that." Already she was messing up, saying too much as usual. She'd have to work on that. Being an agent for Obsidian was going to be hard, but she wanted to do it, wanted to succeed and secrecy was tantamount.

Sarah smiled reassuringly before bending to put items in the refrigerator. "No worries. I'll get the scoop out of Rick eventually. Would you like to stay for some tea? I was just about to make a cuppa for us."

"No. I'm under strict orders to deliver this and then return back to Leesburg."

"Where?"

"My sister's home about an hour from here." *Damn! I did it again!*

"Ah."

"Is Rick around? I have to talk with him." Feeling nervous, she glanced down the hall at the closed door, suddenly wanting to bolt. There would be no charming him with playful banter and levity. As nice a guy as her new boss was, his business is death-dealing and she had unwittingly effed with an op. She couldn't joke or flirt her way out of having possibly ruined Operation Macarena and having put everyone in jeopardy.

"He's just down the hall in the office. Jane, thanks again for dinner. I wanted a real American pizza pie but steak is just as good."

With a smile, Jane glanced back over her shoulder. "Sure!"

She liked Sarah and so would Liz. Her smile was warm, but her hairstyle needed some work. Further, she was glad that Rick had moved on from the viper. A guy like him deserved a sweet girl at his side, and this British girl must be something special because no one was invited into the inner sanctum unless they were trusted.

"Hey Rick," she timidly greeted peering around the doorframe. His relaxed look reminded her of the first time she met him in Marrakech. She thought him handsome then, and now.

"Jane! Come in! Thanks so much for the food and meds. I'm sorry to have put you out."

She sat across from him, noting the pain in his eyes and the furrow to his brow.

"It's no trouble at all. I had to swing by my loft in Georgetown anyway, so I just hit the supermarket before making my way back to Pemberley."

He frowned and she took that as displeasure in her.

"Don't worry … I was careful. No one followed me."

"Well that's good to hear. You should always be aware of your environment." He shifted in his seat then grimaced.

"How are you feeling? Is Sarah taking good care of you?"

"Yeah. Don't worry. Nothing a little R&R, TLC, and those pain meds you brought can't fix. It's been a hell of a month."

"Well, if you need anything, don't hesitate to ask. I know you have Sarah, but I can be of any assistance at all to both of you—her having one good arm and all."

"Thanks. I'll remember that."

She nervously looked toward the door, then toyed with her hoop earring. "I like Sarah. I think she'll fit in well around here."

He smiled. "I like her, too."

She fidgeted in her seat. She was never very good at pulling off a Band-Aid when it came to confessions. This was awkward. "Um, Rick … Charlie has instructed me to be absolutely honest with you if I'm serious about training with Obsidian, and, well, I know you think I'm sort of a bubble head, but I want you to know that I *am* serious."

A warm expression crossed his face and he placed the stylus he held on the desk, giving her all his attention. "I'm sure you're not a bubble head."

"Well, the thing is … I did something a little underhanded and sort of bubble head-*ish* but I had the best of intentions."

He raised an eyebrow.

"I helped Liz go to Paris."

She burned bright red, pausing before continuing in absolute embarrassment. According to Charlie, accountability was paramount in this business and she had to learn a lesson.

"Charlie felt that I should be the one to tell you since I had arranged it all. I helped my sister with disguises and camo communications. I taught her how to pick the lock of Caroline's briefcase, and assembled the pistol contents of the case for her. I even gave her some of my spy tools from the museum. Together we fabricated a completely different persona, contact lenses and wigs and all." She couldn't help grinning now, feeling simultaneous pride. "I made her into *me* with a southern accent!"

Astounded, he tented his fingers before his lips to keep them from smiling. She couldn't help noticing how his fingernails were no longer meticulously manicured. There was a hint of dirt below them.

"And why did you do this?"

"So she could confront Darcy and Caroline. She thinks they're having an affair … which I know now is not the truth, at least I don't think. But he did lie to her and, well, you and I both know that Caroline has had the hots for Iceman …" *Oops! Damn!*

He cocked a brow again.

"I'm sorry. I shouldn't have said that, but Liz is sort of crazy these days, living on the wild side of things—which I wholeheartedly approve of—but she wanted to save her marriage, and I wanted to help. But, you know my baby sister isn't the BDSM type and she needed my experience. I know about this sort of stuff."

Rick's eyes grew wide. "BDSM, because Obsidian agents were headed to a kink club?"

"Right! See, I knew you'd understand. Bull whips aren't her thing but she has other skills. Don't fault her—fault me."

"Jane. If I seem a bit taken aback by all this, well, it's because I am. Charlie hadn't conveyed your interest in joining the team. So this is the first I'm hearing of it."

"He said that he sent you an email."

"I'm just reading them now."

"Oh. Well, he's been training me alongside Liz. We've been making plans."

"I see." He thought for a long minute, picked up his stylus again then tapped his laptop screen. Maybe he was looking for Charlie's email, maybe not. Maybe he was getting ready to scold her. She took a deep breath, nearly holding it until he spoke again.

"I'll tell you what, if you can manage to play things a little closer to the vest, then we can find something for you to do with Obsidian, maybe not out in the field just yet but it sounds as though you have other vital skills we can use. You're already employed at the dance school and clearly have demonstrated you're comfortable with the art of deception and allusion using disguise."

He hesitated, his eyes locking with hers. "I see change on the horizon for Obsidian. You could be part of that change ... *if* ... you learn to function in the chain of command and keep secrets ... all secrets. They used to have a saying during WW2: Loose lips sink ships. In our business that is our unofficial motto because if someone talks, the wrong person is dead."

"I've heard that. It's about the Fifth Column."

His astonished look told her that she had impressed him.

"Your first lesson is to trust only those in Obsidian. That's it. What we do is so classified that not even the top brass in most of the country's intelligence organizations know about us."

"So ... you're not going to discipline me for my role in helping Liz? For putting Operation Macarena at risk?"

"It was in service to a most beloved sister. I'm not going to fault you for that. In fact, it does my heart good to know that she's willing to fight head-to-head with a ninja master to save her marriage. My cousin is a lucky man."

"And she's a lucky girl. Between you and me, I owe her a lot. You know, with dealing with our father for so many years." She stood and he smiled up at her. "So, I'm okay … we're okay?"

"We are. Thanks for talking with me straight on."

"Sure! Charlie was right. Honesty is best from the very beginning."

"And be cautious heading back to Pemberley. I can't have anything happen to our newest recruit." He winked at her and she grinned ear-to-ear. "I'll see you next week when Operation Macarena is over and we have our first meeting as a team."

"Thanks for everything. I won't let you down—you can trust me."
Cool! It's official. Pussy Galore, here I come.

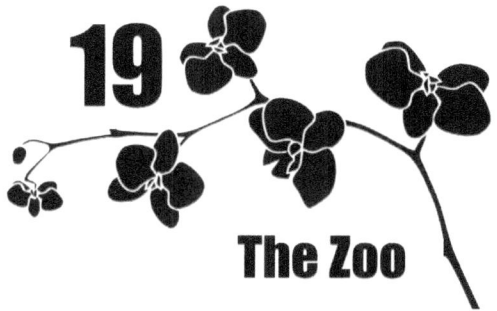

19

The Zoo

This was not the romantic trip to Paris with Liz that Darcy had always imagined, and it killed him to think that they would never come back to enjoy it as they had planned. It was tainted now by the very association of Operation Macarena, the evil woman still lying comatose (thanks to Caroline's carotid pinch) on the surveillance van floor, and the mistrust that had caused his wife to fly—by herself!—to catch him in the act, an act he never had any intention of executing. He did this; he messed this up by not telling her absolutely everything from the start. Hadn't both Rick and Charlie warned him of that? Liz stirred in his arms, shaking him from his thoughts as they sat at the back of the van, jostling from the ride to the *Jardin d'Agronomie Tropicale* in the Vincennes woods. She was out like a light, oblivious to it all and that worried him. Normally, she was a light sleeper and, even though she couldn't hold her liquor, he was surprised that the champagne would have affected her so. Passing out—that quickly? Something wasn't right.

He glanced down at the derringer still clutched in her fingers, his hand resting over them, and he considered the other items Caroline had explained were in the case. His free hand, the one draped around her body, slid down Liz's back and tucked under the corset, wrapping around the compact she said she had.

"Hey, Caroline," he said, tossing it to her over the prone body of Nadya. "Is this one of Bennet's inventions?"

She smugly smiled as soon as she caught it, its gold tone illuminated by the headlights of a passing truck. "Yes. This is the one she stole from my case."

"Tell me about it."

"It's most likely the reason we have all this intel on our target. Karakurt must have touched the mirror, which registered her fingerprint. The powder isn't so innocuous either; it's actually chloroform. Depending on how much the little woman … Liz … used, maybe that's what knocked her out."

He didn't say anything, so sure that was the cause of her crashing. It could be just minutes—or hours—before she came to. He pulled her closer to him and kissed her forehead for the umpteenth time. A tender whisper left his lips. "I gotcha, baby." He'd make sure she went for full bloodwork when they got home; that chemical agent was dangerous stuff.

The four sat in silence until they reached the 100-year-old, rotting *torii* entrance of the infamous "human zoo." Spotlighted in a moonbeam, the ten-foot Japanese gate bid them death and welcome, its shadow eerily cast on the muddy ground they traversed. From the open windows, Darcy could feel the spine-chilling aura in the air and it wasn't because he knew what was coming, or because he was in protection mode with his wife's head tucked in the hollow of his shoulder. Even Caroline seemed on edge, looking upward out the dashboard window, her mouth downturned, her ginger brow furrowed.

"I only heard about this place," she said. "Never thought it was real. It's creepy."

"Yeah. I once read about it. Not one of history's finest ideas. Imperial Europe at its worst."

"You surprise me, Knightley. I wouldn't think you up on your French Colonialism."

"I'm sorry to disappoint you, but I *am* an educated man. Most SEALs are, you know. Even America had one of these so-called zoos. I bet *you* didn't know that."

She must have been affected by the zoo; she stifled her comeback, and that was fine by Darcy. He was in no mood to listen to her make a play for Mr. Clean or for the two of them to start hurling insults at each other.

They parked at the arched gateway, making sure to hide the van within the overgrown bramble and weeds. This place had been long abandoned and even after it was made accessible to the public ten years earlier, its reputation kept thrill seekers away—especially at one in the morning. The reported folklore of ghost sightings saved this place as a carefully guarded secret, the perfect location for a black ops interrogation.

"Will *she* be coming with us?" Caroline sneered.

"No. I'm staying here with her. This is all you, Medusa. Do what you love; do what you do best. Knightley will have your back."

He expected her to tell him that he'd gone soft, but she didn't. Further he thought he saw her grin in the moonlight, like she'd been hoping he'd hand her the reins on this mission. The woman loved being out in the field; not because of any sense of patriotic duty or moral compass in handing out her form of justice, but because, simply put, she instinctively thrived on the methodical kill. It was what vipers did best. Before exiting the van, she toyed with the coiled bracelet she wore, no doubt one of her toys.

"Go deep into the gardens," he advised, watching Knightley holster the 9mm pistol he had withdrawn from the console. "You can't miss the Moroccan building."

"The Moroccan building? Feeling a little sentimental, are you?" she asked.

He was, but he wouldn't tell her that. "Not at all. No one will hear the screams back there."

Knightley reached into the glove compartment and withdrew a high-powered mag light, and she slid open the van door and dragged Nadya out. The woman groaned—half asleep, half awake—but her feet were unable to function so they dragged her through the mud toward their destination. He didn't want to know what the two of them would do to the woman, so long as they came back with the necessary intel: Julia Bertram's location, Morales's location.

Darcy sat listening to the beat of his heart, allowing Liz's sweet scent to overtake his senses. He closed his eyes, absorbing the white noise of silence: a rustle of trees, the crickets from the open window, and like a comforting foundation to it all … Liz's steady breathing.

Her hand twitched and she released the pistol from her grasp. Allowing, instead for her grip to move to something else. He moaned. It must be a reflex but damn it felt so good. His balls hurt from earlier, from the point of where they had left off at L'Enclave.

Gazing down at Liz's delicate features, he admired the slope of her pert nose and the shape of her mouth tinted with plum-colored lipstick. Her long lashes caressed her cheek, a vision of sheer beauty in tranquil slumber.

Only ten minutes had passed since the other two had left them, but his focus was easily redirected when she stroked him. Liz whispered against his shoulder. "Babe …"

"Liz, are you okay?"

"Hmmm."

Reaching up, his fingers brushed against her cheek. "How do you feel?"

"Better. I think." She yawned. "Where is everyone?"

"With your friend from the club."

"Oh! And you're here—with me?" She looked up into his eyes and his heart leapt. She was stunning in the soft glow of moonlight coming through the two back windows. Blue-eyed with black hair and plump lips that begged to be kissed; he obliged with a sweet peck.

"I'm where I should be—with you."

Liz looked like she was going to cry, her shiny eyes reflecting his image in her irises and then she choked on her words. "I'm so sorry."

Shifting his weight, he faced her, cupping her cheeks. "Listen to me. I love that you came all this way to fight for me. I'm the one who is sorry. I should have told you everything." A gentle kiss sparked a deeper one.

"God, I need you," she breathlessly panted.

He chuckled wryly. "I need you, too, but now? Here?"

Suddenly filled with animation, she left his embrace, quickly straddling his lap. Her breasts spilled from the corset when she shirked from his suit jacket, followed by her tug to his tie. One hand raked through his hair.

"Are you still drunk, vixen?"

"No, just feeling emotional."

She moved against his shaft, a flirty smile teased him.

Oh God. Now? "You can't possibly want—"

She cut off his protestation with a gloved finger to his lips. "Yes. I want to make up. I love you," she nearly cried, her voice cracking as her lips neared his. They touched with heartbreaking tenderness, which quickly grew to hungry, devouring kisses until she abruptly stood from his straining arousal.

He was helpless, rendered mute at the sight of her standing between his legs as she slid the panties down. Nothing was more beautiful than the fire in his wife's eyes and her seductive expression. Her bare sex taunted him. He wanted to consume her, taste her, spend hours cradled between her shapely legs, smothered by her raw heat and sweet honey, but—alas—they had not the time. A hurried unzip to his trousers sprung him free.

Even he was surprised at how quickly he'd been aroused, but there was something dangerous and highly erotic about making love to Liz in the middle of an op interrogation. Her ready eagerness and that get-up she wore made it even more titillating.

She raised an eyebrow. "Darlin', your carinatus looks like it's ready to explode," she teased, employing her new southern accent.

"Then sit on it and ride me like your SuperLow. Hurry."

Liz took a step to him, placing one foot on each side of his thighs, her heat only an inch or two from his face and he did just what he had imagined doing. He clutched her hips and pulled her to him, depositing a kiss upon her snake tattoo, then to her soft apex. She moaned when his tongue touched her with a measured tease. He couldn't take much more and guided her down onto his erection.

That first slide engulfing him made him groan aloud. Heaven was between her legs. She rode him hard, giving him exactly what they both needed. Every grind and swivel met his upward thrusts. He was touching her in places that made her wild and crazy, that unleashed her. The feel of her hands clasped upon his shoulders told him she was in control, and he wouldn't have it any other way.

"I adore you," he moaned between bites to her neck. "You're the only woman for me—forever. Do you understand? Only you, Liz."

She floated in her dominance, barely fathoming her reckless eagerness to have him in a van … and with team members not far. But seducing Darcy was more than just wanting him; she needed him, and they both had to set things right between each other. This was where their hearts always met best. Sex was their greatest form of communication; it was in the act that he showed himself and the depth of his emotion. The feel of her husband deeply entrenched in her was like no other heavenly delight. Frenetic synapses flowed through her body, all emanating from each thrust. His hand cupped her backside gliding her upon his hips in back and forth motion, each brush of her pearl against him sent new sparks.

Liz was close … too close. *Together* was her only thought as her mind whirled in absolute ecstasy, feeling as though she was still drunk.

She stilled upon him and kissed him. His lips were warm and pliable; a little nibble held her teasing smile at bay as she rose slightly, inching him from her. He groaned again, and she slid slowly down upon him. Another groan. A third time, left only his engorged tip within, teasing him when she clenched around it.

"Give it to me, Iceman," she cooed and he responded with a shudder, ready to climax but holding back.

He reclaimed the control she had given him, flipping her onto the metal floor and letting himself go, loving her with thrusts so deep she came apart. Her stifled cries matched his, her tears finally flowing as he held her tightly to him, giving her every last ounce of the Iceman. They were one again.

* * *

The building loomed ahead in the pitch dark as Caroline walked *Shinso-Toho*, "like rabbit," behind Knightley with Nadya draped over his shoulder. She silently sniggered at the thought that he was probably enjoying the woman's sex pressed against his shoulder. His free hand shined the light at the entrance to the crumbling structure, but it wasn't necessary for her. She'd been trained to see in the dark. All around them the sound of the forest filled the chilled night air. There was a sweet scent of dead vines mixed with vanilla, probably from a nearby garden that grew wild in the abandoned "zoo." An odd sensation overcame her and it wasn't because her gold lamé dress and sandals belied the ninja warrior guerilla tactics she would employ or the decaying environment they found themselves in. She felt a malevolent spirit or ghosts. Suddenly, a raven landed on the wood beam at the top of the doorway. Its loud, raspy "kraw, kraw" put her on edge. Japanese folklore spoke of the legendary *tengu*, a demon, which came in the form of a bird: the harbinger of death.

They quietly passed through overgrown weeds and entered the Moroccan Pavilion. Decades old blue and gold mosaic tile lined the interior's circumference on the concrete walls illuminated by the wide swath of the mag's brilliant spotlight. There were two doorways on each end of a cavernous room, one leading to a narrow hallway, the other leading to another large chamber with broken glass walls. The entrance archways were surrounded by stone-relief arabesques and Islamic calligraphy, both covered with soot and spider webs. Years' worth of debris and dead vegetation were strewn on the floor. Most likely this room hadn't been entered since the early-1900s at the last shameful exhibition of human exploitation.

Knightley unceremoniously dropped Nadya's unconscious form onto the floor and Caroline laughed noticing how he gaped at the woman's exposed figure beneath the mesh of her teddy bodysuit, his eyes following the flashlight beam.

"I certainly can scratch that itch," she said attempting to shirk off the bad feeling she had, but she couldn't control the steel in her voice.

"No thanks. I prefer arachnids over reptiles even if they are both lethal."

"Humph. Wake her up—let's get on with this and get the hell out of here."

"Yeah. For once we agree. I'm not in the mood to fight off the ghosts of Moroccan Goum warriors. This place gives me the creeps."

Caroline paced before her enemy as Knightley bent down. He glanced over his shoulder. "You're not going to do that tickle torture shit, are you?"

"That's Chinese. Fool."

"Good, because laughing Russians sound like hyenas in heat."

"Ridiculous. Like you've heard hyenas in heat."

"You know what I mean."

But he had a point—the woman before her loved pain. It gave her pleasure. She'd have to employ the techniques of *ninjutsu*, tap into Karakurt's one driving emotion, then manipulate the information out of her by using it.

"Wait!" she commanded before Knightley slapped the woman awake.

"Turn off the flashlight, then strike her and step to the corner. Don't make a move. Don't make a sound. I'm going to use what we know about her to get what we want." She chuckled. "And try not to get turned on by what you see. The last thing I need right now is my back up man with a flaming hard on."

"Yes ma'am," he said and did just as instructed.

Nadya awoke into absolute darkness. She groaned and fought to break the zip ties holding her wrists together.

"Don't fight it," Caroline said, imitating Liz's voice as best she could. She blinked a few times, accustoming her eyes to night vision.

"*Lapushka*, is that you?"

The *kunoichi* detached herself from her actions and walked to her captive. Placing her foot on the woman's sex, she slid it up and down, creating friction and arousal.

"Yes. It's me."

"Hmmm ... do not stop. Did you bring Iceman, too? All that power. He is large man between his legs."

"Yes he is."

Caroline bent, her hand sliding up the woman's torso then over a full breast; the nipple pebbled beneath her palm. She cringed again, attempting to detach herself as she fondled the bosom. She was reaching Nadya's debauched lustful base, using it against her. "He's gone. How does that feel?" A cruel twist to the nipple set the woman writhing in pleasure on the floor.

Then Caroline abruptly stopped.

She could see Nadya's head turn right then left trying to see her as she circled with ninja stealth between the leaves on the floor.

"He trapped you into finding me. I understand."

"Well, he does have a certain sex appeal. A man like this Iceman was hard to resist. I'm sorry I tricked you, but he promised me things."

Nadya laughed. "Yes. I would have done same. Please ... do not stop. I must ... I must have you."

A hand slapped between spread legs.

"Yes!" the woman screamed.

Again Caroline stopped, then circled. "I will continue if you tell me what I was sent to find out."

The Russian laughed. "Not likely, Floria, but I am very much enjoying this role play. Vhat dungeon are we in?"

That's right; she didn't know that they were no longer in L'Enclave. Caroline took Nadya's bound hands and rubbed them against her calf, letting the woman feel bare skin, teasing her with each up and down caress.

"You are so soft. To run my tongue along your thigh—"

The hands fell in a heap on her torso then Caroline removed her bracelet, uncoiling the snake-like metal to use as an instrument of lustful torture. She rubbed its rigid tip between Nadya's thrashing legs, taunting her.

"Oh yes. Yes! Oh!" she cried out. "Just like I did to you. You learn."

"It feels good doesn't it?"

The metal traveled downward, along the inside of a thigh then viciously poked behind a kneecap, a highly erogenous area (at least it was for her.) Nadya rewarded her with a whimper of pleasure.

"I will continue if you tell me where Julia is."

"No!"

Caroline stopped, stepping away from the prone figure.

"Wait!"

She turned back then began the rubbing again, harder this time against the Russian's apex.

"Oh yes!"

"Tell me, please, Nadya," she cooed as if in Darcy's arms.

"She is Muscovite now, but will be Saudi soon." She laughed maniacally.

Caroline raised a brow followed by a slap to Nadya's cheek, a reward for the information.

"You learn fast. There is only pleasure in pain. Give me more. Harder."

A crack of the metal bracelet across the woman's pubis caused her to cry out. "Yes!"

But Caroline withdrew the woman's means of pleasure and walked away. She wondered if Knightley was aroused in the corner, needing a little action himself.

"Are you there, *lapushka*?"

She said nothing, the only sound to be heard was the spider woman's heavy breathing until finally Caroline asked, "Tell me where Diablo is? And I will come back. Then you may have me to do what you like. Then I will lead you to Iceman and we can both take our reward."

Silence fell heavy.

"I will ... tell you, but only if you keep your promise."

Caroline could see that Nadya now stood, holding out her bound arms attempting to find her way in the pitch of the vast room. She was looking for her, her dark shadow traversing the room, hoping to bump into her. Little did she know that a ninja could see in total pitch. Knightley stepped out of the Russian's reach.

"I will continue," Caroline said, moving to stand behind the woman, her hand caressing the exposed flesh in the cutout of her backless bodysuit, sliding down to her leather-clad backside. She unzipped the bottom, snickering at the labored breath of anticipation from her victim. Nadya moaned when the steel separated, exposing her skin.

Suddenly the spider woman turned with hands free from their plastic restraint. In one quick move she sliced at the ninja's neck with the pointed leg of her spider ring. "You are not Floria!" She said.

Knightley fired the Glock, the flash of the muzzle in the darkness preceded the burst of the mag light, the latter shining on Caroline falling to the ground and Nadya running to the exit. The cable tie, disintegrated in two, lay on the floor.

"Did I hit you?" Knightley asked running to her prone body.

"No. Dammit!" She clutched her neck, feeling a slight wetness where the ring grazed flesh. It was either blood or poison, maybe both. Willing her blood pressure to lower she focused on her heartbeat in the event of it being a neurotoxin. She could fight this; she had built toxic immunity over many years. Her throat constricted. Whatever was in that ring had obviously melted the cable tie and was working its way into her system.

She gasped, now having an anaphylactic reaction. "Get me to the van. Fast."

In the beam of the mag light, Knightley's switchblade popped open. "Hold still. This'll kill me more than you." After slicing an *X* around the cut, he bent and sucked at her neck, followed by a spit of whatever poison he had procured.

20
Almost Doesn't Count

There was no sign of Nadya in the zoo as Knightley ran balls out with Caroline draped over his shoulder in the same fashion as he had with the Russian thirty-minutes prior. Although known for her mithridatism, he feared that the toxin coursing through her blood was something uniquely concocted by Karakurt, given it was her specialty. It was only a small scrape to her neck, but the right side of her face had gone numb; clearly no amount of poison immunity was going to help her unless she had a trick up her sleeve.

"Fuck!" he panted, his face getting lashed by trees and vines just as it had in Sierra Leone. The Japanese gate was up ahead, the van only strides from there.

"Don't worry about the vines on my account. I can't feel my right arm nor my face," she slurred, as though she'd been boozing."

"Fuck!" he cursed again. "Darcy!" he shouted as he flew beneath the *torii* structure.

Within seconds he was in the bramble and the door to the van sliding open. By the expression on his face, it seemed that Darcy was anticipating the worst. He grabbed Caroline from his arms and settled her into the passenger seat.

"She was scratched by that bitch, and having an allergic reaction."

Quickly Darcy asked questions as he grabbed the plastic water bottle from the dashboard and doused the blood and fluid from her neck. "Where is Karakurt?"

"She got away."

Caroline grimaced, more in anger than in pain. She clawed at her neck but felt nothing, both hands now had no feeling. "Liz! I … need your help," she declared in raspy pants to the surprise of the men.

"Me?"

"The pills … that were in the case. Where are they?"

Crouched between the front seats, Liz held out her right hand and looked down at the skull ring she wore. "Oh, the acetaminophens?"

"Yes. Do you have them?"

"Sure." Liz popped open the ring and fingered the two pills within. "I don't think they'll help though. I mean apart from just taking off the edge of pain. Are you in pain?"

"Blue one," she struggled to say. "Looks like Aleve … epinephrine."

Again, both men looked at each other. Liz seemed to be the one saving this op from hell in a handbasket. She had systematically captured Nadya, facilitated their escape from the club, and now was about to save an Obsidian agent with her freaky ring.

Caroline swallowed the pill then rested her head against the back of the seat. "Thanks," she panted. "I … owe you."

Knightley raised his eyebrows at that monumental statement then climbed into the back of the van. He'd never heard her thank anyone before.

Liz wanted to gloat, truly she did, but played her best and only card, "Just keep away from Fitzwilliam and we'll call it even."

Although not the delivery method of choice, the effects were almost immediate as the drug lessened Caroline's response to the toxin. She began to breathe more freely.

Attempting to move her inert arm that lay across her lap, she blurted out, "How … did you knock me out on the airplane?"

Shocked, Liz hesitated. "Um … Just an over-the-counter sleeping pill in your drink."

"Damn," she breathed, obviously displeased that she had been bested by yet another generic lightweight.

Knightley turned on the computers and Darcy climbed into the driver's seat, awaiting further instruction.

"Where to now, Caroline?" he said.

"You and Knightley are headed to Moscow. I'm dead in the water."

"Do you know *where* in Moscow? Eleven million people, you know … it's pretty big."

"I don't know but … if we fail there, then the girl is headed to Saudi Arabia. She'll be lost for good. Knightley, contact my brother. I think he should pay Bertram a little visit and force him to get one of his old friends in the Kremlin to help us."

"Christ, the man's not going to agree with that!" Knightley objected.

"Then we go public with his affiliation to Mother Russia and let his daughter get sold to the highest bidder." She shrugged ambivalently.

"You're cold, Caroline."

"Isn't that why you all call me a reptile?"

"And what do we do with you? You can't come with us," Darcy asked.

"I could stay in Paris, and—"

"Fitzwilliam, I can take Caroline home."

He glanced over his shoulder, eyes meeting Liz's. That wasn't easy for her to say, and his reply surprised him. "No. I want you with me."

"I don't—"

His furrowed brow stifled any objection she had. Had she not learned anything in the last 48 hours? Trust. She must trust him on this. Sending her home to the "possibility" of danger without him was now an untenable option, and he'd rather her face guaranteed danger *with* him.

"Hey, Darcy," Knightley said from behind her, staring at the computer screens alive with intel. "You're not going to believe what I'm going to tell you."

"I'd believe anything at this point." He rolled his eyes, unable to conceal his frustration. "See, this is why I prefer sniping alone—I don't have to deal with this crap. When an op fails, it's because my finger chooses not to pull the trigger, not because of lack of intel and flying by the seat of my pants." Again, he looked at Liz, recalling his last failed op. Best damned decision he ever made in his life.

"Well, this may not be as such a blowback as you think. We might have a fix on Karakurt. I'm getting GPS coordinates. Maybe it's her because someone is cruising north on A3 at a pretty good clip straight toward the airport."

"What?"

"It can only be the camo beauty mark," Caroline said, turning to look at Liz, gifting her with a sort of appreciative half-smile. "It must have attached to the bitch when it fell off Liz. It has a microdot GPS tracker inside."

Knightley laughed. "Looks like Liz here is our star operative on this mission. Man, you sure know how to dance the Macarena, Mrs. Darcy."

And with that, she grinned, executing the moves of the well-known dance, putting out one arm then the other, then folding them in genie fashion. "Thank you, Mr. Clean. Maybe it's a good thing that I'm going on to Moscow. Who knows, I just might catch Diablo and kick his ass with the new knife skills that Wentworth taught me. Jane gave me a lipstick pick knife!"

Darcy growled from the driver's seat when he turned the key in the ignition.

"Hey, since we're headed to Russia don't we need to re-name the op now? Maybe some squat-kicking dance?" she asked. "I got it! Floria kicks ass in Operation Kazatsky!"

"Sit down, *Mrs. Darcy.*" he groaned. "Before you hit that big head of yours on the roof of the van."

Caroline chortled.

* * *

Two in the morning, Virginia time, Wentworth paced the southern wall of the estate. He couldn't get his mind off Liz and felt bad about it. He didn't come all this way to fall for another man's wife, but there was something about her that he felt drawn to. Visually, she was his type in every way, but there was more. Her absolute devotion to her husband made him yearn for that kind of love. She had no conception just how alluring she was, and that, too, made him want her. The chemistry between them wasn't real, at least on her part, he knew; she was just missing her husband. Halting his steps, he gazed up through the trees at the half-moon, brilliant in a cloudless sky dotted with stars. He rubbed the stubble on his chin, admitting that he was glad she had cancelled their tutorial sessions, unsure if he could have restrained himself from kissing her. And that would have been a mess. He'd heard about Darcy's temper. The man had ice in his veins and would have no compunction in reacting to something as heinous as sexual advances toward his wife.

The night air was chilly and he finally burrowed his chin into the lambswool at the neck of his leather bomber jacket then continued as sentry. There was absolute silence tonight, an eeriness that crept into his bones, shadows across the forest floor, and he silently crept until stopping to lean against the thick trunk of an oak tree.

He liked this time of night. Further, he didn't mind the solitude—needed the solitude—the escape from the chaos of war, but sometimes he missed the brotherhood. After his friend Ken's death in Iraq, he swore to always keep people at arm's length. It was female companionship that he yearned for though. Women came into his life, but left just as quickly. Who could blame them? The long-term effects of war were here to stay—but damn, he needed a good woman to stay beside him, help him to, at least, get over the sleeplessness. Not to mention, he wanted more than to just get laid. Uncomplicated rolls in the hay were common—emotionless passing of time in someone's arms—but they were getting old. He sighed. Darcy and Crash were lucky men.

A branch snapped under the weight of something in the near distance and jolted him from his thoughts; he turned to face the direction, ears piqued even for the slightest shuffle, and then he saw it: a shadow pass in the moonlight.

Stealthily he moved to another tree and withdrew a knife. The shadow moved equally as covert, making its way to the forest edge. A break in the trees illuminated the small furry animal with glowing eyes. It was just a raccoon. Wentworth breathed a sigh of relief and continued his patrol.

21

Turandot

Even though Liz inadvertently proved to be of great help in Paris, Darcy wasn't sure if he was doing the right thing by putting her in direct harm's way tonight in Moscow. When the words "I want you with me," had escaped his lips unchecked, he had yet to know that they would be headed to Russia, but something in his gut cautioned him not to let her out of his sight, not to send her home. He was determined that Liz would stay by his side. Hopefully, she would follow his instruction, but one thing was for sure: Operation Macarena would end tonight one way or another and then he'd be done with Obsidian.

As they had surmised, Karakurt had departed Charles de Gaulle Airport for Moscow on a private jet, and he, Liz, and Knightley followed on a charter flight sixty minutes later. Air travel had briefly halted the beauty mark's GPS signal, but they were sure that the Russian would lead them directly to her hidden web and Julia somewhere in Moscow. He had to admit, Bennet had done well. The man had a talent in counter-intelligence gathering and surveillance gear. Once landed, the spider woman's signal was back on the move. However, it was lost somewhere on the outskirts of the city. They feared she'd found the transmitter or entered into a satellite dead zone, which was more than likely. Time would tell, but at least Charlie had gleaned fortunate intel from Bertram following the jackass's reluctant call to a former KGB comrade, now with the FSB. Valentina Donkova had indeed shown back up on the Ruskie's radar, and on a hunch the FSB hacked into her former lover, Alexei Petrov's email and phone recordings. Now Deputy Secretary Petrov, with the Federation's Security Council, was about to have dinner with her. Why had she resurfaced as her former identity? What was she planning?

From his position at the threshold of their hotel suite's ornate living room, Darcy holstered the Desert Eagle from Caroline's case under his jacket. Concerned, he furrowed his brow, observing his wife lost in thought as she gazed out the window of the St. Regis Moscow Nikolskya. Either in awe of the view of the Kremlin and the historic district at sunset, or maybe oblivious to both, she toyed with her snake necklace, a reminder of the danger in last year and the worry of danger ahead. His beloved was a portrait in study, and he wondered what her exact thoughts were.

"I'm glad you thought to bring that with you." he said, feeling somewhat disconcerted by her silence.

Liz turned to face him with a false, bright smile trying to be brave but he knew that even though she tried to live a little more recklessly, she wasn't confident for what lie ahead.

"I won't leave home without this necklace. It's too dear to me."

"Then it's a good thing I fixed the microphone. You know, in the event of anything. I feel better hearing your voice."

Her hazel eyes fell to the shirt sleeve peeking out from his suit jacket. "Right, and you brought your cufflinks."

"Always." He walked to where she stood so sensuously majestic in the strapless designer dress he had purchased for her upon their arrival into Moscow: a form-fitting bronze ensemble. Her merlot-colored lips matched the ruby and diamond necklace and matching bracelet, and her chestnut waves cascaded around her face. "You look gorgeous," he said quietly, captivated by the image she presented back-dropped by the fading purple and pink hues of the vibrant skyline.

"Do I? I don't feel it." Her hand went to her stomach, her singular gold wedding band drawing his eye.

"Trust me, you are."

She nervously laughed. "I feel like I did in Monte Carlo. Remember? When you first came into my hotel room without knocking? I couldn't breathe."

"Because you were nervous what the night would hold, what would happen if we saw Crawford."

"No, not because of that. Because I was nervous to be with *you*. I was falling for you and then you touched me, kissed me. You made me yours that night." Her eyes welled with tears and she blurted in near panic, "Tell me it doesn't end here in Moscow. Tell me we'll get home and continue where we left off."

"On my honor." He wrapped her in his arms, holding her close to his chest. His heart broke at her fear. "I was yours ..." he swallowed hard, "when I saw you through my riflescope."

"I know. I keep thinking ... is it better to die together or apart? I'd rather go together than to live without you." She looked up, her eyes searching his. "I'm glad I'm here, glad we're here doing this together just like before."

"Me, too, but neither of us are dying tonight."

"You can't promise that."

"No, but I can promise that I'll protect you with my last breath." He kissed her forehead. "If something happens to you, I'm following."

"Don't say that, Fitzwilliam."

"Then don't worry. Look, you've got your necklace so I can hear everything and it makes me feel better having you near me. This way if you do something unexpected, I have your back." He raised an eyebrow, hoping she got his inference. He hated to steer the conversation in this direction but the air still hadn't been cleared between them.

"Don't worry about me. I'll behave. I'll do exactly as you say."

"Because you always listen to me. You always trust in my experience."

Her head tipped down, her chin near touching the snake diamonds. Sure, she didn't like being called out on this, but he had to make his point; he had to get to the bottom of her distrust. His finger raised her chin, eyes fixing on each other with understanding to speak the truth.

"Before I left for Peru, I asked you if you trusted me and you said you did, that you always had. What changed?" The tremble to her bottom lip nearly broke his heart.

"Caroline."

He frowned, angry with himself and accepting full responsibility for her mistrust. "I'm sorry I wasn't forthright about her. Had I just been honest when you first asked about her you would not have doubted my constancy and flown to Paris."

"It hurt more knowing that you lied."

"You're right. It was wrong of me. Lying and not telling you are the same thing, and not that it's any excuse but I was ashamed. Ashamed that ... she and I ... Please forgive me."

"Fitzwilliam, I do, but understand that I'm afraid of losing you not just to Obsidian, but to another woman, to anyone or anything more exciting than Lizzy of Longbourn. Can't you see that I'm not enough for you?"

"Oh, babe." He sighed, his eyes hurting taking in the sorrow on her face, his hand brushing the waves at her temple. "You have never been more wrong. You're Liz Darcy, but you are no more defined by that name than you are by referring to yourself as Lizzy of Longbourn. You are spirited, alluring, intelligent, and you captivate me with your beauty both inside and out."

"So you say, but I can tell you wanted to come back to this adventure. Obviously, something is missing in your life."

"I only came back to Obsidian to *protect* you and to bring Rick home. Nothing more and certainly not because I missed the life. I cherish *every* moment I get to spend with you. Both the quiet ones where we just sit and read together as well as the adventurous ones. You're a gift; you're my redemption."

"But I'm—"

"The only thing worth living for. Surely, you must know that, Liz. I thought you trusted in us—forever. Trust me. I am happy, but I can't be happy unless I know that you are. Are you … is life everything *you* hoped for … with me?"

"You ask this because I bought the Harley before I was ready, because I feel the need to travel at the drop of a hat, because I like to speed and that I actually had fun playing the heroine in Paris?" She paused, clearly considering her words. "I *am* happy, but feel so liberated from life at Longbourn. I just want to experience everything, but *with* you. And … in truth … I thought by being a little more free-spirited … you'd be less likely to second guess your life with me."

He sighed deeply, his contrition heavy. "That's the one thing in my life, I have absolutely no regrets over. I'm so sorry I made you feel that way."

"You didn't; it's just my insecurity, probably due to my mom, but …," she said softly, looking away from his examination.

"But? Tell me; tell me everything."

Stepping from him, she wrung her hands together. "No. Now's not the time to get into it. We have to go."

"Now *is* the time. There's something heavy on your mind; please share it with me."

"This from the man who hid in the barn listening to Led Zeppelin because he was too afraid to open up to me."

"Well, I've learned a few important things in the last week."

"Okay, then … to put it bluntly you don't trust my judgment; your mollycoddling of me is going to be the death of me."

Flabbergasted, his body went rigid, not expecting that reproach. "Oh God. Is that right? Have I truly turned into your father?"

She laughed lightly. "Not *that* bad. Maybe I'm exaggerating. I don't mind you being protective, it's just …"

"I'm *over* protective."

"A little."

"Why didn't you tell me I was acting like a jerk?"

"Probably for the same reason you didn't tell me about Caroline. I didn't want to hurt you. I mean, it's not *that* bad, but it felt good back in Paris—you and me in the bathroom interrogating Nadya. You trusted me."

"I did; I was petrified for you, but you did just fine. In fact, you made Caroline and me look like Keystone Cops last night."

A wide grin lit her face and glad to see her smiling, he kissed her, re-sealing the deal they had made on their wedding day: together, not apart, trusting each other no matter what.

"Let me help you tonight."

"I won't say no, just … we'll see what happens. If I learned one thing about this op: nothing goes according to plan."

"Tell me again what you are at least expecting."

He let go of her and walked to the desk, picking up Caroline's Smart Watch. Thank God it hadn't been with Liz when L'Enclave and everything in it was fried by the EMP. He glanced at the time considering if he should tell her what his gut suspected or how he hoped the night would go down.

"Knightley will be carrying most of this op. As for you and me, we'll be having a few cocktails, maybe some dinner and acting as his second set of eyes until the time comes to follow her home. We'll penetrate the facility, disable her, save the girl if she's there, then go home."

"So, really, we're not needed at the restaurant. Knightley could very well do this part of the night alone, right?"

"He could, but I'm not comfortable with him going in naked. Besides I'd like to take you out to dinner since we're in Moscow."

"And after dinner?"

"Then you come back here, pack, and wait for me to arrive with Julia, if we find her. She's going to need you. Charlie has arranged for extraction at Ostafyevo Airport."

"It all sounds so very 007."

He chuckled wryly.

"And this Russian government official?" Her fingers tapped her thigh.

He walked back to her and took them into his hand, caressing her knuckles. "Thanks to your lovely little wire beauty mark, we'll find out what that's all about."

"You hate this, don't you?"

"Of course I do. I'm not a spy. I'm a lone assassin."

"You *were* an assassin. You retired; remember?"

He didn't answer, just half-heartedly smiled before glancing at the watch still held in his left hand. Nadya's signal was back on track, most likely headed to the restaurant. It was amazing that the beauty mark was still attached to her body somewhere.

"C'mon. It's time to go."

"To a restaurant named Turandot Palace" She snorted. "Oh the irony."

"It's fate."

"Ill-fated?"

He touched her lips with his index finger. "No, a *good* omen. That's *our* opera, and it has a *happy* ending. Now, do you have the derringer and the knife in your purse, just in case?"

"Yes. And you're sure she won't recognize us, right?"

"Not likely. I didn't recognize you in disguise in the dark club, and I'm your husband. She only saw us masked. Further, she's never seen Knightley.

"Let's test this," he said, fingers clasping the necklace and activating the microphone from behind the stones. He then pressed the small receiver in the curve of her ear, which started transmission. Enacting that familiar pose that she remembered on last year's adventure, he raised his wrist to his mouth then spoke into his right cufflink. "Are you wearing panties tonight?"

Liz snorted. "You have repeatedly told me that this wouldn't be like Monte Carlo. Therefore, I am wearing underwear."

"Damn."

Draped over the chair, was a Russian sable that completed her ensemble. "You should be warm enough," he reflected, lifting the jacket then draping it over her shoulders.

"I better be for $35,000."

From behind, he gently guided her to lean against his chest, wrapped his arms around her and kissed her ear. "You're worth every penny and more."

* * *

In Liz's opinion, Turandot Palace was even more opulent than the Casino Monte-Carlo. She tried not to look overwhelmed by the Florentine courtyard they passed through at the entrance. Neptune and other Roman statues backlit by amber lighting and Venetian lanterns in the atrium bid welcome to a night she knew she'd never forget. It *was* the same as Monte Carlo and she fidgeted.

Darcy rested the flat of his hand upon her back, allowing her to lead the way toward the 18th Century French décor. His index finger pulled along the fabric, tickling her in his soothing manner. The scent of his aftershave wafted to her, and heels clicked on the antique marble flooring as they followed the hostess to a dining room.

"This was once Rimsky-Korsakov's mansion," he whispered.

"Truly?"

"Yes. See, a good omen."

Baroque, French Regency, and Italian Renaissance occupied the same space of grandeur in Turandot's Central Hall. Gilded stucco walls ascended to the domed heaven of sky blue and clouds. Painted Chinese dancers graced paneled walls below ambient sconces. In awe, she felt transported to a place beyond Versailles and her eyes lit with excitement at the magnificent quartz and amethyst chandelier, brilliantly illuminating the two stories.

They climbed a winding staircase, arriving at a table for three overlooking the floor below. A costumed waiter seemed to magically appear to slide out her velvet-covered chair, the piano song rising upward to them. "Scheherazade," blended beautifully with the soft murmur of dining patrons. This was an opulence unlike anything she had yet to experience, but Darcy seemed oblivious to it all. His gaze cast down to the floor below, his expression hardened until he felt her stare upon him. He glanced up to her, a tender smile transforming his face, soothing his brow. "They're playing our suite."

"Yes. Maybe you're right. It certainly seems lucky." She glanced at the menu, her eyebrows rising in shock. "How … how do people afford to dine here?"

"Moscow has the highest number of billionaires in the world—about 80 or so. Welcome to the playground of the nouveau riche."

"Some playground. It's elegant, in yet a magically tacky way." She laughed, although still nervous.

"Can I join you two love birds?" Knightley interrupted the light conversation, his joking manner immediately changing the tone of the evening when he arrived at their table, wearing an expensive suit and a lively smile. "Karakurt is here, and good evening to you Mrs. Darcy. You're looking *très* chic tonight wearing vintage couture. A little something you picked up over in the Red Square?"

"Yes. Fitzwilliam bought it for me."

"Who would have guessed you for such a fashion maven, Darcy." He slid out the chair reserved for him. His bald head and crooked teeth contrasted his dashing figure and sophisticated knowledge of women's apparel. This was the John Knightley she had met in Monte Carlo, not the Mr. Clean of Obsidian. She wondered how he could always be so cool and cavalier when faced with danger.

"I know what looks good on my wife," Darcy replied matter of factly.

"What you mean is that you know what you like to *see* her wearing." He winked at her.

"That's what I said," Darcy challenged with an eye roll, promptly signaling the waiter then quietly ordering three cocktails.

"He's been purchasing my eveningwear since Monaco last July."

"Let me guess: black and barely there."

She chuckled, recalling the Versace. "Something like that. I trust his taste—among other things."

"Shall we get down to business, Knightley," Darcy interrupted, clearly feeling like a third wheel again since conversation was about him as though he was not in the room."

"Sure. She's downstairs, cozying up with Deputy Secretary Petrov."

"Is the beauty mark still working?" She was astounded that her father had created such a thing but pushed from her mind the legal ramifications of his having done so.

"Like a charm and so is the matching receiver." He turned his head, showing her the black mole's placement in his ear. "Right now, they're talking about summers in the Tomsk Oblast since that's where they are both from. She's asked him about his wife, but he declined answering. There's a bit of awkward tension between them. It's clear that they have a past."

The waiter placed a Kir Royale on the table before Liz and two neat vodkas in front of the men.

"When did you learn Russian?" Darcy asked.

"Well, if I tell you, then I'd have to tell you who I worked for in Monaco, and that's not going to happen until long after he and his associates are dead."

"Right."

Knightley's fingers pressed the receiver in his ear. "Wait a sec … she's asking him what he knows about American black ops organizations?" He paused, listening intently. "Does the Security Council have any intelligence on a CIA operative or contract assassin referred to as Iceman?"

Liz gasped, and Darcy's hand reached out to hers on the table. He gave her a reassuring look. "That's nothing new. Every country wants information about American agents."

"Please, don't try to placate me. I'm keenly aware of the fact that you just had a run in with her, and she and her lover want you dead. She may ask about American operatives without raising suspicion, but to inquire about Iceman specifically? I don't think so."

"Okay, how's this for not placating you? It's likely that she knows I am here and this is all a ruse—a trap. It's not as though she didn't tell Caroline that Julia is in Moscow."

Her eyes widened in fear.

"Don't worry, Liz. He said he didn't know. Besides, Iceman is bad ass even if it's a trap," Knightley assured, his deflection obvious when he abruptly snapped open a menu. "Let's order, shall we? We may be here for a couple of hours and I'm starved. Gee, the Peking Duck looks outta this world. Go figure—Chinese fusion meets Louis XIV. Weird."

Apart from the tension, dinner was turning out to be a diverting affair. Occasionally, Knightley would pause, and listen more intently to the conversation going on inside his ear, but they allowed the night to unfold, waiting for a crack in the door to the rest of the evening.

Over dim sum, the break they needed came. Petrov threw his napkin on the table in a huff.

"She's breaking her deal. He can't have the girl she promised him. And because she's reneging on their business arrangement, he wants her to pay him the full million his waiting client had offered for Julia," Knightley reported.

"You mean to say that the Deputy Secretary of Russia's Security Council is a human trafficker?"

Knightley laughed sardonically, completely attentive to the conversation taking place in his ear. "I guess so and he's not happy that Karakurt has cost him a fortune. He also wants an extra shipment of cocaine. Fuck Diablo, he says. Sorry Liz."

"No worries. This is so tragic. They're going to sell her? Fitzwilliam you didn't tell me that."

"Karakurt's not happy about it either, but Morales wants the girl delivered to him—tonight. He's flying in on his chopper," Knightley interrupted.

"Good. We can end this here."

"Petrov is seriously pissed but she's promising to make it up to him, renew their sexual relationship in her dungeon after her business dealing with Morales tonight."

"That's back at her house," Liz said.

"How do you know?" Darcy raised an eyebrow.

"Something she said to me in the bathroom at L'Enclave. Don't forget, she wanted me for her lover."

"Don't remind me."

"Petrov has begrudgingly agreed to go with her to where one of her underlings is bringing the girl to Golyevo Heliport for delivery to Morales. Darcy, I think we should split up on this. You keep eyes on Karakurt and Petrov in case something goes wrong, and I'll head on over to the heliport before she gets there. I'll try to secure the girl."

"Sounds good, but like I said. I think it's a set up. Just like Rick's kidnapping, the girl's for the same intent: to get to me. Move the girl, draw me out into an open field."

"True. So let's give them what they want. You for the girl." Knightley grinned mischievously.

Liz gasped. "No."

"Trust me, Liz," Darcy said.

The deputy secretary rose and then left the table, maybe to the men's room, maybe not—but now was the time to act.

"I'll be back," Darcy assured with a sexy wink and a smile before rising. "I need to use the men's room."

What would be the point in telling him to be careful or to hurry back? She just smiled half-heartedly and watched his retreating back. Her heart squeezed as she sat silent beside Knightley, who played with his car key while she mindlessly jabbed her fork into the single prawn on the dish. She tried to channel her nervous energy into killing the already dead shrimp, but her imagination went wild thinking what her husband was about to do, even though she really had no idea. Finally, she tore her eyes from the crustacean and peered over the wrought iron balcony, observing Nadya (who looked stunning in red) lean back into her chair, cross her legs, and sip her champagne. A chill ran up Liz's spine.

"She's a knockout; isn't she?" Knightley questioned, his eyes also fixed on the spider woman.

"Yeah. I can see her allure for any man. Sort of like a black widow—really sexy looking until she kills you."

"Hence the name Karakurt."

"I wish I could be the one to kill her. That poor Julia."

"Liz, you don't wish for that. 'Cause once you go there, it's hard to get back the person you used to be. Just ask Darcy. The Iceman is embedded in your husband forever."

"Oh, I don't think so, John." She glanced back down to Nadya as she considered Knightley's opinion of her husband. That wasn't true.

It was only a couple of minutes later when, from behind her, Darcy cleared his throat, and she glanced up to see him adjusting the knot of his tie.

"What did you do?"

"What does one do when they go to the bathroom?"

"Wise guy."

He sat, followed by a pull to the remainder of his vodka.

"Did you hurt him?" she asked.

"No. I had to take a leak, but kept one eye trained on him."

"Oh." She watched Petrov take his seat across from Nadya again, wishing Darcy had hurt the evil human trafficker.

"You sound disappointed. Would you rather have had me drop a dirty diaper bomb into his suit pocket?"

"Ha! You must admit, that was a very good tactic, but I'm afraid that for Petrov, I was wishing for something more to the point—maybe using that Baretta you have become so proficient in using."

"You're right, not nearly diabolical enough for him, but impressive in its own right. I just never thought you'd employ something like that on Caroline. Not that I object, you know."

Darcy gazed at her. He, too, loving this familiar banter despite the looming danger—so similar to when they looked for Crawford at the casino.

Playfully pursing her lips, she admired his sly smile, feeling so much better following their honesty in the hotel. Neither Caroline nor

Obsidian would take him from her ever. She was confident of that now. All they had needed to do was clear the air.

Knightley pushed back his chair, stood, then downed his second vodka. He smiled with a lopsided quirk. "Time to go. I'll get the car to take Liz back to the hotel. Then I'll meet you at the target area, Iceman."

"Right. If you get a shot, take it."

Knightley grinned. "God, it's good to be back in the game. See you later, man."

Darcy held out his hand to her, smiling with reassurance. "Are you ready, Lakmé?"

Her stomach lurched and not from the sashimi or the egg rolls.

"Don't worry. I told you. I'll be fine."

"I know. It's just that you hate this stuff."

A little wink accompanied by his playful tease comforted her. "Not anymore; I get to have you as my Bond girl."

22
Hell on Wheels

D on't listen to Knightley. You know me better than him," Darcy said, eyes fixed forward as he held Liz's hand, walking through Turando: Palace's Florentine courtyard. It seemed to come out of nowhere and, on her part, an obvious statement.

"I would hope so. I am your wife, after all."

He abruptly stopped and turned to her, both hands clasping hers. The lines on his forehead crinkled as he considered his words carefully, and she grew concerned.

"What he said about me was incorrect, and I thank you for letting him know it. Iceman isn't embedded in me. That's not who I am. I don't kill because it's in my blood or because there's no turning back."

"I know that. What you did … what you *do* is because you have to in order to protect innocents."

"Yes."

"Others don't know your heart and your struggles, where you came from and what you witnessed but I do, Fitzwilliam." She reached up, her hand smoothing his furrowed brow before she sweetly kissed him.

"How did you know our conversation?" she asked.

"The necklace."

"Ah. I forgot."

"Like I said, I enjoy having you near me—even when apart." He smiled and, just like that, his concern ended and they continued walking to the restaurant's exit doors.

The chilled night air didn't bother her as much as she'd expected. The sable was luxuriously warm and, besides, her blood was boiling with fear, but she tried to conceal it from Darcy. Her powers of quick observation took in the scene around her. Perhaps it was because of her nerves and the fact that this could possibly be the last time she would see him, but still, she noted everything from how some dining patrons waited for the valet to bring their car to how a few others walked across the street for a midnight stroll through the park. Twinkling lights wrapped around tree trunks and Turandot Palace was lit in goldenrod against the black sky. Her eyes fell on Knightley waiting in the Mercedes for Darcy to escort her across the street so he could drive her back to the hotel before heading for the Golyevo Heliport and his half of the Macarena. Three cars down the avenue was her husband's rented white Lamborghini, waiting for him to follow Karakurt. Behind Knightley, two traffic *politsiya* straddled BMW motorcycles as if they were anticipating someone to run a red light or double park. The officers conversed through raised helmet face shields.

She took a deep breath of the invigorating air then squeezed Darcy's hand clasped in hers. As expected, he raised them to his lips, depositing a gentle kiss. "I'll be back at the hotel before you know it. So stop worrying."

"Easy for you to say."

"C'mon, Knightley's waiting."

Suddenly, their eyes snapped to each other's in panic when they both observed Nadya and Petrov prematurely exit the restaurant behind them. Damn. Both Obsidian men had erroneously assumed they had time before Nadya and the deputy secretary finished their dinner.

"Shit," Darcy said under his breath.

Mr. Clean's fingers tapped the steering wheel in nervous release, motioning with his head for her to hurry.

It felt like slow motion with each rapid step she and Darcy took across the quiet street, but in actuality everything happened so fast, like in a blur where only reaction and endorphins played their part. But, again, Liz saw it all clearly—a series of events that spelled disaster when put together. The Russian targets walked toward an exotic sportscar at the end of the street, and the police climbed off their motorcycles. One walked to Knightley where he sat drumming his fingers against the wheel again, and the other officer pulled out his ticket pad, walking up toward the Lamborghini. Nadya and Petrov climbed into the car. Liz saw it all playing out before her eyes and all she could think of was that Knightley needed to get to the airport before them and Darcy needed to follow them—now. There would be no stopping at the hotel.

The asphalt gap between them and the police lessened as though mere seconds were long minutes. She approached, her body closest to the motorcycles as one officer harassed Knightley and the other gave the Lamborghini a ticket. In panic, her heart thundered in her ears as she moved seemingly on autopilot. She glanced up at her husband's furrowed brow and instantly recalled his explanation about Caroline's new large pistol, designed by her father. Her fingers let go of her purse, dropping it onto the avenue before shoving her hand below his suit jacket, unsheathing the massive handgun. Darcy didn't even have time to respond when she reacted without thought, only spontaneous action. Mere seconds elapsed and, with both hands, pointed the gun at an empty bus stop shelter, pressed the button on the grip and sent a red beam 50 feet across the avenue. The heat-guided laser exploded the shelter in a loud burst of flame, nearly knocking them backward. The police reacted, a cacophony of car alarms and screams filled the air, people ran and Nadya's car peeled out. Before Liz even knew what she was about, she tossed Darcy the now inert pistol, bolted to the motorcycle, hiked her skirt, and climbed on.

"Holy Crap! What did you do?"

"Get on!" she yelled to him when she pressed the starter button bringing the bike to life. The Mercedes peeled out, tires leaving smoke and two trails of black tar as Knightley sped away, his tail lights disappearing down the avenue.

"We'll take the Lamborghini!"

"Just get on or we'll lose eyes on her!"

"Then let me drive!"

"There's no time." She felt wild and crazed, adrenaline coursing through her veins when he straddled the bike behind her, wrapping his arms around her waist.

With a wide-open throttle, she gassed the accelerator and burned rubber in getaway.

"Don't forget to counter steer," he commanded, steel and wonderment dueling in his voice, "Push left, turn left. Push right, turn right."

She couldn't help boldly laughing, yelling back at him in definite response, "If you back seat drive, Fitzwilliam, you can walk to the heliport! Just tell me where I'm going."

Unrestrained by a helmet, her hair blew back into him and he leaned forward looking down at his wrist on her tummy, eyes on the GPS tracking on the Smart Watch. Traffic was slowing at an intersection but that didn't stop her. Again, she hammered down, speeding in and out of traffic, lane splitting and doing everything that he had taught her over the last seven months. As though a levee had broken, she felt like a wild child, "Highway to Hell" playing in her head, competing for dominance while he did exactly as she knew he would.

"Take this corner wide.

"Look where you want to go."

"Stop it!" she shouted back to him until he finally said, "I'm sorry. You're doing great, babe." His palm rubbed her stocking-clad exposed thigh. "You must be freezing."

"I'm okay. A little chill in the air doesn't affect the Iceman's woman."

His approving laughter and following response of "You bet you are!" was all she really needed. To her it was his own release of being so over-protective, but, even still concerned, his hand reached up to the dashboard controls, flipping two switches. She felt the immediate warmth in both the hand grips and the seat and then her waist when he tightened his hold around her. His body anchored against hers, prompting her riding with leaning pressure and turn cues, just as he always did with his polo ponies. She gunned the bike down an empty cobblestone street at his direction then turned down another, trying to close the gap on the tail lights of Nadya's vehicle in the distance as she entered the highway north toward the heliport.

Once on the empty expressway, just like Nadya's sports car, Liz opened the bike up full tilt. The wind was cold against her face but she was grateful for the large windshield. She could hear her husband's labored breath in her ear, "Remember what I taught: predict, decide, and execute. You're doing 90, so focus on control, turbulence is normal."

Even though her knees were anchored to the bike as she rode, he must have known that her four-inch heels were having a hard time balancing on the narrow foot pegs when he said, "Lift your feet one at a time," then slid his below hers, giving her a larger solid anchor. Together, they were quite a team.

Ten minutes later, Darcy spoke into her ear. "Knightley's in. Gun it, baby."

She did as instructed, pushing the bike to the limit, the wind velocity attacking her face, but damn if the whole thing was exciting.

* * *

Knightley shut off the Mercedes headlights when he entered the service entrance of the Golyovo Heliport, then parked behind an old metal toolshed not far from the gate. Apart from the cars passing on the expressway beside the heliport, it was quiet, the facility closed for the night. The walk to the helipad and three hangars was only about forty meters ahead. If not for the intermittent red light, he might have missed the two closed circuit cameras up in the trees on the way to the security gate. Stealthily he moved behind a tree, withdrew his silenced .45 and shot out the cameras with precision.

He felt calm for what lie ahead; perhaps the vodka had taken off the edge. Examining the eight-foot-tall wire security gate before him, he chuckled, grabbed a hold and climbed until he was on the opposite side, swinging over with ease. He may have been out of circulation for some time, but he was still fit and still didn't give a crap what was beyond the fence. His secret death wish hadn't left him yet. In the end there was no one and nothing to go home to. And honestly, unless someone similar to Liz Darcy and her bravery catapulted into his life, there wasn't much to look forward to either.

Bright lights up ahead surrounded the hangers, air traffic tower, and several sheds. From his covert position, he could make out a couple of helicopters parked on the helipad but one was clearly occupied; both cockpit and cabin lights were on, illuminating the 75-foot-long AugustaWestland 101, one of the world's most expensive and luxury armored choppers. It was clear that this was Diablo's transport. Four machine gun-toting sicarios surrounded the waiting helicopter and a Jeep SUV. He breathed a sigh of relief that he'd made it before Karakurt and her cohort. Thankful for Liz's fast thinking, he'd driven balls-out to get to the girl before the spider woman's arrival.

Knightley's dark suit blended into the night, and he made his way along the perimeter from one building to the next, shooting out each CCTV as he made his way to attack position. It felt easy … maybe too easy. A single no-brainer shot could fall each sentry without even breaking a sweat. Diablo wouldn't be that careless. As he neared the Augusta, he could see a blonde woman through a rear window of the cabin, her mouth gagged with a red scarf. She was obvious bait. Yeah. Iceman was right; this was a set up. The adrenalin coursed through his body. It felt like breaching the Amazon again, only he was coming in naked. Creeping behind one of the metal hangers, he thought he heard voices from within and paused to pay closer attention. Silence. It must have been his imagination; the blood was now rushing to his ears, and he moved to the building closest to his first target. He peered around the hanger and fired. One down, bullet to the head: three remain before he could enter the helicopter.

Confident that Darcy and Karakurt were only minutes behind him, he moved fast this time. Blood boiling, face set in stone when he came out into the clear, surprising the target to his left. Pistol held out as he swiftly approached. Bang. The second fell.

Now visually concealed by the chopper, he dropped to the ground, rolled under the cabin and came up on the other side firing. The third fell and Knightley rushed the fourth enemy at the stairs before he could get off a shot. Down he went just as quickly as the other three had.

He took the steps two at a time, his breath steady when he entered the helicopter, pistol held to his chest at the ready. But for the girl, both the cockpit and massive cabin were empty. No Diablo. Julia's eyes grew wide when she spotted him; wrists bound to the leather seat, she struggled to get free, making noises. "Ssh. I'm gonna get you out of here," he quietly said before rushing to her.

Quickly, he cut her ties, pulled down the gag and grabbed her hand. "Are you hurt?"

"No. Oh God! Thank you!"

"As we exit stay behind me on the stairs. Do you understand?"

"Yes. Did my father send you?"

What he wanted to say and what he did say were two different things. After what she'd been through now was not the time to call him a traitorous jackass. "Your father helped us to find you."

"There are more guards. They're with the man who brought me here."

"Let me worry about them. Outside this plane, parked to the right of us, is a gray Jeep. As soon as you step onto the tarmac run for cover there."

Her head bobbed in a quick succession of nods and she swallowed hard before walking in his footsteps down the small staircase. Only a few steps down from the helicopter, he heard the metal hanger door open when Karakurt's sports car entered the heliport. Damn.

Diablo's unbuttoned overcoat swirled in the wind around his long legs with each step he took as he walked toward the helipad with his security team flanking him three and three to each side, one behind him. Several of whom also had machine guns.

"Run," he commanded to Julia, opening fire. Fuck.

Tapping his left ear, he shouted, "Iceman, hope you're around the corner. The girl's not secure and you better come in hot because I'm about to get my ass kicked. Diablo and Karakurt are in sight. I repeat; I have eyes on the targets."

Now surrounded, trapped in wide-open space, the girl sprinted to the SUV as hell broke loose in a hail of bullets around them. Knightley withdrew a second pistol, two hands shooting in two directions as he made his way, ducking and firing toward the Jeep for getaway. Machine gun fire sprayed the tarmac.

Just then, the blades of the chopper slowly began to turn as if by remote control. Several of Diablo's men went down but the man himself seemed to be made of armor both in body and resolve. Visually unarmed, he walked with purpose toward the helicopter, unfazed by the bullets as though invincible.

* * *

A billboard directed Liz and Darcy to the exit for the heliport and as she anticipated her husband had more instruction, but she suddenly didn't feel so obstinate, welcoming his direction on cornering the bike. Admittedly, his advice was invaluable and needed. In excited anticipation, her blood pumped into her frozen ears with each loud thump. Who the hell knew what they were riding into? Was Knightley safe? Was Diablo dead from his bullet? What of Julia Bertram?

As the bike slowed onto the exit ramp, she felt her husband's warm kiss on her earlobe then a suckle to warm them. Ahead they could see the entrance to the heliport, the metal gates wide open and welcoming. It was no wonder—they were right on top of Nadya; she had just arrived.

"This is it, babe. We're going in hot. Knightley's under fire."

Cold fingers clenched around the grip and Liz gassed the throttle, barreling through the entrance driveway, the zipping hum of the bike drowning out the sound of gunfire. "Stay low, chest to tank behind that bulletproof windshield," he ordered, withdrawing the Baretta strapped to his ankle.

Her blood raced through frozen veins when they entered the heliport. She felt one with him in that moment. Everything depended upon her and Iceman and she pushed all fear aside.

The chopper blades cut the air in fast rotation, the drone filling the air, competing with the roaring rev of the motorcycle as it flew across the tarmac.

At 50 mph Darcy picked off the remaining sicario security force as Knightley helped Julia into the Jeep under the welcomed cover fire.

Petrov and the spider woman exited the sports car—no doubt expecting to join Morales on the chopper for safety—firing at the motorcycle.

Liz weaved and turned the bike, narrowly missing getting shot but lining up a perfect shot for Darcy when the motorcycle faced off with the woman who had bested them in Paris. Nadya's eyes locked with hers.

Again, it all happened so quickly as Diablo and one of his henchmen climbed the stairs of the helicopter for getaway. The drug lord—his menacing scar evident—stopped and turned in the doorway just as Darcy executed two perfect shots. Karakurt, then Petrov, fell dead.

Liz's focus remained on Diablo as if in slow motion when he removed a pistol from the inside coat pocket. He, too, had a perfect shot set up: her husband, open and exposed with his attention diverted to his own targets.

Morales fired.

"Hold on!" She shouted in split second decision, abruptly letting up on the throttle and turning the bike, wheels spinning like two gyroscopes as she leaned low to one side, almost skidding out.

Diablo's bullet made contact: the bike's exhaust pipe as it did a 180-degree turn of burning rubber and smoke.

More shots fired, but neither she or Darcy could see. By the time she skillfully righted the motorcycle, the helicopter door was closed and the chopper had lifted off the ground. Both Knightley and Darcy fruitlessly fired at the impenetrable armor as it flew away.

On the highway beside them, a steady stream of police lights and sirens were making their way to the heliport.

"We gotta get out of here!" Darcy shouted across to Knightley.

Liz gunned the bike, following the Jeep's lead out the service entrance from which he had originally come.

Morales had gotten away. Assassins and target failing in Operation Macarena, but Julia and Knightley were safe.

23

Flight

Morales settled into the leather seat, his body filled with rage but he tried to conceal it as pain shot through his shoulder.

"Are you comfortable Señor Morales?" his pilot and second in command lieutenant asked through the intercom. It was just the two of them on the helicopter; his enemy had taken out his security force.

He depressed a button with his good arm, his vision locking on the receding night landscape as the colorful minarets of St. Basil's Cathedral grew smaller. "*Gracias*, Cortes. It is just a flesh wound. Nothing I cannot see to myself."

Finally, he tore his gaze away and stood, peeling off his blood tinged overcoat, most of the blood from one of his sicarios when he got shot. He bent, slid a knife from its ankle sheath then tore at his sweater, unable to lift it above his head in order to care for his wound. Then finally came the difficult removal of his Kevlar vest before he stood in just a T-shirt ready for a minor patch job to his arm.

"It is a shame about *Diablesa*," the pilot said.

He didn't answer beyond a grunt as he tugged the first aid kit from an overhead compartment. No, it wasn't a shame. He'd planned it that way and had no remorse—no emotion whatsoever. Nadya had outgrown her usefulness and enjoyment. She'd created a resilient and prolific crop of coca and she'd given him some of the most virulent strains of biological weaponry. Her connections to corrupt foreign dignitaries and government officials gave La Muerta Mundial the face of legitimacy as she helped to form networks of trafficking on five continents. He couldn't deny that her ready companionship had fed his hunger for the sexual liaisons he craved. She met his every need both in and out of their bondage world. He could forgive her the cheating dalliance with Ivan, even this Petrov dog she had returned to after all these years, but the woman had crossed the line when she attempted to sell Bertram's daughter without his consent. Ah, what great irony that he used the very man he sought revenge on to do his dirty work by killing Nadya. Julia, at least, had served the purpose to draw him out, and Nadya had delivered him. It was the least she could do. He had not planned it this way but, in the end, it had all worked out so seamlessly when she telephoned him to say she expected Iceman in Moscow.

"I'm sorry you missed the Iceman, sir?"

"Next time I will not miss. I did not expect a second man at the heliport. His bullet hit just as I took aim at the motorcycle."

"The woman—steering the bike. Someone you think is special to him?"

"Possibly. Carlos is working on that. He has a lead since following Richard Fitzwilliam back to the States." He chuckled wryly. "Apparently, my former captive has a liking for blondes. One came to see him where he and that reporter are held up in Washington, DC, an unbreachable fortress."

"You are taking your revenge slowly."

"*Sí.* It is best to know your enemy, his strengths *and* his weaknesses, his pain will be greater when I can attack his heart, revenge will be sweeter this way."

"And what will you do with Bertram?"

Morales spoke through clenched teeth as he pulled the suture through the wound on his bicep. "On the surface, I have kept my bargain. I have released the girl and as soon as the facial recognition software analyzes the photographs taken from the chopper of Iceman and the woman on the motorcycle, I will enact my revenge. Perhaps it is best that I missed that shot; I prefer to torture a man's soul as much as his body." He closed his eyes and sighed, his mind's eye drawing to Nadya as she dropped to the tarmac, bullet between her eyes. He shrugged, feeling nothing. "Nevertheless. Bertram will arrange for delivery of the weapons in 48 hours and his death will look accidental."

"Very good. Which home would you like to go to tonight, sir?"

"Maria and the children have gone to Krakow."

* * *

Even at this early morning hour, Ostafyevo Business Airport was open for international travelers but the parking lot was empty. Gazing out a window of the Jeep SUV, Liz sat in the back seat beside Julia, mindlessly thinking how the glass terminal resembled an office building. The men silently sat in the front seats as their vehicle pulled through the open gates, heading toward the hangers at the back of the airport.

That flight or fight response had disappeared. Her heart no longer raced, her body and pulse finally calming in the reality that, for the time being, danger had passed—and they had all survived. She tried not to let her thoughts wander, yet again, to the fact that Darcy had come within an inch of death. Of course, her mind overpowered her will and she found herself thanking God that her husband had taught her to look ahead when riding a motorcycle, look to where she wanted to go. Had she not, then she wouldn't have had eyes on Diablo and his gun—pointed directly at Darcy. It could all have ended: his life, their future, and hers.

Shaking her head, she cleared her mind, attempting instead to focus on the aches in her backside from the hard police bike seat and the blisters forming on her heels from her new shoes. Secretly, she longed for her comfortable stable boots. It would only be another day until she was back at Pemberley. Her feet may desire to go home—but her spirit wasn't quite ready to do so. This dangerous adventure, far from the gambit she had thought it would be when she set out with pink bubble glasses, had pulled at so many emotional chords within her. Going home—right now—wasn't what she needed. She glanced to her left at Julia draped in Knightley's suit jacket. The young woman looked blank faced and ashen, her eyes glazed over, lips set. Obsidian's first priority was to get her home to her family.

"Are you okay?" Liz asked for the hundredth time, recalling how banal that must sound to her. Following her own father's kidnapping, that question was ridiculous to pose. No, she wasn't okay.

"I suppose."

"It's all over, Julia. You're out of danger now. That sick, evil woman is dead, and we're taking you home to a safe place."

"To New York?"

"No, to Bethesda; your parents are anxious for your return."

The young woman made a dismissive snort then mumbled something under her breath before looking out the window. That reminded Liz of her own experience last year, having refused to agree with Jane's blind trust of Darcy and Charlie following the wedding-day shoot-out. Trust had been hard for her back then, and she regretted that some measure of *general* mistrust (and insecurity) had been tucked away within her until this adventure. Like a familiar safety net, those emotions had lay dormant, and not because of Darcy, but because of habit, experience, Bill, and both her parents. She wondered if Julia was waking up to the fact that her father had a hand in this nightmare that she had become the victim of. Both Darcy and she could attest to the pain associated with parental deceit and, in her own case, abandonment. Would Julia ever trust her father again once she learned the truth?

Liz draped a comforting arm around Julia's neck and her head gave up the fight, dropping to rest on Liz's shoulder. "You've been through a lot. Going home will be good, you'll see." A slight tremble to Julia's body alerted her to the fact that she was crying and Liz tugged her closer, patting her bicep.

A reassuring glance from Darcy comforted her as his lips twitched attempting to convey a little understanding smile just as he had done when they'd arrived for the first time at the safe house on his motorcycle. Of all the things, she realized on this trip was that she did have *absolute* confidence in her husband's faithfulness and trustworthiness. He had proven it—along with his love—time and again and she felt ashamed for having ever doubted him. *Pfft, Caroline.* How could she have even considered that ridiculous notion? She wistfully smiled back at him.

"Bingley sure is living large, isn't he?" Knightley noted when the business jet came into view, spot lit on the tarmac. "Now that's a sweet plane."

"It's his father's newest one: a custom designed Challenger. They keep it in Prague."

"He has a house in Prague?"

"An apartment, in addition to his houseboat in Maryland, villa in Capri, and a safe house chalet in St. Moritz. In time, you'll be loaded, too."

The Jeep drove toward the flight line and Julia sat up. "Thank you, Liz. I'll survive." Wiping her tears, she tried to smile. "I have a lot of questions for my father, and I'll be demanding honest answers. So I guess it's good to go home and face it head on."

"You may not like what you hear, but I have no doubt that your father loves you. If he didn't, then my husband and John wouldn't be here. I have no doubt that Director Bertram is torn up over your kidnapping."

"I suppose." She looked away, again, tears brimming.

Liz felt inept and ill-equipped to deal with Julia's trauma, unsure what to say or do until Darcy looked back at her, again. He pointed out the window. "I see Charlie brought your sister with him."

Reminiscent of the year prior, Jane waited on the tarmac, nervously bouncing on the balls of her feet as Charlie descended the plane stairs behind her.

"We'll take care of Julia; go to your sister. I know you're anxious," he said with a wink.

When the Jeep stopped, she took off her shoes, opened the door, and, barely waiting for Knightley to turn the engine off, jumped out the vehicle, bolting toward Jane. Flooded with emotions of all kinds, what she needed most was Jane's wacky levity *and* she needed to thank her because without her sister's help, she would not have gone to Paris. Operation Macarena might have had a very different outcome, and poor Julia, not to mention Darcy and Knightley, might not be alive.

"Lizzy!" Jane shouted, running to her with open arms, their bodies crashing together. "Thank God you're safe. I was so worried. Are you okay? Charlie wouldn't tell me anything other than that Darcy was madder than hell that you showed up in Paris. I'm so sorry!"

"I'm okay, really. Don't be sorry at all. In fact, I owe you a big one for encouraging me to go. Oh, Jane! I was so wrong. He wasn't cheating."

"Yeah. I didn't think so, but you had to find out for yourself." She set Liz back, but her hands lingered on the sable. A sly smile formed before she said playfully, "Well don't you look like you just stepped off a Paris runway. Love the dress, the fur, those shoes in your hands. Your snake necklace matches perfectly. Damn! Iceman sure hooks you up on these 007 ops. You really are a Bond chick now."

"Ugh, you can have these miserable shoes; for $4,500 you'd think they'd be more comfortable. They are *not* for motorcycle riding, that's for sure!"

Jane's jaw dropped before holding out her hand for the coveted stilettos.

"Shame you have no other clothing to pass my way," she said.

"We had to leave it at the hotel. I even lost my new clutch purse, along with my passport. That handbag set Fitzwilliam back $900, but it couldn't be helped. I had to reach for his pistol and needed two hands to fire that monster."

"Listen to *you* … one trip to Russia and you're coming home a certifiable bad ass!"

(Snort) "Caroline called me certifiable, too." She hugged Jane again. "God, it's good to see that you're okay, that nothing dangerous happened back home."

"Nothing a little late-night spying on the swimming pool couldn't take care of."

"You are so bad!"

"I know, but you were right!—a wet Wentworth is a sight to behold."

"I know he's hot, but do me a favor don't mention him ever again. Fitzwilliam foolishly thought I was cheating with the guy."

"I told you Caroline would fill his head with bullshit."

As though without a care in the world, Charlie walked up behind them, greeting Liz with a cheerful "Hey, Liz! Good to see ya'!"

"Hi, Charlie. I feel like this is a repeat of Seville with you coming to rescue us with a plane."

"Well, at least this time we're headed home. Mission accomplished."

She swallowed hard. "I owe you a huge apology for putting you in such a position at Pemberley. I'm really sorry about lying to you and bringing Iceman's wrath down on you."

"You don't have to apologize, really. I get it. We all do crazy things for love. Look at me—I'm training Pussy Galore how to whip my ass into submission. Did you two at least work things out?"

"We did," Darcy stoically said, arriving to their conversation with Knightley and Julia trailing behind him. "We need to get up in the air and get out of Moscow."

Yes, it was evident that Iceman's chilly persona was back in place. No greeting, no smile, and nothing but frost in his veins as he led the way up the stairs, suit jacket slung over one shoulder and mobile phone in his other hand.

"Is that Julia Bertram?" Jane whispered, ascending the staircase far behind the others.

"Yes. We've all been put through the wringer but Julia's been through hell."

"I bet. I'll pour her a drink when we get on board."

"It'll take more than a glass of wine to set her back to normal. I have so much to tell you, Jane."

"Well, you better start with telling me about that BDSM club … shuga!" she laughed, back to making jokes.

They entered the Challenger's cabin in single file and Liz's eyes grew wide at the six leather reclining seats and sofa, galley kitchen, television, and the tiny sleeping cabin. This was far beyond any plane she'd ever been on. Even the CIA rendition aircraft was nothing like this.

In a manner that Liz remembered well after their mother had left, Jane spoke to Julia in a calming tone as she held open the door to the private room across from the lavatory. "If you'd like, you can rest here. We'll be making a couple of stops to refuel on our way back to the States. I'm sure you could use a sound sleep."

A meek smile accompanied a small "thank you" and both sisters watched with concern how Julia crawled onto the narrow bed. She laid there, head on the pillow, hands tucked under her cheek without saying a word—just staring at the wall.

"Can I get you something to eat or drink?" Jane pressed but received no reply.

Liz's heart squeezed and she covered Julia with the lap blanket draped at the foot of the bed before closing the door behind their departure.

"Is she in shock?" Jane asked.

"Fitzwilliam says no. She's like I was the day of Dad's kidnapping, sort of deer in headlights. I think she knows her father is a traitor."

"Yeah. Sucks when you realize that. Speaking of fathers ..."

"I'd rather not. I'll deal with his extracurricular activities when we get home. I want to be mad at him but right now I'm torn. His little toys saved our lives."

The engines started and Liz looked down the narrow aisle to where Darcy stood, motioning to two seats.

"Take the window seat," he directed as she approached him. His jaw clenched, clearly in that place where he had a difficult time straddling two worlds: warmth and ice, life and death. Apart from making sure she was okay, he hadn't spoken much in the Jeep, but he didn't need to. His expression told her so much: the weight of what had almost happened to her at the heliport was burying him, pushing him back down into that place that Iceman had risen from after their conversation at the hotel.

No doubt, he was battling with his conscience, having insisted she accompany him to Moscow, thereby putting her in direct danger versus sending her home to the threat of perceived possible danger.

As the others prepared for departure, she sat and looked up at him, their eyes locking when he stilled above her. His hair was tousled, his tie gone and the top button of his shirt opened. There was a tenderness growing in his dark eyes and then she saw something unmistakably warm: that subtle quirk to his lips. Barely perceptible but it was there and she grabbed that moment to mouth "I love you." And then he did it—that small yet powerful gesture that had the strength to break every tense situation—he ran his index finger down her cheek before sitting beside her. It felt so good to, once again, have him next to her after what they'd just survived. Like a warm blanket, his physical presence—even just the connection of their hands and his arm pressed against hers—comforted her.

The plane began to taxi, and Knightley buckled himself into the seat beside them on the opposite side of the aisle; already he had a scotch waiting for him in the console cup compartment. His bottom crooked tooth showed itself when he said with a hearty laugh of realization. "Damn! I knew I recognized Diablo's helicopter! That was the one they used in the Bond movie, *Skyfall*. Kick ass movie—kick ass scene."

"Oh yeah?" Charlie asked. "That Augusta can go like 192 mph, and the range … way impressive at about 850 miles give or take."

Darcy turned his head to look at Charlie stretched out on the sofa beside Jane; neither of which were concerned when they slid to the end as the jet lifted off the runway. "Eight hundred miles, you say? That gives Obsidian a radius as to where his home may be. If he was headed farther, he wouldn't limit his transportation to a chopper, nor inconvenience himself with several fuel stops."

"So you'll go after him?" Charlie asked.

"Not me but maybe Rick will. I'm sure he wants some payback."

"I'll go," Knightley said. "What the hell do I have to lose?"

That comment broke Liz's heart. She had never learned his story from Darcy, knowing full-well that it wasn't her husband's story to tell and he'd hedge, but she could tell that Obsidian's newest recruit was lonely. Knightley harbored a sorrow that was so deep that it showed itself in his obvious death wish and blasé attitude about danger.

Neither Charlie nor Darcy commented and Knightley slugged back the liquor, looking out the window into the darkness. For long minutes as the Challenger reached cruising altitude, Obsidian's agents and friends sat in silence, each contemplating the events of the evening and the future of Operation Macarena. Liz wondered what the next op name would be should they decide to go after Morales.

When the plane leveled and the "unfasten seat belts sign" came on, Jane went to work in the galley, preparing everyone a drink. Music filled the cabin and the television came to life. Rick's smiling face came on the screen.

"Looks like you are all celebrating. Good job, everyone!"

"Hey, Rick," Jane greeted, passing before the TV with a tray of cocktails in her hands.

Apart from the bandage to his head, he looked well rested, better than Liz expected given Darcy's claim of him being in a bad way, but she surmised that was more for her benefit so that he could go off half-cocked to Paris without her knowing.

"How are you feeling, Rick?" Liz asked.

"On the mend. I have good nursing care." He smirked and she knew he meant Sarah not Caroline who was still hanging out in Paris— probably at L'Enclave.

"We lost Morales," Darcy said morosely then sipped the Jack Daniels that Jane had placed on the table before him.

"We'll get him."

"We were just discussing that. You're on your own on that operation. I won't be involved, Cousin."

"I've heard that before, but we'll discuss it when you get back, after the dust settles. Mr. Clean, consider yourself off shit detail from this point forward. Caroline was impressed with your field work and assistance in interrogating Nadya Karakurt. What's the spider woman's status?"

"Dead," Knightley replied. "As is Alexei Petrov the Federation's Security Council Deputy. Darcy took them out at the extraction of Julia Bertram. Man, was that a show!"

"We'll have hell to pay for taking out one of the heads of the Russian President's national security team, but I suppose Bertram will have to dance around that issue with the State Department. Serves that jackass right, he got us into this mess in the first place."

"Yeah. Let him explain drug trafficking, gun running, and a sex slave trade," Darcy said.

"And how is Julia?"

"Marginally worse for the wear, but I think her bigger fight will come when facing her father," Liz said.

"Right. And what happened to the target? Morales?"

"I was able to get off a shot before he fired at Iceman and Liz on the bike. I think it hit—and he missed. Hey, Liz, you and me worked in tandem—didn't we? Without some serious skills on that police bike, our man Darcy would be toast."

Feeling proud, Liz glanced up at Darcy; he had yet to say anything about the events of the night and she wondered what he was thinking. Her shy smile was met with that quirk to his lips but nothing else.

"Good work, Liz. Maybe one day you'll join Obsidian, like your sister."

"I'll leave the femme fatale stuff to her, Rick. Jane has more skills than I do, and honestly, I don't think my husband would approve."

"Well, you all completed Operation Macarena's true purpose: brought me and Julia home and that's what matters. For the time, we'll forget about Morales. Come on back to the Beltway. Thanks, everyone. Our complete debriefing meeting is scheduled for next Tuesday at the dance school. See you then."

"Later, Rick," Charlie said before the TV went blank and the music raised.

Darcy placed Liz's hand in his, thumb caressing the pad of her hand in gentle strokes, as they ignored Charlie and Knightley's continuing conversation. She snuggled into Darcy's other arm draped over her shoulder, and pulled her legs up, tucking her feet up onto the seat. His fingers toyed with the messy strands of hair at her shoulder.

"I didn't say, you know, earlier … you were amazing … back there in Moscow. You saved my life," he quietly said.

"I … well I—"

"Let me finish … You really knew how to handle that bike like you'd been riding for years. I'm proud of you … you were so brave, so proficient and I've been an unmitigated ass trying to keep you from cutting lose on the bike."

That made her heart soar. He'd always been encouraging to her, but *that* compliment demonstrated that trust was never the issue behind his smothering and lecturing.

"You weren't an ass, nor holding me back. You taught me to ride; you gave me the skills and in the end the confidence."

As if a veil had suddenly lifted, Liz considered her earlier claim to Darcy that he had been *too* overprotective of her. She took a cleansing breath, clearly seeing that his need to wrap her in proverbial bubble wrap was not about his concern for her lack of judgment or inability. It was simply because his own fear of losing her to forces outside his control made him react as only a former military man would: with decisive guard for the one he loved most in the world.

"Um … I have a confession to make, Fitzwilliam."

"Oh?"

"I was wrong, so wrong. I know now that it wasn't about you *not* trusting in my judgment."

He furrowed his brow. "And what made you see that?"

"Your overprotectiveness is no different than my own for you because I'm *terrified* of life without you. Had that not been the case, then I wouldn't have feared Caroline taking you away from me. My insistence of you leaving Obsidian last year—my dislike of you going back for this op—was born from that fear alone. I know it sounds silly—given my own love of speed on the bike, but it's for that reason that I worry every time *you* get into the Ferrari without me."

"You worry about that? You never said."

"What would have been the point? As much as you have tried to hide your need for an adrenaline rush from me, I know what feeds you. But just as you have been afraid of me on a motorcycle, I'm equally terrified of you in that sports car doing 100 mph around Dead Man's Bluff. I died inside when Gus mentioned that your "lunch with Charlie" was actually skydiving in West Virginia."

"Oh, babe. I'm sorry."

"I'm not admonishing you. I'm only saying that I 'get it' now."

Completely de-iced, he chuckled wryly. "So I'm not a possessive, controlling, smothering jerk after all?"

She turned in her seat and placed both hands on his face. "You, dear man, are just achingly in love, as is your wife, and we both know that without the other it would be a half-life." Her quivering lips touched his and his reply was a soft lingering caress of sweet agreement. She literally could feel his emotion pour out.

Parting, he whispered. "Did that kiss wipe out the image of a hot, wet Wentworth from your mind?"

"What?"

"You forgot, Lakmé, the necklace is still transmitting. I heard it all."

"Is that why you went all Iceman when we boarded?"

He blushed, called out for that stone-cold reserve. His fingers clasped the diamond necklace to turn off the transmitter before finally removing the receiver from his ear.

"Hey, I'm still learning. Don't fault me for being jealous."

"We're *both* learning, but I think on this trip, we've come a long way."

"Are you ready to go home, babe?" he asked pushing back the hair from her face.

She wasn't but after what he'd been through she was sure he most likely wanted to go back to the horses, solitude, decompression before Gigi's wedding. Further, he was probably anxious to resume her tactical training.

"I'm sure you want to go home, so we will. It's been a wild rush and going back to Pemberley to recharge makes sense, right?" she said, looking away, afraid that her expression would give her true desires up.

"Liz? Be honest with me. Do you want to go home?"

"No."

His smile told her that he didn't either.

"Well I do owe you for saving my life back there. I think a romantic detour is just what you and I need," he said.

* * *

An hour later she was fast asleep, curled up in the seat beside him. He had an idea and was sure she wouldn't mind taking their anniversary trip a little early. The cabin lights were dim and he texted Charlie who was stretched out on the couch two rows back: *Instruct the pilot, we're getting off in Santorini, Greece.*

24

Reset

Two jet skis sped across the deep blue waters off the volcanic Greek island of Santorini, leaving a misting wake and a trail of white foam behind them. Power and exhilaration coursed through Liz's suntanned body as she raced Darcy toward the clear waters of Amoudi Bay and its stunning cliffs.

The Mediterranean sun beat down on them from a cloudless azure sky, but she didn't feel the heat at all. In fact, she felt cool and refreshed, though her cheeks and arms might tell a different story at the end of the day. No doubt the sunburn she acquired three days ago would renew, but it was worth it.

"You won't win!" she shouted into the wind, her spirit unfettered and carefree.

"Bulldinky!" he laughed back, teasing her with her own silly swearword as he opened the throttle, pushing the watercraft to go faster.

His laughter carried back to her when he turned, a torrent of spray hitting her face. She wasn't angry; she was having the time of her life. Even at that speed, she couldn't help admiring his backside squatted over the seat, rising up and down with each thump of the watercraft meeting the chop.

She, too, took it up a notch, her blood racing, closing in on her husband, careful to keep her focus ahead 50 meters (and away from his backside). "Winner gets to jump the cliff first!"

"Deal!"

Neck and neck the jet skis competed. Both she and Darcy leaned forward, every once and again looking to the other for a millisecond and grinning.

"Are you having fun?" he shouted.

"A blast!"

And with that he leaned, turned, and sprayed her with his wake again.

"You'll pay for that!" She, too, turned her jet ski, breaking the surf in a 360-degree turn and showering him with a steady wave of seawater.

"Ha!" she shouted, gunning the watercraft, the two of them neck and neck toward the small island.

Their crafts tripped the chop until finally the winner was declared when Darcy threw up both arms in victory when they entered the rocky inlet near the cliffside village of Oia. Both slowed, exhilarated and panting with smiles plastered across their faces. Her heart pounded against the watersports life vest she wore.

"You cheated," she said petulantly.

"I didn't; you're just a sore loser. What happened to my hell-on-wheels girl? I thought you said you were going to kick my ass?"

"She was bested by a former Frogman."

"Yes she was," he teased, climbing off the jet ski at the landing jetty on the small triangular-shaped, mountainous island of St. Nicholas where he tethered them.

Standing on the ancient stone, he gazed down at her still seated on the watercraft. She was spellbound by his beauty and watched as he removed his life vest, baring his tanned, broad chest. His muscular arms and tight abs held her fascination with each movement of his upper body. A little contented sigh left her lips—the events of last week almost forgotten; the uncertain future yet to be written. The present was now her focus. Damn, they only had a few days left to this heaven before they had to go back to Virginia.

"You're staring," he teased again.

"How can I not? You're so damned sexy."

She thought she'd die when he playfully flexed his bicep followed by the outstretch of his arm in invitation. "Let's go, gorgeous. Are you ready to climb then jump?"

With a supportive tug and lift, she ended up in his embrace surrounded by his strong arms. "Yes. Sort of."

"You're nervous?"

"Sort of. I've never done anything like this."

"I'll be right there when you bullet in. Nothing will happen to you."

"What about the cliff?"

"Nothing will happen to it either. I promise."

He kissed her, warm lips surrounding hers with delicious wetness. God, she could definitely die in his arms—just like this—with that twinkle of mischief in his eyes and soft lips consuming hers. Ever attentive, he unhooked her life vest then placed it upon his on the jetty. Now bikini bare, she clasped his hand, threading her fingers with his as they climbed the stone steps toward the platform overlooking the bay, the sun beating on their damp backs. At the top of the staircase, they turned, taking in the panoramic vista of the caldera, the snow-colored village of Oia atop the red cliffs, and the colorful fishing harbor of Amoudi at the shoreline. Several boats and swimmers dotted the iridescent combination of aqua blues and greens sun kissed in shimmering gold.

Awestruck by the picturesque view, she reveled in the tranquility and squeezed Darcy's hand. "I have no words. I can't describe just how breathtaking it is," her eyes finally gazing up to meeting his.

"I can."

He wasn't looking at the sea when he said that.

"You're such a mush."

Behind them, neatly tucked into a dugout within the rock was a centuries old white chapel. Unlike the blue-domed churches indicative of Santorini, this simple Cycladic cubic building spoke to her. She wasn't religious and hadn't been inside a house of worship in two decades, but to enter didn't require religiosity, just respect.

"Can we go in before I jump to my death?" she half-jokingly asked, met by her husband's unexpected smile of agreement. She wondered if he had considered the same before she suggested it.

He led the way, pushing open the weather-beaten wood door, and her eyes adjusted to the dimness within, having just come from the brilliance outside. Several silver icons adorned the simple plaster walls. There was no altar, just a few wooden pews that faced a wall of colorful icons. To the right, beside an elderly woman dressed in all black, was a table on which to place lit candles. It seemed a natural thing to do when Liz fingered a white taper, lit it from someone's already burning prayerful petition then stuck it into the sand. From the corner of her eye, she witnessed Darcy do the same. Neither spoke or made eye contact until they left the silence of the chapel.

"What was your prayer?" she asked, shielding her eyes from the sun as she looked up at her husband.

"That you don't chicken out in cliff jumping."

"Wise guy."

He examined her face. "What was yours, babe?"

She shrugged. That was one secret she would keep to herself. "The same."

Laughing, he took her hand again to follow the footpath leading to the side of the mountain, a sort of patio made of ancient stone and shells that overlooked the bay—a popular place for jumping.

"This is it. Do you want to go first?" he asked.

"No. I'm sure I can do this. Tell me again that it's safe."

"It is. Trust me and more importantly, trust yourself."

She peered down at the clear water, eyes settling on the boulders deep within on the right. "Are you sure I won't hit the rocks?"

"Yes, I'm sure. It's deeper than it looks. Just propel yourself with your knees, body perpendicular, arms above your head and keep straight. Don't free form it like some of these kids do."

"Sounds complicated." Her fingers tapped her thigh, unsure where the fear was coming from.

"Okay then, we can do this together. I can hold your hand and we'll jump at the same time."

"No! I *do* want to do this by myself and besides you won fair and square. You jump first."

"Just remember what I have always said about fear and danger—it's the Ferrari in Monaco all over again—enjoy the experience, just like you've enjoyed all the daring adventures you've taken this year. This is nothing in comparison." He smoothed a finger down her cheek before depositing a peck to her lips. Then, as if an eager child, he rubbed his hands together, stepping backward, back against the rocky mountain. His eyes locked with hers and he grinned before he ran to the cliff's edge then catapulted himself off without a modicum of fear.

His powerful body, straight like a bullet, hit the water seamlessly, disappearing below. Seconds later, he came up with a huge smile and a wave.

Clammy palms and a thundering heart almost made her bolt back down the stairs, but his shout of encouragement bolstered her resolve.

"Do it, Liz! You're gonna love it! There is no counter steering involved!"

Stepping back to the rock wall just as he had, she whispered, "Yeah. Trust him. No fear. You ride a SuperLow for Christ sake." She could do this. This was nothing compared to the motorcycle shoot out in Moscow. Besides, Darcy was just below. He wouldn't let anything happen to her. Ever. He was right, she had to trust in herself in yet another new adventure and push the fear aside.

And with that thought, she ran, amazed when her body leapt from the cliff and, a second later, dropped into the bay. Down she went into the sudden enveloping refreshment, her water shoes touching the bottom, and before she could even get her bearings to swim to the top, she felt Darcy's hand on her wrist, tugging her upward into his arms.

She panted, clinging to him, their wet faces only inches apart as they both tread water. "I did it! It was so easy. Let's do it again."

"You got it, babe. This time, can we jump together?"

* * *

Darcy sat comfortably on the terrace of their luxury accommodation at Aria Suites in Santorini. Tucked alongside the rocky cliff and overlooking the Aegean Sea, its whitewashed Cycladic structure provided some of the best views of the volcano. Luckily, *this* last-minute reservation had been available; the room he had initially thought to be perfect—the Tosca Suite (in honor of Floria, his tangoing, derringer-wielding, jealous wife)—lacked the luxurious amenities he sought for her. Instead, and probably more fitting of late, the Carmen Suite was ironically suited. His liberated, spirited, seductress wholly approved of the private terrace, sea view, and the sun lounge. He couldn't help but smile at the memory of her expression upon their arrival; her shock and near-tears adoration of him had bowled him over. A small step, given the weight of his sins, on his way to setting things right between them. The road to a perfect marriage and absolute understanding of each other would take time but they were well on their way after Moscow. He reflected confidently that by their first wedding anniversary they'd have ironed out all the kinks.

Dinner had just been cleared away and their private chef left for the evening; *Lakmé*'s "Flower Duet" played from their sitting room and he smiled. It was the piece that began it all for them, and he recalled with fondness the op that would change his life: lying in Longbourn's field, the growing intensity of the music, Liz's hair flying around her in the Jeep. The image through his rifle scope had affected him profoundly and that memory alone made his heart and mind feel even lighter than it already did as he nursed an ouzo. He waited for her while she slipped into something more comfortable to watch the sun set over the submerged caldera. His fingers wrapped around the glass, bringing it to his lips before sweet anise touched his throat in delicious warmth as it went down. It was their last night and enjoying the magnificent panoramic view with each other was just the way to end the trip. He'd make love to her tonight, like he did every night, but tonight would be different. His heart—more than ever—felt something so deep that he couldn't explain it. As she said the other day before cliff jumping, he had no words.

The corner of his lips quirked, thinking how much Liz was enjoying their time together in Greece. Her wildness seemed less reckless; his suppressed adrenaline need had found balance. Actually, both of them had found a balance in the other. Together, they were untamed and daring, and other times tranquil and lazy—yin and yang, sharing every moment. This trip had set them right. They had hiked and jumped the cliffs, enjoyed every water sport available, and allowed their free spirits to soar. Conversely, they relaxed on the beach, strolled the alleyways and dined quietly. Some nights they read to each other from their terrace, or simply watched the sun set with after dinner drinks, such as tonight.

She joined him on the terrace, wrapped in a pink silk negligee and wearing a glorious smile on her sun-kissed face. He couldn't help the involuntary action of his palm resting over his heart. She'd taken his breath away countless times, but now, feeling as he did, he was utterly enraptured.

"What is this look you are giving me?" she asked.

He just smiled, feeling so damned happy.

"Aren't you going to say something?"

"A man who felt less might." He held his hand out to her, guiding her to sit on his lap, his other hand smoothing around her slender waist as he held her to him. Breathing in, he delighted in her familiar strawberry scent when she snuggled into him, resting her head on his shoulder.

"You know, Fitzwilliam, you say so much even in your silence. I can read your kisses, the furrow to your brow. I'm even learning to read what is behind your Iceman expression."

"Hopefully, you won't ever have to see that again."

"One can hope, but I cannot help but to think that Diablo is still out there. That you're still not sa—"

"Ssh. We vowed not to bring it up while here."

"You're right. I'm sorry."

The sky and the sea were aglow in brilliant orange as the sun touched the horizon. They sat in silent awe, their thoughts their own, their heartbeats one. Darcy's fingers toyed with the delicate gold band encircling her finger and despite the knot in his throat he spoke softly, "I love you, Liz."

She lifted her head from his shoulder, gazing into his eyes, her own filled with tears and he continued, attempting to give voice to the overwhelming emotions he felt tonight.

"I know it's an overused phrase, three small words, but … for me …

"For me, they are the only words you need say."

"No. There is more in my heart but I just … I just don't know how to say it. You're a part of my soul, and … there is no one in this world that I can or will ever love as much as you. Truly, all the love I have in me is only for you."

"And one day our children."

He smiled then gently kissed her lips. "Soon, babe, but until then, each beat is yours."

She stood from his lap and took his hand. "You're afraid, I get it. But I'm not afraid of the future anymore. You're right. It's the Ferrari, the cliff jump, the motorcycle—all of it. We can't allow fear to rule us. Together we shouldn't stop living the life we've dreamed because of Obsidian." Pausing, her sparkling eyes spoke to his soul. "Make love to me tonight, Fitzwilliam. Let's create life from our love. Trust in *us*."

Their gaze continued to hold each other's. He said nothing, the corner of his mouth raising in a tender smile, his breath caught.

"*That* was my wish when I lit the candle in the chapel," she said.

In that moment, with the sun setting behind her and the powerful emotions coursing through every cell in his body, he listened to his heart. He stood and scooped her up into his arms then carried her to the bedroom. Starting a family had been his wish, too.

Epilogue

The bride looked gorgeous as she walked down the fabric runner holding onto her brother's arm, and the summer morning couldn't have been any lovelier for an outdoor wedding. From the processional, Bach's "Air on the G String," to the weather and the guests' spirits, everything was sublime. There was a freshness—a newness—in the country air surrounding Pemberley. The horses ran in the east field and the scent of freshly cut grass wafted in the morning air, mixing with the roses and honeysuckle entwined within the wood trellis. Liz sighed in absolute contentment, feeling optimistic for everyone's future. Happy barely described the euphoria she felt inside watching her sister-in-law and Fitzwilliam, all smiles, greet the pastor under the floral wedding canopy. The chiffon drapes, along with the delicate lace of Georgiana's fingertip veil blew in the gentle breeze. As though it was her own wedding day, seven months earlier, her heart skipped a beat; her tummy fluttered. What a glorious day and an equally beautiful man. She loved her husband more at this moment than ever; each day doubling in intensity than the one before if that was possible.

Still tanned from their spontaneous trip to Greece, he looked dashing in his light grey suit and pink dress shirt, and she resisted a chuckle at the recollection of what they had done last night with that silk tie he now wore.

When he placed his sister's hand in Justin's following a kiss to her cheek, Liz smiled thoughtfully and toyed with one of the ruby and diamond earrings Darcy had purchased for her in Seville last year. Her gaze continued to drink him in and she could see what most people probably overlooked: there was a trace of glistening to his eyes. He was such a sap under that hard SEAL exterior. She'd seen the Iceman do dangerous things in the name of justice and for the ones he loved, but none of that hard-core shell was who he really was. Only a handful in their inner-circle knew the real Fitzwilliam Darcy. She chanced a glance at Rick seated beside his girlfriend, Sarah. She, too, saw the real man beneath that Obsidian front that Rick had honed throughout the years. Her observation traveled to Charlie and Jane, both fun-loving and free spirited, but committed to making the world a better place through Obsidian's covert impact. Although she was still miffed with her father for his housebound projects (even if they had saved the day time and again), it was unfortunate that he was unable to attend due to his house arrest—some things the government was unbendable about and rightfully so. Heck, they hadn't even allowed him to attend her own wedding.

"How did I do?" Darcy whispered settling beside her on a white chair as the ceremony began, anxiety rolling off him, but all smiles.

"Wonderful. She's so happy."

He took her hand, entwining their fingers then raising their knuckles to his lips. "As am I."

"You're such a sap."

"Yes I am, beautiful."

They sat in quiet rapt attention, stealing furtive glances at each other, seemingly oblivious to all the other guests and loved ones surrounding them. Both their hearts swelled at the vows "I do," getting choked up recalling their own declarations of forever. Yes. Forever. That was the vow and they both learned the hard way about trusting one another wholly, and about being completely forthright with the other. Operation

Macarena had succeeded in at least that: opening communication even on difficult matters. Clearing the air in Moscow had bridged the small gap between them. The Darcys were once again a unified force—one to be reckoned with and completely simpatico in understanding the other. They'd been home for over three weeks now, but there hadn't been the need to rehash what had happened in Paris and Moscow. They may have rescued Julia and killed Nadya, but Diablo was still out there somewhere, having escaped in his helicopter. Her self-defense lessons would recommence tomorrow and she was looking forward to training side-by-side with her husband.

These past weeks home, they didn't discuss the unbelievable events they'd been through, instead discussing happy things: their plan to visit the Florida Keys at a secluded resort on Sunset Key for their wedding anniversary in October and reminisce about the impromptu reset getaway to Greece following Moscow. In Santorini, Darcy had spoken of his dream to buy a sailboat and the two of them spending three months in the Caribbean next year, and the hope of children and how it would all work together, but never once had he brought up the subject of entering the polo circuit. When the time was right, she'd ask him about that.

"I know I said this before but … I'm sorry," she whispered leaning toward him and he furrowed his brow. "That I mistrusted you and showed up in Paris."

He shook his head, disagreeing with her and, as was his way, forgiving her and taking the guilt upon his own shoulders. He whispered back. "And I said, that it wasn't your fault. It was mine. Remember?"

"I do."

"Besides, without you, we never would have saved Julia. Don't forget that."

She smiled wistfully, recalling the pride she had felt in the van, having unintentionally handing them Nadya, time and again. Of course, instigated by a series of mishaps and coincidences, but she'd take the credit.

The preacher declared, "You may kiss the bride."

And Darcy did. Turning to face her, his palms cradled her face and he kissed her full on the lips.

Everything was as perfect as it should be. His kiss told her that.

* * *

Under the double-peaked reception tent, guests tapped their glasses with utensils, encouraging the new Mr. and Mrs. Hamilton to kiss. Justin waved them on, grinning to the symphonic clinks until his lips met Georgiana's.

"Look how adorable they are," Liz said. "You couldn't have asked for a better man for her."

"Yeah. He's all right." Darcy joked, his face beaming. "I won't kill him."

"Sheesh. What are you going to say when one day it's your daughter getting married?"

He laughed wryly. "If she becomes anything like her mother, she won't start dating until she's in her thirties."

"And what's that supposed to mean?"

"Just that you fell for the first *real* man to come along and had you any sense at all you would have run far from me. I've brought you nothing but danger."

"But you also saved my father, aa…nd gave me incomparable and insurmountable love, not to mention the sex alone was worth hanging around for."

"Yeah. That, too." He kissed her sweetly, but a tap to his shoulder interrupted them.

"Can I steal you away for a few minutes, Darce?" Rick asked, a timid smile upon his face, visibly embarrassed to pull him from the kiss.

"You can't have him! He was just about to dance with me," Liz joked, eyes sparkling as she hooked her arm into their cousin's. The band was just kicking up following the main course.

"I won't keep him long and then you can have him all to yourself." He winked. "Man-talk if you know what I mean."

"She's a keeper, Rick."

He glanced over to where Sarah stood talking with Aunt Catherine. "She is. She's considering my offer but, after meeting our aunt, she just may high tail it back to London."

"Your aunt is all bark, no bite. Sarah will learn, just as I did, how to tolerate her. She means well even if her manner is off-putting."

"Not that the topic of Aunt Catherine's overbearing intimidation tactics doesn't have comic value, but you can't expect me to miss that little bomb you just skirted over, Rick." Darcy cocked an eyebrow. "What offer did you make to Sarah?"

"Ha! It's not the one you think. We sort of came to an agreement, I'd come clean about Obsidian if she didn't print it. Once she knew, I asked her to join the team. A journalist is not only an effective cover, but also a great source of information coming in and out of the Anglosphere and its overseas territories. Not to mention, her many sources. It's all intel we can't possibly acquire now that Bertram's gone, and along with him our security clearance. His replacement, Elliot, hates what we do almost as much as the jackass did."

"Maybe it's time to shut down Obsidian. Without my father-in-law's help you've lost a small edge."

Rick laughed. "That's not going to happen. C'mon. Let's talk away from all this celebrating."

Darcy bent, leaving Liz with another kiss followed by a caress down her cheek with the back of his index finger. "I won't be long, Lakmé. Save me a dance?"

"Absolutely, darling. You and me on Operation Tango as soon as you get back."

Grinning, Knightley approached her with an outstretched arm. "C'mon, Liz. They're playing our song," he said. "Hope you don't mind, Darcy. Your lovely wife should never be left alone at the edge of the dance floor."

"If it was anyone else, I'd say hands off," he called after their already departing forms through the crowd.

The cousins strolled toward the front of the estate, the music fading behind them with each step. They casually discussed the wedding and Georgiana's beauty. They reminisced and even pondered how Darcy's parents would have been so happy with her choice of husband. Careful of being overheard, conversation was about everything but the elephant in the room. Down the drive, they walked beneath the lush green canopy of trees, the horses grazing at the wood fence beside them.

"How are you feeling, Rick?"

"Good. I feel good. The ribs are still a bitch and I'm gonna have one nasty looking scar, but I'm tough."

"The scar'll make you look like a mean sonofabitch, contradict that fastidious image of yours."

"Hey, I may look all metrosexual and gentlemanly, but I *am* a mean sonofabitch."

"You're right. Speaking of mean … how is Caroline recovering?"

"From our break-up or from her poisoning?"

"Both, I guess."

"Healthwise, she'll be okay. She has full feeling back in her arms now. I think her pride was hurt more than anything. Fierce *kunoichi* miscalculated her opponent and it almost cost her life, let alone kept her from going to Moscow with you and Knightley."

"And owing Liz a great debt in the process."

Rick laughed. "Oh that must have killed her."

"Yeah. And how did it go between the two of you?"

"That went easier than I thought it would. We're through but she'll remain with Obsidian."

"Was she surprised by Sarah's arrival on the scene?"

"Of course. That was yet another blow to her ego." He snorted. "I tried to convince Knightley to take one for the team, to make her feel better about being dumped, but he said he wasn't that desperate for a roll in the hay; he's not completely without a conscience."

"There's always that *Wentworth*. He obviously has no issues with coming onto another man's woman," Darcy said sarcastically.

"I thought of that, but I don't think she'd like to do it in the back of a pickup truck. She might break a fingernail."

"Good point."

"She's through with you, too, Darce. You know, thanks to Liz's drunken set down and life-saving. So I'm not surprised that she declined the invitation to the wedding. I think she's afraid of your wife."

"That makes two of us. Liz *seems* to have moved on from her anger about my not telling her of my past romantic entanglement with Caroline, but I have no doubt that she'll zing me with it during our next argument about something totally unrelated."

"They do that, you know."

Darcy nodded. "Yeah. I'm learning that everything is fair game. Women … marriage … it's as tough as I expected, but more rewarding than I ever imagined."

"Yeah. I suspect so. But you're a man in love."

"With the best woman who is, right now, still foolishly feeling responsible for Operation Macarena going to shit. But truth is, she helped us. Obsidian was ill-equipped to go after Diablo, and I wasn't on my game—with or without—her there."

"I have to agree on both points. Bertram really threw us to the wolves and you'd been playing with polo ponies for too long. But we'll be better … wiser for it going forward."

"I have to credit him for coming through in the end, but I'm glad he's gone."

They reached the foot bridge, the place of his marriage vows. Salaam was not far off in the field; the koi swam below them.

Rick took a deep breath. "He's dead."

"Who's dead?"

"Bertram. The administration is claiming it an accidental drug interaction, but I don't think so. My guess is Diablo got to him with that same shit they injected me with but only in lethal dose."

"Just proves my point how unprepared we all were for dealing with Morales."

"Are you ready now? Is the Iceman back?"

"Why? What do you mean?"

"Are you ready to finish the job we started? I have intel where Morales might be. And truth is, he's always going to be looking for you, for Liz, for anyone you care about. Besting him in Moscow no doubt added fuel to the fire."

"That's a risk I have to face. I'm training Liz to protect herself. And, as you've already witnessed, Pemberley's perimeter is secure. No one's getting past the former military team I hired to safeguard the estate. I'm taking precautions, and she's aware of the danger." Dark eyes examined his cousin's cool blue ones.

"But is that enough? Neither of you can hide inside your compound forever. Come back to Obsidian—off the books—for the sole purpose of taking out Diablo. You and Bingley scouting and sniping. It's what you do best. None of that spy crap I sucked you into."

"No. If you want to go after him, then go after him, but I'm done."

Rick tented his fingers before his stomach. "I don't think you mean that. I know you. I know what feeds your blood: your abject sense of justice. Thanks to Liz, you found the man you once were, but *because* of Liz, and the love the two of you share, you just can't walk away from being the man you *became* after your parents' death."

"Yes I can. For her, I can."

"I disagree, Darcy. Iceman is part of you no matter how far you try to run from him."

Darcy ran his hand through his hair. "Why does everyone think that I can't move on from Iceman? Knightley said the same thing to her back in Moscow. Yes, my sense of justice is impenetrable, but I'm not that stone-cold killer you or he speak of."

"Okay, but I know that protecting Liz is your life's mission, and you would become that stone-cold killer once again when called upon. I'm giving you an opportunity to end this once and for all. You know damn well, that so long as you are alive, she is in jeopardy."

Darcy expelled a deep breath, gazing out at the tranquil landscape before him. He knew he shouldn't even consider this, but his cousin was 100 percent correct. There was no room for his scruples or the softer side of him when it came to protecting Liz. He'd die—and kill—for her safety and happiness.

He spoke with a sense of foreboding, "Where is this job, and where did you get the intel?"

"A lead Sarah has from a contact in Bermuda. There are whispers of cartel submarines trafficking between South America, Florida, and the UK. Her contact swears that a man named Sanchez-Morales has an estate on the south shore of Paget."

"And you're sure you trust her?"

"Without a shadow of doubt."

"They don't dance in Bermuda."

"To hell with the op names. This'll be done your way."

Rick could see the wheels turning in Darcy's head. The consideration, the finality, the peace at the other end of the tunnel.

"We're vacationing in the Keys for the month of October for our wedding anniversary."

"So do it when you get back—or before you go. You know you have to do this."

A heavy pause settled in the fresh air. The two horses ran across the field as Darcy pondered the disconcerting future until he finally expelled a deep breath in defeat. "This one job. Just this job, and only when *I* say that I'm ready and *only* after discussing this with my wife at length and getting the go ahead from *her*. If we agree as a couple that I should go, then I'll let you know."

"Good. I don't want you going back out there then have regrets."

"Rick, I'll go out there in good conscience, doing what I have to to keep her safe."

Rick held his hand out. "Okay, then. When you're ready, get that bastard."

The Iceman and Liz will be back in book three.
In Good Conscience

Glossary

Bang and Burn – Demolition and sabotage operation

Blowback – Spy term for unintended consequences of secret operations abroad

Burned – The compromise of an agent's identity

Caldera - A large cauldron-like volcanic crater

Camo communications – Camouflaged communication devices

Counter steering - At speed a motorcycle is controlled by pushing the handlebars away from direction you want to turn

Dangle – A double agent for the purpose of intelligence collection or disinformation within an agency

Dorogaya – Russian for darling, sweetheart

Decoy – Spy term for a person used to distract the adversary

Company – What Central Intelligence Agency employees call the CIA

EMP – Electromagnetic Pulse

Femme Fatale - A mysterious, seductive woman who uses her charms to ensnare her lovers

FSB – Federal Security Service, Russia. A successor agency of the KGB

Going dark – Termination of communication, going silent

IAFIS – The Integrated Automated Fingerprint Identification System, maintained by the FBI

In flagrante delicto - Sexual misconduct

Joule – One joule is the equivalent of one watt of power radiated or dissipated for one second

Klick - Kilometer

Kunoichi – Modern term for female ninja

Lakmé - A priestess from opera *Lakmé* by Léo Delibes

Mallika -Slave of Lakmé, opera *Lakmé*

Mithridatism - Immunity building against the action of a poison by taking the poison in gradually increased doses

Off the net – Going off the general network of communication

NSA – National Security Agency, a branch of the U.S Department of Defense ensuring the security of American communications

Naked – A spy operating without backup

Russian Security Council – A council that consults with the President on national security affairs

Torii - Traditional Japanese gate found at the entrance of or within a Shinto shrine

Music References

- "Ghost Riders in the Sky" recorded by The Outlaws, Arista, 1980
- "Leave Your Hat On" recorded by Joe Cocker, EMI, 1986
- "Arabesque No. 1" composed by Claude Debussy, 1888
- "Love TKO" recorded by Teddy Pendergrass, Philadelphia International Records, 1980
- "Symphony No. 7, Movement 2" composed by Ludwig van Beethoven, 1812
- "The Magic Flute – Overture" composed by Wolfgang Amadeus Mozart, 1791
- "One Step Closer" recorded by Linkin Park, Warner Bros., 2000
- "Un Bel di Vedremo" from opera *Madam Butterfly*, composed by Giacomo Puccini, 1904
- "Scheherazade, 1st movement" composed by Nikolai Rimsky-Korsakov, 1888
- "Whole Lotta Love" recorded by Led Zeppelin, Atlantic 1969
- "Vesti La Guibba" from opera *Pagliacci*, composed by Ruggero Leoncavallo, 1892
- "I Put a Spell on You" recorded by Nina Simone, Philips Records, 1965
- "Temptation" recorded by Diana Krall, Verve, 2004
- "Epoca" recorded by Gotan Project, Ya Basta, 2006
- "Highway to Hell" recorded by AC/DC, Atlantic, 1979
- "Flower Duet" from opera *Lakmé*, composed by Léo Delibes, 1883
- "Suite No. 3 in D major /Air on the G String" composed by Johann Sebastian Bach, 1730

Acknowledgements

There are many to thank for helping to bring *Without a Conscience* to publication, and frankly, I couldn't have done it without my Facebook friends' constant and, sometimes, not so subtle needling to get to work and finish what I had started. Thank you for your encouragement, patience, and support.

Big hugs and girly kisses to Sheryl and Pamela, my dearest friends who have stuck with me through thick and thin, lifting me up and slapping me upside the head when my confidence left me. I love you both.

Gail, Chasity, and Kathy—you girls ROCK. Thank you for your friendship.

A special thanks to Kristi for working so hard on editing, keeping Iceman's voice, and helping Liz to do her thing. Your talent helps clean us all up! I am a lucky girl to have you as not only part of my publishing team but also as a friend. Super hugs of appreciation to three of Iceman's greatest fans: Zoe, Serena, and Debbie C.H. for all your assistance!

One last shout out to a hunky naval officer, WaC's military technical advisor. I am honored to know you and thank you for your brave service to our nation and for your assistance!

About the Author

Cat Gardiner loves romance and happy endings, history, comedy, and Jane Austen. A member of National League of American Pen Women, Romance Writers of America, and her local chapter TARA, she enjoys writing across the spectrum of *Pride and Prejudice* inspired romance novels. From the comedic Christmas, Chick Lit *Lucky 13* and bad boy biker Darcy in the steamy adventure *Denial of Conscience*, to the romantic comedy *Villa Fortuna* and the sultry 1950s Noir *Undercover,* these contemporary novels will appeal to many Austenesque lovers.

Her greatest love is writing 20th Century Historical Fiction, WWII–era Romance. Her debut novel, *A Moment Forever* was released in May 2016. She is currently working on her next, *The Song is You.*

Connect with Cat here:

Catgardiner.blogspot.com / facebook.com/cat.t.gardiner
vanityandpridepress.com / twitter.com/VPPressNovels
cgardiner1940s.com / twitter.com/40sexperience

Other Books by
VANITY & PRIDE PRESS

Undercover – An Austen Noir
by Cat Gardiner
Inspired by Jane Austen's *Pride and Prejudice* characters, a mid-20th Century steamy romance

"Forget Bogey and Bacall. Cat Gardiner's Darcy and Bennet have chemistry that will make anyone need a fan and a long cool drink of water. Undercover is riveting reading that had me completely sucked into the moment and the action. It's fantastic."

Villa Fortuna – Pride, Prejudice, & a Haircut
by Cat Gardiner
Inspired by Jane Austen's *Pride and Prejudice* characters, a contemporary romantic comedy
* Voted Just Jane 1813's Favorite Modern Adaptation for 2015
* Honorable Mention, 2016 Hollywood Book Festival

"Romeo and Juliet meets Pride and Prejudice in this hilarious, sweet, and oh so sexy modern adaptation."

Lucky 13 – Matchmaking & Misunderstandings
by Cat Gardiner
A contemporary Austen-inspired, *Pride and Prejudice* novel
* Austenesque Reviews Favorite Modern Adaptation for 2014

"What a phenomenal read! The attention to detail and the clever way the author immersed her audience in the story was such a terrific experience!"

Denial of Conscience

by Cat Gardiner

A fast-paced contemporary, Austen-inspired
***Pride and Prejudice* novel**

* One of Austenesque Reviews Top 10 Favorite Austenesque
novels for 2015
* Margie Must Reads Favorite Modern JAFF for 2015
* More Agreeably Engaged Favorite Modern JAFF for 2015

"Denial of Conscience smolders with action, adventure, and romance. Darcy and Liz are hot together! I'd beat down Jane Austen herself for this Darcy!"

Guilty Conscience

by Cat Gardiner
A Conscience Series bonus novelette to *Denial of Conscience*

"What a great little glimpse into Darcy and Lizzy's early marriage! Cat certainly knows how to get her readers ready for new thrills and chills between Darcy, Elizabeth, their family and friends."

A Moment Forever

by Cat Gardiner
A compelling WWII historical fiction romance
* Of Pens & Pages, Voted Favorite June 2016 Read

"A Moment Forever is a masterwork of comparisons.
A mystery reveals a romance and the romance reveals two worlds of conflicts and comparisons."

Dearest Friends

by Pamela Lynne

A heartwarming, *Pride and Prejudice* Regency variation
* Bronze Medalist, 2016 IPPY Award in Romance

"Dearest Friends is one of those rare stories that quickly grabs hold of the reader and never lets go; it is a thrilling ride filled with danger, seduction, romance, and humor. I never wanted it to end."

Sketching Character

by Pamela Lynne

A romantic Regency *Pride and Prejudice* what-if variation
* One of Austenesque Reviews Top 10 Favorite Austenesque novels for 2015
* Margie Must Reads Favorite Original JAFF for 2015
* More Agreeably Engaged Favorite Variations for 2015

"Such a book, the kind you don't want to stop reading until the end. It was fantastic! I must say I was pleasantly surprised. I laughed, I cried and so much more."

Family Portraits

by Pamela Lynne

An Austen-inspired Regency continuation of *Dearest Friends*

"This book took on me on an incredible journey and answered many questions left over from Dearest Friends. A truly great read and what a talented writer, one who is on my auto buys."